D0638310

The Mystery of Breathing

Books by Perri Klass

Fiction

RECOMBINATIONS

I AM HAVING AN ADVENTURE: STORIES

OTHER WOMEN'S CHILDREN

LOVE AND MODERN MEDICINE

THE MYSTERY OF BREATHING

Nonfiction

A NOT ENTIRELY BENIGN PROCEDURE:
FOUR YEARS AS A MEDICAL STUDENT

BABY DOCTOR:
A PEDIATRICIAN'S TRAINING

The Mystery of
Breathing

▼

Perri Klass

A MARINER BOOK
HOUGHTON MIFFLIN COMPANY
BOSTON · NEW YORK

ACKNOWLEDGMENTS

I would like to thank Eileen Costello, M.D., Mitchell Katz, M.D., and Mark Mirochnick, M.D., for reading and commenting on the manuscript; any errors of medical fact or unreasonable flights of medical imagination remain, of course, exclusively my own.

First Mariner Books edition 2005

Copyright © 2004 by Perri Klass

ALL RIGHTS RESERVED

For information about permission to reproduce selections from this book, write to Permissions, Houghton Mifflin Company, 215 Park Avenue South, New York, New York 10003.

Visit our Web site: www.houghtonmifflinbooks.com.

Library of Congress Cataloging-in-Publication Data
Klass, Perri, date.
The mystery of breathing / by Perri Klass.
p.   cm.
ISBN 0-618-10961-7
ISBN 0-618-56207-9 (pbk.)
1. Women physicians—Fiction. 2. Anonymous letters—Fiction.
3. Boston (Mass.)—Fiction. 4. Neonatologists—Fiction.
5. Medical ethics—Fiction. I. Title.
PS3561.L248M96 2004
813'.54—dc21   2003050854

Printed in the United States of America

Book design by Robert Overholtzer

MP 10 9 8 7 6 5 4 3 2 1

In memory of my father,
Morton Klass—who read everything
his children wrote

It was neither sane nor healthy; it was, in fact, a nasty, dirty and lunatic scribble. Harriet stared at it for a little time in disgust, while a number of questions formed themselves in her mind. Then she took it upstairs with her into the nearest lavatory, dropped it in and pulled the plug on it. That was the proper fate for such things, and there was an end of it; but for all that, she wished she had not seen it.

.　.　.

"Here's where the real things are done, Harriet—if only those bunglers out there will keep quiet and let it go on. God! How I loathe haste and violence and all that ghastly, slippery cleverness. Unsound, unscholarly, insincere—nothing but propaganda and special pleading and 'what do we get out of this?' No time, no peace, no silence; nothing but conferences and newspapers and public speeches till one can't hear one's self think . . . If only one could root one's self in here among the grass and stones and do something worth doing, even if it was only restoring a lost breathing for the love of the job and nothing else."

—DOROTHY L. SAYERS, *Gaudy Night*

Part One

▼

1

Who Do You Think You Are?

A TINY NEW BODY SLICK WITH BLOOD, limbs unfolding for the first time into air. The very first time she saw a baby born, Maggie knew: This was her moment. Like a farmer who follows an unexpected breeze blowing out of a hillside and finds himself in an endless, fabulous underground cavern: This is the glory that was there all along, just waiting for me. Maggie finds herself in all kinds of unlikely places thinking of birth — in the shower, on line at the bank machine, or now, driving to work. For the first time, for the first time — the air of the world inflates a brand-new set of lungs, air sacs like tiny bubble wrap. And a heart no bigger than a golf ball beats and beats again. Maggie will never get over it.

She is on her way to work, and this is her job, taking care of those babies in the first moments and hours and days, making it go right when it starts to go wrong, helping the hearts and lungs that cannot do it on their own. Maggie will never doubt her choice: This is her moment, this is her window, this is where her game is played. You get only certain moments, certain sequences, certain golden hours, even in medicine, times when every decision makes a real and true difference for a whole life's stake. She was raised with religion, Maggie was, and she has reimagined and reinvented herself as a woman of science and a woman of medicine, but she knows holy when she sees it. She knows a miracle. And this participation in the miracle, this knowing what to do, is her job, her place in the universe. If she prayed, which she was raised to do but which she doesn't do — if she prayed, she would probably pray, Thank you for letting me be here, thank you for letting me help, thank you for a brain that understands what to do, and hands that can do it. But she doesn't pray; she works. She does her job.

She drives to work, a little too fast because this is Boston and that's how everyone drives but also because she wants to be there. She doesn't eat in the car, though at red lights she notes the coffee drinkers and bagel and muffin eaters in the other cars with a certain fellow feeling, admiring their commuter privacy as she savors her own. She likes her car, she likes even this little piece of being in control — well, what doctor doesn't? Alone in her comfortable car, Maggie sings. She puts a gospel tape into the tape deck and sings along, loud enough sometimes to leave her throat slightly raw, bouncing her voice off the luxury tan leather interior, taking her curves with the swing of the melody. It is Maggie's most unbuttoned moment of the day, though in fact she is buttoned tight into respectable woman-doctor clothing.

Maggie parks her car in the doctors' lot, picks up her briefcase, and off she goes. Into Blessed Innocence Hospital for Infants and Children not through the main lobby doors but through the sliding-glass emergency entrance, which is that much closer to the parking lot. Through the green entrance hall and right into the bright white corridors of the emergency room, quiet and calm at this early hour, charging in as if she's coming off an ambulance. I belong here: a good way to come to work. Here I am, where I belong.

Upstairs in Newborn Intensive Care are the new babies brought in overnight, hooked up to their heart monitors, lungs bathed in oxygen — to Maggie, they are the most important patients in the hospital, and she thinks of them, always, as she comes in — but today they belong to someone else. Today she is on her way to her mailbox, then up to her office, on her way to spend the day writing up a research project, yakking on the phone with colleagues, sorting through papers. But though all she is heading for is her mailbox, her desk, her computer, though she doesn't ever work in the emergency room, she still walks into the hospital with a deep breath of ownership; she still claims these corridors as home turf.

And this morning the emergency room claims her in return; someone pops out of a trauma room and grabs her arm. Mark Kristensen, a senior resident she has supervised in the past, up in that newborn intensive care unit. A wiry, deft boy, conscientious and intense, rumored to be destined for a brilliant career in endocrinology.

"Dr. Claymore!" he says, and she notes that he looks genuinely rattled. He clings to her arm. What does it take to rattle a senior resident at the end of a long night in the ER? Mark Kristensen is very smart, but maybe not the person you want calling the shots in a crisis; more of a thinker than a doer. A little cerebral — a research guy.

"Maggie — Dr. Claymore — what a piece of luck!" Then he swallows, takes a deep breath, and says to her more calmly and more formally, "We need your help here, please."

"What's going on?" She walks through Emergency every damn morning, and even when it's insanely busy no one tries to rope in a passing neonatologist.

But he does not let go of her arm; he is pulling her into the trauma room, which turns out to contain all the purposeful medical chaos absent from the quiet hallway.

"I got a fourteen-year-old here been in an MVA."

So what? Maggie could answer. What do I know about fourteen-year-olds? What do I know about motor vehicle accidents? But she has already guessed the punchline, and though some small part of her is grumping about not getting upstairs to her desk and why can't the residents do their job for crying out loud, most of her is suddenly eager and buzzing and *on: Let me at her!*

The girl on the table is chunky and childish in appearance. She wears a loose sweatshirt and ratty jeans, which are being efficiently cut off her body by two nurses with shears. She is writhing, moaning on the metal exam table, screaming when the intern jabs in the second IV line. But her movement is limited; she is strapped to the table, and her neck and shoulders are immobilized with large red

5

foam blocks. Until an x-ray shows no injury to the spinal cord, they don't want her to move her head or neck, and they cut her clothing off rather than roll her or jar her, rather than pull anything over her head. The shears clip rapidly up the front of the sweatshirt, splitting the lettering in half. Parkdale Country Day. Underneath, just above the girl's left breast, is a tattoo of a snake encircling a rose. Maggie herself reaches for a box of surgical gloves and sorts rapidly through the sealed packets. Eights, eights, nines, what the fuck do they think, that all doctors are big men with big hands? Ah, a seven.

Mark Kristensen has been over at the bed, checking the girl's vital signs. Now he comes up to Maggie, nervously thanks her one more time.

"How far along is she?" Maggie asks.

"We've called over to St. A. They're sending an OB —"

"How far along is she?"

"Best guess is maybe twenty-two, twenty-three weeks. Doesn't really show." He gestures to the abdomen of the girl on the table. An abdomen Maggie has already noted: looks plump but not particularly pregnant. An abdomen that suddenly arches up off the table as the girl screams out a long, quavering howl of pain and terror.

"Baby's crowning," says one of the ER nurses, employing the patented I've-certainly-seen-all-this-before tone of ER nurses everywhere.

"Looks like OB isn't going to make it," Maggie says cheerfully to Mark. Pats him on the shoulder. "You do the delivery, I'll take care of the baby." As Mark seats himself on a metal stool at the bottom of the table, as the nurses gently bend the girl's legs and fit her feet into the stirrups, Maggie sets up for the baby. Selects the smallest endotracheal tube out of the crash cart drawer, turns on the wall oxygen, turns on the warming lights that a nurse has just wheeled in for her, a metal tree on wheels with a cluster of lights at the top like pointy coconuts. She rips open the pack of gloves and snaps them on to her hands, tight and taut as the skin.

"Where are the rest of the doctors?" she whispers to the nurse.

"The intern's out sick —"

"What if I hadn't been passing by? Is Mark supposed to handle the mother and the baby all by himself?"

"Here it comes!" says one of the people over at the big table, around the mother.

Maggie is ready. The lights burn down on the back of her neck, a familiar and oddly comforting warmth, warming up a table ready for that wet, cold little passenger. Was the girl in labor before the car accident happened? Was she being driven to a hospital, perhaps, or did the trauma send her into premature labor? Who was driving, one of her parents, her boyfriend? Is the driver alive or dead? All vague questions, all of very little interest right here and now. The oxygen is hissing and Maggie wants that baby, wants that baby in her hands, wants that baby to be a little further along than Mark Kristensen thought, wants that baby to have a chance.

A very premature baby, whatever other problems it may encounter, doesn't usually have a hard time passing out of the birth canal. It's easier to push out a one-pounder than a seven- or eight-pound full-term baby, even if your head and neck are immobilized and you're screaming and you're only fourteen years old and not very big. The baby comes out in a slow corkscrew, blue and glistening into Mark's hands, which catch it and ease the final half-turn of buttocks, legs, feet. Mark holds the baby, which fits easily into his hands, and looks from side to side. The nurses hand him cord clamps, scalpel, nudge him along. Mark probably hasn't caught a baby since medical school, but at least his hands don't shake; he isn't afraid of the baby itself. Babies are his business, but they're Maggie's business too, and this one is hers. Let Mark deal with the fourteen-year-old pediatric patient on the table. He swivels on his stool and Maggie takes the tiny thing from his hands and lays it gently down on her table, in the warm spot under the waiting lights.

The baby is limp and gray, not a good sign. It's not really a baby yet, to tell the truth, but what the residents call fetusoid. A disproportionately large head, bruised and tinged with blue, like a thin-skinned fruit fallen victim to an early frost. Arms and legs like chicken bones, and no tone in the muscles at all.

Maggie is not thinking any of the things you might expect her to think. Not thinking, Oh, how sad, how perfect. Not noticing the perfect fingers, so whisper thin and slightly curled (though she would probably notice if there were not five on each tiny hand). She has no awe to spare right now for life and its formation, no grief. She has bonded with this baby, become this baby: This baby is hers and she is his. *His* — she has registered the bean-sized penis, and the smooth sac of testes.

"Looks a little older than twenty-two weeks," she says to no one in particular. Her fingers have checked the pulse, squeezing the thick coiled umbilical cord where it meets the baby's stomach; the cord twists between her fingers, its slippery vigor the most alive thing about the baby. But way down deep where this baby is rooted at the cord, there is a pulse beating. Not as fast as it should be, but beating. Maggie's other hand is applying oxygen, and she is annoyed; this could be done by a nurse, and would be, in a real delivery room, with a real delivery room nurse. The nurse she had expected to help her has gone over to check on the mother, who is having some bleeding. *I am in charge. You are helping me.* Maggie tries to put this thought into her gesture as she beckons the nurse to join her at the table. I have done this hundreds of times, and you are all damn lucky that I happened to be passing by.

"Heart rate's about fifty and dropping," she says firmly. "Let's put the tube down, give him some breaths, and see how he does." Looking down at the limp body, which in its thirty seconds of independent life has not yet tried to take a breath, she adds, "I think he's gonna be a real fighter."

There is no one second when she turns it around, no one instant when the baby makes the choice to live. You could argue, in fact, that the baby does not get the chance to make that choice; Maggie's history is his destiny. She spends her entire working life concerned with the saving of sick and premature infants. She knows her business. She is more than a hundred times his weight, she has been alive twenty million times as long as his couple of minutes, and she does not question her right.

She gives the baby breath. A tube narrower than a drinking

straw, though made of a much firmer plastic, is down in his airway. The nurse's hand is ready on the oxygen bag, but Maggie pulls the bag away. A newborn's lungs are stiff, particularly a premature newborn's, and she wants those first few breaths to go in with sufficient pressure. She squeezes down, watching the hand swing on the face of the pressure gauge.

At one minute of life, the baby got his first score; Maggie awarded it automatically as she requested a dose of adrenaline and shot it down the breathing tube. The one-minute Apgar score was one out of a possible ten; the baby got one point for having a heart rate. Nothing for breathing, nothing for color, nothing for muscle tone, nothing for a grimace when the breathing tube went down. Maggie was already focused on the five-minute score as she got ready to slice off that stump of umbilicus and insert an emergency intravenous line into the big vein leading up inside the baby's belly. The drugs slide in through the line threaded through the umbilical stump: adrenaline to kick the heart, some normal saline fluid to get the blood pressure up.

Oh, the joy of it! No one who has not personally and individually saved a life and started a heart will understand it, and perhaps only those who have been fortunate enough to save a life right at the beginning. The heart rate comes pumping up, and the nurse, listening through her stethoscope, calls it out with pride. "Heart rate's sixty. Heart rate's eighty. Heart rate's up over a hundred!"

"He's pinking up!" Maggie says, and the two of them exchange a nod over the little body, which is no longer quite so ghostly a gray. As the trunk first turns a bruised lavender color and then gradually takes on a more convincing rose, the hands and feet by comparison look shockingly dark and dead, dull purple steel molded into baby toes as small as ball bearings. And the five-minute Apgar is four, and by then the baby is committed. He's on his way.

And then, somewhere between his five-minute Apgar and his ten-minute Apgar, as the obstetrician finally comes running into the room to take over at the gurney, the baby kicks. Flexes his legs up into the proper chicken-wing folded position, finally, and kicks out.

"We got us a keeper here," Maggie announces, a little bit too loudly, in that strange fishing jargon that becomes second nature in the delivery room, as if you could actually throw a too-small specimen back into the welcoming warm waters of the womb. "He's a fighter, all right." And she straightens up for a minute. The scalp at the part in her hair feels baked by the warming lights; there is sweat on her forehead, and her shoulders ache from bending and from tension. It is a familiar combination of discomforts, just as it is a familiar joy; it is the composite delivery room moment when the pressure eases enough to let her be aware of her own cramped and sweating grown-up body once again, when she is no longer wholly and completely focused on the physiological functions and responses of a newborn body, when she knows she is winning.

Hospital routine takes over. The mother, her bleeding under control, is wheeled off to a bed on the postpartum ward of the adjoining adult hospital, St. Ambrose; she'll get her spine films on the way, and, the obstetrician points out brightly, now that she's no longer pregnant, she can have belly films too, just to make sure there was no abdominal trauma from the car accident. The resident from the newborn intensive care unit has arrived to take the baby upstairs, and Maggie, having carefully supervised the baby's placement in the rolling incubator, has yielded her prize, this heartbeat-powered newborn, this — yes, go ahead and say it — this miracle of oxygenated cells and mechanically expanding chest.

As Maggie strips off those snappingly tight gloves, flexes her shoulders, rolls them up toward her ears with a pleasurable ache, as she systematically washes her hands and imagines all the while the progress of that incubator — down the hall, into the elevator, up to the fifth floor and Newborn Intensive Care — Maggie is also conscious of a responsibility that is still hers, still undischarged. All these things fit together in her mind at this particular moment: the let-there-be-light glory of the life-giving touch, the mechanics of hospital cleanliness, the incubator's journey down those familiar corridors, and then one last disagreeable but undeniable duty. A rather interesting mix of the cosmic and the petty, though she herself would see no particular contrast here. She may have left religion and prayer far behind, but fundamentally she is a believer,

Maggie is, and she knows that from the petty to the cosmic is never more than one short step in a hospital. As in, *Good attention to gloving and hand-washing will reduce the spread of hospital-acquired infections and help save lives.* She would say this, she would mean it, and she would practice accordingly; she scrubs thoroughly and conscientiously at the sink, each finger soaped and rinsed. Proper attention to detail will save lives — she knows it's true.

As will prompt attention to the derelictions and misjudgments of residents. She does not particularly set out to humiliate Mark Kristensen in public, but, in all honesty, it never occurs to her to take him out of this room, still full of nurses and other emergency room personnel. She has something to say to him, and here they both are, and she wants to say it and be done and get on to her mailbox.

"Mark, nice job on the delivery." The OB resident and a nurse are wheeling the mother away.

"Thanks," Mark says. All pleased with himself and proud. "You really bailed me out there, though. I appreciate it."

"What if I hadn't been walking by in the hall? You're the emergency room senior — you need to be prepared for whatever might happen. You panicked, Mark, when you figured out she was going to deliver. You left your patient! You left your patient and went rushing out into the hallway — and you were lucky, you bumped into a neonatologist. But what if I hadn't been there? Were you planning to just keep going till you found someone, anyone, to come hold your hand? Or were you planning at all?"

Maybe the drama of the occasion has gotten to her; her voice is a little shriller than she'd meant to pitch it, her tone more severe. Mark has that stunned, slapped-in-the-face look that means he may yell and he may whine and he may make excuses and he may even, god help us, cry.

Maggie corrects her tone. Softer, gentler, firm but constructive. "You need to think ahead, Mark. There's no way you should ever be here alone. You get tied up with one patient, someone else rolls in — if the people who ought to be here don't show up, you need to call in reinforcements, and the time to do it is before the emergency happens. Do I make myself clear?"

The nurses are looking at them, or rather, not looking at them rather too carefully. Mark is reading off a list of excuses about a sick intern and the junior resident away interviewing for fellowships and the attending went to a code upstairs, and the sick call resident is on her way in but she had car trouble, and he himself only left the room to call for backup.

"Well, next time," Maggie says, looking pointedly at the phone on the wall, "call from here, or send a nurse. If you're the only physician in the place, you stay with the patient. But the other thing I'm trying to say is, don't put yourself in the position of being the only physician in the place. This time you were lucky, she was lucky, the baby was lucky. Next time someone might be unlucky."

She nods at him in dismissal, strides briskly past the not-staring nurses, out of the room and down the hall, off to pick up her mail.

See her down in the basement, see her march along. Tap tap tap of pumps on concrete, swish swish swish of woolen skirt. In a week the month will end, the new month will begin, the hospital wheel will turn and she will be on service, in charge in the newborn intensive care unit, and then there will be medical action and plenty. Babies and deliveries and ambulances; her head will be full of ventilator settings and medication decisions. And that sounds only good to her. Today was meant to be a day of reading and writing and academic work, set back, removed from the blood and breath on which her profession is built, but that morning intrusion of reality was welcome enough. What I do is real, what I am is real.

Her mailbox, one square cubby in the honeycomb that covers the mailroom wall, is stuffed with envelopes and journals. Maggie grimaces automatically; so much junk, so much nonsense mail. Into the big plastic garbage bin by the door goes a fat wad of mail too dreary to be opened — notices from physician recruiting services and cellophane-windowed envelopes from medical publishers thick with cards to be returned so that one or another brand-new, overpriced textbook can be sent to her immediately.

She is left waiting at the elevator with her more real correspondence. A manuscript from a colleague, sent for her comments, another from a journal sent for review. A small pile of letters. The *New England Journal of Medicine* and the *Journal of Maternal Fetal Medicine*. Around her the workday and the hospital chug along in their usual patterns, undisrupted by the small drama of the emergency room premature birth. And Maggie herself is focused now on other details, her fingers eager to finish sorting the mail. In the elevator, scan the contents of the journals, see if there's anything interesting or anyone she knows getting published. In her office, close the door and open the envelopes and go through them quickly, put the garbage in the garbage, deal with what needs to be dealt with. In even this small and trivial planning of this small and trivial moment of her working day, here are Maggie's strengths and her weaknesses: She is organized and disciplined and neat, she is reliable, faithful, and competent, but she is smug and sometimes arrogant and far too wedded to her own arrangements. Not such a bad balance sheet for a doctor, is it? And she was right, after all, in what she said to Mark Kristensen: Why should his feelings matter more than an error of judgment that might have meant a patient hurt or sick or dead?

Upstairs, in her unnaturally orderly little office, she slits open each envelope with a letter opener, not above the small pleasure of neatly torn paper. Piles up the three or four things that need answering in the in-basket. Turns over the next envelope, notes automatically, even as she slips the point of the opener into the slight gape at the corner of the folded flap, that this is interoffice mail, a letter from the Department of Cardiology at Blessed Innocence Hospital for Infants and Children. A report on a patient? An invitation to a seminar? Probably not a personal note of any kind, since there is no doctor's name scrawled in above the Cardiology logo on the envelope. And then, as she slits the paper, placing her incision precisely on the fold, she notices something else: There is nothing else on the envelope at all, not her name, not her address. A blank Department of Cardiology envelope — is it really for her?

Maggie unfolds the letter, takes her last innocent breath, and sits staring at it, recognizing what it is. Look at this. See what this is. Oh my god, would you look at this? Who would send this to me? Can you believe it, look what came in the mail. And finally, under it all, maybe, a little bit of here is the letter I always knew would arrive some day.

The formal salutation: *Dear Dr. Maggie Claymore.* A correct and secretarial beginning, which makes the lack of a sign-off or a signature that much more blatant. But then, what sign-off would you use in an anonymous piece of hate mail? Sincerely? Very truly yours? She reaches nervously for her beeper, fingering the on-off switch. It is on, of course. She is not one to leave her beeper accidentally off, or to delay replacing the battery.

> *Dear Dr. Maggie Claymore,*
>
> *Maybe you think you stupid evil self-satisfied woman that everyone is fooled by you but it is not true!!! who do you think you are??? When you parade through the hospital the people are whispering to each other that you are a cruel and harsh bitch and that you do harm to your patients and to young doctors who come to you for training in fact everyone hates you and is always sorry to work with you and if you think that no one is aware of the disgusting lies and cheap tricks which got you where you are then you are wrong and some day you will be more than wrong you will be found out and you will have to leave but why don't you just make it easy on everyone and QUIT NOW!*

And then she pushes back her chair, leaves her desk, leaves her mail in a heap, and she is out in the hall, moving fast, almost running. Tap tap tap, her shoes tear up the linoleum tile. She disdains the notoriously tardy elevators, she pushes open the door to the stairwell and pitches herself forward down the stairs, pulling herself along on the banister. All morning she has looked somewhat dignified, queenly in her kingdom, but now she is a woman dressed for business running down stairs faster than her shoes will allow, her blouse pulling out at the waist; she is distressed and disarrayed and, by the last of the five flights, puffing. Back in the mailroom, she stands staring at the mailboxes, confirming what she already knew: there are no names on the boxes, only a number neatly printed in white on a dark green label below each space. Maggie has no idea what her number is; she locates her box by eidetic memory. Here it is, this is mine, in this particular location, I'd know it anywhere, I could find it in the dark. In fact, she now sees, her box is number 372.

The mailroom director is sorting medical journals into boxes. He is a big man, tall and also very fat, with black hair down to his shoulders, a smoothly shaven almost ridiculously pink face, and a diamond earring in his left ear. He wears a denim work shirt and immaculately white painter's overalls.

"How do I know which box belongs to someone?" Maggie asks him, hearing her own voice out of breath and inappropriately intense.

"Who?" He sends a pile of copies of the *Journal of Pediatric Infectious Diseases* pinging neatly into one box after another until a whole row has been serviced, neat blue covers protruding from each and every cubby. "You could check the address labels on those magazines and you wouldn't find a single one out of place."

"But what if I wanted to leave something for someone — if you weren't here?"

"I'm generally here." He smiles at her, a pink and maybe slightly creepy smile. But then, she is in a mood to find things creepy. "You're always free to leave things in the basket there." He indicates a large blue plastic laundry basket prominently displayed on the counter and labeled with a sign in fluorescent orange letters: MAIL DROP.

"Do you keep a list somewhere of which box belongs to whom?"

He jerks his thumb at a small crowded bulletin board in the far corner of the room and pays no attention at all to her as she goes over to look. His *Boston Herald* is spread out there on a small table, next to a portable radio and cassette player and a stack of cat breeding magazines. There are several Polaroid pictures of strangely shaped orange-yellow cats on the bulletin board as well, space-creature animals with big moony eyes and round disc ears, along with lists of mailing costs, hospital security directives, and an invitation to a support staff picnic from a couple of months ago, complete with elaborate directions and a carefully drawn map of Brookline.

Under this, she finds the list of box numbers, pockmarked with holes from all the notices that have been pinned on top of it. She verifies that her name is there, next to 372, and stands wondering what to do next. Should she ask him whether he had noticed anyone putting anything in her box yesterday or very early this morning? Ask maybe if anyone else had come looking to find out who went with which box? It seems suddenly embarrassing, as if he will know immediately what is in that letter upstairs on her desk — and it is then at that moment that she realizes that she does not want anyone in the hospital to see the letter. Not even the mailroom guy.

It might be worth pointing out that Maggie has never really been particularly aware of the mailroom man before, though she is scrupulous about emptying her mailbox every day and therefore sees him regularly. Sees him but doesn't see him; the truth is that like many doctors, she more or less accepts the hospital support system without examining it closely. The halls are cleaned and the food is served in the cafeteria and machines are repaired and she is not really aware of the people who do these things, of the dark blue maintenance boiler suits and the light green housekeeping dresses.

And instead of asking any detective questions, she nods assertively to the mailroom guy, though he either doesn't see her or chooses to ignore her, and she goes briskly out of the mailroom. Furious with herself, but also flat and defeated, she goes back up those five flights of stairs, locks herself in her office, and reads the letter again, for the second, third, and fourth times. She is peculiarly troubled by the absence of commas and almost finds herself reaching for a pencil to add them in, as if the letter would be less strange if only it were properly punctuated, less suggestive of the run-on hatreds of a boiling angry mind.

Maggie would rather be, oh, how she would rather be, in the newborn intensive care unit. While she sits at her desk and tries to make herself work on various important things, a grant proposal, a journal article, a lecture outline, they are taking care of her baby in the newborn intensive care unit. Her baby, single-handedly and handily snatched away from death — are they taking proper care of him? Paying full and proper attention to his many needs? And anyway, who would send her an anonymous letter? *You do harm to your patients* — what an outrageous thing to write. *Everyone hates you.*

What kind of settings is her baby requiring on his ventilator? Does he have an umbilical artery line in? What did his blood count look like? Will the ventilator blow holes in his lungs? Will he bleed into his head and wind up neurologically damaged? No, she believes he's bound to come through just fine; he's the probably unwanted child of a high school girl, and those babies do better than you expect them to. It's a basic superstition of newborn medicine: The unwanted, casually conceived babies do well, and the so-called premium babies are in danger. If this were the desperately wanted child of a well-to-do couple in their forties who had spent expensive years going through the dark maze of infertility treatments to bring about this glorious result, well, then you would have a setup for disaster. Or so thinks Maggie, who is herself half a well-to-do couple, who is close to forty, who has not managed to get pregnant in several years of trying, and who has avoided all intimations of infertility treatments. Someday. Maybe. Maybe not.

The team in the NICU is three interns supervised by a resident, all in turn supervised by an attending neonatologist. In a week it will be Maggie's turn to fill that slot, but right now it is being filled by Hank Shoemaker, who would definitely not be Maggie's first choice for her baby. Still, he knows what he's doing. What he's doing right now is this: He is trying to make the intern on call, a clueless woman named Marjorie Fallon, think intelligently about ventilator settings, and it is a losing battle.

"So if the baby isn't oxygenating well you're going to —" He pauses, waits for her to supply the information. Instead she makes a great show of considering this incredibly basic question, waiting for him to answer it himself so she can nod and agree.

"Well, which would you increase, the pressure, the rate, or the oxygen concentration?"

"You wouldn't want to increase the rate," she ventures.

"Marjorie, it's the middle of the night, the baby isn't getting enough oxygen, you're the only doc around, the nurse comes and asks you what to do. Don't tell her what *not* to do, tell her what you want done."

The two of them stand looking down at the baby, who is completely still on an open warming table under lights. The breathing tube that Maggie inserted down in the emergency room is taped to the baby's upper lip, a little silver heart sticker fastens a temperature probe to the rib cage, a gauze bandage holds an oxygen sensor on the toe, the plastic umbilical venous line runs into the abdomen, and a nurse has just put a regular intravenous line into the arm. Still, to Hank, this baby looks insufficiently connected up; he looks at the baby and thinks, That endotracheal tube should probably be changed, the baby needs an umbilical artery line. Plugged in, he thinks. We need to get this baby well plugged in.

"Increase the oxygen?" Marjorie suggests, though without conviction.

"Yes, you could do that, but remember, very premature babies do have these stiff little lungs, and I think I'd personally go up on the pressure before I went too far with the oxygen." Marjorie nods, as if to say, My sentiments exactly.

In fact, Marjorie keeps on nodding her enthusiastic agreement with whatever he says, and he feels a little sorry for her; she is one of the poorest excuses for an intern he can ever remember seeing, and she is trying so hard to cover her inadequacy by employing these transparent medical student tactics, by staring into his face to try to read the answer he wants, by earnestly presenting him with data he hasn't asked for and doesn't need. She stands there now, chewing her lower lip. It's a pretty lower lip; she is actually very good-looking, in a sort of sexy schoolgirl way. She has long wavy brown hair pulled back with a plaid headband, and she wears neat Shetland sweaters and plaid skirts. When Hank first met her, he expected her to be smart and competent; she looked like the person who would pop up with the right answer. But she isn't smart, or maybe she has just come to the limit of what her brain can do, and Hank knows it, and the other interns know it, he supposes, and so does just about everyone else.

"Hey, Hank!" Justin, the resident, all excited about something. A new baby coming in by ambulance? An interesting delivery across the bridge in St. Ambrose, the adjoining hospital? With relief, Hank turns away from Marjorie, who is now studying the ventilator with a bright, excited expression, as if she hasn't ever seen one before.

"Hey, Hank, get this! That baby, the one Maggie Claymore saved in the ER this morning?"

"What about it?"

"His grandfather is a state senator or something — and get this, his daughter was pregnant and he didn't even know it! She sneaks out of the house at night and runs around, and she was driving around with her boyfriend, and everyone was drunk, naturally, and they get into this accident at five A.M., and the next thing you know, she delivers in the ER and Maggie resuscitates her twenty-three-weeker!"

"Between twenty-three and twenty-four weeks, I thought we agreed."

"When I was an intern, I once saw Maggie try for a twenty-two-weeker." Justin is half admiring, half derisory; he admires the medical skill, but he knows he is talking about an extremist.

"She doesn't like to give up," Hank acknowledges. He would agree that Maggie is often too aggressive about resuscitating borderline babies, and certainly much too aggressive about prolonging extreme and heroic care for very premature babies who are not doing well. He would not pretend to admire her, or even to like her. But this particular resident is getting a tad too cocky for Hank's taste as well. "Maggie was the one on the spot this morning," Hank says firmly. "The doc on the spot makes the call."

"Yeah, well, there are four men in suits out there and a newspaper reporter and a lady from the hospital PR office. You want to talk to them or you want me to? It's all because of who the grandfather is."

"I'll talk to them," Hank says, fumbling at the neck where his yellow precaution gown is tied. He can't get the knot undone, and Marjorie the intern reaches over and does it for him. "Thanks," Hank says. "Justin, you might just go over this baby's plan with Marjorie, review the ventilator management." And he lumbers off; he is a big and ungraceful man, and he knows it. He is most at home in the world when he is doing procedures, when he is threading a tube into a newborn artery, for example. His stumpy finger-tips can rest with feather delicacy on an infant wrist to sense a pulse, his slumping shoulders and awkward elbows can hunch in over a tiny troubled baby and guide the needle, the tube, the scalpel, to where they need to go. He had once been portrayed in a hospital Christmas show by an intern wearing a Smokey the Bear mask, and in his most secret foolish fantasy, he had entertained the notion that the nickname might stick, that he might become known in the hospital as Smokey or The Bear, suggesting an affectionate regard for his size and his strength. But as far as he knows, no one has ever called him by either name, and if he has a hospital nickname he doesn't know it, which means he probably doesn't want to know it.

While Hank talks to the men in suits, offering guarded hospital catchphrases about the medical condition of this newborn baby, Maggie is sitting, frustrated, at her desk. She has tried to edit an article, tried to work on her grant proposal, and she is getting nowhere. Usually she has no trouble focusing, shutting out everything else, but today there are two separate worries nagging at her, and they seem to draw strength from each other. She keeps thinking of that baby, wondering whether even now they are giving up on him, deciding he is too small and too sick to live, and she keeps thinking of that letter. The result of these distractions is that she is left edgy and irritated, though without quite knowing who is irritating her, since after all, she doesn't know what is going on with the baby, and obviously, she doesn't know who sent the letter.

She tells herself she is just going down the hall to use the bathroom; there is actually a bathroom closer to her office, but that one is used by patients as well as staff, and Maggie, who is fastidious, doesn't think it is cleaned often enough. Also, she once found a mother in there snorting cocaine. Therefore she has every excuse to take the longer walk to the staff bathroom near the NICU and, after she uses the bathroom, to stand for a minute or two looking through the window. The NICU is set squarely into a corner of the hospital building, and the corridor tracing the angle of its inside walls is glass from waist level up. Thus, two sides of the NICU are mostly window; the design is supposed to offer parents a literal window into the weird world inhabited by their sick newborns. Curtains had to be added on the inside so that the nurses could prevent parents from looking in on particularly gruesome procedures, or deathbed scenes. Nurses, and most especially residents, often neglect to draw the curtains before getting down to the business of extracting blood from a one-pound premie, and the director of neonatology occasionally receives an angry letter from a casual passerby who has witnessed something particularly unpleasant.

So Maggie pauses at the window, peering in, imagining herself on the other side. She feels, as she always does, a small surge of pride, looking into this, her rightful place. Neatly spaced rows of babies, the sickest out on warming tables, the rest in plexiglass incubators, boxes for babies who no longer need to be observed quite so closely. The banks of monitors, the chrome and tube arrangements of ventilators, the purposeful nurses. And it's easy to see where her baby must be, over there on the warming table where the intern and the resident are talking. But as she watches from behind glass, Maggie can clearly see that something is going wrong; the intern and the resident have broken off their conversation and are looking down at the baby in concern, and the nurse is bending over the table, fussing with the monitor, suctioning the airway.

My baby. My baby. And so for the second time that day, Maggie rushes into a room where she is not really supposed to be the doctor, this time without an invitation. She is at the bedside, she is pushing in next to the intern, a woman she doesn't know, a pretty and competent-appearing young woman clutching a clipboard. Marjorie Fallon, M.D., on her nametag. "What is it, what's wrong?" Maggie asks.

"The ET tube is clogged," says the intern importantly, though she does not appear to be doing anything to either diagnose or correct the problem. The resident, a good-looking, cocky guy named Justin, with whom Maggie has worked before, is listening to the baby's chest with his stethoscope, and the nurse is suctioning the tube once again with a thinner plastic straw.

Justin takes the stethoscope out of his ears. "I don't think it's clogged," he says to the nurse. "I think it's out. I think it's in his esophagus."

While he is speaking, the nurse has hooked up a bag and mask and another nurse has come over to join them, pushing a metal cart with many drawers.

"Are you sure?" Maggie reaches over and unhooks a stethoscope hanging from the warming table. But the resident, Justin, has already untaped the tube from around the baby's mouth, already slid it out, like someone unhooking one of those proverbial fish: throw him back, he's too small. Now the nurse has the transparent plastic donut of the face mask clamped over the baby's nose and mouth and she's squeezing the oxygen into his lungs while Justin gets ready to put in a new tube. The numbers on the oxygen monitor, which had dipped down into the sixties, start trending slowly up toward a hundred percent again.

"Okay," Maggie says, "go ahead and bag him up. Justin, are you comfortable with this, you can tube him?"

For the first time, Justin turns and looks at her, really registers that she is there. Maggie supposes that she has tweaked his ego by asking this question, but what the hell; this is a very tiny baby and a very sick baby and her baby, and she is not so sure that endotracheal tube needed to be pulled so hastily; a little more suctioning, a little repositioning, and maybe the baby could have been spared the trauma and danger of a second intubation so soon in his life.

Justin does not actually speak to her; instead he speaks past her to Hank Shoemaker, who is approaching at an ungainly trot across the room. "The new one's trying to die," Justin calls out. "That tube had an awful lot of play in it. It came out of the airway and I had to pull it. I'm going to reintubate him."

Hank, as he reaches the warming table, nods quickly to Justin, and what he says to Maggie is "Checking up on your big save?"

"I came by to see how he was doing," Maggie says. "I happened to be here when Justin decided to pull the tube."

"The tube was *out*," Justin says. "It was in his esophagus."

"Okay," Hank tells him, man to man, maintaining strong eye contact, just to let Maggie know how little she's needed. "Now let's put it back in."

22

Maggie steps back as they bustle around. The baby is Hank's patient, Justin's patient, not her patient. She knows this. She would like to push them both out of the way, dig an elbow into each back, clear the runway, and put that tube in herself. But she steps back and stands next to the intern, watches from a short distance away as Justin intubates the baby, not completely smoothly, not on his very first try, but reasonably competently and reasonably efficiently. On the second try, he gets the tube where it needs to be, down through the vocal cords. As they are taping in the tube and hooking the baby back up to the ventilator, Maggie smiles at the intern and makes her way out of the NICU. In a week she'll be in charge. She'll maybe have to take Justin down a peg or two — but on the other hand, she likes him for being decisive, sure of himself, and skilled. Justin is the kind of resident she was herself. Hank, on the other hand, is an asshole, but that's hardly news. Too bad if he thought she was checking up on him, too bad if he can't understand why she's invested in this baby. Too bad if he can't deal with women doctors, she thinks, remembering how he failed to include the intern, Marjorie, in any way when they were intubating the baby.

As Maggie walks back to her office, she is making a variety of promises, to this young woman who needs teaching, to Justin, who needs a better medical model than Hank Shoemaker, but above all to the baby, who is indeed and triumphantly still alive. And she has, for the moment, stopped thinking about the letter.

2

In a Cavern, In a Canyon

GROWING UP, Maggie did not go on vacations. Well, only
Prayer Camp, those two weeks every summer, but that was
staying in New Jersey. Other kids visited relatives up and
down the East Coast or drove all the way out to Mount Rushmore.
Maggie's mother's family was in upstate New York, some assorted
aunts and uncles and cousins, but Maggie's mother, Annalisa, was
out of touch, as she said. Out of touch — an occasional Christmas
card, never, never, a phone call — but back then, in the 1960s, long
distance calls loomed large. And there was never a trip to see those
upstate New York relatives. Never a trip at all, not anywhere. It was
part of being poor. Other people went on vacations. No one Maggie
knew ever went to Europe, but there were children in her school
who had been to Puerto Rico and Acapulco. Not children she knew
well, though, not children she went to church with. There was a
Holy Land pilgrimage one year at church, but that was only for
adults, and Maggie's mother, of course, would not have been able
to afford to go, and would not have had anyone to take care of
Maggie.

But one year, the year that Maggie was nine, her mother took her
to Virginia to see the Luray Caverns. They didn't drive because
Annalisa was really a very uncertain driver — driving, Maggie later
decided, was one of the things her mother still somehow expected

that a lady should not have to do. Life had not provided the requisite gentleman, and so Annalisa drove, but never easily and never happily or naturally. Now and then they had a car, a car bought used from someone at church, and Annalisa drove it tentatively and well below the speed limit, driving herself to work at the accounting office where she was a secretary, driving Maggie to school, driving them both to church. She signaled every turn from at least half a block away, paused for the count of five at stop signs, and parked with a small sigh of relief: another journey over. And when these cars died, as they inevitably did, Annalisa and Maggie returned to their usual patterns, Annalisa catching the bus to work, Maggie walking to school, a friend picking them up for church.

So they went to Luray Caverns by Trailways Bus, starting with a local bus trip all the way into Manhattan to the Port Authority bus terminal, through which Annalisa steered her daughter steadily, gripping Maggie's shoulder so tightly that it was sore for the first part of the bus ride down to Washington. It took several buses and then finally a taxi ride to get them there, to a motel right near the caverns, and the motel room, bare and cheap as it was, seemed quite novel and exotic to Maggie. It was no boarding house, like the places they stayed in at Prayer Camp; here there was a small private bathroom, and a strip of white paper around the toilet seat, and tiny wrapped soaps, and a general sense of industrial hygiene and anonymity that made it quite exciting to sit on one of the double beds and listen to traffic rushing by outside.

Annalisa was a small and pretty woman, and when Maggie now remembers this trip, she remembers her mother looking very young. Which of course she was; she was not even thirty. And thirty, Maggie now understands, is very young. Maggie herself, after all, at thirty, almost ten years ago, was not only childless, but still in training, still only a junior-status doctor, not fully formed. Maggie reminds herself of this from time to time: she was so young, my mother. She was the age of a medical student, the age of a resident, and there she was, alone with a daughter.

When Maggie studied American literature her first year in college, she came across the F. Scott Fitzgerald line, the one about no second acts in American lives, and she immediately thought of her mother, her mother's whole life set and decided and determined. The great explanatory disaster of Annalisa's early life was Maggie: the pregnancy have-to-get-married-before-the-age-of-twenty, the rupture with her shamed and grieving family, the move to small-town New Jersey. And all over and done before Annalisa turned twenty.

She is wholly and completely glad, Maggie is now, that her mother's life turned out to hold a second act, after all, a second marriage, a comparatively prosperous southwestern adventure. And all of it, thank goodness, far away from the kindly patronage and suspicious scrutiny Annalisa lived with as a young single mother in that New Jersey town of well-to-do complete households, in that PTA, and above all in that church. And, not to put too fine a point on it, far away from Maggie herself — easily and cordially in touch, now that long distance calls are no big deal, but far enough away that Annalisa can be proud of what Maggie does without having to look too closely at who Maggie is.

Maggie the adult thinks back on her mother's struggles with carefully determined sympathy and admiration: She was so young, she tried so hard. On all those years as the underpaid secretary in the accounting office, on the tiny "garden apartment" in a town in which everyone, everyone, everyone lived in a suburban house, on the covered dishes brought to relentless church suppers and summer picnics, at which her mother always took special trouble to be courteous to the wives, to offer help with the babies, so that no one could ever say she was paying any attention at all to the men. It was, Maggie knows now, and even knew then, a careful and a limited life, and a life lived in only a very few settings. That is why she remembers, so clearly and with such unaccountable delight, her mother in that motel room near the Great Smoky Mountains in Virginia, in the only motel room they had ever shared — or, as it turned out, would ever share.

And her mother seemed just as excited as Maggie to be there, in the hotel room, in Virginia. To be on their own and anonymous. Maggie did not question the destination; all through her childhood, a geode had glittered on the top shelf of her mother's curio cabinet, a mysterious crystal geode perched on a wooden base painted with gold letters: Luray Caverns, Virginia. The geode had been brought from Luray Caverns by Maggie's father, back from the army. Sometimes when she let Maggie handle it, Annalisa would sing the chorus of "Clementine," and she sang it now, in the motel room, with Maggie joining in.

"In a cavern, in a canyon, excavating for a mine,
Dwelt a miner, forty-niner, and his daughter, Clementine,
Oh my darling, oh my darling . . ."

Annalisa was small and pretty and yes, so young. She should have been something altogether more sheltered, a matron in the park with three little ones and a red wagon, a patient supermarket mommy with Kleenex at the ready and a penny for the gumball machine. She was made not for luxury, but for genteel suburban ease, for the certainty of being taken care of. She dressed, of course, with scrupulous modesty, but also as prettily as she could manage on her tight budget; she favored small floral prints and lace edgings. Her blond hair was slowly darkening to brown, and as the color changed, she shortened it. Maggie could remember her mother with pale ringlets, which over time became light brown waves. Makeup and hair dye were frowned upon in their church, and though many ladies bent that rule just a little bit, Annalisa, already under watchful suspicion as dangerously single, did not. Most of all, Annalisa stayed bright and determined and cheerful, come what might, but from a very young age — certainly long before the age of nine — Maggie could clearly hear the desperation behind the cheer.

Well, then, said Annalisa, let's go to the coffee shop and have ourselves a little dinner. But when they saw that across the highway was a Howard Johnson, they risked running across, holding hands and singing "Clementine" and giggling like two friends the same age, so that Maggie could have her special favorite, the open hot roast beef sandwich, while her mother had a tuna salad plate.

Maggie came out of the teeny tiny motel bathroom, showered and happy and in her pajamas. It was a small thrill even to use the rough too-small white towels. Annalisa had already stripped back the stiff padded bedspreads from both double beds, and she had climbed into bed and conked out. Maggie stood looking down on her mother, her exhausted, sleeping mother in her pansy-patterned nightgown. Maggie knew the second bed was for her use, and she was young enough to be a little excited about it — having her own motel double bed! But she stood and watched Annalisa sleep for a long and gentle moment. And then she slipped quietly into bed beside her mother, who stirred slightly but did not wake.

The Caverns were more beautiful, more astounding, more everything, than Maggie had expected. They took the tour and stood there underground as the guide flashed colored lights on the stalactites and stalagmites, and the whole time Maggie kept hold of her mother's hand, and the whole time her mother squeezed her hand. Maggie was afraid to be underground and thrilled to be underground in this unbelievable place. Who could have dreamed, ever, that a crack in the earth could lead you into great grand chambers of magical growing rocks? It was enough to make you dizzy.

They moved on into the greatest room of all, and the guide played a song for them on the famous stalac-pipe organ — little rubber hammers, he said, produce these musical notes by hitting the stalactites — weddings happen here, he said, great grand parties. Maggie looked over at her mother. Annalisa's eyes were closed and her lips were moving, a face Maggie knew well — her mother's praying face. She is saying thank you, Maggie thought, she is thanking the lord. She closed her own eyes. Yes, her mother was right — this called for some acknowledgment beyond the routine, everyday thanks for life and daily bread. Into Maggie's mind came the gold star that her fourth grade teacher, Mrs. Brandt, pasted onto particularly good compositions, and the vision of Mrs. Brandt's admirably regular handwriting: *Good use of your imagination!*

On the long bus ride back, Annalisa seemed more lighthearted, more giddy, than Maggie had ever seen her. She had bought Maggie a necklace in the Caverns gift shop, a gold chain with a polished pink crystal pendant, and she had bought herself another small geode, and she sat holding the geode, turning it to catch the sun coming through the window and saying silly things about the places they passed: Well, would you look at the way they spell those words! Kwik-Kleen-Korner! Well, I'm not sure I would want to eat in a place that advertised world's hottest chili dogs!

The bus had turned off the highway and stopped in some small town, no one getting off but a few new riders getting on.

Her mother held the geode up, admired the way it caught this new angle of light, and sighed happily.

"Wasn't it a good time, honey?" she asked, her face young and excited and all alight itself.

"Yes, Mama," Maggie answered, already beginning to worry it over in her mind — why can't you always smile like this, why can't we always go on trips together — when she looked up and noticed that two young men, coming down the aisle of the bus, had stopped and were smiling back at her mother.

They were in army uniform, with crewcuts and dog tags. They were tall and straight and, to Maggie, blindingly good-looking, both of them. She had never seen real soldiers before.

"Hello, there," one of them said to her — to Maggie! "I have a sister just about your age!"

"That's a beautiful stone, ma'am," the other said to Annalisa. "Where did you happen to come by that?"

"We bought it at the Luray Caverns!" Maggie announced, answering her mother's question, and she was thrilled to see the two men exchange a glance and then settle into the double seat right across the aisle. The soldier with the little sister took the seat on the aisle, and Maggie was on the aisle, and he offered her a piece of a chocolate bar, first thing, right off. Maggie looked doubtfully at her mother; there were so many rules. A stranger, a man, a soldier, candy . . . but Annalisa gave a tiny little nod of permission, and the chocolate bar was full of almonds.

And Annalisa gave permission again for Maggie to move across the aisle and play cards with the soldier who had the little sister — he had a deck, he said, and he'd love to play a few hands of Go Fish to pass the time. Maggie had never ever touched a playing card — card-playing was as bad as liquor or lipstick, wasn't it? — but she learned the rules of Go Fish in a minute or two and played one absorbed hand after another.

And meanwhile, her mother sat beside the other soldier and talked and talked. Maggie had never seen her mother sitting beside a man and talking and laughing; the only men that Annalisa socialized with were from the occasional formal setups at Prayer Camp, and those always happened in a group. This was different — they were on the bus, they were across the aisle — but they were also, somehow, in a state of privacy. Maggie heard the beginning of their conversation — the soldier made a joke about how Annalisa and Maggie must be sisters, not mother and daughter — but then their voices got a little softer and Maggie's own soldier made some silly jokes that set her laughing, and she stopped wondering why her mother was allowing her to play cards, stopped trying to listen to the talk across the aisle, and just played Go Fish for all she was worth.

She would remember, Maggie would, the way the soldier's bristly, short golden hair stuck straight up from his almost shaven head. She would remember the slightly raw, scraped look of his cheeks, as if he had tried to deal severely with himself on all fronts. She would remember and repeat all the verses he taught her to "I Don't Want No More of Army Life," including the ones that were slightly risqué — "The nurses in the army, they say are mighty fine; some are over eighty and the rest are under nine!" ("I'm nine!" she said. "*Under* nine," said the soldier, and they both laughed.) And she would remember, without quite understanding it, that there was something slightly charged, slightly flirtatious, about asking the questions: "Do you have any sixes?" But there was also something powerful and interesting about being asked: "Do you have — any jacks?" her soldier asked, drawing out the question, pondering it, making it sound as if something grand were at stake. "No!" said Maggie triumphantly. "Go fish!"

But what went on across the aisle? And what went on at the next rest stop, when Maggie's soldier, Dwayne, took her in to the coffee shop and bought her a Coke, while her mother and the other soldier took a stroll together "to stretch our legs"? Oh, Maggie does not imagine anything very extreme — there were no tantalizing hints, no strange disappearance, no disturbing sight of her mother flushed or rumpled. In fact, Maggie could see the two of them clearly from the counter stool at the coffee shop; they went walking along the grassy slope that led down from the rest area to the highway, then out past the picnic tables, and then finally they were out of sight for maybe five minutes, and then they came strolling back again. But when they came strolling back, Annalisa had taken his arm. Her mother, holding a man's arm! And even more than that, Maggie, now waiting outside near the bus while the driver fussed with an unsatisfactory windshield wiper, could see the way her mother turned her face up to the soldier, who was so much taller, and smiled, and shook her head very slightly so the waves of her hair bobbed in the sunlight.

Maggie wanted suddenly to run to them, to butt her way between them so that their arms would separate, to grab her mother's hand and swing on it like a small child. She wanted also to turn away and leave them walking together that way, so her mother would go on smiling and laughing and making her hair dance. Instead, her own soldier, Dwayne, suddenly bounced a pink rubber ball at her across the pavement, and Maggie, surprised, caught it and bounced it back at him even harder, so that, tall as he was, he had to leap into the air to grab it on the bounce.

The soldiers got off even before Washington, D.C. They said goodbye, and Dwayne said, Thank you for the card game, and Maggie could hear Thank you for the pleasure of your company, ma'am, from across the aisle. Dwayne gave her the pink rubber ball and tried to give her the deck of cards, but Maggie told him, No, thank you, and then a lie: I have my own at home. And they went down the aisle of the bus together, tall and straight, and Maggie looked out the window and saw them, shouldering the big olive duffel bags that had come out of the luggage compartment, putting on their caps, two nice, polite, big strong boys.

She thought about it a lot, of course, Maggie did. All the way home, and then for weeks afterward, and then on and off for months and years. She did try saying experimentally to her mother, *Weren't they nice,* as they sat together again, rolling further north, and her mother said something Maggie did not quite, at that moment, understand — she said she hoped they would be okay. That they wouldn't be sent anywhere. And Maggie, a fourth-grader who did not read the newspapers, and had, at that point, barely heard of Vietnam, let it go.

The trip, the Caverns, the soldiers — it was more to think about and puzzle over and remember and twist her brain around than Maggie had ever had. Her life was regular and predictable and very, very bound by rules — probably every nine-year-old lives that way, and perhaps did even more so back when Maggie was a child, and even yet again more so in a small town, in a strict church, and on a tight budget. But what a richness of material this was, what a suggestion about the miracles underground as we walk, about the possibilities of chance meetings and a world full of wonderful strangers!

When she got a little older, Maggie began to wonder more and more explicitly what had happened between her mother and the soldier — whose name, it seemed to her, she had never known. Maggie began to hope, in a slightly patronizing way, that there had been *something* — a passionate kiss, or maybe even more than that, his hands on her body, the two of them falling together to the grassy ground. But they had been out of sight five minutes or so, and they had come back calm and composed, and perhaps, really, Maggie did not want to envision her own mother going past a certain point. But still, she wished her mother something to remember, something with this soldier who would have been, Maggie came to understand, the same age Maggie's father had been when Annalisa met him. And the truth is that over time Maggie revised her own harsh picture of her father — the man who abandoned his wife and child and went on to drink himself into an early grave — to look more like a tall, strong soldier, buzz-cut hair catching the light like magic crystals, swinging sure-footedly along the road with Annalisa on his arm.

3

The Luxury of Marriage

DRIVING HOME, Maggie is astonished by how much she wants her husband. To see him, to touch him, to tell him everything. *How I saved the baby. How I got the letter. How the letter made me feel.* She has shown the letter to no one and she will not, she thinks, show it to anyone — except Dan. And she is eager, suddenly, for his eyes to see it, for his voice to scorn it and dismiss it. She does not usually drive home so eagerly; she takes him, she thinks, reproaching herself, perhaps a little too much for granted. Her sweet husband, her sweet, smart, silly husband. The one she can trust enough to let him see the letter. He will call the writer nasty names, he will make serious, interested guesses with her about who it could be, or, if she likes, silly, extravagant guesses accusing all the most important doctors in Boston, and he will be shocked and angry and outraged on her behalf, of course, of course. All honor to him, to Dan.

Abruptly, without signaling, she pulls off the road and parks next to Ollie's All-Natural Gourmet Emporium. She has a desire to spend money on Dan, to bring him home rich foods and extravagant surprises, along with this goddamn letter. Most weeknights they don't make a very big fuss about dinner, they are well stocked with upscale low-fat frozen entrees, they have takeout menus for the local all-natural burrito place and the local pizza place and the

Chinese place that delivers. But tonight she wants to come home bearing gifts. Maggie explores the crowded aisles of Ollie's, leans into the freezer cases, deliberates carefully between the Ollie's olive salad and the spicy Mediterranean mix. She buys a whole round little Camembert, because the man at the cheese counter promises it's ripe and perfect — "positively deliquescent," he tells her, and she likes the word. She buys pâté because Dan loves pâté, and she buys two different kinds of pasta — Dan believes that Ollie's entrees should always be judged by the number of useless adjectives in their names, and these two are perfect; Maggie carefully memorizes the little cards in order to be able to tell her husband what he is eating: homemade wild mushroom tortellini in virgin olive oil and sundried tomato pesto; organic hand-cut buckwheat basil fettuccine with hormone-free veal ragu.

Ollie's food, as Dan has often said, is fundamentally ridiculous, but he says it with his mouth full, and she buys a box of out-of-season raspberries that costs more than the Camembert, and a little black and silver carton of chocolate gelato. The expense and the extravagance and the cholesterol and calories of it all please her so much that, as the young woman with the eyebrow ring and the lip ring and the big silver ball on her tongue rings up her purchases, Maggie reaches out and snags one more thing: imported German dark chocolate wafers with blood orange cream. Good.

You would perhaps have to know their usual evening routine, their generally conscientious attention to the health rules set by their own dear profession, their tendency to get dinner out of the way quickly, to understand how lavish this all looks to Dan, home first and waiting for Maggie in the kitchen, when she arrives and unpacks her pretentiously folk-art Ollie's shopping bag. His eyebrows go up, his dear, bushy eyebrows, thinks Maggie sentimentally, and then he moves her deeply by joining right in, by ignoring health and protocol and even mealtime convention by reaching, right away, for the box of German chocolate wafers, and ripping it wide open with the exuberant gesture of a man who knows that by evening's end there won't be a single cookie left.

*   *   *

To tell the truth, after all that, she isn't very hungry. She contrives to give Dan larger shares of all the food without his really noticing; they are that somewhat familiar, very unfair couple, the man who can eat pretty much what he wants without gaining weight, the woman who has to watch and weigh and guard herself at all times. But Dan is deeply, deeply moral about following the advice he hands out all day; his patients are adults, and he spends so much of his working life struggling with the long-term effects of smoking and drinking and eating too much, or too much of the wrong things. He practices at a clinic in a poor neighborhood, and his patients suffer from what he calls poor people's diseases: hypertension badly out of whack for years, diabetes never really properly controlled, years of stress self-medicated by chain smoking and too many beers. And of course, since many of his patients are the working poor, many of them try hard not to go to the doctor; they are uninsured or poorly insured or afraid of expensive prescriptions.

You could not get much further, medically, from what Maggie does, and she honors Dan without for one minute understanding how he can take it. There she is, poised among these tiny newborn things, right at the beginnings of whatever lives they will have — incapable of damaging themselves, trying for life with all they have, with whole life spans hanging in the balance — how can anyone choose the battle for the last two or ten or even twenty beaten-down years, struggling all the time up the hill of the patient's own death wish? Where does he get his dedication, Maggie wonders — or, sometimes, less exaltedly, Why doesn't he get bored? Why doesn't he get frustrated? She gets drama and decision and the highest of stakes; he gets to explain yet again why salt is bad to people who live on fast food meals, from cigarette to cigarette.

Dan is a good person, Maggie believes, in many ways a better person than she is herself. He has no academic ambition — quite the opposite, in fact. He chose his job, his path, his place, because he liked the idea of what is called in the trade *working with underserved urban populations,* and liked as well the idea that he would never ever have to wear a tie to work. He cheers Maggie on in what she does, but he does not like Blessed Innocence very much; it is, so clearly and absolutely, a place where every male doctor wears a tie, and often a starched white coat into the bargain.

And now, after all, she does not want to show him the letter. She sits across from him in their small, bright, neat kitchen, white tiles, white cabinets, white walls, and she chews on a couple of wild mushroom tortellini, watching him fondly as he takes the stuff in by the forkful, and she does not want to show him the letter. Here is Dan, the one and only person in the whole wide world to whom she feels she can show this letter, show it to him and he will not even for one moment look at it and wonder, *Is this true?* But she doesn't want to show it to him after all, any more than she wants to spill black paint on the white countertops.

Let him talk about his swimming club. And he does. "I brought home the newsletter" is what he says. "Wanna help me stuff envelopes after dinner?" He manages to ask this with a wink and a leer, as if he is making her an indecent proposal, and she nods: Yes, of course. What could be better?

"You should see this one kid, this Cape Verdean boy," Dan tells her. "This amazing kid — he has a butterfly stroke like you hardly ever see — just comes naturally to him."

"How old?" She watches him take the last of the fettuccine.

"That's the thing — he'll be applying to colleges next year — if we can just get some coaches to scout him. I'm telling you, this kid could go places." Dan grimaces around the strands of buckwheat basil fettuccine hanging out of his mouth. "Listen to me — I sound like a fucking guidance counselor."

"Well," says Maggie, not meaning to sound accusing, "*aren't* you his fucking guidance counselor? For all intents and purposes, I mean."

And she is thinking, I love this man. And she is thinking, Why am I so sentimental tonight?

For the past couple of years Dan has been involved, more and more and more, with a local organization, offering low-cost swimming lessons to urban children, at an inner-city Olympic-sized pool. Dan, you see, was a swimmer way back before Maggie knew him, in high school and in college, and when the two of them go on vacation, he still occasionally astonishes her with his perfect disciplined form, his endless tireless laps. All, he insists, pale shadows of his adolescent skills, but still, she can tell, he enjoys her admiration. She finds him beautiful and exotic, unfamiliar and appealing, when she watches him in the water, doing this thing that he practiced and practiced for years, all before she knew him, all in the essentially unknowable territory of his past. There are pictures of him from college, even from high school; the teenage certainty of his muscles. The shaved body, the regulation bathing suit, and the muscles.

But he no longer swims regularly, and certainly not competitively. He had given it up even back in medical school, or at least, demoted it in his life to the status of workout. And now he has become involved with this pool and made himself into some kind of elder statesman of inner-city swimming, the patron saint of the non-white kids who, in the fantasy at least, come out of nowhere to astonish everyone at a meet held in some lavish suburban facility. That's the fantasy; sometimes it comes true. Dan rides the bus and cheers them on and, above all, he raises money.

Now he clears away the dishes, though they have not yet had dessert, and though Maggie would like dessert — the rest of the chocolate wafers, the gelato, the raspberries. Of the two of them, Maggie cares more about sweets, especially chocolate, and she would like dessert. But, in fact, she is slightly ashamed of her chocolate fantasies, of her tendency to reward herself with a candy bar from the machine if she has worked hard all morning, of the Three Musketeers bar she has already eaten today, reward for saving a baby's life, compensation for that terrible letter.

She watches Dan arrange piles of newsletters on the table, piles of envelopes to stuff, sheets of printed labels to be peeled off and stuck in place. They have done this many times before, and Maggie obediently starts folding the four-page newsletters, looking down at the victorious team photograph on the first page: a textbook multicultural assortment of children, black, white, Hispanic, Vietnamese, Cape Verdean, grin triumphantly for the camera, still sleek and dripping from their swim. And next to the photo, a letter from Dan himself, saying in slightly stiff, slightly stilted prose what Maggie knows he really believes: that the discipline of swimming, the joy of pushing your body as far as it can go, the necessity of team-work, can replace so much that is missing in the lives of inner-city children. She folds and stuffs, folds and stuffs.

"I got this letter today — this kind of awful letter."

"About what?" He is sticking on labels, she is still folding. Every time they do this, one of them says to the other, You know, we could just pay some kid twenty bucks to do the whole job, and then, a few months later, Dan brings home the next issue. They must both secretly like the companionable do-good job of it, Mag-gie thinks.

"Well, about me," she says. She puts down her last few folded newsletters and goes to her briefcase. She takes out the letter, which she never wants to handle again, and carries it over to Dan, who has also stopped what he was doing and is watching her.

When she doesn't hold out the letter, when she stands there clutching it, trying to think of what to say to warn him, not, after all, wanting to show it to him, he stretches out his arm and takes it from her, pulls it from its blank envelope, and reads it slowly and carefully. Maggie, watching him read it, tries to fold more newslet-ters, but stops even trying when she hears him say, "Oh, Maggie. Oh, for Christ's sake! What a disgusting, horrible, stupid letter to get!"

It seems to Maggie then that she has been waiting all day for someone to say that. This is the true luxury of marriage: two for one and one for all. Someone who is on my side. Okay, I have an enemy, but I also have a friend.

Dan has gotten to his feet and come around the table. He stands beside her, waiting for her to stand up and hug him, which she does. She presses her face into the soft blue shirt on his chest; it is a matter of principle with Dan, like not wearing a tie, that all his clothes must be easily machine washable. In their domestic econ-omy, in fact, he does all the laundry, since most of it is his, since Maggie's work clothes all have to be professionally cleaned, dropped off and picked up. Dan orders his khaki pants and his but-ton-down shirts, short sleeve in the summer, long sleeve from fall

38

to spring, out of nice, thick, sensible catalogues. His clothes always smell slightly herbal from the extremely expensive organic laundry detergent that he buys. Maggie presses close to him and inhales.

"So do you have any idea which of your delightful colleagues might have sent this?" Dan asks.

"I don't know." Of course she has been thinking. Of course names have occurred to her.

"I mean," he says, "I can't say I'm entirely surprised, in some ways. That place is such a pressure cooker — I mean, in a certain sense you should probably look at this as tribute — you have an enemy because you're such a hotshot. Which of your colleagues would you say is feeling most insecure lately?"

"This isn't from a doctor. This is from a crazy person."

"Well, the two are not mutually exclusive. There's plenty of overlap. I think you have to read this letter inside out, if you know what I mean — where it says everyone hates you, what it means is 'everyone likes you better than me.'"

"A crazy person," Maggie says again.

"Who was that nurse — the one you had the fight with last time you were on service?"

"Erika Donnelly. But she's not crazy." None of the nurses who know me and work with me could have done this thing.

"David Susser. Claire Hodge. Hank Shoemaker."

Why is he naming off the other neonatologists? For heaven's sake, this letter, this is not something a doctor would do.

"This is not something a doctor would do," Maggie says miserably. And into her mind comes a news photo of a urologist in New Hampshire, recently arrested in connection with the mysterious disappearance of his wife.

Dan may imagine himself as looser, more free-spirited, but in many ways he is just as controlled and orderly as Maggie herself. He believes in paradigms and algorithms, differential diagnoses, which are, after all, ordered decision trees of possibilities and probabilities. If you get an anonymous hate letter, sit down with a pad of lined paper and make a list of the people at the hospital who might have sent it. The people who you know in your gut don't really like you. The people who have always seemed a little off, a little crazy. The people with whom you've actually had angry words from time to time.

And Maggie tries, really she does. She sits at that same kitchen table, the supper dishes cleared away, now the newsletters, folded and stuffed and labeled, back in their carton. Maggie sits at the table and picks over her life, pulls possible names reluctantly out of her brain and reluctantly writes them down. A hematologist with whom she had a little brouhaha last year; he passes her in the corridor without saying hello. Erika Donnelly, a sharp-tongued but very good nurse.

"Doctors don't write anonymous letters to other doctors because of an argument about how to manage a patient — everyone would be writing letters all the time."

"Maybe some of them are — maybe some of them do."

And here at last is her dessert. Dan puts it on the table next to her yellow foolscap pad, like a reward: a big dish of chocolate ice cream, at least half the carton, liberally sprinkled with raspberries, two chocolate wafers sticking out like rabbit ears. With unmixed joy, Maggie abandons her pad and her guesses, picks up the dish and pushes back her chair. Dan follows her out of the kitchen and into the living room.

"And why would a nurse do something like that? Why wouldn't she just complain about you — about me — to the other nurses? Nurses pass judgment all the time — they don't need to write anonymous letters. I bet you anything you like that this is some person I barely even know exists. Some crazy fringe character."

"People know you're going to get promoted, Maggie."

"How can people know it when I don't even know it?"

"In your heart, you know it's going to happen. They're going to expand your department, they're going to colonize more hospitals. And they're going to put you in charge of it. And someone is pissed. Really pissed."

Maggie protests: Nothing definite yet about those expansion plans, no reason to think it will be me — if, in fact, it's anyone. If it happens.

The ice cream is so good. The ice cream is the best thing she has ever eaten — or at least, the best thing she has eaten this evening. She does not want to talk about the letter while she is eating the ice cream. She takes another bite and, trying to make her voice light and teasing, she asks Dan how he's doing in his new career as a telephone solicitor. For the sake of the pool, he has been hitting up doctors all over the city, shamelessly calling all kinds of acquaintances and acquaintances-of-acquaintances, even treading a little bit close to the line to lean on various wealthy specialists who get referrals from his clinic and would presumably like to keep getting referrals. In his place, Maggie would worry about professional etiquette and professional ethics, but Dan worries about neither, so deep-down sure is he that his cause is just. The pool needs extensive renovation work to bring it up to standard, the locker room amenities are not what the kids deserve. He calls up medical school classmates of his and Maggie's, people he hasn't seen for years, and leans on them and leans on them until they give. Hey, he says to them, you know a hundred bucks doesn't mean anything to you one way or the other — well, I'm telling you now, it means a hell of a lot to the swimming pool. How about it?

Did he reach the two guys from their class who became plastic surgeons? How about the ophthalmologists, the guys with all the money? And for a minute he's distracted: Can you believe this guy — he's an otolaryngologist, his wife's an ophthalmologist, you know they've got money coming out of their eyes and ears, so to speak — told me he'd send me a check for twenty dollars! Twenty dollars! I told him, don't bother, save it for a rainy day. That's not a donation, that's an insult! I said, Let's put it this way: you give me one tenth of whatever you gave the richest medical school in America this year. One tenth! So he laughed, like it was some big joke, from out in Wellesley or Weston or wherever the hell he lives, and he said, well he couldn't quite do that, but he'll send me a nice check.

Maggie nods, looking fondly at her husband, this most unlikely crusader.

"Maggie," he says, "Maggie, I worry about you going back there.

You have an enemy — you have to figure out who it is. It's someone who hates you — and it's probably one of your very closest colleagues."

"This is not something a doctor would do. This is not something that one of my colleagues would do. This is something that a crazy, unstable person would do." But her voice is not any too steady, any too stable.

"And doctors are never crazy or unstable? Come on, Maggie. There's probably not a fully stable person in your whole department."

"Stop talking this way — please?" She is on the edge of losing control, and she almost never loses control. She argues, she fights, she wins and loses, but she does not cry and scream. She will not cry and scream. She stands up, holding her empty bowl, automatically reaches out and politely takes his as well, and carries both into the kitchen. She looks around wildly, and thinks of herself outside, taking some deep breaths of cool night air. She calls out to Dan in the living room, hardly able to trust her voice, that she is going out for a minute, and then she goes stomping down the stairs. And when the cooling air outside hits her cheeks, she can feel wetness. She turns her back on her own house and walks briskly away, down the hill, around the corner.

When you stomp out on a domestic scene, leaving your sparring partner behind, shocked by your sudden and decisive action, what you really want, of course, is to hear the running feet behind you, to be chased and caught by a penitent and guilt-stricken fellow who has realized with sudden, drastic force as the door slammed behind you that you are the sweetest and most precious thing in his life. Maggie, pretending to herself that she was not listening for those footsteps, and also, of course, a streetwise urban woman out alone after dark, listening always for quite another kind of footsteps, is for various reasons delighted to round another corner and come upon a scene of emergency and activity; lights and noise and action, an ambulance newly drawn up to the curb, red light flashing, in front of a bar. Harrigan's.

She moves through the thinly gathered crowd, most of them just out of the bar, giving off the smell of smoke and old beer. Two EMTs are kneeling beside an elderly man, collapsed, thin and frail, on the cold sidewalk. One is taking a pulse, the other is calling questions into his ear: Can you hear me? Have you taken any medicines? The man's eyes are open; he looks weak and confused but awake and breathing. Not the red face of the drunk you might expect collapsed outside a bar; he looks instead pale and almost elegant, with a small, well-groomed white beard and mustache. He lifts one hand as if it is heavy, his long fingers waving gently at the young men — and then lets the hand fall back to the pavement. Heart attack, stroke, alcohol, Maggie says to herself, all unfamiliar adult diagnoses. He wears a red and black checked wool shirt. Unbutton it, Maggie thinks professionally. Get some leads on his chest.

Ordinarily, to be honest, Maggie would not offer to help, would not say a word. The EMTs know what they're doing; with adult patients, especially, they know much more than she does. And they know their equipment, and what can be done on the street corner. So why does she step forward, identify herself as a physician, ask if they need any help?

"I think we're okay here," one of the EMTs says, slightly condescendingly, but he turns his head to say it, and so he is not looking at his patient for a crucial instant in which the old man's eyes roll back and his arm jerks.

"He's seizing!" Maggie announces, and drops to her knees beside them.

They do not want her help, of course, do not need her help. They tend to their patient perfectly efficiently — but Maggie has already turned his head to the side, and she holds it there, her hand cushioning the old man's papery cheek, his brush of a beard, protecting his face from the sidewalk as his body stiffens, his back arches, arms jerk.

Anyone know him? Maggie hears the EMT call to the crowd. Anyone know what medications he takes? But she does not look away from the old man's head, she holds him as gently as she can. The seizure is over almost immediately, and now his eyes are closed, his head drooping limply against her hand. What a strange feeling it is, holding an adult's head, an old man's head. Maggie's

43

hands are used to the fine-haired heads of newborn babies, to the soft indentations of the fontanels, the newborn openings in the skull. She kneels there on the sidewalk, cushioning wrinkled cheek and beard and thinks, I wonder what I am missing.

No one in the crowd knows anything about him. The EMTs strap him onto a stretcher, and still Maggie holds his head. She takes her hands away only as they get ready to lift him into the ambulance, then stands, silent, with the rest of the crowd, watching it speed away, feeling a certain longing: I wish I could go along and help. I wish I could be there when the ambulance arrives. I wish I were sure I would know what to do.

But in Maggie's job, the ambulances always bring new babies, starting out their lives. Sick, yes, born too soon, yes — but always new, always at the beginning. Always there, as Maggie's friend Claire has said, to play for the whole gazonga.

So despite this peculiar sadness, she can summon satisfying thoughts as that other ambulance speeds away, laden. And even more satisfying: Dan is walking down the sidewalk toward the little knot of bystanders and bar patrons. Dan has come to find her.

They buy more ice cream, a pint of Oreo fudge. Dan insists on buying it for Maggie, and they take it home to their house. No, they don't eat it in bed; they are not food-in-the-bedroom people, as a general rule, and Maggie would not go to sleep without brushing her teeth. But they eat it in their pajamas, and they peacefully, happily, mutually, do not discuss Maggie's job or Maggie's anonymous letter. Dan, with unusual tact, has removed the yellow pad with the unfinished list of names.

They go up to bed after Dan has watched the ten o'clock news on his regular channel. They have, these two, a remarkably orderly house. It would be easy to imagine Maggie and Dan sitting down at the personal computer in the little study off the living room and making an inventory of their possessions, the good china, the everyday dishes, the microwave, the area rug in the hallway, the medical journals, the six table lamps and the two floor lamps. Maggie is compulsive about throwing papers away, about getting rid of anything broken or worn out; there is one small closet in the upstairs extra bedroom where certain unwanted wedding gifts are stored, and that neatly stocked and not completely full closet sometimes bothers her like a guilty secret.

So Maggie walks into a bedroom as fresh and sorted into place as any chain hotel room. The pillows straight, the comforter centered on the bed, the box of tissues on each night table, the books in the small bookcase aligned shelf by shelf. And yes, if you were to search her drawers or her closet, there would be no satisfying squalor to discover. Maggie gets into the bed, props her pillow up against the wall, and leans back, leafs through a journal. Turns down the corners of two articles she wants to read later with some attention. Well, she is thinking, I certainly got myself wrought up over nothing. A stupid letter from a stupid unbalanced person and I've been crazed all day. Time to let it go. Time to think about more important things. She looks down, eyes slightly unfocused, at the abstract of an article about a rare heritable neurocutaneous syndrome, but what actually crosses her mind is a specific and very intense sexual thought. She imagines Dan's voice, saying in a very specific tone and at a very specific moment, *Oh yes, like that.*

Maggie looks up from the journal, the type smearing now on the glossy page under her thumbs, and sees her husband come into the bedroom. Whatever else happens, we are a fixed unit in the great wide world. And the two-for-one-and-one-for-two side of marriage strikes her now not as a guarantee of mutual defense and loyalty but as a secure and remarkable promise of pleasure. She pictures Dan in a hotel pool somewhere or other, the rhythmic splash of his crawl, the smoothness of his arms reaching out with each stroke, streaming water.

He is doing his little routine, her husband, gangly in his flannel pajamas; he likes them cut loose and roomy, so the shoulders slide down his upper arms, the cuffs are turned back over his wrists. She watches him, she appreciates his swimmer's body, the strong shoulders, the powerful arms, the tapered waist. Blurred now a little bit by age and lack of practice, but the lines are there to be seen, and the power. He is laying out his watch on the dresser, checking the time against the alarm clock, setting the alarm clock. He will check that the windows are securely closed, even though no one has opened them since last night, pull down the blinds, make sure the closet doors are fully shut, close the bedroom door, turn on his bedside light, turn off the overhead light, take a tissue from his box, blow his nose, throw away the tissue, and get into bed, all in that order. Maggie pulls the comforter up around her shoulders. Moving as little as possible under the blanket, she unbuttons her nightgown and slides it down over her shoulders, down around her waist, kicks it off entirely. When Dan finally lifts his side of the comforter, his own medical journal in hand, let him find her waiting and naked. She knows what she is doing. It is no small thing, knowing that.

4

Beach

MAGGIE, eleven years old, a solid, stocky child whose body had not yet really begun to change. At the Jersey Shore with her mother for the two-week session of Prayer Camp, staying in one of their usual, slightly run-down boarding houses off at the southern end of the beach, her mother, as always, busy and breathless with her flock of summer girlfriends, with the annual possibility of a husband. The summer before, Maggie had been a Mustard Seed, and she still wore around her neck the little seed, in its tiny Lucite teardrop. She had liked being a Mustard Seed, but she was finding it slow going in the Nazarenes, led by a relentlessly enthusiastic woman named Frieda, who always wanted the group to sing in public as they marched along. Maggie walked on the boardwalk alone, though she was supposed to go only with another Nazarene. She skipped late-afternoon prayer gathering and took a book to a remote corner of the beach.

She was, for the first time in her life, very aware of herself, of who she was and how she looked. She saw the way people glanced at the group of Nazarenes, following along behind Frieda and murmuring an accompaniment to her martial hymns, her off-key but jubilant "I've got that joy joy joy joy down in my heart!" She stared at herself in the rippled mirror inside the closet in the boarding house room she shared with her mother; there were girls in the

Nazarenes who already wore bras, who tucked their shirts into the waistbands of their skirts to suggest slim middles, concave bellies, girls with pale, wispy hair or ringlets. Maggie was, as far as she could tell, straight up and down — and straight in front. Some of the other girls complained about the dress rules; at home, they said, they hemmed their skirts up above the knee — one even said she had worn a halter top. Maggie, looking in the mirror, was for the first time grateful for clothes as concealment.

Her mother never did have much luck with the few available men at camp. A stern-faced widower with five children, Maggie remembered from one year, or a terribly nervous high school math teacher, who brought his own water filter to the table and talked on and on about the dangers of invisible gamma rays. After these stiff communal dinners, Maggie's mother and her girlfriends would shake their heads together and laugh quietly in corners, always with an eye out to whether Maggie was listening.

This particular afternoon, Maggie had left the Nazarenes early, complaining to Frieda that she had a stomachache, and had stopped back by the boarding house for a book that she had hidden behind an old trunk in the communal living room. She had found the book, corners crumbling off its pages, in the drawer of her nightstand and had instantly slid it between her Bible and her book of meditations for young girls. She had already read it through once and was reading it again, more slowly. It was called *Thunderball*, and it was easily the most interesting book she had ever read.

Maggie climbed off the boardwalk and made her way down the beach. The afternoon sun was still hot, the noise of the waves still punctuated by the cries of people in bathing suits, people she mostly left behind as she moved away from the smooth, sandy stretch, found herself walking between sharp rocks, around warm green-edged lakes of seawater. She walked to the very end of the beach, where the sand was cut off completely by a tumble of rocks, beyond which she could see cars going by, picking up speed as they drove out of town. She settled herself down, back against a boulder, spread her skirt neatly over her crossed legs, and opened her book. All afternoon, waiting to get away, she had been imagining James Bond himself waiting for her here among the tide pools, and so when a man suddenly rose from where he had been sitting behind another rock, a few yards away, her first reaction was disappointment: wrong guy.

"Hi, there," said this tall, thin young man with untidy, brown curly hair, with a brown beard and mustache, this man in blue jeans and a denim work shirt. And an instant later a young woman stood up beside him, turned around to see who he was talking to, and the sight of her confirmed Maggie's slightly shocked, thrilled inkling that she was alone with a pair of hippies. The young woman had long, straight brown hair, wore cutoff blue jeans and a bright pink sleeveless shirt. She was a little bit plump and immensely friendly; she had barely said hi before she was next to Maggie, examining her book to see what she was reading. And the next thing, she was offering Maggie one of their sandwiches, and Maggie, for the first time in her life, was eating sprouts.

They were not really hippies, not exactly, Maggie decided. The man, Jonathan, was a doctor just finishing up his training, he told her, and the woman, Deborah, was his wife and taught art in a big junior high school in New York. The Old Testament names, the gold ring on her finger, his respectable job (she had never before met a doctor, when she wasn't actually going to see one). What they really were, Maggie has realized in retrospect, was extremely nice, friendly, gentle people who met an eleven-year-old girl reading alone on the beach and included her in their picnic, in their after-picnic stroll. Deborah knew the names of the various barnacles and seaweeds, knew them matter-of-factly. Jonathan explained at some length about how he was being trained to be a doctor, about medical school and residency — the first time Maggie had ever heard the words. They noticed her book, and they talked about James Bond movies — Maggie, who had only been to the movies twice in her life, both times with her youth group, once to see *Born Free,* once to see *Mary Poppins,* was dazzled to learn that James Bond was waiting for her at the movies.

Maggie was late to supper, running back along the boardwalk as fast as she could, book tucked into the waistband of her skirt. No one noticed, no one minded; her mother had saved a seat for her at the long table and nodded absently at her as she sat down. Her mother was involved in a long whispered conversation with her best friend, Ella, and continued the conversation all through dinner, while Maggie ate mechanically, the book pressing against the bare skin of her belly, the sound of her new friends' voices in her ears, and James Bond himself in the air, so close she could almost smell the gunpowder.

It happened the following night, after supper. Maggie and her mother were sitting on the boarding house porch, her mother in the rocker, Maggie on the front steps. It was a peaceful evening, just darkening down, and Maggie was altogether peaceful. She had obeyed all day, she had made herself part of the Nazarenes, sung the songs that Frieda wanted to sing, collected shells to make a decorated border around the scripture verse. The verse itself Frieda had written out on a board in Elmer's glue, which the girls had carefully sprinkled with sand tinted with food coloring. At the end of the week, at the final prayer meeting, each of the children's groups would contribute a decoration, something made with God's own natural materials. Maggie looked forward to gluing the shells around the board, a tight mosaic work of seashell patterns, like the little shell-covered boxes and picture frames that she had coveted along the boardwalk.

Maggie and her mother skipped the Gathering that night; the guest preacher was Reverend Hills, who had preached the summer before as well, and Maggie's mother had not enjoyed his nasal voice or his graphic descriptions of the tortures waiting in hell, which had given Maggie nightmares. Besides, as Maggie's mother had said, smiling conspiratorially at her daughter, a person can get a little tiny bit tired of always being in a group. Ella and the others had gone off, and Maggie's mother had prinked herself up a bit in front of the mirror, then settled herself in the rocking chair in her flowered dress and her pretty white cardigan; she kept looking up and down the street, and it had dawned on Maggie that her mother was expecting someone.

But instead of her mother's guest, it was Deborah and Jonathan who came strolling leisurely along the sidewalk, arm in arm, who saw Maggie sitting on the steps and stopped to talk. There were probably a number of reasons why her mother let her go off with them, with these two strangers. There was Deborah's outfit, a long, loose ankle-length dress made of Indian cotton, which from where Maggie's mother sat must have looked modest and old-fashioned. There was the polite way Deborah asked permission to take Maggie with them for their walk along the beach, the respectful tone of Jonathan's voice, his little speech about how clear the constellations were at night here at the shore, how nice it was to be able to pick them out. "My wife knows them all," he said. And then, of course, there was probably Maggie's mother's urge to be alone with the man she was expecting. Maggie never knew who he was, or even whether he came; her mother didn't marry him, any more than she married any of the men she met at Prayer Camp. When she finally did remarry, a decade later, she married the accountant for whom she had worked for many years, and she brought him into the church; they eventually moved to Arizona and opened a bed-and-breakfast patronized mostly by the traveling faithful, decorated with expensive antiques and framed Bible verses done in elegant calligraphy. Way above those shabby boarding houses at the southern end of the beach. Now Maggie's mother is far away from the beach, from the Jersey Shore, from any shore at all.

Maggie could not believe she was really setting off into the night with Jonathan and Deborah. Neither of them seemed to think it was the least bit extraordinary, neither seemed aware that something was happening in Maggie's life, happening right there, beside them. They strolled along the deserted beach, admiring the cloud formations in the dim sky, waiting for true darkness. It was there, sitting down on the sand beside Deborah, that Maggie realized something new, something that seemed to her at once absolutely right and true, and at the same time part of that same uncomfortable, new awareness that had plagued her the whole summer: There was something wrong with her life. If she told them what a big deal it was, if she told them she had almost never before been alone with adults who were not her teachers or members of her church, if she told them that to her they seemed exotic and remarkable, they would be surprised, they would probably pity her. Never walked along a beach at night before! Never sat on the sand and looked up at the stars! Maggie closed her eyes, and leaned her face forward

51

onto her knees, listening to the erasing noises of the surf. There is something wrong with me, wrong with my life, she thought, seeing herself, this afternoon, stomping along the beach behind Frieda, singing, "I'm going on that journey that begins today." I will always only be marching down the beach with Frieda, always be singing louder than I want to, always be part of that different and slightly ridiculous group — while all around her, people like Jonathan and Deborah would walk in pairs, having chosen each other, talking in gentle voices or walking in companionable silence, appreciating the sun on their backs and the satisfying warm sand at their feet.

Deborah stood up, her skirt billowing around her legs. "Let's run."

Jonathan stood up immediately, as if that were a perfectly normal thing for one adult to suggest to another, and the two of them started to run, then Deborah stopped, turned to look at Maggie, who sat frozen — turned and called to her to come on, to get moving. "Sand is the best thing for running on," she said, and then she took off after Jonathan. And Maggie came after them, felt her own feet clop down confidently on the hard-packed sand, which received her every step with a very slight shock of resettlement. Maggie caught up with them; they weren't racing, were just loping along at a comfortable pace, Deborah's granny gown streaming out behind her like a dark flag, Jonathan pumping rhythmically with his arms. They ran, the three of them, all the way down the beach, as far as the boulders where they had met the day before.

It was finally, truly, dark. The moon was rising, a bright quarter-moon that did not light up the sky at all. Maggie and Jonathan and Deborah walked along the very edge of the incoming tide, each new wavelet lapping just beyond their feet as it gave up and retreated into the darkness of the ocean. Jonathan found Cassiopeia, and Deborah showed Maggie the evening star, and the lyre. Maggie had been shown before, on a nature walk last summer, how to trace the Dippers and find the North Star, but she let Deborah show her again.

And then the three of them turned and stood gazing out over the water, looking not above the horizon, where the constellations were coming more and more clearly into view, but instead at the unbroken darkness of ocean.

And then she realized the other two were taking off their clothes. They did not even look at her, did not seem to be the least bit self-conscious, just piled the clothing neatly on the sand, set back a little from the water line. Deborah had simply lifted the long dress over her head; under it she wore only a pair of bikini underpants, which she immediately removed. She had small, round breasts and abundant pubic hair; Maggie was embarrassed to be looking at her and embarrassed to turn away. And then Jonathan, out of his shirt, his jeans, his underpants, was standing there completely naked. Maggie had barely seen an adult woman naked before; her mother was very careful. She had, of course, never ever seen a man, and was so shocked now to be seeing one that she wasn't sure whether or not she was surprised by what he actually looked like.

"Are you coming in?" Deborah asked, her voice as pleasant and friendly as it had been before, as casual and by-the-way as if she were not standing naked with a naked man on a public beach.

"No," Maggie managed, afraid that the sound of her own embarrassed voice would make the other two realize the shame of the situation — but instead they started walking toward the water. She could see their pale bodies hazy in the darkness as they waded in, giving out little yips as the waves caught them; she thought she heard the single more definitive splash as Jonathan threw himself forward into the water, and then another as Deborah followed suit, but perhaps she was only hearing the breakers.

And then Maggie could not see them anymore. She sat down and drew up her knees again, but she did not hide her face and cry. She remained staring straight ahead, hugging her legs, trying to imagine the two of them out there in the ocean, their naked bodies moving through the black seawater, Deborah's breasts hanging down as she floated, Jonathan's penis waving between his legs. Maggie did not wish she was out there in the water with them; that was very simply unthinkable. But she hugged to herself a sort of triumphant gladness that she was waiting for them on the shore, hugged it to herself like a promise to be redeemed.

The night air was warm on her skin. There was no one she could see, no one she could hear. If she turned around she would see the lights of the town, but if she stared out to sea, there was no sign of any other person. There were two naked people in the water; she knew that because their clothes were here on the ground beside her, and she reached out and felt the thin cotton of Deborah's dress, just to be sure.

And then they were coming toward her, out of the water, laughing, complaining that it was cold without the sun, and Maggie leaped to her feet and offered them clothes to dry off with, Jonathan's shirt, Deborah's dress, handing them those items without the slightest shyness, smiling at them as they smiled at her, as they dried off and hurried back into their clothing, and then all three walked slowly back toward the boardwalk.

And that was it, that was all. The next day, presumably, Jonathan and Deborah left town, went back to their home and their jobs. Probably they grew up and had children, he practiced medicine and she taught art, probably they never gave a second thought to one night on a deserted Jersey Shore beach, when the warm air and the beautiful night sky seemed to demand a late-night swim. And for Maggie, a sweet memory, a night she hugged to herself all the rest of that summer, all through the following winter, the thought of Deborah and Jonathan, naked on the shore.

But over the next few years, as she found herself returning again and again to her memory of those moments on the beach, something changed. She was no longer enjoying the secret friendship that had placed her in that spot at that moment. Instead, she was lingering over some glances that might have passed between Deborah and Jonathan as they came out of the water; instead of remembering the glorious daring of her own nonchalance in regarding their nakedness, she was thinking of them looking at each other. What would have happened if she hadn't been there? Would they perhaps have kissed each other? Done everything that James Bond did, that the girls whispered about, that Eleanora Davenport had seen in the movies when her sister came home from college and took her to see *Butch Cassidy and the Sundance Kid,* on the condition that she never told their parents?

She edited and reedited her vision of Jonathan and Deborah on the beach. But something in it was not right; they walk out of the water and look at each other, and there is a special smile on Jonathan's face as he looks into her eyes. They move into each other's arms, and his hand comes up to hold her shockingly naked breast. It was troubling and dazzling, but it was not right, and it took Maggie almost a year to take it to the next step, so that it was not Deborah walking wet and naked from the nighttime ocean, but instead she herself, Maggie, triumphantly and shamelessly unclothed, Maggie who had left her long hippie dress in a pile on the beach, Maggie who had plunged fearlessly into the waves, Maggie who had slipped her bare body through the salty water, who came walking out onto the beach beneath the stars, and Maggie who had turned to Jonathan and looked into his eyes and seen that smile on his face.

And it was still that same moment, that walking out of the water onto the beach with Jonathan, that Maggie returned to in her mind, even now, decades older, making love with her own husband, who perhaps not so coincidentally was himself a brown-bearded Jewish doctor — not to mention the swimming motif. It was an image that had solaced her sexuality all through adolescence and still never failed to arouse her, whether or not she continued into the now far more complex and explicit fantasy of what went on to happen on the beach. She had other sexual daydreams, momentary recastings of grapplings on the movie screen or idle responses to the occasional good-looking man in a boring meeting. But she had only one serious recurring fantasy, one set of images that automatically came to mind almost every time she made love, with Dan as with all her boyfriends before Dan. It was silly to be pushing forty and still be using (her word, *using*) the same fantasy as when you were fifteen, but it would have been even sillier to reject this gift, this easy, familiar transition to arousal. She had even imagined herself, elderly and widowed, Dan long gone, same fantasy, comforting herself in her room at the old age home. It was perhaps silly to be stuck in a fantasy about something that happened, or didn't happen, to an eleven-year-old, but it worked, it made her happy. Maggie, who was fond of hospital aphorisms, would probably have shrugged self-consciously and offered, "If it isn't broke, don't fix it."

5

The Tremor of Inaction

THE REASON I'M ASKING is because both yesterday and today something got into my box that didn't have my name or address on the envelope."

The same letter in her mailbox this morning. Same exact letter. *Who do you think you are???* Maybe a photocopy, maybe just another copy printed out of the word processor. *People are whispering to each other that you are a cruel and harsh bitch and that you do harm to your patients . . .*

And the mailroom guy will not look at her; he answers her automatically, bored, irritated. "You got somebody else's mail?"

"No, it was meant for me." She is standing right in front of his little table, hooking her hands together like a bad actress reciting lines on stage. *If you think that no one is aware of the disgusting lies and cheap tricks which got you where you are then you are wrong . . .* Self-conscious and posed and speaking her piece. "It was what I guess you would call an anonymous letter. A piece of hate mail."

But now he does look up, abandoning the pile of cat photographs he has been sorting on the table. He looks straight into her eyes. Is the expression on his mildly plethoric face shock or sympathy — or is it perhaps prurience?

"Is that starting up again?"

"Who else has gotten them?"

"It's happened," he says, somewhat uncomfortably. "Probably happens every now and then in any big institution."

"What's your name?" She means to establish contact, to treat him with more respect, not less, but the question comes out sounding like a challenge, as if she intends to write down the name and report him.

He pushes back his chair, heavily, stands up, turns to face her. The diamond in his ear catches a beam of light from the ceiling fixture and flashes once. He puts down the deck of photographs; cats and more cats, Maggie can see.

"Frank Gruenwasser," he says, and smiles at her, and holds out his hand. His grip is warm and firm; his hand is big and incongruously decorated with three small gold rings, almost lost between his thick fingers, but it is the grip of a man who knows how to use his hands, and knows how to meter out his considerable strength.

"Maggie Claymore."

Frank Gruenwasser suddenly breaks his eye contact with her, steps past her without excusing himself, though it seems to Maggie that he comes unusually close to her; his large body almost fills the mailroom doorway, where he is accepting an express delivery from a courier he obviously knows well, who speaks with a strong Haitian Creole accent. Maggie can't see him around Gruenwasser, whose hair, long and flowing to his shoulders, is as black as his sweater, so that from the back the effect is of a man wearing a hood, enormous and anonymous and sinister.

The invisible courier departs, and Frank Gruenwasser turns back to Maggie, holding a pile of express envelopes. "Before there was overnight delivery, things came in the mail. They took a couple of days extra and it didn't make a fucking quarter-pound of difference to anyone in the fucking world." He opens a small drawer in the counter, takes out a square plastic container. Several rows of exquisite marzipan fruits and vegetables are neatly arranged on silver foil, and the foil mirrors the curved undersides of the pink and golden peaches, the blood red cherries, the incongruous royal purple eggplants, all done the same size, all perfect and unblemished and remarkably real. He takes a black-specked yellow pear delicately between his fingers, lifts it to his mouth, then holds out the box to Maggie.

"How beautiful," she says, but does not take one; she does not particularly like marzipan, and there is something weird and not-so-appetizing about this man and his candies. Besides, she has been promising herself a treat from the candy machine again this morning, maybe a Kit Kat, and if she eats candy now, she can't let herself buy candy from the machine, and she would rather have a Kit Kat — she can taste the thin chocolate flaking in her mouth over the cookie wafers. She will buy her mass market candy from the machine and eat it in private, all alone, just she and the chocolate, thank you very much. So why does he keep waving the box at her? "They're too beautiful to eat," Maggie says.

He pops the entire candy pear into his mouth and begins to chew; a faint smell of almond.

"I can always make more," he says, somewhat indistinctly, and she finds herself reaching for a properly dimpled orange, complete even to the tiny dark disk of stem at its northern pole, trying to picture this enormous man shaping these minute fruits.

Frank Gruenwasser swallows, visibly. "I don't know who put that letter in your box. No one did it while I was in here. But I'm out of here for maybe twenty-five minutes, taking the fucking Fieldston Research Building's fucking mail over to the fucking Fieldston Research Building. And if they don't want me to leave the mailroom unattended every morning, then they can fucking make the Fieldston people come here, just like everyone else, or they can set up a mailroom there."

Maggie chews the marzipan orange; her teeth sink easily into the dense stuff, and for an instant they feel stuck, her mouth glued closed, as her tongue is flooded with intense sweetness.

Maggie makes a to-do list every morning, no surprise. And checks off almost everything almost every day. *Harvey Weintraub, 11:00,* she wrote on her list, not that she would need any reminders. Harvey is her boss, the head of neonatology. He is also her mentor, the man who has bet on her again and again. An early morning call from his secretary, a politely worded request: Does she have a few minutes to stop by his office? This is a summons of importance to Maggie, who can easily imagine that it might mean something big, something wonderful.

Neat and busy in her tiny, tidy office. A little rueful: *that damn letter again*. But she will put it in its proper place and move on. She shakes her head. Look at her and see a satisfied matron remembering marital exchanges under the sheets, or an ambitious professional looking ahead to a crisp and tantalizing interview later in the morning — she is back to being the various things that she wants to be, that she has made of herself. Her office is remarkably neat by hospital standards; the articles are filed, the journals are in chronological order on the shelves. Her desk is clean, and the African violets, arranged in a row along the window, are blooming. A clean utilitarian office, an office in which you could believe serious work was done by an organized person.

Who do you think you are???

The irony is, Maggie is not in the habit of thinking of herself in that smug way: a neat person, a person who needs her world to be neat. In fact, it has been a point of pride with her, the idea that she can work anywhere; in medical school she shared an apartment for a year with a woman who was and still is a phenomenal slob, and Maggie worked happily in the chaos. The clean office is a convenience, or maybe a way of keeping her own private secrets. The work is what matters, the work is the essential. I am a person who can work anywhere. But is she really, on any level, anymore, a person who can work happily in the midst of mess?

If you think that no one is aware of the disgusting lies and cheap tricks which got you where you are then you are wrong and some day you will be more than wrong you will be found out and you will have to leave . . .

In fact, her customary take on herself is that she is putting up a front, that she is disguising an inner self that is still recognizably the superficially sloppy but keenly focused graduate student she had once been. That is to say, the person she had been before medical

59

school. A graduate student in molecular biology, a twenty-two-year-old who had escaped her childhood and adolescence, escaped church and family and the confused but thundering certainties by which her mother still lived, and found instead the promises of science. The promise that truths are there to be found, but the joy is in the finding. The true Maggie. That twenty-two-year-old, sure of her place in the science world, wearing perhaps an old sweatshirt and a pair of jeans with fraying cuffs, would have marched cheerfully into a lecture hall to attend a talk by some famous scientist or other, would have bicycled back to the lab afterward to work late at her desk, crammed behind the lab benches littered with articles and computer printouts, all punctuated with the ring indentations of coffee mugs. Would have biked home again some time after dark, wearing reflectors on her knees and another on her forehead, never thinking twice about how she looked as she sweated her way along the street.

That graduate student person, Maggie reflects, Maggie the compulsively neat and professional doctor, surveying her office with satisfaction but also perhaps with some nostalgic regret, that person is pretty dressed up now, in every sense. But I still know who I am, she answers the letter in her mind. And, no, I will not be found out because there is nothing to find out. I am what I say I am. I know where I came from and I know where I am going. So there.

And in this same determinedly satisfied, ambitious spirit, Maggie sits in Harvey Weintraub's ostentatiously large, ostentatiously messy office — large to show his power in a hospital where space is always at a premium, messy with reprints and journals to show he hasn't lost touch with the medical literature just because he golfs with the president of the hospital and spends most of his day in meetings. Maggie remembers him as a practicing doctor, and lord, he was a marvel. She trained under Weintraub; his is one of the voices she hears whispering in her ear when it's time for a tough decision. And he watched her, as she was watching him, and he believed in her, encouraged her, gave her her first job. They recognized each other, you might say. In some formal, tightly constricted teacher-student way, Maggie loves him, and she mourns his moves

60

up the ladder, which have taken him, finally, completely away from patients.

Weintraub is a small, neat man — expensive blue suit, meticulous striped tie. As polished as his desk. A formal posed picture of his dark-haired, foggy-eyed wife and three stepladder daughters is centered on his desk, framed in glossy wood; next to it, in Lucite blocks, are the candid family shots: the girls tadpoling off a raft on a lake, the wife and two older daughters on horseback. Maggie has met them from time to time, over the years. She has some trouble making conversation with the wife, who is one of those traditional doctor's wives; the little asterisk next to her name in Maggie's mind is to remind her for conversational purposes: *Very interested in Impressionism, works as a volunteer docent at the Museum of Fine Arts.*

The preliminaries: How's it going? Are you in the NICU this month? Not till next week, but I'm really looking forward to it. He is far from clinical practice himself, and by now for all his best efforts probably a little out of touch with the fast-moving field of neonatology, but Weintraub likes to hear that his chosen lieutenants love their work. His phone rings, his secretary has put a call through, and he grimaces apologetically and picks up the receiver. Maggie stares off into the distance, registering and vaguely approving the framed degrees and certificates, the large Gauguin exhibition poster. She *does* love her work. And she *is* looking forward to being on service.

You do harm to your patients and to young doctors who come to you for training in fact everyone hates you . . .

It crosses her mind to mention, just mention, the anonymous letters, but she puts the thought away. Maybe it's all over. Or again, maybe it's just something she'll have to learn to live with, a crackpot letter every morning. Weintraub would expect her to be tough — he helped her learn to be tough in all the right ways. He may not look it, in that fancy suit in this fancy office, but he's pretty tough himself. She remembers him at the end of a terrible, terrible night in the NICU, back in the old days when there was so much less they could do for meconium aspiration, a baby dying before their eyes — telling the weeping parents that there was nothing they could do, encouraging them to rouse the family priest at three A.M. for the baptism — and then the baby, inexplicably, agonizingly, getting a tiny bit better, a tiny bit better, as Weintraub hung over him and adjusted the ventilator and the priest stuck around and prayed. Maggie remembers Weintraub, much younger, of course, dressed in rumpled, bloody scrubs, of course, and with that exhausted, exhilarated, life-saving light in his eye, saying to her, with what seemed to both of them profound meaning, that old hospital aphorism: "Remember, Maggie, what doesn't kill you makes you strong."

He hangs up the phone. He looks her in the eye and picks the conversation up again, no lags, no hesitations.

"I don't know if there's been any talk about this, Maggie, but we're thinking of linking up with Saint Catherine's — taking their nurseries under our wing, so to speak."

"I've heard it mentioned." A finger on every pulse, that's me. Blessed Innocence and its expansion plans: what Dan would call, a little cynically, imperialism, empire building. And not only Dan; Blessed Innocence is already something of a two-thousand-pound gorilla, and other hospitals watch its moves pretty carefully.

"They've got a high volume of deliveries over there, and they're very interested in upgrading to a real level-three nursery — now they're at about a two point two, I'd say."

Maggie permits herself a discreet chuckle at this often-repeated witticism. A level-two nursery can care for newborns with some medical problems, while only a level three can handle babies on ventilators. St. Catherine's has a couple of ventilators, but they are notorious for transferring out any sick baby. The Blessed Innocence residents' standard wisecrack on the subject is that the ventilators are just to keep the nurses breathing until help arrives.

"We might start sending our people over — rotate the residents through, give them a taste of a NICU in a smaller hospital, retrain their nurses — nursing education is very excited about the idea."

"It does sound exciting." Every possible alarm buzzer is going off in Maggie's mind as she nods appreciatively and makes the appropriate *um-hum* noises of interest. Weintraub has bet on her before. He likes her style and she likes his. He knows how hard she works — how hard he taught her to work. And there's something else going for her too: They need to promote a woman. And yes, she deserves it, and yes, she's published plenty, and yes, Weintraub likes her. But also, let's face it: Who else do they have? Hank Shoemaker — too hard to get along with, too weird, always looks like a slob. Not executive material. David Susser — lab rat supreme, happy only when talking science to scientists. Claire Hodge — still isn't really back from her maternity leave, spends her life trying to get home to her baby. Elissa Gravenstein — smart but abrasive, always fighting with the nurses, telling Weintraub where to get off, sometimes right but often wrong, too tall, too fat, too loud. They need to promote a woman, but let's face it — it isn't going to be a woman like that. And Freddy Bellavista — sweetest guy you could ever hope to meet, but his research project flopped bigtime.

And now Weintraub is off down some other alley, and not her favorite. Not his either, she would guess: this new employee support program that the hospital vice president is so enthusiastic about, this New Age bullshit, Employee Empowerment Through Sharing. Has she had a chance to meet the director, Graham Shipley? Well, the hospital is hiring Shipley and his staff as "change consultants." When he says that, Maggie notes, he almost cracks, almost laughs, almost shrugs — but he doesn't. Oh, Harvey, you are a company man, Maggie thinks, but she thinks it fondly. There is no one that she would rather have running her department, no one she respects more — and if the price of power is that he has to play along while the hospital wastes money on some flavor-of-the-month consultants, well, so be it. Nothing, after all, can be as bad as the year they hired the alcoholic cultural sensitivity trainer. She almost says as much to Weintraub, but if he can be restrained, well, so can she. Here, he says, take a look at one of Shipley's survey forms. I just think you should understand that the entire hospital administration is committed to this at the very highest level. They'll notice who participates, who seems to be open to this whole change process. Have a leaflet. Passes it across the desk: Would you be interested in taking part in a staff support group facilitated by a hired professional?

Maggie looks it over, thinks, Give me a break. Nods enthusiastically. "Looks fascinating."

But now Weintraub isn't looking at her anymore, he's looking here and there around his office: diplomas, journals, that white coat hanging on a hanger on the back of the door, as if he's just one shrug away from practicing medicine.

"Your work is so important, Maggie, I'd like to see you go on publishing, and go on with the clinical work, of course. I've been very proud, watching you."

"I had good teachers." Well, it's the politic thing to say, but it's also true. He was a great teacher, once upon a time, the kind of teacher who changes your life, the kind of teacher she would like to be herself. But where is this leading?

"These are important years for building your career — I'd be sorry to see you taking any kind of long hiatus, or losing any of your dedication. Of course, I understand that sometimes there are other imperatives, other ties . . ." his voice trails off, and he reaches for his pad again.

She understands, of course. And she's suddenly so angry that it shakes her: How dare he? He's asking if she's planning a baby, if she's going to be disappearing on him, taking a maternity leave. He has no right to do that. He has no right! But her anger is almost immediately replaced by a sense of excitement: He's got to be sounding her out for something good. He just wants to be sure he isn't going to be hit with a long maternity leave right after he appoints her, that she isn't going to turn into Claire Hodge, into one of those women who suddenly want to work part-time, or leave the hospital by five.

"Harvey, before you know it, I'll be forty." She smiles. "Dan and I talked about having a baby a few years ago, but to tell you the truth, it didn't happen, and maybe that was just as well."

He's nodding now, agreeing, and she gets another jolt of anger: smug bastard with his daughters sitting there on his desk. How dare he agree that it's just as well?

"And you know, Harvey, I can't help thinking that for someone with no children, I have an awful lot of children. All those babies — when I think about them out there growing up!" How can she mean this as truly as she does, and yet also offer it up as cynically and calculatedly as she does? Dan would despise me for this, she thinks. Would he? Wouldn't he? Would he just smile?

"I know exactly what you mean," Weintraub says, and she knows that he does. She learned some of it from him, the long-term, shadow joys of being in at the beginnings of lives — and the skills, of course, to do that all-important good job. "It's the great blessing of this field," he says, gently. "The greatest joy there is."

Still, Maggie seethes a little inside, even as she smiles at him past the family pictures, which would of course never occur to him as having any relevance to their conversation.

In the corridor outside Weintraub's office, she is shaking very slightly, a tremor she recognizes from tense moments in the unit, waiting for a very sick baby to be transported in. It's the tremor of inaction, of holding back, waiting for the moment when she can give the orders and do what needs to be done. It always disappears promptly when she actually has the baby under her hands.

She is up on the roof because when her friend Peter Cannon, her best friend in the hospital, says, Want to have coffee? he really means, I want a cigarette. It is his major sin, this in a doctor about whom many jokes have been made along the lines of Saint Peter, or Peter Cannonized. So she meets him in the hospital cafeteria, where he buys not only coffee, but also an order of french fries, wilted from sitting under heat lamps since lunchtime, and a piece of Boston cream pie. Balancing these on a cardboard tray, he leads the way to the elevator, and Maggie, clutching her austere cup of hospital coffee with skim milk, trails him obediently.

They take the elevator to the top floor, then climb a last neglected metal flight of stairs and step out carefully through a doorway that has been, as usual, left illegally propped open by the maintenance workers, who have taken to smoking on the roof since the entire hospital was declared a smoke-free zone. There are a couple of blue-coverall-wearing environmental services workers up there now, smoking in the windbreak created by the old, dead brick chimneys. The day is crisp, the wind strong and laced with city grit, and Maggie finds it an unexpected pleasure to be outside.

Peter is the head of the clinic that cares for children with birth defects; he is a tall, thin, dapper, fast-moving man with a receding hairline and a handsome, square face. He has the eating habits, but not the waistline, of everyone's lovable roly-poly uncle, the one who finishes up what the children leave on their plates at Thanksgiving. For Maggie, he is a comparatively new friend, though she has been sending patients to him for years, children with congenital problems who graduate from the NICU and need continued care. Peter is such a notorious hospital saint, it made Maggie wary at first; he takes care of these complicated, devastated, depressing kids, the kids no one else wants. The kids who are not curable. But there is nothing at all pious about Peter, unless you count his regular attendance at Mass, of course. And his investment in his patients, Maggie has come to believe, is not so different from her feelings for the very premature babies: Cheer them on for what they can do, even if what they can do is limited. It is an achievement to live a little longer, to gain a little more control over your limbs, your speech, your bodily functions. And if those are the only achievements within a child's reach, then so be it. Every life is worth care and money and time and expertise.

Maggie gets a glimpse of it sometimes, and it takes her breath away — herself, Peter, all her colleagues, taking on these questions almost casually, as if they had every right to go to work in the morning and make these decisions. This mix of job detail and career talk with something else — call it arrogance and ambition of the highest kind, or call it goodness and the need to unsettle a cruel universe — but you have to give them full credit for what they are. For what they think is all in a day's work. For what happens when they get it wrong.

You do harm to your patients . . .

Peter, she thinks about saying, casually, ruefully. Peter, the craziest thing . . .

Peter is lining up his french fries neatly along the ledge at the edge of the roof. Maggie digs her hands into her skirt pockets, waiting for the squirrels to come, and looks out on the medical kingdom around her. Buildings connected by caterpillarlike bridges, multistoried parking lots squeezed in at odd angles, tight, choked streets crawling around the always expanding hospitals. Old buildings now used as laboratories, shiny new window-faced buildings built after successful capital campaigns, the whole complicated mess of interconnected institutions can be seen clearly from the roof of this particular older building, Blessed Innocence Hospital for Infants and Children.

The squirrels are coming now, two of them fighting over the first french fries, ignoring Peter and Maggie. Peter admires their survival among the hospital buildings, he remarks on their impressive size, their vigor, their lack of fear. And, of course, coming up to the roof to feed the squirrels allows him to sneak a smoke as well; like the janitors, he is puffing away.

He gestures with his half-eaten piece of Boston cream pie. "The cholesterol tastes better with nicotine," he says, smiling. "You ought to try it."

Maggie shakes her head. "I'm a self-righteous lifestyle puritan, like everyone else."

"You do still allow yourself the occasional glass of wine?"

"Dan just subscribed to a wine magazine."

"You see? Self-improvement through alcohol — there's the work ethic for you." Peter puffs manically on his cigarette, then stubs it out on the rough gray cement of the roof. He gobbles down the last of his pie, takes a long, happy breath of roof air, and points out a particularly plump squirrel, bushy tail held in a proudly erect scroll.

"Look at that sucker. You ever notice any babies missing, you know who sneaked in and ate them."

"Clinic busy today?" she asks.

"They love me, they can't keep away." He lights another cigarette.

"Are they going to give you money for another physician?"

Peter shrugs, a great big exaggerated shrug, palms up helplessly toward the heavens, mouth twisted quizzically. He does not write papers. He does not get big grants. All he does is take care of the hardest patients, and the hospital does not help him as it should — in fact, the hospital has repeatedly suggested to him that if his clinic needs another doctor, perhaps he should get grateful parents to raise money and establish an endowment.

Suddenly he grabs Maggie's arm, pulls her around a corner behind a boarded-up skylight. Two security guards, somewhat sheepish in their demeanor, have come out the propped-open doorway onto the roof. Peter and Maggie stand silently behind the skylight while the guards march over to the cluster of janitors and begin checking ID badges.

"Speaking of self-righteous lifestyle puritanism," Peter mutters into Maggie's ear.

"What's going on?"

"Don't you read your memos? Don't you ever go to your mailbox?"

"Yes," she says, a little grimly, "I go to my mailbox."

"Smoking on the roof has suddenly been discovered to be a terrible fire hazard, not to mention that it makes a mockery out of our glorious new smoke-free building policy. You know our slogan, Healthy Hospital, Healthy Sick People. They've got the security guards doing sweeps — they're taking down names."

Indeed, one of the guards is laboriously copying names off badges onto a clipboard.

"C'mon," Peter says. "So we can live to commit our crimes another day."

He guides her around a low wall and down a short flight of brick steps onto another level of roof. This section is a forest of square brick chimneys, each only a little taller than Maggie herself.

"Old ventilation system from the laboratory floor. Good place for playing hide and seek." He puts his finger to his lips, and then she hears it too, footsteps from somewhere among the chimneys. Maggie, feeling the not entirely pleasant tension of waiting to be caught, tries for a superior amused smile. Then she sees a man emerge from between two square chimneys maybe thirty feet away from where she stands. His back is to Maggie as he leans against a column; he is so large that he takes up most of the space between that column and its neighbor. She has no trouble recognizing him, even from behind, the faded low-riding jeans, the red thermal shirt, the black sweater, the hood of hair. Frank Gruenwasser, standing with his back to her, leaning his shoulder against the chimney. He looks calm and almost monumental as he stands there. He might be holding up the building. He does not, from the back at least, appear to be smoking. "It's the mailroom guy," Peter says, no doubt in relief that it isn't the security guards after all, but this time she shushes him.

"Something's going on," she hisses. "I want to see what he's doing up here."

When Maggie peeks around the chimney again, she sees the mailroom director talking to a nurse she doesn't know, a woman in her fifties with jet black hair in a Cleopatra cut, wearing a trim white tunic and closely fitting white pants. Okay, big deal, so the mailroom man has a friend. Maggie feels foolish, but also determined. She will stick this out and see whether they are here to talk, or smoke, or kiss. And then at least she will know something about this man.

"Holy cow!" Peter whispers. The nurse, her manner undeniably furtive, has just slipped some small object over to the mailroom man, who has instantly pocketed it. And from his pocket, digging deep into the jeans, which slip even further down, he withdraws several bills, which he hands to the nurse.

Maggie and Peter, without any discussion, whip back behind their pillar. They stare at each other, but neither speaks for a moment. In that moment, they hear footsteps once again, and when Maggie sneaks another peek at where the other two had been standing, they are both gone.

But still Peter speaks in a whisper. "Did you know about this?"

"No," says Maggie, weakly. "It was just a joke, following him."

"So while the heroic security guards are stamping out cigarette smoking —"

"Look, we don't really know what this was about —"

"Come on, Maggie. We just saw what was probably a drug deal, and a drug deal involving a nurse —"

"Do you know her? Who she is, where she works?"

"No," Peter says. "But I think I should find out."

Maggie's baby is still alive, but he's had a rocky night. Lung disease and more lung disease, lots of disturbing drops in his heart rate, and all the other things that go with being the youngest of the youngest. Maggie is not about to make the same mistake again, not about to barge right into the NICU and put everyone's back up. But she just happens to be passing, and that young woman, the intern, whatever her name is, Marjorie Fallon, is coming out, so she stops and makes conversation for a minute. Bad news. The head ultrasound shows bilateral bleeds into the brain, a common problem in very young premies.

"Too bad," Maggie says, a little gruffly, she's known a lot of premies, she's seen a lot of head bleeds — but damn it, this is *her* baby. She's tempted to give this intern a short lecture on head bleeds: Yes, they can mean brain damage, but there's no way to predict how much, there's no knowing with this one particular baby what the outcome will be. Maggie would bet Hank Shoemaker is all gloom and doom: damaged baby, devastated baby, a strong subtext of *should never have been resuscitated*. Well, if Hank Shoemaker wants to go throwing babies away — oh, just wait until they promote her!

And there's really no foolproof way to prevent an intraventricular hemorrhage in a very young premie.

"Well," she says to the intern, who is still standing there, staring at her with this blank, perky look on her face, "guess I'll see you next week, right?"

"Oh, right, yes! You're going to be our attending —"

"So you'll be here and I'll be here, and that baby will be here too," Maggie says. And then, because it is not yet her territory, she leaves the young woman standing there and heads for her office.

And finds another young woman standing outside the office door, a very different woman, and one she is much gladder to see.

"Theresa!"

"I was just writing a note to leave you —" Already Theresa is apologetic, soft-voiced, hesitant, as if making her excuses, as always, for the space she takes up, the attention she requests. She is a gentle, soft-edged woman, huddled in clothes too big for her: shapeless turtleneck, sacklike skirt, and an enormous white lab coat over it all.

"Do you want to come in —" Maggie digs in her pocket for her keys.

70

"No, I should be going." She is already backing away. "I just wanted to show you, I did get the catalogue for the winter extension school courses. I wondered if when you had a chance you would take a look at it and give me some advice —"

"Theresa, that's terrific!" Maggie hears her own voice as unusually bright and loud, contrasted with those gentle, almost whispered words.

Maggie has been encouraging Theresa for almost two years now as she has climbed, slowly, hesitantly, even painfully, the imposing mountain of the pre-med courses; taking them in the evenings, one by one, paying tuition for each — and now, when they are almost all finished, there are still the Medical College Admission Test, the applications, all the fees to pay. Theresa does not believe that she will ever be a doctor, or even a medical student; Maggie, a believer, knows with all her heart that science, medicine, authority, knowledge, will save Theresa's life — as she believes they have saved her own. This is Theresa's reward, like it or not, for her intelligence, for her astounding competence in the lab, for the almost embarrassing but still pleasant respect and awe in which she holds Maggie. What Maggie knows, and what Theresa is able to believe only sometimes, is that Theresa is wasting her life working as a lab assistant and bottle washer, that the same interest that drew her to work in a hospital setting will pull her through all the years of studying, and most especially, that she is as smart as any of her bosses, any of the doctors. Theresa, three years out of college, with a 4.0 four-year transcript from the University of Massachusetts, Boston, and two parents who were absolutely dead set against her original dream of medical school, veers back and forth between Maggie's confidence and optimism and her own tendency to believe the chance is gone, the die is cast.

. . . and to young doctors who come to you for training in fact everyone hates you and is always sorry to work with you . . .

"Let's have a look." Maggie grabs the catalogue away from her. "Here, Theresa, come on in for a minute." And then, as she digs in her pocket, pulls out her keys, she suddenly knows absolutely that someone has been in her room. There is nothing to see, just the closed white hospital door with her name printed discreetly on the little brown plaque off to the left, M. Claymore, M.D. There is nothing at all, except a terrified certainty, as she puts her key in the lock, that someone else has come through this door, that her office is not as she left it, is not waiting for her and welcoming her home.

The smell hits her as soon as she begins to push the door open. For an instant she wants to stop, pull it closed again, run away from the office. Find a security guard, send him in instead. But she pushes the door open all the way, breathing through her mouth, the way you would at the bedside of a patient suffering from particularly nasty diarrhea. Smells are a hospital fact of life. She switches on the light.

Smells are a hospital fact of life. As are bedpans, even bedpans full of someone's particularly nasty diarrhea, but that doesn't mean Maggie is prepared to encounter one sitting in the exact center of her desk. It is a standard dark yellow hospital bedpan. Her African violets have been shredded neatly into it, on top of the odiferous contents. Maggie averts her eyes, breathes through her mouth. She picks up the bedpan, holds it out, away from her, and walks rapidly into the bathroom down at the end of the hall near her office. She dumps what is in the pan, flowers and feces, into the toilet, flushes, flushes again, drops the pan itself in the enormous trash can. Someone will be in soon enough to empty it. Standing at the sink, she washes her hands several times. Then catches sight of herself in the mirror and is horrified to see that she looks like someone else, some horrified, terrified hospital victim, a patient and not a doctor, overwhelmed and undefended.

6

Makeovers

THIS IS THE MOST BEAUTIFUL THING *that I have ever seen.* Maggie, eighteen years old, late at night in a cluttered college dormitory room. The beat of somebody else's record player is coming dimly through the walls or up through the floor. A sludgy coffee cup at her elbow, a very roughly made bed behind her. Her hair is pulled back with an elastic into an uneven ponytail, under the too-bright keep-me-awake bulb of her desk lamp, her nails chewed with the tension of midterms. All the neatness and order in the room on a sheet of paper on her desk where she has just drawn out for herself, in black and blue and red ink, the lac operon.

It is the era of record players and typewriters; Maggie's second-hand manual portable Olivetti, a high school graduation gift from her mother, sits inert, between term papers, pushed to the back of the desk and piled with photocopied worksheets. But here on her notebook paper she has drawn a piece of eternal technology and explained it to herself.

She will remember this all her life as her first real and true moment of adult intellectual understanding. Her conversion experience. High school was all about being a good student, and she was a very good student in all her subjects, Maggie was, and she had aced high school biology and high school chemistry and high school physics, all without really paying attention. She had read a few books on animal behavior and listed "biology" as her interest going into college, and signed up cheerfully for more rounds of frog dissection and drawing and labeling neat diagrams, and whatever else they might throw at her. And she had, she now realized, spent the first month of college biology in the same note-taking, underlining daze: *Teach me something and watch me repeat it back.* But she was scared of the midterm, scared of the hungry pre-med students all around her, scared of the density of type in her molecular biology textbook, and so, facing the midterm, late at night, she had made herself read through the text with a different kind of line-by-line decoding, and then made herself write it out again, diagram it not for neatness but for meaning, as if the lac operon were something true and real to be explained, and not just the next stage in the great test-taking game of school.

The lac operon. It was the first system of gene regulation to be worked out and dissected and understood. The DNA sequence in *E. coli* bacteria, the dearly beloved subject of so many millions of experiments, the genetic switch that controls the metabolism of a particular sugar — lactose.

And Maggie understood it. She understood all of its many moving parts, its bits and pieces. She felt full of the delight of it — turn on the genes, turn off the genes, yes sugar, no sugar, induce, repress — and all of it built perfectly into the tiniest of spaces in the tiniest of organisms. Maggie had barely believed in bacteria up till now; bacteria in general and the famous *E. coli* in particular were just items on the list of schoolbook constructs, like electrons and potential energy and ancient Sumer. And now all of a sudden she was ready — eager — to go and preach, to stand up somewhere and explain, with fanatic excitement, what she had just understood about the workings of the world and the true meaning of life.

She wants to speak it aloud, she does. She can hear her own voice declaiming, explaining. She looks a little self-consciously around the room, but, as she knows, she is alone. Her roommate is at an all-night group-study session for the famously difficult introductory government survey course. Softly at first, then with more certainty and more volume, Maggie explains the lac operon to her wall. The genes, the enzymes, the promoter, the operator. "So, then," she demands, "what happens when there is only glucose present? The repressor protein stays bound to the DNA of the operator, and no transcription takes place — obvious, right? Who needs to transcribe the enzymes that break down lactose, when there isn't any lactose to break down and all you have is glucose? And then, if all you have is lactose, well, then the lactose binds to the repressor and that means the repressor doesn't stay bound to the DNA — and that means transcription can go on. So far so good — no lactose, no transcription, yes lactose and you pull the repressor off, so the lactose has induced the enzymes needed to break it down. Okay, but look at this: What if you have glucose *and* lactose both present? You might think that the lactose would turn on the transcription, but no!" Maggie pushes back her chair and begins to pace. She is talking now in exactly the tones and cadences that she will use all her life when she is teaching something she cares about, in the tones she will use twenty years down the line when she teaches young doctors how to turn on the hearts and lungs of newborns. Maggie has found an essential truth, and she wants to explain it.

Her voice gets louder still. "The bacteria *prefers* to use *glucose,* not *lactose.* So even if there's lactose present, as long as glucose is there, the bacteria wants to use that. So there's another whole mechanism built right in! If there's glucose available, the cell doesn't make any cAMP." She pauses dramatically, then puts on a fake confused voice: "*cAMP,* you ask, *what's all this about cAMP?* Well, without cAMP, the CAP protein can't bind to the DNA. And if the CAP protein can't bind to the DNA, then transcription can't happen. And glucose lowers the cAMP — so there you are, the lactose may be there, the repressor may be pulled off, everyone may be ready and waiting for the transcription to go on — but no deal! No go! Null and void! The glucose has turned down the cAMP, which has turned off the CAP, and you can't have any enzymes to break down your lactose, so there!"

Let me at it, Maggie is thinking. Let me at that exam. Or maybe, Let me at that fucking exam! Let me at those fucking pre-meds! And also, of course, let me at this, let me throw myself against this, let me understand it, all there is, and thereby understand everything.

And it lasted, it stuck, it took. She was in college at the right moment for the early intoxications of genetics and cell biology, worlds exploding and opening from moment to moment and crowded full of incredibly smart, eager people who understood one another's secret language and who knew they would be the ones to write all the new rules of the universe. Yes, of course. Welcome to the club. And she was in college at a good moment for joining the club; there was scholarship money available for a smart student. Summer research money. Lab fellowships — Maggie as she finished college knew exactly what she was going to be: a cell biologist, a scientist, smart and serious, unadorned and hardworking, and close, remarkably close, to the core of real life and its waiting secrets. She came out of college and went diving down into the graduate school years of total science, total lab life, with the eager abandon of a creature finally released into her natural element. Goodbye forever to New Jersey and to adolescent turmoil, goodbye to the aimlessness of college parties and the silly ups and downs of college love affairs, and goodbye to everything else extraneous and distracting that people made up for themselves because they weren't doing the things that really mattered. Religion, for example. Even, to tell the truth, most relationships. At her college graduation, Maggie was patronizingly gentle to her mother; of course Annalisa would never understand who her daughter was and what she studied, never learn that secret technical language that allowed Maggie to read and understand life itself.

She liked the lab, or some aspects of the lab, and she liked the life — she still looks back on it as a halcyon, pure period, and she still thinks of that serious young self as the first, true Maggie, that scruffy twenty-two-year-old graduate student who had evolved out of that slightly less scruffy college student. How she looked, how little she cared. Well, perhaps it was a scruffy era, especially for science majors, jeans and army pants, thermals and flannel shirts. Certainly the medical students who parade nowadays through the hospital under Maggie's watchful eye are much much spiffier. On the other hand, she herself has gotten dressed. That's why she looks back with such affection: how happily free from all the adolescent pulls of competitive beauty — and from the opposing messages that had been so strong in her childhood, in her high school years, the stern injunctions of modesty in the sight of God, and the need to regard her body as a holy temple. And of course free also from her own reaction and rebellion — her body as temptation, her body as weapon, her body as instrument of the devil — she was free of it all. Free to regard her body as a working machine. In the lab, she had been among people who thought about almost nothing larger than a cell; they talked grants and science and scientific politics, and if they had their little outside interests, experimental jazz or some solitary sport (rock climbing, long-distance bicycling), they chased those down on their own time. They didn't talk about their feelings, they didn't talk about current events, they didn't talk about their personal lives — those were subjects of conversation for people who didn't understand molecular genetics. And as for sex, well, everyone needs a little of that, and every so often Maggie would take up with some new postdoc for a little while — someone with whom she could go home, still talking science.

Khaki pants and pullover shirts every day of the year, turtlenecks in the winter, T-shirts in the summer, just like the male graduate students; haul a bag of laundry over to the laundromat once a week, and replace the sneakers when they get too ratty. Anything else would take time from the lab. And, of course, she had worn her hair down below her shoulders, neatly braided back every morning and fastened with a rubber band. Practical and efficient, not dressed to distract or be distracted.

But somehow, Maggie did get distracted. Or dissuaded, or turned aside, or maybe just turned. She liked the lab and she liked the life, but as she balanced that complex equation of talent and luck and time and place, she found herself, over the next several years, shifting course, shifting ambitions, shifting her sights. The cell biology program was poised between the university biology department and the medical school, and there was Maggie, once so scornful of pre-meds, now starting to look with more interest and more envy at the scientists who were also doctors, who moved in

77

and out of the cell biology laboratories and their mysterious medical lives. Maybe without knowing it, Maggie started to get hungry for a job in which she would directly touch people. Maybe she started to doubt herself as a pure researcher — doubt her aptitude, doubt her dedication, doubt her chances for success. Or maybe she was just growing into her own next phase, her next conversion. *I want to do something that's bigger than cells, something that actually affects other people.* And, of course, *I want to be sure I can get a job doing what I'm trained to do . . .*

And in medical school she made herself over. All right, allow her a genetic metaphor harking back to that first heady moment when she glimpsed the truth of gene regulation, and therefore of the universe, and therefore, in college student ascending order of importance, of her own destiny. That was an essential reinvention or conversion — call it transcription, as in DNA into RNA. And then, the shift from scientist to physician — call that translation, as in RNA into protein. The very structural stuff of life. What happened in medical school was far more trivial, and yet in its own way all-consuming, cosmetic, yet essential — call it the tweaking and folding, the external modifications that allow a protein, once the amino acids have been linked in line, to perform its function in the cell.

All right, as Maggie herself, in teaching and speechifying mode might have said, *all right,* enough of this metaphor. What are we talking about here? We are talking about how I decided to turn myself into a dressed-up, grown-up doctor so that the other goddamn doctors would take me seriously, okay?

She made herself over and advanced to meet her destiny, her job, her husband, her place in the world. Maggie met Dan in medical school, both of them living in the medical students' dormitory, but both older, coming back to school after a couple of years away, she in the lab and he doing do-good work, setting up rural migrant health centers in Florida. They were a relief to each other among their young and eager classmates, two slightly older people who knew what they wanted, who were in medical school to get out on the other end and get on with life.

She went to medical school. And along with the loss of science, for so, after all, she felt it, along with being plunged into memorization and multiple-choice test taking with a group of high-achieving, newly minted college graduates, came a certain loss of that happy unconsciousness, that scientific-world immunity to the foibles of ordinary people.

What happened to Maggie's appearance was a calculated campaign. It was clear enough, looking at the few women who came to lecture to the medical students, that doctors did not enjoy that science-wonk immunity. Doctors dressed for work, doctors looked like professionals. Successful women in medicine, attendings at the important teaching hospitals, wore stockings and skirts and makeup, and their hair was not haphazardly pulled out of the way into random ponytails. Perhaps that made them look more reassuringly doctorly to their patients; certainly it made them acceptably feminine to their older senior male colleagues.

Maggie was not a person to expend her energy fighting something that would never change. She was not eager to be seen as a rebel or even as a rugged individualist. On the other hand, she felt, she had missed the education that other women seemed to have acquired effortlessly along the way. Her adolescence, she supposed, had been warped by obeying the dictates of the church or fighting them; Annalisa's below-the-knee frills or her own secret halter tops. And college had been about something else, about finding out what was real and true and essential and getting rid of the trimmings. And now she needed trimmings. Okay. Problems are there to be solved. She bought the goddamn magazines and the goddamn makeup, and she learned to do it. She clocked the new routines into her day and her week and her month, shaved her legs every night in the shower, paid a ridiculous amount for a haircut every eight weeks. Bought clothes, cheap during residency, now more expensive; skirts below the knee, button-down blouses with feminine collars, little ruffles down the front, bows at the neck, like the silly bow ties of dandified but transcendently nerdy male doctors. Wool and linen and cotton jersey, challis, paisley, maroon, navy, gray. She is, after all, a doctor, and this is, after all, Boston.

She has made herself over. None of it comes naturally. It has been laborious, uncomfortable, and, she sees clearly, only partially successful. But it was necessary, and if the cultivation of female rituals and vanities has not come to feel quite natural, it has at least come to seem absolutely routine. And yet, and yet — fundamentally it all feels wrong, every bit of it. She gets dressed in the morning feeling that she is enclosing herself in a shell, a mask, a costume. She scrapes her legs, tweezes her eyebrows, protects her manicured hands when she does the dishes, all with the strong sense that she is putting on a moderately successful act. And because it is an act, because none of it comes from the heart, she does not dare let down her guard. Other doctors, when they have no patients to see, might come to work dressed casually, might risk running shoes or a day without earrings. Maggie feels, however ridiculously, that if she lets go once she might lose it all; the hell with the carefully conservative jewelry, screw the pantyhose, now and forever, never belt another dark wool skirt.

Interestingly, despite other messages from these same magazines, not to mention from the culture as a whole, Maggie has no particular anxiety about how Dan feels about the way she looks. They had, after all, become involved when she still looked like what she thought of as her real self. And his relation to her body and her face was not the appraisal of someone looking over a sexual prospect, but instead some bedrock-deep connection, some sense that they were part of each other. She would not have said "joined at the heart," would have disliked the sentimentality, the aesthetics, and the physiology of that notion, but she might have said "in some way hooked up to each other's neurons."

And anyway, Dan of all people. He had headed straight into a job for which he never had to wear a tie; he does not own a suit. A casual clinic in a bad neighborhood; he goes off each morning in khakis ordered from L.L.Bean and a button-down shirt. He washes his face with whatever he finds in the soap dish. It is his true self, and also his vanity by now: He knows fine foods, he knows fine wines, but he owns nothing that cannot be tossed into the washing machine. Regular cycle. Organic laundry soap, which maybe doesn't get the colors quite as bright as something not as good for the planet, but Dan has his values clear. And yes, maybe he is a little bit proud that he still has the basic swimmer's physique, the broad shoulders and strong arms, the relatively narrow waist, but it's the private pleasure of someone who would perhaps always rather be naked. Who would, perhaps, come to think of it, always rather have Maggie relax and take her own clothes off. He watches Maggie's moderately successful attentions to herself with indulgence but no real interest; if this is what she has to do, then this is what she has to do.

Moderately successful. Only moderately because, of course, there was only so much she could do. What does Maggie look like, after all the routines and all the careful attention to detail? She is still solid, with a waist that remains thicker than she would like despite faithful years of sit-ups on a slanted board. She has an appealing, vigorous walk, a long and almost exuberant stride — but the shoes and clothes she wears to work trim it back, just a bit. She has dark hair cut to below her ears and styled into a sleek frame around her face, hair well tamed and unquestionably professional. Dark eyes set surprisingly far apart, and sometimes lit with evanescent yellow-green lights. Her nose somewhat fleshy, and what keeps her face from being unremarkably pretty is the imbalance between large nose, broad space between the eyes, and a mouth ordinary in size, which looks small in comparison. This was, at any rate, what she was told when the makeup consultant analyzed her features five years ago, and she was advised to draw on a slightly larger mouth every morning with lip liner, fill it in with lipstick, and face the world with a more correctly proportioned face. She doesn't do it, of course; movie stars may need large, full, sensuous lips, even if they're drawn on, but a doctor does just as well with a small, conservatively colored mouth.

What Maggie looks like, when all is said and done, is a carefully dressed, carefully made up, ordinary-looking youngish woman. Facing forty. And for this reason, at certain moments, it seems to her ridiculous to go to so much trouble, so much expense, so much discomfort. It will never make her beautiful; in fact, she does not yearn to be beautiful, but still — all this work! To go through so

7

Damage Control

A hospital with a reputation to uphold such as your own must be aware of the dangers posed by an unscrupulous and unqualified doctor who is well known to everyone who has worked closely with her as dangerous to her patients by virtue of her bad judgment and lack of knowledge as well as her willingness to sacrifice the lives of children or even we could say kill them neglect them murder them. A head nurse such as yourself in a position of power has a moral obligation to prevent injury to innocent patients by keeping Doctor Maggie Claymore off your ward and if possible out of the hospital all together.

IS THERE ANYBODY ELSE who has a key to your office?" The chief of hospital security is looking at her like it's all her fault.

"Probably," Maggie says. "You know, it's one of those little offices they carved out on the fifth floor — it used to be where Fiscal Services was, and before that I think it was part of Social Work. Anyone could have a key — plus, you know, those locks aren't all that hard to open. I've seen someone open those doors with a credit card."

Sandow eyes her severely.

"It was a security guard," Maggie says, self-righteously. "He

83

didn't have the right master key, and my friend was locked out, so he opened the door with a credit card and a hairpin."

"Dr. Claymore, I have only a limited amount of time this morning. Perhaps if we could discuss who you think might be behind these letters." Martin Sandow has a smooth, handsome, corporate face, a nice gray suit, a big bulging chest, and a disproportionately trim waist that suggests regular gym workouts. Maggie, looking at him, feels he is about to try to sell her life insurance, or maybe about to conduct one of those investment seminars they're always sticking in at medical meetings.

He grabs up a yellow pad and a pen. "When did this event at your office occur?"

"Tuesday I got an anonymous hate letter. And I've gotten one every day since then — another copy of the same letter. On Wednesday, someone broke into my office and left a bedpan full of excrement on my desk. And now all these other letters."

A letter to every nursing supervisor in the hospital; Maggie has seen two, received by the nursing supervisors in the NICU and the bone marrow transplant unit down the hall. Addressed to the women by name, warning in somewhat formal language, that Doctor Maggie Claymore was a danger to her patients and had achieved her position at Blessed Innocence Hospital through forged credentials and trading sexual favors for professional advancement. *As a professional woman who is herself of the highest quality both personally and professionally you need to be aware of the danger that this so-called doctor may pose to patients who come to this hospital expecting in good faith to receive only the best of care and also to her fellow employees who do not all of them yet realize the type of person they have among them . . . Sincerely yours, one who can no longer remain silent.*

Letters all over the place. Everyone knows. Anyone could know. It makes her furious, furious enough to storm into the hospital security headquarters and demand action — and come up against this smooth and corporate fellow, Martin Sandow, with his limited time this morning. A gold hospital service plaque on the wall, an absolutely and definitively clear desk, a gleaming gold pen set. Security is what you call if a parent gets violent, or goes crazy and tries to grab a sick baby and walk out, or when some dirtbag goes through the nurses' lounge and takes the coffee machine and the stethoscopes and someone's wallet. Security is uniformed guards with their badges and their static-emitting walkie-talkies, guards notoriously slow to arrive at a crisis, usually big, usually dumb, occasionally helpful. Who would have thought security was also this man and this office, and what the hell does he know about anything, anyway?

"At the time that your office was broken into, what exactly was taken?"

"Nothing. Nothing was taken. Someone just came in, left this thing on my desk."

"You mean, almost like some kind of practical joke?"

She shrugs.

The fact is, she badly wants to believe in this man, in his expertise, in his powers of detection and protection. She has met this mechanism often enough in parents, the desperate desire to repose faith and trust and hope, the impatience with any doctor who tries to explain uncertainty or the limitations of medical powers. It is very heartening to believe you are in expert hands, and to believe that those hands can turn everything around and bring you to the happy ending you so desperately desire. But now, face to face with Martin Sandow, she frankly cannot make that leap of faith. What she feels, with a heavy weariness, is that she will have to explain even the simplest facts about her life, her office, her job, to this too closely shaved expert in nothing, and when she is all done, he will understand less than she does.

"Baby Boy Kennedy."

"Kennedy?"

"Not those Kennedys."

That brand-new too-small baby, the one automobile-accidented into life before his fourteen-year-old mother even knew she was pregnant — they are saving his life, whether he wants it saved or not, whether he will ultimately live or not — but they are doing it by means of sharp points that pry into his tiny limbs in search of blood, a plastic tube curving down into his trachea. This is not what he was meant to live through. Maggie, who is not really a woman without imagination, does not try to imagine the mind of such a baby, though she has sometimes thought about a distant future in which premature babies will bubble contentedly in incubators built like fish tanks, all warm fluids and safe darkness. Soft, nourishing devices waving gently in the currents like helpful plants. A throbbing generator like a heartbeat pulsing through the dimness. What must it be like for a baby so small his eyelids are still fused closed to be assaulted by unfiltered light and noise? Maggie doesn't know, but she needs the noise and the light, and if the baby lives, he will not remember this, of course. Of course not.

His fourteen-year-old mother, one of her arms in a cast from that same automobile accident, sits in a wheelchair next to his warming table. What does she see? She never stays long, on these elaborately arranged visits to the NICU. And she comes accompanied only by nurses; no family members, no boyfriend.

Her important political father, besieged by reporters and rumors, held a press conference at the State House yesterday. A man who all his professional life has been a Kennedy in Massachusetts, but not one of those Kennedys. That's been his burden, his public handle — now he has another one. Grandfather of the car crash baby. Publicly stood by his daughter, reaffirmed his faith in the good doctors and nurses of Blessed Innocence. Who have all, by the way, seized on that designation from day one: Baby Boy not-those-Kennedys he will be as long as he stays in the NICU.

And Grandpa not-those-Kennedys has refused to give any details about the baby's father, or about his daughter's presence in the car during the night. "These are private family matters," he said, publicly. "Private matters to be discussed privately." Dan showed Maggie the newspaper story; the phrase rang in her head when she got to work and found out about all the letters to all the nursing supervisors.

Martin Sandow has taken her seriously. Two hours later, he comes to find her in her office, to inspect the scene of the crime — and he brings along a hospital attorney. For "damage control," he says, introducing the attorney, Elaine Oliphant. Damage control, a phrase

Maggie finds ominous: Obviously, he is not talking about damage to her. To Maggie, the two of them seem to fill her small office with an alien and oppressive presence.

"I know Elaine," she says, cutting short the introduction. When she looks at Elaine, she remembers moments over the years when medical cases spilled over into legal cases: one ugly battle about whether parents could decide to withdraw aggressive medical therapy from a baby who the NICU staff believed was going to do well, one protracted custody arbitration about a mother who wanted to take her newborn home with the oxygen he required, but was constantly being found smoking in the bathroom, one threatened malpractice case concerning a newborn brought in by helicopter from Martha's Vineyard who died on the way. Bad stories, bad feelings — but Maggie and Elaine had gotten along; Elaine had been shrewd and to the point. All doctors, perhaps, distrust all lawyers a little, but in Maggie's opinion, Elaine is okay. But what is damage control?

Sandow is making notes furiously, looking around Maggie's small, neat office as if spotting clues left and right. His handwriting, Maggie can see, is rounded and regular and large, the handwriting of a man with nothing to hide. Nurse's handwriting. "Now, these letters that arrived today were all fully addressed — must have been left somewhere for interhospital mail pickup. Probably used one of the really busy drops where no one would notice an extra ten envelopes."

"Ten?" asks Elaine Oliphant, shifting in her chair; her heavy silver necklace jingles faintly. She is a cheerful, rail-thin woman maybe ten years older than Maggie. Her light brown hair is touched with silver-gray, and she tends to wear tight suits, short skirts — she has amazing legs. But she favors ethnic jewelry — today she wears this rather frightening necklace of carved silver, which covers the entire front of her chest; she might be from a mountain tribe, wearing her dowry on her bosom for all to see.

Elaine opens a folder, puts it down on Maggie's desk. She looks Maggie in the eye. "Do you remember the Heather Clark case?"

"Sure." Maggie is surprised, a little taken aback. "The little girl who died."

Elaine indicates her folder. "I have an anonymous letter that says you killed her."

This letter, different from the others Maggie had seen, had been received by the nursing supervisor on West Seven:

Doctor Maggie Claymore who has no more right to that title than one of the poor innocent babies in her so-called care is as a matter of fact the murderer responsible for disconnecting your patient Heather Clark from her monitors and leaving her to die alone in her room whether from motives of malicious practical joking or perhaps because she se-cretly believes that children with birth defects and other problems are better off dead but in either case she is not a fit person to be allowed to hold power and authority in a children's hospital where people like yourself work hard to provide excellent care. If you investigate her whereabouts you will find that she was indeed in the hospital on that night although she did not arrive to help at the resuscitation or in any way contribute anything to the care of poor Heather after her terrible heartless and murderous criminal action resulting in the code.

In a way, the thing that upsets Maggie most of all, the thing that makes her so mad she can hardly speak to them politely, is that they have actually bothered to check; already Elaine has "verified" that yes, Maggie was the NICU attending at the time of Heather Clark's death, and she has checked the old call rotas and spoken to Leo, the intern who was on duty.

"What do you think Leo thought when you asked him those questions? What do you think he's saying to the other residents? By now, everyone in the hospital probably knows I'm your prime suspect!"

Can anyone, anyone at all, be wondering whether this is true? Could anyone wonder, even for a split second, if she murdered a child because the child had congenital anomalies? Will someone whisper it to Peter Cannon, in his busy clinic full of children, no child born intact? She cannot bear that anyone should say such a thing about her, should hear such a thing about her. She cannot bear it.

Exercising her own form of damage control, Maggie had already forced herself that morning to call Harvey Weintraub and tell him about the letters — clearly he is going to hear about them, so he had better hear it from her. He was concerned and solicitous, and she was shaking when she put down the phone. She had thought, originally, to call Peter next, to say, Peter, the most awful thing is happening to me, come have lunch with me, tell me it will be okay. But she had not done it. She had not been able to do it.

"I have no connection to Heather Clark or her death."

"You were in the hospital that night, though?"

"Yes." Reluctantly. And again, "Yes."

More than a year earlier, two floors up from the NICU, a small child died in the night. Her name was Heather Clark, and she suffered from a whole constellation of problems. She had been born with deformities (or anomalies, as the genetics specialists say, as Maggie says) of her face, her airway, her kidneys, her heart, and her brain. To a very great extent, she had defied expectations. When she was born, her parents had been repeatedly cautioned that she might not survive infancy; they had been told that she would probably be severely retarded, that she might never feed herself, never learn to speak. But she survived her infancy, survived one surgery after another, and though her development was hardly normal, it was obvious that behind the face that had been largely reconstructed in one of the longest plastic surgeries ever performed on a child her size, there was a brain that was livelier than anyone had predicted.

Heather did not roll over at three months and sit at six, she did not babble at nine months and talk at fourteen, but by the age of two she could walk and she was beginning to talk. Her mother, Cordelia Clark, although she was generous in her thanks to the doctors and nurses and physical therapists and speech specialists and developmentalists, never hid the fact that she took personal credit for Heather's progress, divided it only with God.

Heather was hospitalized at the age of three for a respiratory infection. It was not the first time. She had been born with an almost nonexistent chin, leaving her airway unprotected; every time she swallowed, fluid could go down the wrong tube and get into her lungs. But surgery had improved her facial anomalies; among other things, the surgeons had built her a chin, which had to some extent improved both her breathing and her swallowing. But her trachea was still not normal, and she was subject to pneumonias whenever she caught cold, and to occasional breathing problems in her sleep at any time. At home she always slept with a monitor on. After three days in the hospital, she was much better, and her mother felt able to leave her and go home to attend to the new baby, Sean. Heather knew all the nurses, they all knew Heather; she was something of a pet patient on the infant and toddler ward.

So Cordelia Clark went home to Sean, and Heather drank a small cup of chocolate milk through a straw for her evening snack and settled down to sleep, attached to a cardiorespiratory monitor and an oxygen saturation monitor. Because of her vulnerability to respiratory viruses, and because every single child on the infant and toddler ward seemed to have a bad runny nose, the nurses had given her a private room, even though this meant putting her all the way down at the end of the hall. Her two monitors stood on a little metal stand outside the door, their alarms turned up as loud as possible so that they would be heard down the hall at the nurses' station if there was any problem.

And during the night there was a code down the hall; a baby who had been recovering from a bad case of croup suddenly got much sicker and stopped breathing. There was the hustle and bustle of the code, doctors and nurses from all over the hospital. Finally, the baby with croup, safely intubated, had been transferred to the intensive care unit by a flying wedge of senior residents and intensive care nurses, pushing the crib, the monitors and the portable oxygen tank, while a respiratory therapist walked at the head of the bed, squeezing regularly on a resuscitation bag. And then, after that baby was gone, it was suddenly discovered that Heather Clark was dead in bed, disconnected from her monitors, and that the alarms on both monitors, which should have loudly called attention to the disconnection, had been silenced.

No one could say what had happened. Had someone, maybe someone who didn't know the ward and had only come for the emergency, silenced the alarms because they were beeping during the code? Had that person maybe even checked Heather, seen she was all right, silenced the alarms because they were beeping for nothing (a common enough problem), perhaps even meant to come back and turn them on again? Could there actually have been foul play — had someone disconnected the monitor leads and turned off the alarms and left the child to die?

"Did you go to the codes on West Seven — either of them?"

"When I heard the second code announcement, the Heather Clark code, so soon after the other announcement, of course I wondered what the hell was going on on West Seven — so I ran up. But every doctor in the hospital was already there, I couldn't even get into the room. I checked to see that they had senior people there, and then Leo paged me back to the NICU so I left. It was a real mob scene."

Elaine nods. "That would check with what Leo told me." She sees Maggie's face and adds hastily, "Believe me, I'm not accusing you of anything. I'm just trying to decide who needs to know about this letter, and how much they need to know."

Don't show it to anyone, Maggie wants to say. Haven't enough people seen it already? She thinks again of Peter Cannon, reading that sentence, *she secretly believes that children with birth defects and other problems are better off dead,* and she pushes the thought away. Not Peter. Not my colleagues. And, please, not Theresa. Not Theresa, who has already seen my office vandalized — a stupid joke, I told her, and I toughed it out. Don't show this letter to anyone. Not the people who think well of me. Not the people who like me. But please, above all, whatever you do, don't show this letter to the people who already don't like me.

How many people are there, Maggie thinks, who already don't like me? Okay, we know there's one and that one is crazy — well, okay, we know there are probably a few, and they aren't all crazy — that's just life. But how many are there? And how many who like me and think well of me? Please, don't make me start keeping count.

The police investigation of Heather Clark's death was immensely hampered by the immediate hospital response to Heather's pulseless body, which had been to hold another, this time unsuccessful code; by the time the police came to examine the room, the relevant monitors and monitor leads had been handled by the doctors and nurses trying, some of them through tears, to resuscitate the child. And of course there was no hope at all of making sense of the fingerprints on the doorknob, on the bedrails, on Heather's chart.

By firm hospital custom, NICU personnel did not go to codes elsewhere in the building. They stayed with their own — and if one of their own tried to die, they did not call a code, either. That was the point of intensive care; everyone and everything needed for a resuscitation was already there, and the babies were too sick to be left unattended by their doctors and nurses. However, when Maggie heard the second code call in less than two hours for the same ward, West Seven, she decided to run up and see if they needed extra hands. She hurried up the two flights to the seventh floor, only to find the hall already crowded with doctors and nurses and respiratory therapists, everyone who had been assembled for the first code and then some. Maggie's memory is actually very specific; she remembers the senior cardiac surgery fellow trying to fight his way into Heather's room, but the crowd around her bed was so dense that even that famously aggressive two-hundred-and-fifty-pound former college fullback was having some trouble.

Even from the hallway, Maggie had seen that something strange was going on. Code discipline seemed to have broken down altogether; a nurse should have been in charge, sending away the excess people, clearing the room. Other nurses should have been calming the other parents, who were standing in other doorways up and down the hall, bewildered in their nightclothes, some protectively clutching their own breathing babies. Maggie remembers feeling a little puzzled herself — she didn't know what was going on, but she could clearly see that the last thing anyone needed was another doctor. The cardiac surgeon gave one fierce twist of his mighty shoulders and made it into the room; a wall of white backs closed behind him. And at that moment her beeper went off; Leo, the NICU intern was paging her back to ask for some final instructions about a baby's ventilator. She slipped back into the stairwell, back to where she belonged, shaking her head at the disorder on the ward.

The next day, she heard some details of what had happened; it was the talk of the hospital. The autopsy revealed only that Heather had, as hospital parlance would have it, died of her disease. She had died choking on thick mucus containing some amount of regurgitated chocolate milk, clogging her always too narrow and now infected and inflamed airway. She had not been able to breathe, and after a while, her heart, oxygen deprived and never completely normal in its functioning, had stopped. No question that if she had been properly attached to the monitors and someone had come promptly in response to the alarm, her airway could have been suctioned and she would almost certainly have survived.

Cordelia Clark, not surprisingly, had sued the hospital, and, not surprisingly, a year later the case had not yet come to trial. Maggie knew this was going on, as did every doctor in the hospital, but to tell the truth, she had not given the story much thought; it was a bad thing, but it had happened out of her bailiwick, and hospitals are full of bad things. It was someone else's lawsuit, someone else's headache, someone else's tragedy. Maggie was fully capable of losing sleep agonizing over medical mistakes, over things not done or done badly, but there have to be some patients who aren't your problem.

Maggie got home early, before Dan, already somewhat unusual. She looked up from the sidewalk to see the windows on the second floor were dark, confirmed that Dan's disreputable car was not parked on the street, and instead of letting herself into their apartment, she rang the downstairs doorbell, Sarah Hartz's doorbell, and now sat drinking tea and eating homemade honey-nut cookies. I should do this more often, Maggie thought, as Penelope charged across the kitchen to climb into her lap, her red corduroy overalls crusted with bits of the blue Play-Doh she had been rolling out on the floor. I should do this more often, and it shouldn't take a major disaster to bring me down here, looking for company.

Penelope, when she was being affectionate, was a significant but willing weight. Her firm little bare feet pressed hard into Maggie's thighs as she stood up, balancing easily on Maggie's lap. With one hand she continued to work a little blue ball, and the salty, chemical smell of Play-Doh seemed remarkably familiar. Surely, Maggie thought, I haven't touched this stuff in thirty years.

"My Play-Doh," Penelope said. "Blue."

"It's very nice." It always took her a few minutes to relax around her goddaughter, and to accept the rush of pleasure and affection that came with Penelope's recognition, with her status as valued visitor. Penelope flashed her now a very complex, spritelike smile, part wicked glee, part the delighted anticipation of adult reaction.

"I eating the Play-Doh," she said, and raised the blue blob to her lips.

Sarah's maternal hand swooped down and removed it. "Play-Doh is not for eating. Play-Doh is for playing with."

Penelope's face drooped, then contorted, and a first howl startled Maggie. Sarah's hand dangled again in front of her daughter's nose, and therefore, in front of Maggie's as well. This time it had a honey cookie in it. Like a fish rising to the bait, or perhaps more like a large snapping turtle, Penelope jerked her head forward and bit the cookie out of her mother's fingers. Of necessity she stopped crying long enough to gulp it down — no, maybe more like a boa constrictor, Maggie thought, watching her take in the whole half-dollar-sized cookie and apparently send it right down into her gastrointestinal tract.

Then she opened her mouth and sang, spraying cookie crumbs in all directions:

"Puff the magic magic! Puff the magic magic!"

"Magic *dragon*," said Sarah.

Penelope got louder. "Puff the magic magic!" There was a hint of a tune in the line as she delivered it, but only a hint.

Maggie brushed the cookie crumbs off her sleeves and took another cookie herself. She was tempted to sing a line or two herself, or maybe to ask Sarah to sing the whole song, tempted to stuff herself with honey cookies and cover herself with crumbs. She hugged Penelope tight and the child slid into a comfortable sitting position on her lap, allowed Maggie to kiss her antic curls — and then slid down again to run barefoot across the kitchen and sing her one line again, as loud as she could.

It was a very pleasant kitchen. Sarah was one of the world's all-time slobs, and always had been, but she had a certain talent for nest building. True, the sink was piled full of dirty dishes, and true, several days worth of mail and catalogues and circulars was scattered on the kitchen table, but it was a kitchen full of bright metal canisters, tea and flour and sugar, big glass jars of pasta, beans, rice, lentils. A hanging wreath of sage leaves, another of dried red chili peppers. Perhaps Sarah was actually neater than she used to be, perhaps that was one more discipline that motherhood had imposed on her. Penelope's highchair, an up-to-the-minute white high-tech wonder, sat drawn up to the littered butcher block table. Its tray was clean and clear, ready for Penelope to eat her dinner — if she still had any appetite after all the honey cookies.

She tried to take a polite interest in Sarah's seed catalogues. The house had a tiny but sunny backyard, which neither Maggie nor Dan had ever attended to, and which Sarah now gardened assiduously.

"As many red flowers as possible," Sarah said, opening to dog-eared pages.

"MY red red red red!" said Penelope, pushing close to the table.

Maggie reached down and snagged her, hauled her back up to lap level, and Penelope giggled.

"You red red red red!" Sarah said, pointing to Penelope's socks. "What's Penelope's favorite color?"

"Puff the magic magic!"

Maggie imagined the two of them, in next summer's sun, digging among the red flowers. And, clutching Penelope suddenly close, felt a little dizzy. She had no wish at all to confide in Sarah about the anonymous letters, the whole mess. Sarah herself was rather prone to conspiracy theories; each of her jobs had in one sense or another blown up in her face eventually, and she was always full of explanations. People resented her, people tried to take credit for her accomplishments, people plotted against her because her presence made them look bad. She never wondered whether the reason that every job she did deteriorated into conspiracies against her might have anything to do with her own approach to life. Maggie had over the years listened through any number of conspiracies, any number of stabs in the back by women Sarah had

8

Godchild

HAVING SARAH HARTZ FOR A FRIEND in medical school had been Maggie's vicarious rebellion, as she marched straight ahead into residency, fellowship, success, love and marriage, house and job. Had Maggie really known, looking at her way back when, that Sarah was not going to follow some version of the same trajectory? Sarah was a recognizable high-achieving left-over hippie Jewish princess, with the long curling black hair and the definite features, prominent nose, big dark eyes. She dressed the socially conscious medical student part, did medical school in ethnic prints and faded blue jeans and long silver filigree earrings from India, did medical school with clogs and a battered backpack. But all of the other concerned students sorted themselves neatly into residency programs to become gynecologists who really talked honestly to their patients or pediatricians who would work in the inner city or internists with degrees in public health or, most of all, psychiatrists. And Sarah didn't; she fell off the track. She dropped out halfway through her fourth year of medical school, or tried to. The medical school, sticking by its notorious unofficial motto, Hard to Get In, Impossible to Get Out, did not let her go; they told her she was on an extended leave of absence, and when the time was right, she could of course come back and finish.

During those three and a half years of medical school, Maggie had seen Sarah through a phase of Orthodox Judaism, a phase of total absorption in traditional Chinese healing arts — she learned Chinese and made plans to do a fellowship in Yunnan — a phase of superintense surgical ambition, and a phase of fanatic macrobiotic nutritional messianic fervor. Each phase had its appropriate boyfriend, and since Sarah and Maggie had lived first as next-door neighbors in the dorm and then for a year sharing an apartment, Maggie was quite familiar with the intimate bedroom and kitchen details of each new incarnation. So off Sarah went, finally, to Nepal to work in a local health initiative, though Maggie suggested, somewhat dryly, that they might have more use for someone who had finished medical school. Anyway, the key was the boyfriend, Dr. International Health himself, who was going off to spearhead this new program and train the local practitioners to implement public health policy, and Sarah more or less went along for the ride.

But Maggie missed her badly, and was delighted to see her move back to the Boston area after the Nepal relationship had come to grief (and the health initiative had been defunded), and after she had spent a number of years knocking around first India, then France, then Seattle. Maggie, the invincibly achievement-oriented, even allowed herself to hope that Sarah was finally ready to finish medical school and get serious. The medical school would probably have taken her back — Hard to Get In, Impossible to Get Out — and think how good she could have made that Nepal experience sound.

Instead, Sarah worked in a bookstore, until she was promoted to manager and a jealous colleague got her fired for some minor bookkeeping irregularities (Sarah's version). She did some freelance technical editing, but the woman she worked for was threatened by her competence and stopped sending her manuscripts (Sarah's version). She thought about trying to make a living as a backup musician, but it got kind of messy because she was romantically involved with two different guys in two different bands, and then she worked for almost a year as a research assistant to a public health professor who was doing a study of the epidemiology of testicular cancer. She got pregnant by the professor, decided not to have an abortion, and allowed the professor to buy his way out of a difficult situation (he was married to a hotshot lawyer) by setting up a small trust fund for the baby. He immediately accepted a job in Los Angeles and had not been heard from since. Sarah looked around for a new job and was abruptly hired to teach science in a small progressive private high school.

And after Penelope was born, Dan and Maggie offered the first floor of the house, a reasonably priced rental. The people who owned the house before them had made over the first-floor apartment for an elderly mother, modernized the small kitchen, equipped the bathroom with hospital wall-bars to help you stand up off the toilet or keep yourself steady in the tub. And they had widened the entrance hall so that the front stairs instead of beginning outside the door to the first-floor apartment now began in its vestibule and led directly up into the second-floor living room, and to make it easier for the woman on the first floor to travel up and down into their home, they had put in an electric chairlift, which ran on a steep track alongside the stairs. The first-floor apartment was therefore not really separated from the rest of the house, though the staircase was now curtained off and barricaded by a child safety gate.

Sarah and Penelope lived mostly in the back rooms of the apartment, the kitchen and dining room. Sarah, at least in her new maternal incarnation, turned out to be a reasonably quiet and responsible tenant, always happy to take in the paper and the mail if Maggie and Dan wanted to go away, cheerful and relaxed about things like plumbing repairs. She was a flake, of course, to use Dan's usual word for her, but a flake who paid her rent on time and had made their tiny bit of a back garden into a place of beauty. And she was, for Maggie at least, and maybe by now for Dan too, by marriage, a member of the family; it did not seem strange to think that she was separated from them only by a curtain, a baby gate, a flight of stairs.

Maggie, when she agreed to be Penelope's godmother, was already facing her own failure to conceive. She loved her goddaughter first with delight and then with conviction, and by now with a passion that sometimes woke her up nights, imagining she had heard Penelope calling. But there was no way to hear Penelope all the way from Maggie's bedroom; it was her own dreams that were waking her. Sarah knew without knowing the details that Maggie and Dan had thought of having children, and clearly that hadn't happened. Sarah said, with grace and gratitude, that Maggie was taking on some of the mothering, some of the worrying, some of the waking up. And it was true that Maggie found herself, from time to time, sitting up in bed, straining her ears as if she might hear, from two floors away, the safe, regular breathing of her darling. And Penelope was so worth loving, such a triumph of a child, who by the age of two seemed to have all Sarah's intelligence and charm but much more sense and much, much more strength of purpose. A dimpled butterball-type child, dark corkscrew curls, big dark brown eyes, apple cheeks, and a will of iron. Maggie, who had never doted from such a close perspective before, now doted, enjoyed watching Penelope push her own mother around, and then, of course, she got to retreat, finally, to Dan and adult married life with a certain sense of relief.

But yes, it was entertaining to observe Sarah's hip and haphazard style of single motherhood, though it did cause Maggie to reflect on her own mother's far more frightened, far more rigid efforts. Annalisa had done her best, of course — and the older Maggie gets, the kinder she is inclined to be. Yes, Annalisa had known Maggie to be the wages of sin, and yes, she had worried and worried, she had been an intermittently uncertain and intermittently severe parent. But had she had any fun? Pregnant at eighteen, dutifully married in church, then beaten up, abandoned, by a guy who would drink himself to death before he was thirty. All those years of chickenfeed salaries and humiliating jobs and stupid church picnics. You would have to look at Sarah, for all her eccentricities, and know she had gotten the better deal. Maggie strained more than she ever had before to remember sweet moments, moments when she was held close to Annalisa. The two of them on the bus together, singing, In a cavern, in a canyon. Blowing out the birthday candles. The year I was the angel narrator in the Christmas pageant. My poor mother, Maggie would think, occasionally, watching Sarah hug Penelope.

Of course, Penelope was a handful, but that was probably good; she needed to be a stronger character than her mother after all: No godchild of mine, Maggie would have muttered, is going to waste her life doing one half-assed thing after another. When Penelope was old enough, Maggie thought, she needed a serious school; she needed challenge and reward and stimulation. She needed the chance to grow up into everything that Sarah could have been. And I will pay, Maggie thought, confusedly, imagining summer camps so different from the one she herself had attended, picturing, somewhat confusedly, the ballet lessons she had longed for as a very young child (too expensive for Annalisa), the pressured but challenging and stimulating schools, summer programs in Europe, Ivy League colleges. Whatever Penelope needs. And she saw her own role, as godmother, to be an in-house example of nonflakiness.

And Dan had gotten to be fond of Penelope too, once it was clear that for the most part she was going to stay in her own apartment, clear that her crying would, at worst, penetrate only very dimly to the second floor, clear that Sarah was not actually planning to open an ashram or a soup kitchen or a video games parlor in her living room. That Sarah had, in fact, settled down with a serious job and a child. Every so often, on their way out the door in the morning, Maggie and Dan would run into Sarah, desperate to get Penelope to the babysitter, seriously late. Sarah would be dressed for work, khaki skirt and mail-order sweater, carrying, usually, a precarious pile of handouts and student papers. Penelope, keenly conscious that her mother was hurrying, would be on the sidewalk, howling and removing her shoes. Sarah had tried Velcro, double-knotted laces, and cunning little plastic cylinders designed to hide the shoelace knots, and had even wrapped masking tape around the shoes after lacing them, but Penelope always got her shoes off. Rain or snow, sleet or hail, if she thought her mother was trying to hurry her somewhere, she sat on the sidewalk and took off her shoes and howled. Sarah would snatch her up and carry howling child, shoes, Sesame Street lunchbox, handbag, papers, and all-important stuffed bunny to the waiting taxi, and Dan would look after them and think, Maggie assumed, that perhaps there was much to be said for life without small children after all. Maggie, who spent her working life surrounded by very small children, would be thinking the same thing.

9

Warning to All Parents

M AGGIE'S FIRST DAY attending in the NICU, wouldn't you know, and there comes in a baby so sick that no way can she leave in the evening, especially not leave Marjorie Fallon in charge. Six hundred grams, twenty-six weeks, only survivor of a pair of twins born to a woman after five years of infertility treatments. Premium baby, million-dollar baby, her million-dollar brother pronounced dead in the delivery room after an attempted resuscitation. The OBs kept those twins inside as long as they could, even though the mother's membranes were leaking, but they couldn't get past twenty-six weeks, and by the time they were born, both babies were suffering from infection, stress, and, of course, severe prematurity. So the boy died, as boys are statistically more likely to do, but the girl did pretty well, at least at first. But her lungs got worse and worse as the day went on, and the docs maxed out the ventilator settings on the regular ventilator and began talking about possibly using a high-frequency ventilator for her, and then her blood pressure and her oxygen began dropping and she started manifesting a severe bacterial infection, or, as the residents would say, acting septic. Over the course of the night it was one thing after another: playing with her vent settings, bringing in the high-frequency ventilator, pushing fluid into her as her blood vessels leaked out into her tissues, transfusing her with blood products, packed red blood cells, plasma, platelets, starting her on first one and then two pressors, intensive care medications to kick her heart and squeeze those blood vessels tighter, raise her dropping blood pressure, get some blood and thereby some oxygen to her muscles and her kidneys and her heart and, of course, above all, to her brain.

Baby Girl Grassini, surviving sister of the deceased Baby Boy Grassini. With all due modesty, or, maybe better, without false modesty, Maggie knows this: Baby Girl Grassini has been about as sick this night as it is possible for six hundred grams of baby to be. That she is alive, and even getting a tiny bit better this morning, is a surprise to Maggie, as well as a personal triumph. A less fine hand with the ventilator, less skill juggling the pressors and the fluids, and the Grassinis would right now be mourning the loss of not one but two premature babies. Credit Maggie, credit Dorothy, the nurse who tended baby and intravenous lines and ventilator all night long. Go ahead and credit even Harvey Weintraub if you want — this is the man who trained the hand that turned the dial . . .

She does not say this to the interns on rounds, of course, but maybe it comes through in her tone. "This baby basically went into shock last night, and she's been on the edge of shock — septic shock — all night long. Stiff lungs, leaky blood vessels, it was really touch and go keeping her pressure up for a long time there."

"But now she's starting to get better?" asks Marjorie, just as if she hadn't been uselessly in the NICU all night, ignoring the sickest baby, assuming Maggie would take care of everything. Maggie makes another in an ongoing series of mental notes: Talk to this girl, and soon, and strongly. Does Marjorie know what they call her? Maggie heard the other two interns talking, heard Iliana say it to Neil: Just be glad you don't have Swifty to deal with when you're on call. You wouldn't believe how useless she is. Oh yes I would, said Neil, sweet little meek Neil, who wouldn't hurt a fly's feelings.

"Grassini is nowhere near stable, Marjorie. She's on two pressors, she's got bacteria in her lungs and in her blood — and we have no idea how big a hit her organs took from oxygen deprivation over the last twenty-four hours — there could be significant damage."

But yes, Maggie thinks, cautiously hopeful, yes, I think we're turning some very small, very early corner. I think maybe the antibiotics are beginning to kick in, we've found the right vent settings for her, her pressure's not bottoming out every ten minutes. I have been helping her heart and her lungs do their job all night long, and I think I can get her through.

And out in the hallway, Dorothy claps Maggie on the back and they allow themselves that moment of mutual congratulation: Way to go! Dorothy is a sensible and extremely dexterous mother of four who works nights by preference because it gives her afternoons and evenings at home. She has one of the best pair of hands in the NICU; she can get IV lines into veins that Maggie, who isn't bad with her hands, can't even see.

Way to go! In the hallway, Maggie and Dorothy smile at each other; it is not so very often in this life, after all, that two women who have between them stayed up all night and fought death away from an infant can meet in a corridor and look each other in the eye.

There, on the elevator wall.

WARNING TO ALL PARENTS!!!!

Too many exclamation points, a clear sign of a mind deranged.

And then the picture, a black-and-white mug shot muddied by xeroxing.

DO NOT LET YOUR CHILD BE TAKEN CARE OF BY THIS DOCTOR DR. MAGGIE CLAYMORE!!!

The first poster reported to security was found by a nurse from the orthopedic ward who stepped into an elevator at five A.M., pushing a child in a wheelchair, on their way down to radiology for some emergency hip films. The child was whimpering about having left her stuffed Barney doll in her bed.

YOU HAVE THE RIGHT TO REQUEST ANOTHER DOCTOR!!!

The nurse tore down the flier and took it with her to radiology; while the hip films were being done, she paged the night security supervisor and told him. I've heard about this stuff going on with this doctor, she said. The night security supervisor came over to radiology, moving at a self-important jog, picked up the flier, and removed four more from other hospital elevators, congratulating himself that he had dealt with the situation promptly and effectively.

DR. CLAYMORE IS BEING INVESTIGATED FOR NUMEROUS COMPLAINTS OWING TO HER MEDICAL DIFFICULTIES AND HER PERSONAL RUDENESS SHE DOES NOT CARE ABOUT PATIENTS AND THEIR FEELINGS!

The night security supervisor did not get around to checking out hospital bulletin boards, and numerous other copies of the poster were discovered later on in the morning, as people came to work. He also did not think to inspect the hospital bathrooms, and it turned out the large public restrooms adjoining the first-floor waiting room had fliers hanging up in every stall, both in the men's room and in the women's room. These were subsequently found and pulled down by the custodial staff.

YOU OWE IT TO YOUR INNOCENT CHILDREN TO PROTECT THEM AND ASK FOR ANOTHER DOCTOR!!!

Mr. Grassini, Mrs. Grassini. She's on her feet but only just, you can tell. Well, no wonder, one day postpartum, one baby dead in the delivery room. She has that slightly puffy, slack look women get right after they've given birth, or maybe she's drugged. Looks like she's walking around in shock. Looks like she was crying a minute ago, eyes widened and reddened and puffy. Tousled black hair, drawn features. He, on the other hand, doesn't miss a trick. Young, stocky, and obviously thinks he's handsome, carries himself sort of formally, even in jeans and a polo shirt. Attends his wife with slightly aggressive devotion, like he's hoping someone will give him a hard time.

The day-shift nurse is still getting sign-out from Dorothy, so Maggie orients them. Goes as gently as she can, but what can you do? She doesn't say, Sickest baby in the room, nearly died last night and may yet. But she has to say, This is the ventilator, which breathes for your daughter. Have you chosen a name yet? Felicia, how pretty. For her grandmother, how nice. That's her breathing tube — and those two lines going into her bellybutton are going into a vein and an artery — and this tube helps us empty her stomach — here, Mr. Grassini, take this stool. Please, sit, put your head down, sir. Do you need to go out of the room for a while?

At six hundred grams she is about as long as a Barbie doll. Her head is concealed by a thin white band to shield her eyes from the extra set of lights that irradiate her to help clear her blood of bilirubin, a nasty byproduct of broken-down red blood cells, which her immature liver can't clean up. The triangle tip of her nose peeks out from under the eye shield, the endotracheal tube protrudes from her mouth, pulling the corner just a little; one nostril is occupied by the nasogastric tube into her stomach. Both tubes are taped in place, the tape covering her cheeks and upper lip. Below the tape, her tiny mouth droops slightly open, and her whole body is puffy and almost glistening in the light, edematous from the fluid that keeps leaking out of her blood vessels and into her tissues. And the four heart monitor leads, and the heart-shaped sticker on her stomach, which monitors her body temperature. And the two tubes leading into her bellybutton stump. Even one of her pearl-toed feet is wrapped in an oxygen-sensing band, which connects to yet another monitor; the other is taped to a board for yet another IV. Do you need to go out of the room for a while?

"How're you doing, Mom?" asks the nurse coming on shift. "You feeling steady?"

But Mrs. Grassini is perfectly steady, staring down at the warming table as if she's ready to start taking baby pictures. Her husband, on the other hand, hasn't looked back at the baby since that first glance, that first reaction to all the tubes breaching her tiny body, worming their way into trachea and stomach and blood vessels.

"Does she have a chance?" he asks, low and defeated, at the same moment that his wife speaks, clear and demanding. "Can I touch her? Can I hold her?"

"Sure thing, Mom," says the nurse. "You can touch her. You just need to be careful of all our tubes and gadgets, but you go ahead, stroke her arm. She'll get to know your voice and your touch — even very premature babies learn to recognize their parents."

Mom. She's Mom. They're calling her Mom. Mrs. Grassini

reaches out her index finger and strokes the baby's right arm, smaller in diameter than that big adult finger. Strokes it with wonder, like any new mother reveling in the surprise softness of newborn skin. And Maggie leaves them to it, checking as she goes that the husband isn't about to faint, fall off the stool, bang his head on the NICU floor — it's been known to happen.

"Go on," the nurse is saying, "try singing to her. They've done studies to show it lowers their stress level. Let her know you're here."

Mr. Grassini is sitting upright on the stool, white-faced but reasonably stable, staring not at his baby but at his wife, as she leans over the warming table and sings Brahms' Lullaby into the miniature ear hidden beneath the white Velcro mask. Her singing voice is high and pure and true.

Maggie takes a deep breath. She is tired and tense and also at peace. And she is about to see the poster for the first time: Sandow and Weintraub barrel on in, and behind them, Elaine Oliphant and a woman Maggie doesn't recognize. Sandow is waving a piece of paper at her; with shock and immediate recognition, Maggie sees her own picture.

"It's escalating." Elaine Oliphant, with three strings of heavy turquoise and silver around her neck. The whole group crowded into the NICU conference room, the poster on the table. Maggie cannot stop looking at it, cannot stop reading the words, cannot quite bring herself to read them right through.

"Where were you last night, Dr. Claymore?" This woman, this new investigator, Donna Grey her name is, accents the "you" in a manner that suggests quite clearly that Maggie hung up the posters herself. For one second she can't answer, caught between outrage and a shocked sense that her answer will lead her right into the trap.

"I was here, in the NICU. Taking care of a very sick baby. I'm the attending."

Donna Grey nods. "Just as you were the night the Clark child died?"

"Yes," Maggie says tightly. "Just exactly."

Donna Grey holds a black looseleaf binder open on her knee, makes the occasional note. She is tall and somewhat brassy in appearance, with short clipped blond hair and a wise, slightly drawn face. Maggie can't help comparing her favorably to Sandow; she seems so much less corporate, so much more plausible as a detective. She looks like the social studies teacher for whom even the wiseass tenth grade boys behave, or like the older flight attendant who comforts the passengers and talks the terrorist into surrendering his gun. Looks, in short, not quite like a doctor, not quite the right social class (that frosted hair), but maybe like the best ER triage nurse you ever worked with. Wears a black suit that gives the impression of a uniform.

And asks her questions. "Did you leave the room with the sick child at any point?"

"I went down to radiology several times to look at x-rays. X-rays of the sick baby's lungs. I went to the bathroom once or twice as well. But I didn't keep records."

Donna Grey just nods to herself and makes a note.

Maggie, with all the fury of her exhaustion, bursts out loud and angry. "Are you accusing me of doing this all myself? Doing this *to* myself?"

Four sets of eyes are looking at her quizzically, are wondering about her reliability, her sanity. Did she kill Heather Clark? Does she write herself anonymous letters? Did she paper the hospital last night with posters of her own face? After last night of all nights they come to her with this shit, with this trash. I was doing my job last night, is what I was doing. I was doing my job and doing it right and if you guys would do yours then there would not be some lunatic wandering around the hospital hanging up posters.

"Dr. Claymore, whoever is behind this obviously knows your schedule, your job responsibilities."

She looks to her boss, Harvey Weintraub, embarrassed to have this happening in front of him, embarrassed to see him dragged into this, her mess, but also expecting him to stand up for her, protect her. You showed me my job, you *gave* me my job — now you have to defend me while I do it. He is the other doctor in the room; let him defend her, doctor for doctor.

109

But Sandow leans across the table and speaks directly to Harvey Weintraub, man to man. "I think we're taking a real risk having Dr. Claymore responsible for patient care during this period. It makes her vulnerable."

"And the hospital," puts in Elaine Oliphant.

So Maggie is on her feet. Grabs the black binder out of Donna Grey's hand and slams it down on the table. "Are you saying *I'm* the crazy person here? Just because you can't figure out who's really behind this, you decide it's me!"

Elaine Oliphant stands, puts a hand on Maggie's shoulder, says gently, close to her ear, "The only thing we're saying, Maggie, is that someone is trying to discredit you — and whoever it is knows the details of where you work and when you work — and I think there's a real risk a move could be made against one of your patients just to discredit you."

"No," Maggie says. But she imagines it clearly: a figure creeping toward the incubator, a hand injecting something into the IV tubing. Playing with the ventilator settings. Imagines it so clearly and concretely that she frightens herself: Has that figure always been there, lurking at the edge of my imagination?

Sandow is still talking to Weintraub. "I would advise that for the good of the hospital — and for her own safety, of course, you pull her out for now."

"Could you do that?" Elaine Oliphant asks. "Could it be arranged?"

Weintraub, of all of them, is actually looking at Maggie. He shrugs, he looks confused. "We could shift the attending schedule around a little, let someone else work now. Maggie could pay it back later on —"

"That would protect everyone." Sandow.

"It would certainly cover the hospital." Oliphant.

"Might be advisable." Donna Grey, who has reclaimed and reopened her binder, flipping a page or two, eager to go on.

"You can't do that." Maggie, still standing up. Trying for calm and collected, hating herself for feeling close to tears. "If some idiot comes in one night and hangs up posters saying I'm a rotten doctor and then the next day you pull me out of the NICU, how's that going to look? Like you agree, like you don't trust me to take care of patients."

The conference room door bangs open again: her junior resident, handsome Justin. Arrogant and just this side of defiant.

"Grassini's bottoming out her pressure again. And her O2 sats are way down."

"Let's go!" She is out of there. She is at the bedside, staring down at Baby Girl Grassini. The parents, thank god, have gone home. Around this warming table the flow pattern of the NICU changes to reflect the emergency, two extra nurses standing by, a crash cart. Data are being recorded on flow sheets, soft, confident women's voices pass numbers back and forth. Maggie expects this, registers it, but does not attend to it. Under the tape and the tubes and the leads is *her* baby, and that baby is not getting enough blood around to her brain and her other organs.

"Okay, Justin," she says, "let's push a little more normal saline, right now." More fluid into the baby's tiny circulatory system. Let's get this blood pressure up!

Get a chest x-ray, check the position of her endotracheal tube, make sure she hasn't popped a hole in her lungs. Play with the two pressors she's already getting, consider changing one to a more last-ditch kind of drug.

The portable x-ray unit arrives a split second after Maggie does, and she stands back to let them take their film. Sees the quartet of her tormentors from the conference room standing right there, looks Sandow in the eye, and says, "The radiation from this machine can damage bystanders. Men and women of reproductive age are advised to leave the room or wear protective lead aprons." Sees Sandow look nervously around, watches him note that the radiology tech and the nurse are both putting on aprons. Maggie reaches for the third apron, draped over the handle of the portable x-ray machine, and puts it on. Enjoys watching Sandow scurry back to the conference room, protecting his precious gonads. And Elaine Oliphant not far behind. Civilians.

The x-ray is done. Justin will send one of the interns to bring it to the bedside in a couple of minutes. Maggie is listening to the baby's lungs, looking almost angrily at the bedside monitors, which keep telling her, low pressure, not enough oxygen. Now she is telling the nurses how much to dial up the pressors, agreeing with Justin that it's probably worth changing drugs. And we have to give more fluid, she tells Justin — but let's also set her up to get some more red blood cells, so she'll have something to help hold the fluid inside her blood vessels. Order the transfusion, stat.

Maggie stares at the numbers on the monitors, making her own calculations. "I think it's time to start steroids," she says firmly. All night she wondered and worried about giving the baby steroid hormones — sometimes steroids can turn a baby around, but in the setting of overwhelming infection they can also suppress the baby's immune response — but this baby is going under and Maggie has to do something. Okay, Justin, calculate the steroid dose.

Justin looks a little scared, but he also looks interested. They could lose this baby here and now, and they both know it. Okay, she says to him, encouragingly, what do you want to do with the vent settings? He has exactly one second to tell her, before she just goes ahead and tells the nurse, and when he does tell her, and gets it right, Maggie can't help it, she smiles at him: Good, right, you know what you're doing. She feels focused and busy and happy and anxious about all the right and proper things. And as she and Justin close ranks around the warming table with the nurses, all of them hovering close, Maggie raises her eyes to see Weintraub staring at her.

"Let me do my job," she says to him, and he nods.

And they do it, they save Felicia Grassini yet again. Probably it's the steroids, though there's also the substitute pressor, some fancy footwork with the vent, and of course, more and more fluid, so she looks more and more bloated. But her blood pressure is once more compatible with life, and her oxygen saturation comes up, and she's stable again. A long afternoon of the baby being relatively stable and no lawyers or detectives coming around to make life miserable. As the day wears on into early evening, Neil and Marjorie sign out and go home. Justin and Iliana are on call, and Maggie can go home feeling that Justin is on top of things.

On the way to her office, she swings by the laboratory where Theresa works and finds Theresa, who has stayed late as usual, getting ready to leave. Maggie is enormously relieved when Theresa greets her straightforwardly, when there is no comment made about letters or signs. Did they ever find out who put that in your office? Theresa asks her, with casual disgust, as if they were discussing some one-time stupidity.

"Not yet," Maggie says, practicing, "but whoever it is is really out to get me. There's a whole campaign going on, and frankly, I don't have time for it. I'm on service now, you know."

Theresa nods. She knows. She follows Maggie's clinical schedule carefully, partly out of vicarious interest in this career that Maggie has promised can also be hers — the conferences! the lectures! the publications! She comes faithfully to any talk that Maggie gives, and more hesitantly to other hospital lectures, hovering near the door as if she thinks someone will tell her to leave.

"Come to the NICU tomorrow on your lunch hour," Maggie says. "I'll show you what's going on." She has done this repeatedly for Theresa over the past year, including her on rounds, taking her to see interesting patients all over the hospital, letting her in on the medical conversation. This time, Maggie knows, her motives are very mixed; she can feel herself craving the admiration, the gratitude.

"Are you okay?" Theresa asks, very hesitantly, very softly.

Maggie shrugs dramatically: What are you gonna do? "It's just some asshole," she says. "You can't let that kind of thing get to you."

They are standing in front of her office door again, and she is grateful for Theresa's company as she firmly unlocks the door, throws it open. An innocent office. An office at Blessed Innocence. She smiles at Theresa as if to say, See, nothing to worry about.

"I'm going to a birthday party," Maggie explains, taking a package from her desk drawer, a present wrapped by the store in orange and yellow tissue and tied with a mass of curled ribbons. Inside is a whole family of stuffed mice, mother with a frilly apron and a sunbonnet, father with a top hat and a bow tie, two mouse children and a tiny mouse baby. "My goddaughter is two and a half and we're having a party." And she despises herself for the echo in her brain: See, Theresa, I am kind to you, I buy presents for small children, I am an admired and even beloved person. Everyone does not hate me!

Penelope squeals happily when she sees the mice, though of course Penelope by that point squeals happily at almost anything. Penelope is delirious with birthday-party spirit, with cake and candles and singing, and now with wrapping paper and ribbons and gifts. The other party guests are three little girls and their mommies, and Maggie looks those other little girls over, admires the cuteness of their party dresses and the frilled matching panties underneath, but they don't compare to Penelope. Penelope knows so absolutely what makes the world go round. Penelope squashes handfuls of cake into her rosebud mouth with such happy abandon: This is mine, this is good. "Happy birthday dear Penelope!" she sings, over and over, crumbs falling from her lips. Little Sophie from up the street bursts out bawling when her piece of cake falls on the floor, and little Natasha from the play group can't control her tears when all the presents turn out to be for Penelope, and little Taylor from wherever has been whining since the party started, but Penelope glows white hot with energy at the center of her home, her party, at the center of attention. And all the well-groomed, well-bred murmurings of the other mommies, *This is usually her bathtime* and *I'm afraid we're still working on sharing* and *She gets so frustrated when she feels she's been clumsy,* they all sound silly against the clear strong voice of Sarah, proudly and surely calling out to her daughter. Sarah giving her daughter a half-birthday party in the evening, Sarah baking her this stupendous cake with dark chocolate custard in the middle and thin bittersweet chocolate glaze on top, a real and grown-up cake, a cake to bake for someone you love.

And so, instead of sitting stiff and self-consciously professional among the mommies, Maggie basks in the special favor of her goddaughter. Penelope goes racing around the chaotic living room, a stuffed mouse in each hand, and Sophie and Taylor follow close behind — Natasha is still struggling with her mother over her desire to take Penelope's new xylophone home with her. And every time Penelope passes the rocking chair where Maggie sits eating her second piece of cake, she pulls up short, holds out the mice, and she and Maggie lock glances and say, "Squeak squeak squeak!" Penelope doubles up with giggles, and then on she runs, and Maggie, bone-tired, her mouth full of the fabulous comfort of chocolate and sugar, feels that Penelope is running for her as well.

"She has so much energy for this time of day," says Taylor's mother, a little disapprovingly.

"Well, all that cake!" says Natasha's mother, looking up from her whimpering, wimpy daughter. "She won't be able to sleep tonight!"

Penelope comes charging right at Maggie, smashing into her and sending the chair tipping all the way back. And Maggie, fortunately finishing her last bite of cake, pulls the girl up into her lap and holds her close, smelling chocolate and ammoniac diapers and good clean child dirt.

"Squeak!" Penelope screams. "Squeak squeak!" She presses her mice into Maggie's face, tickles her nose with soft gray acrylic fur.

Tears are in Maggie's eyes. Sleeplessness and stress are making her sentimental, and she glories in it. She is thinking of Baby Girl Grassini, of Felicia. Last night I saved a baby's life; she's still here because of me. Let her be blessed, let her be safe. Sleep, my child, and peace attend thee, all through the night. All the stages Maggie knows from Penelope she wishes on those six hundred grams: infancy, toddlerhood, first words, I-can-dress-myself, squeak squeak. And yes, all the things ahead: Let there be birthdays and high school graduation and a wedding, anything else you can name, all because of last night. Let her be blessed.

Penelope wriggles free again, back down to the floor, but Maggie holds on long enough to bend over and kiss the back of her wild curls, the sweet curve of her head.

Maggie's preference would have been to face Donna Grey, that official black-suited presence, in one of her own professional uniforms. But there's no way she isn't going to shower and change; she's been on her feet for thirty-six hours. The hot shower feels as good as a shower feels only under such circumstances; she closes her eyes and imagines she is standing in a thundering hot waterfall, she is in a secret cavern, enclosed and protected and invisible as the water washes over her and around her. It's an old image, she recognizes it from as far back as residency, from other sleep-deprived showers: This is real, this is here, this is good. She has spent her whole working life, her training life, knowing these intervals of bone-deep fatigue, the fatigue of a body and mind truly used, truly pushed past all understanding. And one of the things you promise yourself at those moments is a trip to the secret cavern under the waterfall, to be washed out of the world for a few steaming minutes of water thunder and clean, hot mist. A cavern under a hot waterfall. And she soaps herself a second time just to enjoy the shower a little longer.

Sweatpants and a cotton turtleneck. Sorry, Donna Grey, but it's been a long day. She brushes her wet hair back from her face, no makeup. For that matter, no shoes. A pair of sweatsocks, and she marches into the living room. This is my house, Donna Grey.

Donna seems less intimidating than before, a little tired herself, and she accepts Dan's offer of a cup of decaf with obvious gratitude. Sits down in an armchair like she's glad to, and allows herself to relax into it. She's still carrying her black binder, though, and Maggie finds that in itself somewhat menacing. What the hell is written on all those pages, anyway?

And the first item on her agenda tonight is to dig up dirt on Dan — another waste of time, Maggie thinks wearily. Donna goes through some obvious stuff about where he works and how long he's worked there and how far back he and Maggie go together, writes it all down on a page midway through her binder. Shuts him up gently enough when he starts to speechify about the swimming pool, just notes down the name and address. Then she takes Maggie through some more biography, where she went to college and medical school, then finally asks again if either of them has any idea who might be behind the letters and the rest. Maggie reluctantly volunteers a couple of the names off her list, prefacing them with remarks about how these are just people she had come into conflict with, that it isn't to say any of them is crazy enough to do a thing like this. Erika Donnelly the NICU nurse, Clem Garfield the hematologist, Hank Shoemaker the neonatologist. And then starts all over again saying how really, she can't picture any of these people —

Donna Grey cuts her off. "Is there anyone at the hospital with whom you have had an intimate relationship at any time?" she asks, her pen poised.

116

"An intimate relationship?" Maggie is so tired, her eyes are closing as she sits there. Oh, please, don't let there be anything going on in the NICU. At least not for a few hours. Just let me sleep for a few hours. But where's the beeper, did I leave it in the bathroom? No, it's clipped to the back of her sweatpants — she's practically sitting on it.

"Anyone you have been sexually intimate with at any time, now or in the past?"

Dan, gruffly: "I wondered if you people were going to get around to asking that."

Donna Grey looks at him steadily. "It's a question she might find easier to answer if you went and made more coffee."

"No!" Maggie says, surprising herself with the loudness of her voice. "He doesn't need to go anywhere." Now they're both looking at her. "The only person," she begins, and then stops, looking at the expression on Dan's face. "It was before we got married, long ago," she tells him.

"There is someone at the hospital you were intimate with before you married?"

"There's one person. He's over in heme/onc."

"Hematology-oncology," Dan says politely to Donna Grey, who makes more notes.

"What is his name, please?"

"I just don't see what relevance —" Maggie is slightly surprised to note that she still has the will to object. She knows, after all, that the fastest way to sleep involves answering the questions, but still. Still. And she had gone and told Dan not to leave the room.

"Listen, Dr. Claymore," says Donna Grey, leaning forward, no longer relaxed in her chair. "This kind of thing — people do it when they have very strong emotions about the subject, the target. That includes people you've argued with, but it also includes people you've been intimate with, people who might be in love with you, or once have been in love with you — those are the very people who might be aware of you and think about you and end up being very angry at you."

"Maggie, you need to tell her," Dan says. He comes and sits on the arm of Maggie's chair, lets his hand rest comfortingly on her

117

shoulder. But she isn't comforted. This name is no easier to say, in fact is harder to say, with Dan's body so close to her own. Maggie shuts her eyes.

"Kenneth Weiss."

"We went to med school with him!" Dan, surprised.

"He and I did our third-year pediatrics together at Blessed Innocence and that's when. It's an awfully long time ago. Heme/onc recruited him because they needed someone who did his weirdo kind of cell membrane protein biochemistry. He's basically an adult oncologist with a big lab in a pediatric hospital, and they make sure he never has to touch a patient and everybody's happy." Maggie feels wise and tired, and slightly perturbed: Third-year had been before they were married, she and Dan, but after they were already involved, in their on-again off-again days. Living apart, somewhat troubled, but still allied, still linked, more or less. She had chosen to interpret it as less, had strayed every now and then and come back without telling him about it, but had he understood it that way as well? And would he still care, more than a decade later?

"Forgive me, Dr. Claymore, but when were you last on intimate terms with Dr. Weiss, and what is the nature of the relationship that now exists between you?"

"It was more than ten years ago — we were in our third year of medical school. And it wasn't much, even then. Just a few — a few dates. Because we were doing this rotation together and sometimes we would go out after we left the hospital." And eat pizza and go back to his room in a crummy apartment he shared with two guys from the class ahead and take off our clothes and fuck our brains out. She almost giggles. God, she's punchy. She has to watch herself carefully; she could say anything. "As for now, we aren't even friends. There's no relationship. When I see him I say hello, and I see him maybe once a month, in the elevator, on line in the cafeteria." And he's losing all his hair, she might tell Dan later, and he's trying to compensate by growing the world's biggest mustache. And I never really liked him much, anyway. It was just one of those things.

She closes her eyes and leans against Dan, and after a second he puts his arm around her shoulders and squeezes.

"When was the last contact you had with Dr. Weiss?"

"I don't know," Maggie says, without opening her eyes. "I can't remember."

"She worked all night last night," Dan says. "She's pretty tired. Maybe if you have more questions for me, Maggie could lie down?"

Maggie gets shakily to her feet and heads for the stairs, and she's halfway up to the third floor and her bed when Dan catches up with her, puts an arm around her, leads her into their bedroom. She didn't even say good night to the detective, and now she fights back an impulse to call downstairs to her, Don't waste your time on Kenny Weiss, he hardly knows who I am, he lives for his cell membrane proteins. But why should Dan have to listen to her defend Kenny? She falls down on the bed, turtleneck and sweatpants and socks and all, and he unclips the beeper from her pants and sets it on the bedside table. She is swimming in thick, warm water, the pool at the base of the waterfall. Looks around for Dan, but he is not swimming toward her. Her voice sounds thick and unfamiliar in her ears, reverberating through the water.

"Dan, I'm sorry."

"Go to sleep. You need to sleep." He covers her up gently, but she opens her eyes and looks up into his face as he bends over her, and it seems to her, even as she falls almost instantly asleep, that he is troubled and sad and confused as he stands there with the comforter in his hands, spreading it out over her, warm and smooth.

"Were you aware of your wife's relationship with this Dr. Kenneth Weiss?"

The detective is still sipping slowly at her coffee.

"She wasn't my wife when this was going on — it was years before we got married."

Dan does not sit down again on the couch; he stands, his arms crossed over his chest, in front of the bookcase, swaying ever so slightly back and forth.

"Were you aware that this intimate relationship had existed, regardless of when your wife states that it ended? Were you aware that it had, in fact, taken place?"

"No, of course I wasn't."

The detective stares at him steadily.

"I didn't tell Maggie about all the people I was ever involved with before we got married. I didn't ask her for a list of hers, either. This sounds like some totally minor student thing — and I really think you're barking up the wrong tree. Blessed Innocence isn't about thwarted love and passion and romance — that place is all about power and ambition. That's what you ought to be looking at."

"What do you mean, Doctor?" The detective has set down her coffee mug now, carefully, squarely on its coaster.

"Look, you have to realize what kind of place this is." Dan starts pacing, back and forth in front of the bookcase, hands jammed in his pockets. "My wife — Maggie — she loves Blessed Innocence — she takes it seriously."

"Takes what seriously, exactly, Doctor?" Donna Grey has her notebook open, her pen poised, but she is not writing, she is watching him.

"Look, could you call me Dan? Please? So I don't feel quite so much like this is a hostile interrogation? Even if it is?"

"Exactly what is it that you feel your wife takes seriously, Dan?"

"That hospital — that place, what they're doing there. For Maggie, in the end, it's still all about the babies — about the kids, especially the kids that no one else thinks have a chance. That's why this is ripping her up this way — that little girl who died, she's exactly the kind of kid that Maggie would fight for." And now he does sit down, drops onto the couch facing Donna Grey, and asks her, in a curious high voice, as if he is himself not so far from crying, "Do you have any idea how hard she works?"

Donna Grey makes a note.

"She was there all day yesterday, all night last night, all day today — and any minute that beeper will go off and she'll go back there, even if I try to stop her — I'll end up driving her there myself because I'll be scared she's too tired to drive — I've done it before! And then she'll get into that NICU and all of a sudden her brain will be clear and she'll be like — I don't know how to explain it to you. Like a person on a mission. Like a person saving the whole goddamn world."

"But what did you mean, Doctor —" She sees him putting up his hand to interrupt and corrects herself. "Excuse me, Dan, what did you mean when you said that about what kind of a place Blessed Innocence is, and Dr. Claymore taking it seriously?"

"I mean that it's a shark pond! It's a vicious place, it's full of vicious people, out to make their careers, out to stab everyone else in the back — it's not about the kids, not for most of them! It's about making it and grants and glory and getting ahead and getting promoted — and Maggie has this persistent delusion that if you work hard and you take great care of your patients, it will be rewarded! I mean, talk about blessed innocence!"

His voice has gotten loud, and he stops suddenly. He shrugs, looks slightly sheepish. "Maybe all I'm saying is that it's a big academic teaching hospital, only a little more so."

"And do you have a theory that ties this in with the allegations now being made about Dr. Claymore?" Donna's voice is neutral, as it has been all evening.

"Isn't it obvious? You don't go looking for a crazy lover in a place like that — you go looking for someone who resents her professionally, or is worried that she's going to beat them out for something. It's what I said: The place is not about sex or love or passion — not even sick passion. It's about ambition and success and glory."

"And for Dr. Claymore?"

Dan laces both hands into the hair on the sides of his head, looking down, shaking his head slowly. "She's different. She's so different she doesn't even know how different she is. I don't mean — well, maybe you'd have to know some of these bastards. Maybe they would fool you too, detective or no detective."

"So what you seem to be saying is that your wife — that Dr. Claymore — is not so ambitious?"

He shakes his head. "I don't mean that. Maggie is a fighter. She's competitive, she's determined, she's ambitious. And she's right to be ambitious, she's the best they've got! But for Maggie, it's still all about those babies."

And now, finally, the detective is taking notes again, writing furiously, line after line after line. Dan leans back against the cushions and watches her write.

Part Two

10

What You're Investigating Is Me

OMETIMES, NOT OFTEN, you run through hospital halls. To the delivery room or the nursery or the patient's room where something suddenly has gone wrong. Sometimes you run because sometimes seconds count. And the hospital makes way for you, and your colleagues stand back, recognizing the imperative, the priority, the ticking clock. But it is almost midnight and the halls are deserted and Maggie is running and running; crumpled in her hand are the fliers, more fliers, different fliers, ripped down from the walls, from the bulletin boards, and her breath pounds in her chest. Someone, some hand, someone's hand, put these up, and not so long ago. She was on her way home, leaving the NICU an hour or so ago, and there it was, a poster hanging right above the elevator buttons. There it was, her own picture, hanging on the wall; she recognized herself with the force of a shock moving through her body — the same picture, the same blurred head and neck photo that the detective had triumphantly identified off the hospital face sheet. But a new poster, a new goddamn poster about Maggie, hanging up right there by the elevator for everyone to see: PARENTS BE ALERT AND PROTECT YOUR CHILDREN FROM THIS SO-CALLED DOCTOR MAGGIE CLAYMORE!!!

So what can she do? All she can think to do, and she does it so immediately that it is almost without thinking, is find the rest of them, pull them down, crumple them, shred them, destroy them before people see. And they're everywhere — seven more found by checking just the bulletin boards on the NICU floor! Into the stairwell and down to the next floor — her breathing is heavy, her vision slightly clouded. A poster near the playroom! Another in the conference room. And the bathrooms — she runs back up the stairs and finds one in the bathroom near the NICU. And then back down. Posters could be anywhere, everywhere. Her face could be anywhere, blurred and suspicious and guilty. She imagines posters hidden in charts, tucked under the plastic trays covering hospital meals. Finds another taped like an official notice to the door of the call room where the surgical residents sleep.

Maggie can hear herself panting. But this is my hospital, my place, my world. How can this be happening? Who can this be happening to? Whoever is doing this must have been everywhere, all around the hospital. She will go to the nursing station and ask, Who has come by tonight, have you seen anyone suspicious? But how will the nurses look at her? Will they have seen these posters or the last set, or the letters? What will they think of her, wild-eyed and out of breath and furious?

A deep breath and she reaches out, rips down the notice from the call room door.

"Don't do that!" A woman's voice, sharp, a little angry. Maggie spins to face Donna Grey, complete with binder.

"What the hell do you mean, 'don't do that'! There are posters up — posters with my picture! All over the hospital! And you didn't stop it — you can't stop it! What kind of a detective are you supposed to be, anyway? What the hell use are you to anyone? And for your information, I am goddamn well going to take these down!" And she crumples the flier tight in her fist, a hard little ball of paper.

"Scotch tape might have held fingerprints, Dr. Claymore. The pattern of where the posters are hung would give me the route he took through the hospital. Or she, of course. You're tampering with evidence, and interfering with my investigation." She is looking, steadily, at the clump of paper in Maggie's hand.

"Fingerprints?" Is it possible there is actually technology being deployed? Maggie allows herself a little twinge of hope. "Have you found any fingerprints?"

"Up until now, I haven't had the chance to examine a piece of paper that hasn't been handled by a whole slew of people. I want you to leave these new notices alone — especially if they're taped."

"But you will take them down? They won't be here in the morning when people come to work?" She can hardly stand to go home and leave them in place; in her mind, they glow like poisoned spots of radiation in the hospital building, or like patches of increased uptake on a nuclear medicine scan, marking the cancer, the pathology, the metastases.

Donna holds out her hand for the crumpled fliers. The tampered evidence. The fliers covered now with Maggie's own fingerprints.

One more sick baby, okay? Understand that the whole time, the whole time all this is happening, Maggie's brain is full of babies. Whatever else she does, whatever else she thinks about, she is also thinking about all the babies under her care, breathing with them, digesting or not digesting with them, thinking of the readouts and the numbers and the way each baby looks, every day. All of these people, all the doctors on the team, all the nurses in the NICU — their brains are full of babies. Baby numbers and baby lab results and baby ventilators and baby formulas. They go through the NICU on rounds, Maggie and her little flock of doctors, pushing their metal cart of charts from nurse to nurse, and the conversation ranges from the technical and the terrible to the newborn familiar. So while all this is happening, Maggie's thoughts are always, every day, peopled by these babies, by twenty or more of them. And no matter what else happens, the babies keep coming, and they need to be cared for and the decisions need to be made and the lessons need to be taught.

"Breaking bad news in the DR," Maggie says to her team the next morning. She reaches up and writes it on the whiteboard in green marker: today's topic. Breaking Bad News in the DR. "Always a very big deal to the parents. Even something minor — an extra digit, for example. You know how we always say, ten fingers, ten toes — if it's ten fingers, eleven toes, that's a big shock to parents. Let alone if it's something wrong with the face, cleft lip, cleft palate."

"Or ambiguous genitalia." Iliana Mendes-Ribeira, on target, as usual.

"Exactly. Tell us about that."

"I was taught that the parents will always remember what they are told in the delivery room — what gender you say the baby is. If you tell them, you have a boy, and then it turns out the baby is XX, that you have been fooled by an enlarged clitoris, they may never accept that they have a daughter. For example."

Swifty writing down everything, earnest and sincere. Justin dozing, disheveled and post-call. Neil plainly on edge, an appropriate attitude for the intern on call, waiting for a transport to come in. Full-term baby with probable pneumonia, rule out congenital heart disease. Nothing you can do about it till the baby gets here, Neil.

"Neil, how about some other examples? Delivery room diagnoses?"

"Well, there would be the things you might suspect and not be absolutely sure about. Like Downs." Iliana is without doubt fully familiar with the diagnostic criteria of Down syndrome, so Maggie doesn't ask her to list them.

"Ever had that happen to you, Iliana? Ever look at a baby in the DR and think Downs?"

"No," says Iliana. Then shrugs, somewhat ruefully, and adds, "Not yet."

"I have," Justin says, sitting up. "My first month covering the DR. Saw the epicanthic folds — I mean, this wasn't an Asian baby — and I called it right away. First thing I did was look at the hands — and there was a simian crease."

"Did you say anything to the parents?"

"Not in the DR. Actually, the nurse took over. She made the diagnosis too — and she looked at me and she could see I had made it and I guess she didn't want me shooting off my mouth. She told them they had a healthy baby, ten fingers ten toes" — he grins, a little sheepishly — "and she hustled me and the baby right out of there before I could say a word."

They all smile at one another, these five doctors. Acknowledging the pecking order, the complexities of doctor and nurse.

"Parents will never forget the words you use, the sense you give them of the baby's potential. For you, this is all in a day's work — for all of us." Maggie looks around the little circle, meeting each resident's eyes in turn. "For them, for the parents — well, it's the first time they see their baby, and they will remember it forever. So you'd better be damn sure of your diagnosis, and you'd better think out carefully what you're going to say. And if it's plus-minus, don't say anything at all — wait till you know what you're talking about." She pauses, ready to change gears. She is not particularly fond of psychosocial stuff, but when you have interns covering a delivery room, this is basic: They need to know how to behave when something happens. Okay, duty done, time to get back to the medical. "But then, of course, there are some delivery room diagnoses that require immediate medical action — so you have no choice. You have to let the parents know. Justin, why don't you tell us about last night's delivery? The baby with the tracheo-esophageal fistula?"

And now Justin sees where this was leading — now they all see. Maggie is a good teacher and a good doctor, and here she has led them from the theoretical right smack into Justin's big middle-of-the-night crisis moment. Iliana and Neil paying close attention — this is another "not yet," another possible emergency moment that could fall to one of them on any given night. And Swifty writing things down for all she is worth.

Maggie likes to teach. She found this out about herself in college, found that she could learn difficult material by giving lectures to her empty dormitory room. She remembers herself in college — and graduate school too — formulating what she learned, as she learned it, by teaching it back to herself. Teaching herself was all very well — in fact, she found that after several years of lecturing to herself about cell biology and genetics, it was a little disappointing when she got her first job as a teaching fellow and started explaining these same subjects to undergraduates. They didn't feel the same urgency to understand; they looked at her dully, as often as not, or seemed bewildered by her enthusiasm, or shook their heads and asked unhappily whether this would be on the test. She needed students who were pushed, as she was, by something fierce and hungry — and she found those students, once and for all, when she started working with residents. There is no one who pays closer attention than a half-trained doctor hearing a story about a scenario that might play out tomorrow night — or a couple of weeks or months down the line. These interns are experienced enough to know how inexperienced they are; they know the world is full of medical what-ifs. They listen and they learn, they whisper essential instructions and important mnemonics over and over to themselves, they hold themselves braced and tense for the moment when the lesson may become real. They are the best students in the world, smart and scared and on the line, and Maggie loves to watch them learn.

"First thing I noticed when I came in was, no father," Justin says. You want psychosocial, he'll give you psychosocial. "So she's probably all alone with this."

"Not another teenager!" Maggie can see it coming.

"No, not a teenager. Elderly primip in fact."

Elderly primipara is the old-fashioned but still in use technical term for a woman who is over thirty-five and having her first baby. What Maggie would have been herself, if she had ever gotten pregnant — she is way past taking such things personally, she believes. She no longer flinches at descriptions of infertility, she no longer identifies. And yet, this time, she feels herself brace slightly, as if she expects a blow. But no one can tell, and Justin keeps talking.

"Mom's forty-one. But not your typical — she had this tattoo — you know, on the underside of her arm. Her hands were taped to the boards so I could see it — a mandala."

"A what?" Swifty, worried she's missing a medical term.

Justin draws it quickly on a notecard.

"Yin and yang," identifies Iliana.

"Actually, in Hindu religions it symbolizes the universe. The word *mandala* is Sanskrit for 'circle.'" Justin shuts up, seeing them all looking at him.

Maggie notes the knowledge; she finds it interesting and unexpected, but she chooses to pass it by, as one passes by any one-upmanshiping piece of arcane knowledge in the hospital.

"Thank you, Justin. Now that you've filled us in on the psychosocial context, perhaps we could get back to the life-threatening malformation?"

"What I said was, I want to tell you about your baby. First I told her congratulations, she had a big strong boy, and he was doing fine, but he had a problem. You know, it's always worse when it's something they're never gonna have heard of. I said, His throat doesn't connect up properly to his stomach so he can't swallow his own saliva, and we're sucking it out with a tube — we're going to take him across the connector from Saint A's to Blessed Innocence and have some more doctors check him out, because he may need to have an operation to hook things up the right way, connect his throat to his stomach."

"And how did she take it?"

"She started crying. I think the anesthesiologist turned up her sedative a little. And by this time I'm talking about how good the surgeons are, how well babies do with this."

"And what did she say?"

"She yelled out, '*Why did this happen to him?*'" Justin does not mention what a shock her sudden loud wail had been, how everyone in the room had turned to look at her, the obstetricians, the surgical nurses, Dorothy, the NICU nurse over at the warming table. As if this loud, tormented voice in this sterile, controlled environment was a sudden reminder to them all of the questions better not asked and the answers not easily given. Or maybe just a reminder that this woman had had no place at all in the various conversations of the delivery room, doctor to doctor, doctor to nurse, nurse to nurse; they had all been lowering their voices to keep their words away from her, and now she had reclaimed her place in the drama. He does not mention any of that now, letting Maggie Claymore teach her little lesson on breaking bad news in the delivery room. And he also does not mention that when he was running

131

down the hall toward the bridge to the delivery room, he saw her, Maggie Claymore, when she should have been home long ago, running ahead of him, running like a crazy person. Around a corner, out of sight. Like maybe she didn't want anyone to see her.

After Justin's careful explanation, the woman on the table had completely ignored him. "Why don't they let me see my baby?" she screamed, and, on cue, Dorothy materialized at Justin's side. In her arms she held the baby, now securely wrapped in one of the white blankets, a cap slightly askew on his head. The tube was taped to his cheek.

"I'm going to rush this little fellow right out of here," Dorothy said, "but I wanted to give him a chance to say hello to his mommy first. Now, I'll hold him, and you turn your head, and you'll be able to give him a kiss."

The woman turned her head to the side, pursed her lips, but broke into renewed howls when she saw the baby. "What's that thing in his nose? Take that out of his nose! No one said you could do that to my baby!"

"He needs that right where it is," Dorothy said. "You give him that kiss now, so he'll have something nice to think about when he's on his way over to Blessed Innocence."

She brought the baby's cheek, the side without the tube, right up to the mother, and, obediently, the woman brushed her lips against her son's face. Her eyes opened wide, staring at the baby, then her face worked convulsively, and a new kind of crying began.

"Does he have a name?" Dorothy asked.

"Justin," said the mother. And then she let go and howled it out for all she was worth: "Justin! My baby!"

"Okay, now," Dorothy said. "It's time for me and this doctor to take Justin over to Blessed Innocence, just a few steps away, so he can meet the other doctors who need to see him. We'll be letting you know everything we do, and before you know it, you'll be coming over the same bridge to visit him. And I'll tell you something funny — this doctor's name is Justin too. So come on, Big Justin, come on, Little Justin."

*   *   *

How they look at her on morning rounds. And how she has to look at them, at everyone, wondering briefly, should this person be on my suspect list? Erika Donnelly, a nurse Maggie's never gotten along with all that well, and now she feels mildly guilty for having mentioned her name to Donna Grey, and wouldn't you know it, Erika is bonded tight to Baby Boy not-those-Kennedys. Erika is what a perfect blond California beach girl would look like if you overinflated her with an air hose. Big and round with cartoon breasts and a full-cheeked, pretty face. And she's technically a good nurse, and Maggie knows this. They're all good; the NICU is an unforgiving place for nurses who are anything less than really quick and really smart. But Erika has this style that Maggie quite frankly can't stand; she's superpossessive, makes it clear that no one else has her babies' interests at heart the way she does, makes it especially clear that the doctors are menaces, that her main job is to protect her babies from the doctors' unnecessary procedures and piss-poor judgment calls. Suggest any procedure, however essential, and Erika flinches as though you are personally and deliberately causing her pain. When Maggie pictures Erika Donnelly, she imagines her dramatically blocking the way to a baby, interposing her own pink pneumatic body between the doctors and her patient's tiny form. That's how the big argument between Maggie and Erika climaxed all those months ago, Erika ready to defend her baby to the death. Never mind that Maggie was perfectly right and that baby did in fact need the gastrostomy tube. And got it and did well and went home, thank you very much.

But how Erika looks at her now, as they discuss this baby. Kennedy. Who is doing pretty well, considering how he looked in the emergency room. Considering how he looked when *I* resuscitated him in the emergency room. He's still on the ventilator, of course. Still ridiculously, impossibly small. Still getting all his nutrition intravenously. But it's going to be time to try using his gut soon, and Erika says his ditzhead teenage mom has actually been pumping and storing breast milk. Well, Erika doesn't say it like that. What she says is, Mom's really rising to the challenge. Really invested in this baby.

Thing is, "Mom" also tested positive for syphilis at delivery, turns out. Wasn't ever tested for it before, of course, because she had no prenatal care, because she didn't know she was pregnant, because she doesn't have the brains god gave a rabbit (Justin, summarizing the story for Maggie on rounds, while Erika looks furiously offended). So the baby's being treated for possible congenital syphilis. Doesn't show any clinical signs of it, though.

So when Maggie asks if this mother has been tested for HIV, she's asking a perfectly reasonable question. Defends it as a question by explaining to the interns, Sexually transmitted diseases travel in packs. What puts you at risk for one puts you at risk for all the others. And no, turns out they haven't tested the mother for HIV. So Maggie rules that they can't give the baby the breast milk, not till they've got the HIV test results. Again, perfectly reasonable; breast milk does transmit the virus. But somehow it's also mildly aimed at Erika, who gets a little of her own back as they finish rounding on her baby.

"Dr. Claymore, I'd just like to remind the residents that everything about this baby is absolutely confidential. No matter how many TV reporters show up — you have a professional responsibility here. You guys shouldn't be discussing this with anyone, and I mean anyone. Not the other residents, not your spouses — if anything about the syphilis or any of the rest of the stuff you want to do leaks out, I'm going to make a formal complaint."

Then, as they start to move on, next warming table, next baby, Erika Donnelly says, "By the way, Maggie, a detective came around early this morning to check up on those letters that say you killed that little kid a year ago. What was her name again — Heather Clark. That detective, she came to morning report, she wanted to know which nurses were on that night." Everyone is carefully watching Erika, not Maggie. "I don't see how I'm supposed to remember whether you seemed calm or you seemed agitated. Not from a year ago. You know what I mean?"

An awkward lunch in the cafeteria. Some of the other neonatologists — Claire Hodge, David Susser, Hank Shoemaker — ask tentatively how things are going in the NICU, what's up with that baby who was in the newspapers? And then the murmurs, Heard you're having this problem, Maggie, that's really tough . . . Any idea who's behind it?

"There's a detective investigating," Maggie says. Makes herself say. "A woman named Donna Grey. Has she talked to you?"

She looks around the table, and they will not quite meet her eye, though all their heads are nodding. And she sees Peter Cannon, her good friend, walking past, and she grabs up her tray, with her half-eaten salad, and chases him out of the cafeteria.

"Peter! Wait up! I want to talk to you!"

He stands quietly by while she disposes of silverware, paper goods, tray. Then as they go down the hall, into the main entryway of the hospital, he asks her, "So how are you, Maggie?" with such solicitousness that she knows first of all that he knows all about what is happening to her and second of all that he is hurt that he doesn't know it from her.

In the entrance atrium, there is a group of schoolchildren singing scales. They wear white button-down shirts and dark blue pants, and they are conducted by a pink and bald young man who is shorter than the older boys. A sign on an easel proclaims them the Westwood Day School Chanticleers. Maggie pauses, checking them out. Their voices are tuneful and reassuring, and the conductor's enthusiasm makes her smile.

With the scales as background, Maggie turns to face Peter.

"I should have told you about this, Peter," she says. "It upset me so much that I couldn't talk about it, and I guess I kept hoping it would go away. I know it's silly, but it feels like the worst thing that's ever happened to me."

Peter squeezes her shoulder for a long moment, and she wonders whether this is in fact the first time they have ever touched. She cannot help wondering: Will this somehow be reported to Donna Grey, and will poor Peter, who she suspects is not at all interested in women, find himself facing questions about any possible "intimacy" between himself and the highly suspect Dr. Maggie Claymore?

"This detective came and talked to me about Heather Clark,"

Peter says. "We took care of her for two years in the clinic. And actually, Mrs. Clark and I are still in touch — she was angry at the hospital after Heather died, of course, but she didn't blame the clinic."

Well, of course not — you're a fucking saint. But Maggie doesn't say it. She needs all the friends she can get.

"Does she know about these accusations that someone is making — about me?"

"Oh, I don't think so. There's no reason for her to know about all this — it would just stir up her grief. I told the detective that you had no involvement whatsoever in Heather's care — that I don't think the two of us ever even discussed her."

The school group launches suddenly into the song, "What the World Needs Now Is Love," and Maggie and Peter allow themselves to exchange a quick smile. Peter snaps his fingers absently along with the music.

"I also told her," Peter says, "that you are one of the strongest advocates in this hospital for children with congenital anomalies and disabilities. That it's completely obscene to suggest you're the kind of person who thinks they would be better off dead."

"Is that what she suggested? Is that what she's going around suggesting?"

"Well, she asked whether I thought that was a fair representation of your views."

A small girl with sheets of pure blond hair steps forward from the group and fills the atrium with a shockingly big, rich voice; they interrupt their conversation and turn to look:

"Lord, we don't need another mountain,
There are mountains and hillsides enough to climb!"

How they look at her everywhere. All over the hospital. How the woman who weighed her salad at the cafeteria checkout looks at her, how the messenger picking up the tubes of blood at the NICU desk looks at her, how Dr. Kenneth Mustache Weiss looks at her when he passes her in the main lobby. Or doesn't look at her. Has Donna Grey talked to him yet? What has she asked him, what has he answered? What does he think? Theresa comes to find her; the news took awhile to get to the serology lab, but it's there now. People are talking about the posters, the letters, the accusations. Theresa has come to exclaim in shock and horror, and that makes Maggie again tough and breezy. She turns aside all talk of the posters, the letters, the enemy. Flips through her little pile of today's mail as though there could never be anything in it that would alarm.

"Can you believe this garbage?"

Theresa looks up in sympathetic alarm, prepared for an evil letter full of hate and abuse, but what Maggie is waving at her is just that inane survey, this new little program — the change consultants. Employee Empowerment Through Sharing. EETS. Please complete this survey as a preliminary effort toward defining barriers to employee empowerment. Your efforts will help us ensure that our workplace enables all employees to reach their full potential.

"We have to memorize the structure of all the essential amino acids," Theresa says.

"Very useful information. Comes in handy all the time."

"The first quiz is Saturday."

"You nervous?"

Theresa never seems nervous, exactly. She seems unsure, apologetic, but calm.

"I do well on tests," she says. "I always did. This stuff isn't so hard to learn."

Maggie reads from the empowerment survey. "'My feelings are considered important in my workplace. Strongly Agree, Agree, Not Sure, Disagree, Strongly Disagree.'"

"Maggie, are you sure you're okay?"

"Look, some asshole is trying to wreck my life here. But I'm not going to let him, and the way to not let him is to keep on with my life. Go ace that stupid test."

When I feel bad I can share my feelings with my coworkers. Strongly Agree, Agree, Not Sure, Disagree, Strongly Disagree.

My coworkers support me in an atmosphere of mutual respect. Strongly Agree, Agree, Not Sure, Disagree, Strongly Disagree.

*   *   *

"She goes around behind my back asking the residents to verify my movements. She asks the nurses if I seem agitated! She accuses me of suppressing evidence — I want to know who she thinks she's investigating, me or the crazy person?"

Harvey's office. The same old crowd. Maggie mad but in control of herself.

"You want to know what I think? I think she doesn't have anyone else to investigate, she can't come up with a single suspect, so she's wasting her time checking my comings and goings, my emotional state."

Donna Grey looks straight at her. Maggie finds herself thinking of her own interviews with parents, the your-baby-may-die-tonight interview.

"Doctor," she says, calmly enough, "I'm sorry to put it this way, and I know you aren't going to like this. But say I get called in at a company, there's someone writing anonymous letters about the boss's assistant, letters saying he's embezzling money, say, and the boss asks me, should he make a public statement, this guy is innocent, ignore the letters, they're from a crank. Okay, you follow me so far? I have to say to that boss, How do you know the guy is innocent, how do you know the letters are from a crank?"

"What?" says Harvey to Elaine, hospital bigwig to hospital lawyer.

He sounds outraged, but not, Maggie thinks sadly, not outraged enough.

And Donna Grey ignores him, goes right on with her flat-voiced recital. "See, what I have to consider is, till the investigation is over, how do I know this guy isn't really embezzling funds? He's the boss's assistant, he's got lots of power, maybe someone caught on to him and they're afraid to come out in the open. Let me do my investigation and then we'll see. And then the other thing: What if this guy is sending these letters about himself? That happens, more than you'd think. Sure, someone's a little off-balance, but you don't know who it is, not till the investigation is done. Or then, on the other hand, maybe he's not sending the letters himself, but maybe his ex-wife is doing it because she's mad about his being behind with his alimony payments — maybe it has nothing to do with the company. That's why you have to have an investigation, not just a preliminary report."

Maggie gets the sense that she has just heard Donna Grey's longest set speech. She is again, through her own anger, reminded of herself, of some of her own often repeated welcome-to-the-NICU-I'm-your-baby's-doctor routines.

"So what you're investigating is me." Remembering how she had wanted to believe in Donna Grey, this tough and smart woman. Have to give her credit, at least: Donna Grey is not afraid to say it. And not afraid to look her in the eye; the woman's large wide-set green eyes meet hers without sympathy, without apology, without blinking.

Harvey is angry. "No one here for one minute believes that Maggie is guilty of anything. Let's make that clear. Maggie is the victim, and the hospital is trying to protect her. Maggie is a very talented doctor doing a very difficult job under extremely difficult conditions — I hope I am making this clear to you. Meanwhile, someone was all over this hospital last night, hanging up posters. It surely ought to be possible to figure out who it was."

Donna shrugs. "Hospitals are hard. There's no real security, no check on who comes and goes. And there's a kind of invisibility — you don't necessarily notice a person in a white coat or a nurse's uniform. If there was some street person with a long white beard roaming around last night in striped overalls, sure — but we're not dealing with a perpetrator who takes that kind of chance."

"Well," says Martin Sandow, "it's not that there's no real security. I mean, a hospital is by definition a place with lots of people coming in and out, but we do check IDs, especially at night —"

No, you don't, Maggie thinks.

"No, you don't," Donna Grey says. "I've checked it out over the last few days, and if you really want to know, the night people don't check anyone's ID. You could march in here at night and kidnap the patients and poison the water coolers, and there isn't a soul who would check to see if you had a hospital ID or if you matched the picture on it. Especially if you look okay — you know, white, professional, like you know what you're doing . . . most likely no one will bug you. And if you're wearing a white coat, forget about it. You're untouchable."

"That really isn't true," says Sandow, stiffly.

"Let's hope it isn't." Elaine Oliphant does not look cheerful.

"Listen, folks, last night I had on a white coat and a stethoscope and went walking around this place, and not very late either, just around ten. That's when I ran into Dr. Claymore. I wanted to get a feel for the security and the situation at night. Walked right past that guy who sits in the main lobby, the one you think is supposed to check IDs. He didn't even look up. Walked onto every ward, went into at least one patient room on each one of the general wards, read a couple of patient charts. Only places I got stopped were the operating room, because I wasn't dressed right and a nurse out front told me I couldn't go in, and the unit where you work, Doctor, the newborn unit up on the fifth floor — a nurse started asking who I was and what I wanted, but she's the only one."

Maggie feels a sudden burst of pride, in her NICU, in her nurses. Even Erika Donnelly; easy enough to imagine her blocking the door.

"I really think you may have exceeded your brief here," Elaine is saying.

"Look, it's a good thing I did this. See, I didn't know that this perpetrator was going to spend the night hanging up signs, did I? But now I have a real sense of how easy it would be, and maybe a couple of ideas about how someone might do it. And if you want answers about what happened last night, and what happened that night a year ago when the little girl died, and what the hell is going on in this hospital, then you need someone who knows a little bit about the place, and not just the official line either. Because the official line is that a security man sits down in the main lobby all night and checks everyone's hospital ID." A pause, as she looks around the table, meeting each set of eyes in turn.

"Dr. Claymore, I'd like to talk to you again later today." Donna Grey still sounds calm and unembarrassed.

"I'll be up in the NICU all day." Shove it up your ass, Martin Sandow. You wanted them to pull me out, but I'm still there.

"I'll come find you. I need to go over some aspects of your previous statements — and your husband's." And though the implication is unmistakable, especially after her little illustration about the boss's assistant's vengeful wife, what Maggie actually feels, much to her own surprise, is a sort of trusting relief, the kind that might be felt by a parent who has decided to place hope, fully and completely, in the doctors, has agreed to emergency surgery, and signed the consent. Investigate me — investigate everyone. Snoop and poke and question, and find out whatever there is to know.

11

Babysitting

I T WAS THE ERA when all thirteen- and fourteen-year-old girls in the state of New Jersey babysat. It was the late seventies, and they got a buck an hour, and parents left them happily, thoughtlessly, casually, alone in suburban houses with two or three small children, on toward midnight or even beyond. It was what thirteen- and fourteen-year-old girls did in New Jersey on Saturday nights, at least until they grew up enough to do something better.

It was Maggie's first time sitting for the Federbergs. They had gotten her name, as people did, from some other family in the neighborhood — though their neighborhood was by no means Maggie's neighborhood. The Federbergs lived on one of the nicest streets in the very nicest part of town — a little higher up, a little closer to the golf course, a little farther from the highway. Bigger lots with bigger houses. Swimming pools — no one in the part of town where Maggie and her mother lived had a swimming pool unless it was a wading pool you dragged out of the back of the garage, a big plastic dish you rolled on its side like a hoop, or an inflatable thing you blew up with a bicycle pump and then filled with cold water from the hose.

It was the era when the mothers of thirteen- and fourteen-year-old girls cheerfully sent them off to babysit with families they didn't know. Maggie left the Federbergs' phone number on the little lined pad by the phone and said goodbye to her mother, who reminded her, almost automatically, to make sure they gave her a ride home, to get her homework done early, and not to run up the phone bill — another girl in Maggie's church youth group had recently gotten in trouble, Maggie's mother knew, for making a long distance phone call while babysitting, to her aunt in Virginia. Actually, Maggie knew, Eleanora Davenport had talked at length to her fascinating sixteen-year-old male cousin, who rode a motorcycle. He had promised to take her riding the next time she visited. It was also, of course, that era when long distance phone calls really did seem like a big deal.

Anyway, Maggie found the Federbergs' house, no problem. Mrs. Federberg had a lot of very curly hair, and she was dressed up to go out in something that looked like it came from India, printed with elephants and tigers in big busy blocks of color on droopy beige cotton. She showed Maggie all the things that mothers showed their thirteen-year-old babysitters: This is the television, this is the stereo, be careful if you play records that you put everything back in the right jacket. They had hundreds of records. But what Maggie was really looking at was a big square wooden frame in a little sunroom right off the living room. An apparatus she had never seen before, but still somehow familiar, maybe from a textbook illustration or a museum.

"That's my loom," Mrs. Federberg said kindly. "I've been studying weaving for more than three years now — ever since my younger daughter was born."

Maggie nodded.

"I did macramé for a long time," Mrs. Federberg said. She gestured to a row of plants, hanging in front of the sunroom windows, each in a different net of knotted colored cord. "But it's very limiting, macramé. No matter how good you get at it — and I have to say, in all modesty, I did get quite good — there's a certain dimensionality you just miss. Maybe that's because macramé doesn't really have the same history."

Maggie nodded.

"Weaving, now!" Mrs. Federberg tossed her trailing scarf over her shoulder and glided to her loom. She invited Maggie to admire the partly finished rectangle of fabric, a ruddy brown background with geometric red zigzags. "This is a traditional Zuni pattern," she said proudly. "I mean, it's adapted, of course. But next year I may go take a special course on the Zuni reservation. Don't you think that would be amazing?"

Maggie nodded. Inside her head she was wondering, Aren't Zunis the other kind of Indians? while looking at the print on Mrs. Federberg's dress, which so clearly seemed to come from the faraway Asian country of hippie wraparound skirts and bedspreads.

"I like it," Maggie said, a little shyly. She did like it; she liked the pattern, and the substantial feel of the rough cloth between her fingers, and Mrs. Federberg's pride. Maybe she also liked the size of the loom and the way it took up the sunroom; there was no equivalent she could think of in her own home, no strange and sizable adult toy.

Mrs. Federberg gripped Maggie's arm, stared into her eyes. "Weaving has brought me to serenity," she said. "Weaving has taught me lessons — I wish I had time to explain to you what weaving has been for me! I want my little girls to grow up with this craft, to pass it from mother to daughter. And this is after I had tried so many routes — so many ways — after so much searching!"

Mrs. Federberg's husband, Mr. Federberg, appeared behind her in the living room. He was dressed in blue jeans and a sports jacket, which is what hip dads wore, and he was looking at his watch.

"We do have a reservation," he said.

A Zuni reservation? Maggie suddenly wanted to ask, but she didn't, and Mrs. Federberg was off in a flutter of brightly colored draperies, telling Maggie over her shoulder to go ahead and help herself to the ice cream in the freezer.

But Maggie helped herself to more than that. Oh, she did eat the ice cream, though only after she had read a series of Dr. Seuss books to the two little Federberg girls and turned off their lights. They each had a great big bedroom, which made Maggie envious in a kind of routine way; she herself had the one tiny bedroom at home, a room smaller than the Federbergs' sunporch, smaller, in fact, than the loom. But it was, at least, a bedroom; Maggie's mother slept in the living room on a fold-out couch. Any friend

Maggie visited, any family she babysat for, there was always that quick gulp of envy, and she was more or less used to it. On the other hand, the Federberg girls did have truly big, truly airy rooms, carpeted in sunny yellow, spilling over with dolls and books and toys.

She put them to bed, she left their doors slightly open and left the light on in the hallway, she went downstairs and helped herself to the ice cream in the freezer. And then, of course, she prowled, she snooped, she looked around to see what she could see.

And that is what every thirteen- and fourteen-year-old girl in the state of New Jersey did while babysitting. Grownups went off and left the girls in charge of their houses, surrounded by the trappings of adulthood, and the girls did research. They were not, by and large, very interested in the children, though they did, by and large, conscientiously earn that dollar an hour. No, the babysitters were interested in the parents. That same girl, Eleanora Davenport, with the motorcycle-riding cousin in Virginia, had confided to Maggie and Nancy just last week that even as she was talking on the phone, long distance, running up the bill, she had opened a drawer in the bedside table and found not only condoms, but a copy of a book called *The Sensuous Woman* — and when she tried to tell them about the chapter she had read, she got all embarrassed, and then she started to giggle, and then she told them she couldn't say it. And then she told them it was about spraying Redi-Whip on a man's you-know, and licking it off, and then they all three giggled so hard they got in trouble in study hall.

Fortified by two dishes of ice cream, though without Redi-Whip — there actually was a can in the refrigerator, and the very sight of it made Maggie snicker, a little breathlessly, but she couldn't quite bring herself to eat any — Maggie tiptoed back up the stairs, listened outside the little girls' doors to be sure they weren't awake or restless, and then slipped very quietly into the master bedroom. It was an enormous room with a grand, high ceiling and a big window in the ceiling set right over the bed, but it was the bed itself that held Maggie's attention. She had heard of waterbeds, of course, but she had never seen one. It was a great big waterbed, covered with a furry throw printed to look like a tiger skin. Maggie pressed down on one corner of the mattress — it was a waterbed from back in the early days of waterbeds, when the slosh was quite distinctive. Bravely, she sat herself down on the corner of the bed, then allowed herself to fall backward and ride up and down on the waves of her impact. She was, of course, giggling. She would call Nancy, she thought, right then and there, and tell her, Guess what they have, guess what I'm lying on, right now! Maggie rolled over as heavily as possible, trying hard to create water action.

People can live however they want, Maggie was thinking. She didn't know exactly what she meant, but it was something to do with her mother's own cramped and pinched life, so carefully scrutinized by the good friends who felt so sorry for her poor and single state, so limited, it seemed to Maggie, limited even in what should have been Annalisa's most private, relaxed moments. And of course, Annalisa had very few private moments; she did, after all, sleep on the fold-out couch in the living room. And Maggie herself had kindness and imagination enough, even at thirteen, to appreciate that her mother's life was limited in part because what little privilege and privacy there was belonged to Maggie herself. She could appreciate this on some sympathetic level while still, much of the time, feeling a certain resentful irritation at her mother for not having somehow managed things better — Why didn't you pick the right kind of husband? Why didn't you stay married? Why don't I have a dad? Why don't we have money? Why do we have to go to church all the time? Why can't I wear nail polish? — which actually may not have been that different from the resentful irritation that most thirteen-year-old girls feel toward their mothers.

People can live however they want. People invent themselves, invent their homes, their rooms, their marriages. Weaving. Waterbeds. Zunis. You do not have to grow up to live the life in which you were raised. You can look around at the great treasure chamber of the world and you can pick and choose. And Maggie explored the Federbergs' bedroom, not systematically, but with deep appreciation; she treated it like an art exhibit, drifting here, drifting there, looking closely at anything that caught her interest, anything that seemed to offer especially vital information.

She drifted as well through the bathroom and the kitchen and the living room. She didn't find everything there was to find — she missed the Federbergs' marijuana, for example, not knowing to look for it, not being capable of recognizing it even if she had found it. Two years later, she would have known to look in the oregano jar, and she would have known what she was seeing, and perhaps even have sneaked a small quantity in a Baggie, but by two years later, Maggie was no longer babysitting on Saturday nights. So she missed the marijuana, but she did find and recognize a certain telephone-dial package of pills in the top right-hand dresser drawer, and a large number of intriguing record albums. She put one on the stereo, *Bat Out of Hell*, turned the volume up as loud as she thought practical without waking up the children, and settled herself down on the couch to read her real prize, the book that had been waiting for her, concealed under the pile of extra blankets: *Everything You Always Wanted to Know About Sex but Were Afraid to Ask*. By Maggie's best and most cautious calculation, she had at least two hours before the Federbergs came home, and she intended to use them. There was no point in wasting any time calling Nancy, calling anyone at all — Eleanora Davenport herself, given the choice, would absolutely have said, Read as much as you can, and tell me about it tomorrow.

12

Pumping

T O BE PERFECTLY HONEST, I guess I resent that they even sent me to see you." That they're putting me in bullshit therapy so I can feel really good about how they can't figure out who's persecuting me. That when Harvey Weintraub said, Maggie, we are going to support you all the way, what he meant was, You get some sessions with the hospital's pet shrink.

"That's what happens when employees start to feel disempowered. It always breeds resentment and a sense that you aren't in control of your own destiny. Our goal is to help you take back a sense of control."

"Right, yes, I understand." Not wanting to be too rude to Graham Shipley, institutional psychologist, whatever that is, and hospital guru, director of the Employee Empowerment Through Sharing program, who is obviously in high favor. I mean, would you look at the size of this office? Employee Empowerment Through Sharing indeed — guess who's getting empowered here. And guess which employee is not, repeat *not*, sharing an office. And do you believe that name, Graham Shipley? Why not Shipley Graham? Younger than she had expected, a tall, slightly pudgy man with curly dark hair and crooked front teeth. He looks ready for his TV interview at any time, always patiently explaining the complicated world that is so clear and open to his understanding.

"Now usually, as you know, we're working with empowerment *groups*, but Dr. Weintraub has asked me to do some special sessions with you, because I gather you're having an especially difficult time." Oh, the canned sincerity of the man, the earth-toned, textured sweater, the wire-rimmed glasses, the intense, concerned eyes in the very slightly pockmarked face.

"Maggie, Dr. Weintraub is concerned that what is going on may have affected your comfort level in the workplace."

"You mean, because everyone I've come in contact with for the last month has been looking at me and thinking about these posters and these accusations?"

"I'm wondering if you could share with me some of your experiences — have there been other times in your life when you were concerned about other people's opinions?"

Maggie shrugs.

"Let's close our eyes, both of us," says Graham Shipley. "As adults, we get comfortable in our lives, in our identities, in our selfhoods. Let's think together about when we were shaping those selfhoods, when we weren't so sure who we were."

Maggie leans back in her comfortable chair. She despises his language (selfhoods!), but she knows what he means. Yes, she does, she knows what he means. She has never been to a shrink. This is new to her, the temptation to do the talking, the seduction of being listened to.

It never fails. Here you have two very low birth-weight babies, Baby Boy not-those-Kennedys and Surviving Twin Grassini, and one mom is a didn't-know-she-was-pregnant teenager and one is a million-dollar-infertility workup, so which one do you want to bet is doing well and which one is doing terribly? Karen Kennedy is probably going to have a baby to take home with her in a couple of months. And she's a miserable, lost adolescent who comes in every couple of days to spend some time staring into the isolette, looking dazed. On the other hand, both Mr. and Mrs. Grassini are there day and night, hanging over Felicia, who just gets sicker. Baby Girl Murphy, Justin called her on rounds one morning, Baby Girl Murphy's Law. If something can go wrong . . .

Can't even count the complications, can't even imagine the pages and pages of documentation and order sheets and x-ray reports mounting up. The infections, the IV problems, the stiff lungs, the head bleeds, the skin breakdown. And she just won't gain weight. Maggie is willing to bet there isn't a nurse or doctor in the place who hasn't had the fleeting fantasy: Late one night, Grassini dies, they switch not-those-Kennedys into her bed — if only they were the same gender!

The two mothers in the pumping room: Karen at last cleared to pump her breast milk, her HIV test negative; and she does it — she still comes in and pumps, but not very regularly. I mean, let's face it, she's a high school freshman! And Michele Grassini there day and night pumping out her milk to store for a baby whose stomach has never successfully absorbed a nutritional substance. When Maggie thinks about that stored milk, she thinks of tears; the lacrimal ducts produce tears by a process not totally different from that by which the milk ducts produce milk. Bottled mother's tears, mother's milk.

Jesus, imagine.

"How's your baby doing today, dear?" Michele Grassini, all plugged in, plastic funnel clasped to full, ignorant breast, producing milk for that baby who cannot eat.

"They never tell me anything. They think I'm too fuckin' stupid." Karen Kennedy, recovered, fully dressed and made up, and no longer cowed by the parental firestorm, turns out to be no tender little victim. Well, of course she has to be some sort of loser: Who else ends up impregnated and infected with syphilis and crashed up in a car at the age of fourteen? On the other hand, she's a tough little cookie, not the least bit awed by the hospital, and Maggie kind of likes her. Likes all the earrings and the now pierced nose, a new decoration, appreciates the Morticia Addams look — all black clothes, white powdered face. Likes the way she heard Karen say to the nurse, Erika Donnelly, one afternoon, So who died and made you God?

"They don't think you're stupid, dear. It's just all so complicated. I come in every day and try to figure out whether Felicia is better or worse, and it's a little bit more this but a little bit less that. If they say her weight is up a few grams, I'm just on air, and if it's down or it's the same I practically start to cry — and then today they told me her weight is up but they think it's because she's retaining water and they want to put her on diuretics."

"My granddad takes those. To help with the stress of being a VIP. They're supposed to make his heart work better. But he's always bumming my cigarettes, you know?"

Oh, let them make common cause together, there in that anonymous little room. Let them cheer for each other's babies. Let them take comfort. And let them stay far away from the certifiably crazy mother of Little Justin and her tribe. That's right, her tribe.

You wouldn't believe it. It's the stuff of hospital legend, and for all her groaning and complaining, Maggie would ordinarily probably take some kind of pleasure in being right at the center of a story like this. The problem is that right now it's the last thing she wants, anything out of the ordinary, anything that might make people more aware of her. Like this whole rainbow tribe of leftover Woodstock Nation dingbats camping out in the hallway near her NICU to make sure that little Justin Higgins does not get his karma fucked up by too much soul-destroying Western medicine. I mean, give me a break. Sure, let's chant. Let's massage him and see if his esophagus elongates.

"So the baby goes to the OR, everything goes fine. They repair the TEF, baby does beautifully. Next morning, I walk out in the hall, and there's the mother's whole commune — they've driven down from Vermont. A six-foot-tall guy with his beard down to his waist — he's the patriarch — a couple of women who both seem to be his wives, one of them pregnant out to here, and then this spooky guy who never says a word, he wears mirror shades and a headset all the time. And a girl who looks like a teenage runaway."

Maggie and Peter up on the roof, Peter sneaking a cigarette. No sign of the mailroom guy.

"I didn't know they still had communes, even in Vermont." How happy, how relaxed Peter looks, leaning back against a pillar, inhaling nicotine. Maybe, Maggie thinks, I should take it up. Or drinking. Or something. And then she shudders, feels her shoulders rasp

151

against the brick, imagining how easy it would be to let everything go. Imagining herself as fat and wild-eyed and strange, as a member of the tribe.

"But before they got in their painted school bus to drive here, they stopped in the craft workshop, and they printed up T-shirts."

"And what do the T-shirts say?" Peter is smiling, and Maggie almost smiles too. It's pretty good.

"*Primum non nocere.*"

"No shit?" He's impressed. He's giggling.

"No shit."

And if you think it's funny that everyone coming into the NICU has to run a gauntlet of unwashed freaks wearing shirts decorated with the oldest medical injunction of them all, in Latin no less — well, looked at a certain way, it is kind of funny. *First, do no harm.* The old warning to think about whether your therapies are worse than the disease.

"Shh!" They crouch, the two of them, behind their pillar. The mailroom guy, apparently not a care in the world. Look at him there, monumental in the thin sunlight. Not smoking. He takes a small brown paper bag from one of his overall pockets and begins tossing round candies into the air, catching them matter-of-factly in his mouth.

And here's the nurse, coming out the door. The mailroom guy snaps one more candy out of the air, starts to put the bag away, thinks better of it, holds it out to the nurse. She shakes her head, offers him instead two little vials. Which he takes. Which he pays for. And Maggie and Peter practically don't breathe until the two of them have finished their transaction and retreated into the hospital building. And then, on cue, Maggie's beeper goes off.

Donna Grey was tired and irritated. Blessed Innocence was much more of a pain in the neck than any large company she had ever investigated for sabotage. There was no security, no records were kept anywhere of people's comings and goings, and, once you got up to the level of the doctors, everyone had a kind of surly resentment about being questioned, just as if they weren't employees, just as if

152

they had no obligation to cooperate. What is it about these people? she wondered, watching Kenneth Weiss fidget.

Donna didn't at all mind making people uncomfortable; in fact, she liked it. More than once she had gone digging around in a company to find sabotage, or industrial espionage, or even an anonymous letter writer, and had found in the course of her digging some other completely unsuspected criminal activity. Every now and then people panicked when she interviewed them, told what they knew about all sorts of things, turned in their colleagues for a wide variety of derelictions. The guilty run where no one pursues. And the big question for Donna was this: Was Maggie running?

"I was in the lab," Kenneth Weiss said again, playing with the pens in his coffee-can penholder. "I told you, I have no idea how late I stayed that night. It's hard to look back and pick out one particular night a week ago."

"And no one saw you leave, and no one was at home when you got there."

He shook his head, a little bit sadly. No one knew when he came and went, he seemed to suggest. "All work, no play," he said, with a rueful little feel-sorry-for-me smile. And Donna straightened in her seat, picking up the vibe: The guy, in his way, is flirting.

Maggie, of course, had not been completely honest or accurate when she had reassured Dan, but what wife in her position would have bothered to be completely honest or completely accurate? Kenneth Weiss was losing a little hair, yes, and his mustache was on the large side, yes, but he was in great shape, a famous workout addict, and he enjoyed a mild reputation as a hospital sex symbol. Ran the marathon every year with a group from the oncology division, dedicating the run to patients and families. The whole division came out to cheer them on, and there was always talk afterward about how good Kenneth looked in his running clothes. He was tall and vigorous and competitive in his energies, and Donna had no trouble imagining him as someone Maggie Claymore might once have had a thing with. Have had a thing for.

Maggie's husband, after all, was a perfectly reasonable, nice fellow, good-looking enough, if you liked them casually groomed, but this fellow, in Donna's terms, was a player. Donna had no way of knowing, of course, that in medical school, when Maggie had indulged, Kenneth had actually been in less admirable condition, though of course he had had all his hair on his head, not on his upper lip; she also, fortunately for Maggie, had no way of knowing that at certain times in her life Maggie had been less than rigorously discriminating. Fortunately because if Donna had known that, she would have been much less willing to believe that Kenneth was the one and only Blessed Innocence employee in that interesting suspect category; Donna tended to think along rather rigid lines, perhaps especially where sexual misconduct was concerned. This was not just prejudice on her part; her professional experience was that sex between colleagues was often a root of industrial evil. She distrusted Kenneth and Maggie all the more because Kenneth did manage to generate a certain tingle, a certain suggestive spark, even here in his drab hospital office. She was, in general, pretty strict about misbehavior, Donna Grey; she didn't like people messing up the planet, wasting resources, filling the emotional air with confusion and trouble.

In some ways, Donna didn't like people all that much, period; she cared a great deal about the natural world, she cared about birds and tide pools and giant trees and endangered cetaceans, though you would never have looked at her and thought, Oh yes, save the whales. And you wouldn't have predicted the extremely well thumbed copy of *Walden* by her bed. But there you are: Donna sorted out all kinds of messes between people, and sometimes she thought human beings were one big mess, one big mistake, one big, ugly tangle. And someone who slept around was someone who slept around.

"Listen," Kenneth Weiss told her, "I did not hang up signs about Maggie Claymore. I might have been in the building when someone did it, or I might not, I don't know, but I swear to god, this is the first I've heard of it."

"You and Dr. Claymore have a history of a more intimate relationship."

"That was a very long time ago." But he did sound, for whatever male-vanity reason, slightly gratified.

154

"Dr. Weiss, you aren't married?"

"No," he said. "But that's not because of Maggie — I mean, there was nothing like that between us. Nothing so serious. If that's what that's supposed to mean."

"No," Donna said, a little smugly, "it's supposed to mean that there was no one at home to notice when you got there last Wednesday night."

He could have said, with perfect truthfulness, That's because I tend not to plan my social life on weeknights. Or, with perfect truthfulness, I was planning to get up very early on Thursday morning to make sure I'd get some time in on the climbing wall at the gym before work. He could have said, Do you want to interview the lady who would have been there, waiting, if it had been a Friday night? He could have said, I am deeply in love, maybe for the first time in my whole damn life, and I am trying to figure out how to fit that in without upsetting everything else. He looked at Donna Grey and wondered whether it was safe for her to know things about him.

"If you're through with your questions . . ." Kenneth Weiss said.

"One more thing, Dr. Weiss. During your association with Dr. Claymore, did she at any time say anything that gave you the impression that her credentials were not perfectly well in order?"

"What do you mean?"

"Did you ever hear, either from her or from anyone else, anything to the effect that she had in any way falsified her record?"

"No," said Kenneth Weiss, staring at her, as if she had finally said something truly, deeply interesting. "Falsified her record in what way?"

Donna Grey shrugged and made a note in her ring binder.

"She was a good medical student," Kenneth told her. "I never heard anyone say anything like that. The rotation we did here together — she got high honors and I only got honors." He doesn't see anything strange in remembering that.

"Okay, Dr. Weiss, thank you very much for your time. I realize you have a busy schedule." Donna closed her binder and stood, ready to move on.

"Why did you ask that — about her falsifying her record? Is she in trouble?"

"We're just doing an investigation," Donna said, and smiled, and left him sitting there at his messy desk with his coffee can full of pens and his untwisted paper clips.

"I don't get it," Erika Donnelly said. "What'd she do?"

Donna Grey had chosen to conduct this interview in the nurses' conference room, and it had perhaps been a poor choice. It was so blatantly Erika's territory, as she sat at her ease in one of the black plastic chairs and fiddled with the coffeemaker. At the start of the interview she had slapped down her clipboard with a sigh to show she was interrupting important work, and then she poured out coffee for them both, tasted her cup and made a disgusted face, and then left Donna sitting there as she bustled to the sink to dump her mug and wash out the pot, to the garbage can to dump out the filter, to the cabinet to get new coffee. Even now, everything poured and added and switched on, Erika was still fiddling, giving the glass pot filling up with the dripping dark liquid a little quarter-turn on its hot plate every now and then, dabbing at spilled coffee grounds with a wet paper towel.

"This is an investigation," Donna said, once again. One more time. "Accusations have been made in an anonymous fashion. Is Dr. Claymore a friend of yours?"

"Are you kidding?"

"She's a colleague of yours, then — you work together."

"Sometimes. When she's on service."

"Do you like her?"

Erika shrugged those big round shoulders. "There are doctors I like better and doctors I like worse. She does a decent job."

"What I need to ask you about is an altercation that I understand you and she had a couple of months ago."

"What are you talking about?"

"You got into an argument."

Erika poured out coffee into a mug decorated with a cartoon cat. "I know what an *altercation* is. I was just wondering what particular *altercation* you were talking about." She took a sip of her coffee, hot and black.

"About some changes that were made on a baby's ventilator — you made some changes without asking her and she thought it was a bad idea."

Erika threw back her head, tossed her luxuriant mane of blond hair, and laughed an unexpectedly shrill appreciation. "Somebody should tell you a thing or two about the NICU," she said. "If you don't have a good fight on morning rounds about something or other, then you know morale is low. Sure, I remember Maggie losing it one morning, the usual kind of thing. I didn't let it worry me."

"So you feel no animosity toward her?"

"Look, what is this? Are you trying to say I'm the one harassing her?"

"No, I'm just conducting an investigation. There have been some allegations — some strictly anonymous allegations — about her professional conduct, and then a lot of name-calling."

"They're saying she murdered that little girl, aren't they? Heather Clark."

Donna sat up straight. "When did you first hear that rumor?"

"I don't know — maybe a couple of weeks ago. Someone told me they heard that the hospital investigated where Maggie Claymore was the night that kid died up on Seven."

"Before that, had you ever heard that Dr. Claymore was involved?"

"I don't think so. Well — wait, maybe there was something once."

"Can you remember? When it was, what you heard?" Donna was making hasty notes, leaning forward and pressing the binder down on the table. Erika Donnelly watched her, noting her obvious excitement. Had Donna looked up she would have seen a not particularly friendly smile, a smile that might just possibly have made her wonder.

"What I remember is — maybe a year ago, after that night when the kid died . . . I was talking with one of the other nurses, and she said the police are going to come investigate everyone who was in the hospital that night. So I asked her who was working in the

NICU, and she told me which nurses — you know, this was kind of like a joke, we were trying to decide who would be a suspicious character if there was a cop asking questions."

"And who brought up Dr. Claymore?"

"Well, you have to remember this was a long time ago. But I think what happened was, I said, Who was the intern? And she told me, and we were both laughing because this particular intern was a total wimp — I mean, the last person you would ever think would do anything he shouldn't do — this guy wouldn't even go to the bathroom without asking permission."

"Yes?"

"So then she said that actually Maggie Claymore was there too, and, actually, she had heard that Maggie went to the code to help out — and we looked at each other, and it was like, Well, you said it, I didn't!"

"What do you mean — what did you mean?"

Erika shrugged. "I guess we both meant that it was sure a lot easier to imagine her running out to kill someone than anyone else in the NICU." She seemed suddenly a little unsure of herself, for the first time, as if she half wished she hadn't started down this road.

"Why is that — what were you getting at?"

"Maggie Claymore is a real ball buster," Erika said, with the relish of one who knows the term has often been applied to her own emphatic style. "She's just — you know, there's people you can see doing a murder and people you can't, and she's just one of the kind . . ." Her voice trailed off. "Look, is this going to take much longer?"

Donna ignored the question. "Since that time, over the past year, have you heard anything at all that gave you the impression that Dr. Claymore had in fact had any involvement with the death of Heather Clark?"

Erika stared at her. "She really *is* mixed up in it?"

"I'm not saying that. I am just trying to collect information."

"No." The big woman shook her head slowly, her pretty, flushed face disappointed. Donna had no doubt that she would have told more if she had more to tell.

"I'll need the name of your colleague — the one you had that conversation with."

"It seems to me that I *have* heard rumors to that effect. That she might have, shall we say, enhanced her CV." Oh, yes, indeed, let me tell you about Dr. Maggie Claymore — I am the expert on that subject! And I have much to tell you, but I'm going to let you drag it out of me, because I know exactly how to play you, you so-called detective. Because I am a fucking Avenger. And Maggie Claymore, you cruel, harsh bitch, you might as well give up. You are up against a shadow, a genius, a goddamn fucking top-of-the-line Avenger.

"When?"

"I don't exactly know — I can't pinpoint anything specific. But old stuff, like medical school, maybe her training — that she claimed things she has no real right to claim."

You can say anything. Anything at all.

"No, I mean, when did you hear these rumors? Before all this started or after?"

"I'm not exactly sure, Miss Grey. I haven't kept track — it hasn't been very much on my mind. But I've been hearing rumors about Dr. Claymore for a long time."

"Can you remember any of the people who passed these rumors on?"

"That's the problem with hospital gossip, I'm afraid." Rueful smile. "Especially since I don't really do a lot of gossiping. I just can't pinpoint *where* I heard *what* — it's more of a vague impression than anything else." Follow up on my vague impression, Detective. Look for the disgusting lies and cheap tricks that got so-called Dr. Maggie Claymore where she is today. And tell everyone you're doing it, that's the way. That's the fucking way!

"You've been hearing this kind of thing for years and years and you can't remember even one specific source?" Does she sound suspicious? Unconvinced?

"I do remember one nurse who used to work in our NICU — she seemed to know a lot about Dr. Claymore. I think this woman had dated a fellow who trained with her — anyway, this nurse, Sue

Kelly, she used to worry about some of the things she'd heard. She asked me once if I really thought the patients were safe with Dr. Claymore."

"Does she still work here?"

"I believe she left two years ago. She moved to Ireland." And good luck finding Sue Kelly in Ireland! Especially since she actually joined the air force and went to Germany. Fucking genius.

Late night. I should go home. Iliana knows what she's doing. She's properly supervised. They'll call me if they need me. In fact, Iliana will be offended if I breathe down her neck. But I can't do it, go home and have Dan look at me with that question in his eyes, *Anything new today?* Can't tell him that today there was a new letter to Harvey, to all the hospital big shots, saying that everyone knows I killed Heather Clark. Dwelling on it with loving detail: *Everyone knows that Dr. Maggie Claymore turned off the monitor on which this sick but precious child depended for her life and then stood by while she died because Dr. Claymore does not believe that imperfect children deserve to live but would rather watch them strangle to death on their own secretions in pain and without mercy.*

The irony is, the residents think I'm an extremist in the other direction. They think I'm pushing too hard with Grassini. They think I shouldn't have resuscitated Kennedy. Maggie Pray-more. Maggie Do-more. I'm the last person in the world to dismiss a child or write off a baby just because there's a medical problem. The last person in the world.

Does he know this, the person who's writing the letters? My enemy? Is he smiling at the irony, is he laughing at me? Or she, as Donna Grey would say, by which she means me, by which she means she never loses sight of the possibility that I'm doing this for attention. And I'm certainly getting attention.

Donna Grey knows that Maggie is still in her office. She also knows that someone is lurking — there is no other word for it — in the staff bathroom right down the hall from the NICU. The door is very slightly open and the light is off, and someone is in there. When she passed the slightly open door she heard a rustle, a lightly caught breath, but she kept right on walking. And why would anyone be in there if not to watch the NICU? Donna has taken up a position herself a little farther down the hall, patiently waiting behind a large trash receptacle. The hall is bright, of course, day or night, with hospital fluorescence. Bright and empty, aqua-green walls and muted checkerboard carpet and the strange, distant pulse of a building full of sleepless people. Donna is not usually troubled by ghosts, but she finds herself thinking, as she watches for the watcher, of the stretchers that have been rolled out of that NICU door, the medical failures, the little dead bodies. And she is right, of course. The corridor in which she is crouching has seen its share of funeral processions; the morgue attendants know the way. And the resilient institutional carpet would take no marks from the stretcher wheels, the lights would hum, efficiently bright and pitiless on whatever human scraps were passing through. Donna thinks of the Blue Hills, of mulch under her feet and the rich, complex smell of reality and life and death outside. She walks alone and without fear in the woods, but she is tense as she waits in that antiseptic hallway. Waiting for the watcher to show himself. Or herself.

My Day: Some Hospital Vignettes, by Maggie Claymore. The one all the trouble is about.

Vignette number one. I lead the NICU team into the x-ray reading room to go over the morning's films with a radiologist. And it's not our usual radiologist, it's Tom Chen, whom I barely know. And instead of reading the first film, he looks at me with tremendous concern and says, Maggie, I'm so sorry you're still having all this trouble. Who do you think can be doing this, do you have any idea?

Vignette number two. Maggie Claymore hurries down the hall, doesn't look where she's going, trips over a bucket. Two women in the light green smocks of Environmental Services stare at her as she catches herself, grabs the bucket, apologizes. Then, as she walks away, she can hear them whisper, hear them start to laugh.

Vignette number three. So Baby Girl Grassini needed a new arterial line, and I got one into her foot, first try. Expected that even Erika Donnelly would be impressed. Instead, as she's taping in the line: "The dad was asking about you, Maggie. He had one of those papers with your picture on it — he recognized you. He wanted to know what it was all about." Blood pulsing back into the art line, bright red arterial blood, pumping with the force of this marble-sized heart, which I have kept beating now for two weeks. "I mean, you can't blame the guy for being nervous. He's already lost one baby." Erika holding out a piece of plastic tubing; I plug it into the line with steady hands: must not jerk the catheter, must not lose the art line. Erika wiping the foot, the board, with gauze and alcohol, intent on her tidying up. "I had to tell him I'm not exactly sure what the procedure is if you want your child to have a different doctor and the baby is in the NICU. I told him that there isn't really any other doctor."

The bathroom door opens a little further. The watcher inside is checking the hallway, looking up and down before making a move. Donna tenses her leg muscles, ready to spring forward. When the figure comes out of the bathroom, she moves, catches up, grabs his arm. Firmly: Come along with me, please. Identifies him without surprise: the husband.

"I'd like to speak with you, please."

Dan looks considerably more surprised; she can see him identify her but with a slight delay: the detective.

"What are you doing here?" he says.

"What are *you* doing here, Doctor?"

"What do you *think* I'm doing here? The nights Maggie stays late, those are the nights that asshole does his stuff in the hospital. I'm going to find him — I'm going to watch until I see who's doing this, someone who's watching her, or hanging up posters, someone who has no business here."

"And then?" Donna Grey is still holding his arm.

Dan pulls away from her and says, as if he's been waiting for someone to ask, "And then I'm going to beat the shit out of him!" It does not sound like something he has said — or meant — very often in his life.

"Doctor, to me *you* look like someone who has no business here."

Now he gets it. Now she watches it sink in. "Are you trying to tell me that instead of tracing this guy, you're wasting your time thinking it's me? Is this supposed to be a step up from thinking it's Maggie doing it to herself? She's out there with those babies, totally unprotected, this crazy person is running around the hospital somewhere, and you're chasing *me*?" His voice cracks, as if he is about to scream or maybe even cry.

To her own surprise, Donna finds herself explaining. "I had no idea it was you hiding in there. So by playing these little games, what you do is distract my attention when I could be looking elsewhere, which is not helpful. But I agree that the nights that Dr. Claymore stays late are the significant nights, and I could tell someone was waiting in that bathroom."

"Good for you! Congratulations! Give the lady a medal! What ace detective work!"

Donna keeps her voice level, ignores his sarcasm. "Does Dr. Claymore know that you're here?"

And now Dan looks slightly abashed. "No. Actually not. She's so determined to tough it out — she might not have wanted me here."

"She would be right, Doctor."

"Dan," he corrects, almost automatically.

"Dan. She would be right. It's not a matter of toughing it out — but her situation is complicated enough, her position is difficult enough. You can't go shadowing her around the hospital and threatening to beat people up."

"Her position! Her position is impossible! And you people aren't doing a damn thing to help — it goes on and on, and there are more letters and more posters and people insult her and it's all she thinks about, all the time — I can tell!"

"Dan — I think you should lower your voice, please," Donna says. She sees the empty parent conference room and gestures him in, switches on the light.

"She gets up every morning and comes in here to this place, she tries to do her job — if you did your job the way Maggie does hers, you'd have caught this guy by now, damn it!"

Donna does not like the way all of these people, all of these doctors, jump to the conclusion that she is inept, at fault. She knows that she is very good and very thorough, and she allows herself to imagine, for an instant, the joy of turning the question around: How come your patients don't all get better? Don't you know your job, Doctor?

But Dan is beyond noticing her annoyance. Dan is not really talking to Donna at all, she thinks; he is just saying what he has to say.

"I'm supposed to be at a swim meet," he says, and Donna does not understand what he is getting at. "Maggie thinks I'm at a swim meet — this pool I'm involved with, this swim program — never mind, it's not important."

"But you're not at this swim meet," Donna says, and there is, no question, an accusation in her voice, that echo of *You're not where you should be.*

Dan pulls a folded paper out of the back pocket of his chinos and hands it to Donna, who opens it, looks at it with some confusion.

"That's tonight's roster for the meet — I was supposed to drive out with the team. I help the coach. I called in sick."

"So you could come here and protect your wife?"

"Somebody has to protect my wife!" He is almost yelling again.

"We are trying to do that," Donna begins, but he cuts her off.

"She pushes too hard, she pushes herself, she pushes these babies — Maggie always believes it's better if you push. But you look at her eyes, you listen to her voice, and you know something's missing — this is wiping her out! Wiping out everything that she is, and she wants me to pretend that I don't notice!"

"What do you mean?" Donna keeps her voice quiet and unsurprised; very deliberately, she does not make it sound like an official question (What, exactly, do you mean by that, Doctor?).

"Maggie's not like me," Dan says, looking at Donna very intently, so intently that Donna feels obliged to nod, though she has no particular idea what he means. "I don't need these guys — I never did — I don't think I'm a better doctor or a better person just because a lot of big-ego academic types say I am!"

He stops, shakes his head. He seems to think he's explained what needs to be explained.

Donna prompts him. "But Dr. Claymore?"

"Maggie *needs* to believe in these guys — in this place. It matters to her — I can't tell you how much it matters to her. We pretend it's like a game — making it, getting ahead — but we pretend that so she won't be embarrassed — or so she won't think I disapprove . . ."

"*Do* you disapprove?" Donna Grey is no longer sure exactly what she is asking, or what he is explaining. Or even how to move the conversation back to more important matters.

Dan shakes his head. "This is wiping her out. If this goes on much longer, I think — it's wiping her out. That's all."

And Donna finds herself liking him, even without fully trusting him, even without fully understanding what he's talking about. And she is immediately on guard because she finds herself liking him; her tone gets sharper and more sarcastic.

"So you thought you would surprise her by catching the bad guy?"

"I'm here to protect her," Dan says wearily.

"So am I, believe it or not," says Donna.

Antibiotics for purebred cats, believe it or not. It turns out that's what it was all about. Maggie blurts out the drug deal story when Donna Grey turns up at her office in the middle of the night, towing Dan like some kind of suspect, for god's sake. Dan is pissed as hell, as you might expect, Donna seems completely convinced that she's caught the perpetrator, and the two of them stare at Maggie like there's something wrong with her, like she must be out of her mind, sitting in her bright little office at a completely bare desk. Absurdly, the sign that hangs over Dorothy Ramirez's desk outside the NICU flashes into Maggie's mind: A CLEAN DESK IS THE SIGN OF A SICK MIND. Because there is her desktop, a perfect rectangle, blinking at them blankly.

So Maggie loses it, quite frankly. When she understands the situation, she just gets totally fucking furious. An old-fashioned foul-mouthed doctor-telling-off-a-dangerous-incompetent tirade. You couldn't find your nose with a pair of binoculars. You couldn't identify a criminal if he came and pissed on your shoe. You blunder around the place getting in everyone's way and you act like you think I'm doing this to myself and you make my husband feel I'm so completely unprotected that he has to come to the hospital himself in the middle of the night — and he's right! He's fucking right! You have no idea who's doing this, you have no idea how to get an idea who's doing this, there are probably a hundred clues every day, this maniac writes letters, he hangs up posters, he's right there out in the open, and you are completely without a clue! And so on — Maggie in full swing. There is an occasional unfortunate intern, even a nurse or two, who has heard her speak in this tone, but she's suppressed it pretty strictly over the years. She knows she's loud and she knows she's mad, but it's kind of a relief.

So she throws in the drug deals. You've got your head up your own ass, you don't know anything that's going on in this hospital unless someone tells you in words of one syllable. Some detective! The guy from the mailroom is involved in some kind of illegal drug deals with one of the nurses from West Seven, but do you know anything about it? Do you think it's interesting that the guy who actually sorts those letters about me into the mailboxes is buying drugs from a nurse who works on the ward where Heather Clark died? Where I'm supposed to have killed her?

And so on, indeed. But there is Donna Grey, opening that damned binder, taking down the particulars. The times, the place, the description. Maggie feels compelled to say, somewhat more calmly, that probably this has nothing to do with her own problem. Probably. But Donna seems interested, and, after all, Maggie deeply disapproves of anyone stealing and selling hospital drugs, and if the nurse really is passing morphine to the mailroom guy, she deserves everything she gets.

So Donna Grey and two security guards bust the nurse the very next day, and after she's been told that she's been witnessed selling drugs on at least two occasions, she breaks down right away and tells them what's going on. Antibiotics for purebred cats. She passes along the leftover medication in the bottles that contain way more than a little baby needs, medication that would otherwise be thrown away.

And because no morphine or other controlled substances have been reported missing, and because the mailroom guy confirms the story and even produces some vials of the antibiotics, the nurse won't actually get fired. She'll get a report in her personnel file, she'll get a severe warning, she'll get put on probation, she'll get in deep shit. And somehow or other, probably because Donna Grey will let it slip to one of the security guards, who will let it slip to someone else, the one thing that every nurse on West Seven and most of the nurses all over the hospital will know by the end of the week is that it was Maggie Claymore who made the accusation, who got a nurse into terrible trouble, just because she was giving some antibiotics that would have been thrown away anyway to a guy who needed them for his kittens. Yes, *that* Dr. Claymore. The one all the letters and signs have been about. The one who — you know. Heather Clark.

"You came to catch him. You came to save me."

"Boy, is she useless. Is she in the wrong place at the wrong time, or what?"

"I could see she was suspicious of you from the very beginning. All her corporate examples are about how it's really the boss's wife, it's really the jealous husband."

He turns to her as they sit stopped at a traffic light, rain pouring down on the windshield. In his car, having left hers in the hospital parking lot. I'll take a cab in the morning, she said, wanting to be with him, wanting to be driven, wanting to be tended.

"Maggie, you don't think for a minute that this is me . . ."

"Are you kidding? Are you out of your mind?"

Did she, just for a minute, for even a split second, when Donna Grey showed up at her office with Dan in tow? Was that part of why she got so angry, was she convincing herself? Nonsense, ridiculous. She trusts him, she loves him, she knows what he is capable of — and not capable of.

"I never for one split second have even wondered whether it's you. I love you. I trust you."

He leans over and kisses her. The light changes, and since this is Boston, even at this hour of the night there is an impatient car right behind them, eager to zoom on the first photon of green, honking at them impatiently to get going.

Which they do; they drive home and go to bed and Dan tends

her, loves her, gets her going. It's a bit of a turn-on, having let herself get that angry, having yelled and screamed and stomped. Not knowing, of course, what the result will be, what every nurse will know by the end of the week. How many enemies she will make, in addition to the one enemy who is already made. For now, for tonight it's a turn-on, and his wanting to protect her is a turn-on. I know what he is capable of; he knows what I am capable of. I love you. I love you. That was wonderful. Thank you for taking such good care of me. I wish I could do more. I wish I could make this stop, all of this. I wish you could too. I wish I could. But thank you for trying. Thank you for loving me. I do, I love you. I love you too. Good night, my dear. Good night.

13

Their Sex Life: Maggie and Dan

THIS PARTICULAR MARRIAGE, these two people, Maggie and Dan. They think about their sex life and talk about it and plan for it and keep track of it. They do not take it for granted by any means; they are conscious of it, maybe even a tiny bit proud of this connection, as something they have achieved together and maintained.

But Maggie does not discuss it with anyone else, not with Sarah, for example, with whom she cheerfully chews over the regularly occurring dilemmas of Sarah's own life: a suggestive remark from a married colleague, or a serious, well-meaning suitor so boring you could cry, or whether to place a personals ad versus whether to answer a personals ad. Certainly Maggie would never discuss anything so intimate with Peter Cannon, who never mentions any personal life at all, although perhaps one day he will trust her with what she presumes to be the religiously tortured details of his probably gay impulses. Or take Claire Hodge at work, so eager to describe the details of her episiotomy, so eager to sit over lunch and focus conversation on her reproductive tract — never a whisper of what's happened to her sex life since the baby was born, what was it like before. Never ever.

Maggie is somewhat curious, as a matter of fact, especially because she and Dan do tend to keep track. So are they typical, do they in fact make love more often and with more satisfaction than other married couples? What do other couples do to keep sex interesting, does it work? And so on. This sort of interest has been known to sell magazines and how-to books, but not, in Maggie's life at least, to influence conversation.

Dan is not someone who believes in letting things happen as they happen. He believes in industry and energy and intention, he believes in reading up on important subjects, he believes in following instructions. He approaches their sex life with goals and objectives, and he, not Maggie, reads the relationship articles in the magazines she sometimes brings home; he even, quite unembarrassed, buys the occasional women's magazine at the checkout counter. The kind of advice and information that Maggie went searching for as a teenager. Keeping the Home Fires Burning. Staying Sexy for Each Other. Ten Ways to Put the Magic Back. What Your Husband Hopes You'll Do for Him. All such articles ultimately turn out to be more or less the same, but that does not mean their advice is worthless.

Dan wanted to keep the home fires burning, wanted them to stay sexy for each other. Well, so did Maggie, of course, but she would have been embarrassed to mention it, let alone buy the magazines. Embarrassed to bring it up, back years ago when Dan first brought it up, cheerfully and matter-of-factly. And they worked at it together, and made appointments with each other, and conscientiously made love every Saturday night, and at least one weeknight as well, usually Tuesday.

Dan is more or less in charge of thinking of fantasies to act out, and his fantasies are pretty mild — run-of-the-mill, you might say. So they rent the occasional dirty video, or order lingerie from a catalogue, you know the kind of thing. And then some little bright ideas that make Maggie slightly more uncomfortable, not in private, so much, but with the thought of anyone ever knowing. Anyone finding out. Things Dan sometimes orders from other catalogues, not lingerie. Actually, it makes Maggie uncomfortable that he is even on those mailing lists, no matter how much they promise discretion and plain brown wrappers and classy, tasteful sensitivity.

Makes her a little uncomfortable but also occasionally gives her a private smugness, a sense of deep secrets and a more interesting life than other people.

It is a promise they have made each other and kept, that's what. A real private side, not just homogenized marital consummations. A story, a secret, an extra pocket of meaning in their lives, at the center of their house. What they have created together, a deliberate connection, an achievement.

They went through this strange strange period a few years ago, those carefully monitored months and years when they were trying so hard to conceive a child. The first months were light-hearted, Maggie and Dan both expecting that all would be easy, they'd just throw out the diaphragm and soon she'd be on her way, but then, as the failures added up, it lost all lightness. They tried to pretend it was all in good fun, tracking her periods and her ovulations, the obligation to have sex frantically at least every other day for one week out of every four — but it wore them down, as month after month went by and Maggie never got pregnant. In fact, there developed a cramped and unpleasant rhythm in their sex life and then in life in general. A week of conscientious, calendar-watching love-making, then a week of pretending to be pregnant — no alcohol, no over-the-counter medications, no x-ray exposure — and then the inevitable disappointment of menstruation, and then two weeks of waiting, free to drink and take the occasional analgesic or antihistamine, until the right time came round again. After six months or so of this, Maggie realized that she and Dan rarely made love anymore except during that ovulation week; after more than a year, she found she had stopped having sexual fantasies, stopped looking at her husband with occasional lust, and in fact, almost stopped touching him.

So it might be fair to say that when they finally agreed to give up the project, to get off this fertility treadmill, it was in part for the sake of their sex life. They were reclaiming their connection — the hell with calendars and keeping track. And they built it back to where it is today.

They have their specific routines, and of course their familiar variations. They know each other so well by now, of course, in this and every other way. And they are proud of themselves, and their pride in their commitment, in their vigor, their pride in this their secret, dark-side life, that is part of what holds them together, and they know it. These two hardworking true believers, Maggie and Dan.

14

Ambulance Dreams

MAGGIE HAD DREAMED about being inside an ambulance, and sure enough, here she was, inside an ambulance. It had been a vivid dream, and also one of those dreams that seem to go on and on, to absorb the whole night, with half-forgotten episodes and complex dialogue that it seemed to her in the morning she could remember but not understand, like a foreign movie with blurred subtitles. A dream about being in an ambulance with a baby who had died on the journey, about doing CPR in a moving chamber, jouncing along the road, yelling to the driver to for god's sake go faster, as if it would really matter to this baby for them to arrive five minutes earlier. A long dream about a long and futile ambulance drive, and in fact, the drive she had once taken along Massachusetts highways, trying her best to resuscitate a dead infant, had felt like a very long drive indeed. So three ambulances here: Maggie in an ambulance, remembering last night's dream about an ambulance, which was based on a real ride of years ago, which, though real, would be referred to always as a "nightmare ride." She is complicated; she is layered over with babies and histories, histories in the medical sense. She is a woman without a child who leaves a long trail of children, alive and dead. Her mind is full of complicated things. And full of babies.

Maggie had been a fellow in training, and the baby had been

born in a tiny hospital way south of Boston, clearly and obviously unstable from the beginning, and Maggie went out on transport, Maggie and a nurse, and they did what they could, intubated and got the lines in, then loaded up the ambulance and set out. Didn't even talk to the mother, who was still recovering from the emergency cesarean with general anesthesia. No time to lose — let's get this baby back! Fifteen minutes into the forty-minute drive, the baby got worse, got harder and harder to oxygenate, and Maggie made the decision to keep going rather than to turn around, and then, of all things, they got stuck in truly terrible traffic near route 495 and had to proceed by stops and starts, siren howling, horn honking, as the cars edged to the shoulder, nosed one by one out of the way.

A newborn baby has to make the switch over from the fetal circulation pattern, in which very little blood goes to the lungs since oxygen is taken from the mother and not from the air, to standard air-breathing circulation, right side of the heart pumps to the lungs, back to the heart, left side pumps to the body. That's what it is to make the transition from the womb to the air, to master the complex mystery of breathing. Sometimes, when a baby is sick with one thing or another, that changeover doesn't happen. The baby in the ambulance had persistent fetal circulation; didn't matter how much pure oxygen they pumped through her endotracheal tube into her lungs, because none of her blood was going to her lungs to pick up any of that oxygen. Her blood was shunted around through her body and back to the heart and back to the body, and her brain and her other organs died of oxygen deprivation, right then and there in that ambulance, with Maggie trying every trick she knew and the nurse twisting her neck around every now and then to stare at the jammed-in traffic to either side of them, and the driver cursing and accelerating dangerously every time he got a little clear space, only to brake abruptly again at the next logjam of goddamn Boston drivers heading back from their weekends on the goddamn Cape.

And by the time they got to Blessed Innocence, the baby was clearly dead. They had been doing CPR for more than twenty minutes in the ambulance, and the baby's first blood gas in the hospital showed there was very little oxygen in her blood, and much too much acid. They would have been doing her no favor to revive her, even if it had been within their powers. To Maggie's immense relief, an autopsy revealed only evidence of respiratory distress and persistent fetal circulation, no secret disaster she had failed to diagnose and treat. Nothing she could have done. The baby had died of her disease, and though those nightmarish moments of CPR would stay with Maggie (this was not her first dream about that ambulance ride), she could still face herself, her colleagues, the nurse, even the baby's parents and say, The baby was just too sick to save. I'm so sorry.

It hadn't left her unsure of her job or worried about her own competence or even nervous about ambulance rides, at least not after she had made herself do a couple more to take the taste away, to remind herself that most of the time an ambulance ride is just the fastest way possible to get a sick baby to a safe place. In fact, she had never since then found herself riding with a dead baby, though there had been some close calls. And she no longer thought much about that particular ride; she had seen a great many babies die, one place or another, and the ones who came back to haunt her were the babies who had lived in her care for days and weeks and months. Not a baby she had known for only half an hour, however dramatic and harrowing the circumstances of the death might have been.

But sometimes she did dream about it, that ambulance creeping forward while the baby slipped away. And last night she had dreamed it, and the sense of her dream, reminding her of those memories, was very strong in her as she climbed into the ambulance today, for real, for the first time in months. She wore her scrubs, and two precaution gowns wrapped around her for the few steps through the sharp cold air. Marjorie Fallon climbed in behind her, then Dorothy, staying late after her night shift to do nursing transport duty.

The EMTs slammed the doors shut and went around to climb into the front; the engine started. The regular transport team was already out, getting a baby from way the hell somewhere or other in New Hampshire, and wouldn't be back for some time, and this second baby, so much closer to home, right out past Framingham, obviously needed to be transported in, and the sooner the better. And Justin had been tied up with a family meeting over Little Justin. Make that a commune meeting. They had been praying and chanting in the family room last night, and some idiot had started a fire. For ceremonial purposes, no doubt. Alarms going off, the fire trucks, just what you need in an intensive care unit. So today's meeting: Update them on the baby's progress and set some limits. Naturally, Justin would have loved nothing better than to slip away and leave Maggie to deal with the whole situation, but tough. She outranked him.

And plus, Marjorie was on her mind; she hadn't really straightened Marjorie out. So, fine: she would go do the transport with Marjorie, give herself a chance to watch the girl in action, see if she was making any progress, spend a little time with her one on one.

They sat on benches like seats along the side walls of the ambulance, lightly cushioned benches but basically uncomfortable slippery perches. They leaned back against awkwardly placed panels of cushioning on the wall, just a little too high for anyone's comfort. The ambulance had gained the highway; nice and clear today, nothing like Maggie's dream. She occupied herself by quizzing Marjorie in a friendly but demanding kind of way: What are some things we have to look out for in a full-term baby with unexplained respiratory distress? What do we want to do before we leave? What else?

Marjorie knew some answers, and she trotted them out gamely, but as usual there was no particular connection to reality; she might suggest something basic, obvious, life-and-death important, like "We have to secure the baby's airway," or then again, she might want to go draw blood on the parents for chromosome studies, just in case that became important later on. Maggie, who found it unexpectedly exhilarating to be whizzing through the bright cold day on her way to grab a baby, was reasonably gentle with Marjorie, she felt, not losing patience, not cutting her off and rapping out the right answers. Okay, she would say patiently, let's think that through. Why might you want to do that, Marjorie?

Therefore Maggie was genuinely surprised and upset when Marjorie started to cry in the middle of their conversation. No sobbing, no facial convulsions, just tears oozing up out of her eyes and making little snail trails down her cheeks, while she pretended nothing was happening and strove to answer Maggie's question: What labs might we need to check before we leave? Maggie had returned to this question three or four times already, each time after Marjorie had tried to track the conversation off onto some largely irrelevant issue, some lab test that might just possibly become important three days down the line. But Maggie's voice had been gentle enough. She looked away from Marjorie, from the pretty young face and the crying, met Dorothy's eyes and shrugged slightly, lifting her own eyebrows to signify *I'm sorry— what did I do? So sue me.* There was silence in the back of the ambulance after that, Marjorie, sniffing once or twice and wiping her nose and eyes, Maggie twisting around to look out the back window at the cars they left behind.

Dear Mr. Danziger, as chief executive officer of Blessed Innocence Hospital who is very concerned to uphold its deservingly excellent reputation you have probably already heard rumors about a certain Doctor Maggie Claymore. I regret very much to have to inform you that in fact all of these rumors are true and worse but most alarming and most important for your own purposes is to know that her credentials are false and your entire hospital is placed at risk by allowing her to see patients here and I must warn you that her resume is a lie from beginning to end and that she may perhaps be a pathological liar which would explain the way she has put herself into this position and which may perhaps require therapy for her but in the meantime she must not be allowed to endanger innocent children who come here believing in the hospital and the doctors who work here. You may perhaps think that it is cowardly to make such an accusation and then not sign the letter but Doctor Claymore is powerful and only someone such as yourself can take the step of exposing her and righting this wrong and this danger.

The baby was sick, all right. Not deathly ill, nothing weird or uncommon, but plenty sick. He probably had pneumonia; Maggie squinted at the fuzzy shadows in his lungs, at the too-small x-ray hung on the too-dim wall box. An x-ray done by someone who didn't usually do newborns; instead of timing it by the baby's crying and catching the chest at full inspiratory inflation, the baby had already started to exhale when the film was taken, so the chest volume was reduced and it was that much harder to see what was going on. But it looked like pneumonia. They had drawn the appropriate blood tests and given the appropriate antibiotics, but they had done all those things last night, when the baby began breathing too fast, and then they had more or less sat on the kid as his respiratory status continued to deteriorate, and now, most unforgivable of all, there was no doctor waiting here to hand over the baby. The pediatrician had approved the transfer, scribbled a note in the chart, and gone on his merry way, leaving the nursery nurses to hover over the sick baby and check the clock, wondering when the hell the ambulance would arrive.

Maggie felt impatient and furious; she was half inclined to call some big shot and complain, get this pediatrician, whoever he was, into serious trouble. But obviously she wasn't really going to waste time now making angry phone calls. She stood back and watched Marjorie do a preliminary exam, fussing with her stethoscope and checking for skin lesions — Marjorie, after all, was the intern who last week had described a new admission's three tiny cherry angiomas in careful detail and missed the loud systolic heart murmur. Maggie herself felt she knew most of what she needed to know about this baby from looking at the way he was breathing, at his fast, shallow little gasping breaths, at the hollows that appeared near his shoulder bones with every breath he took as he used his extra muscles to force the air into his lungs. You could watch him breathe, take a quick look at that lousy x-ray, and your fingers should be getting ready to put in the tube. Maggie picked up his nursing sheets and looked at the results of his lab work — the last blood gas was more than two hours ago. The doctor probably looked at the results, called for the transport team, then took off like a bat out of hell.

Maggie looked the baby over. Not imminently dying, needs another blood gas, and then in all probability he should get tubed. Stabilize his airway, make sure there are no sudden downturns on the ride. Put in another intravenous line; they have one running into a vein in his scalp, but it doesn't look any too secure.

Dorothy was already unpacking equipment; obviously she was planning to get that other IV started. Fine: The nurse knows what she's doing. Now, what about the doctor? Okay, Marjorie, look at this sick little baby whose respiratory status has been deteriorating, and tell me that you need a blood gas to see where you stand. And then if you want, another chest x-ray. I wouldn't say no, though better to tube him first, because then you can check his evolving pneumonia and the endotracheal tube placement all at the same time.

Marjorie had turned to the nurse who was caring for the baby, put a hand on her arm. All traces of tears were gone; she looked concerned and professional in a young and earnest style, and even Maggie, looking at her, almost believed in her competence. "Was this mother tested for group B strep, do we know?" Marjorie asked in portentous tones.

"If this is bacterial pneumonia, and I think it probably is, then you're right, group B strep is a likely organism — but the point is, the baby's already gotten the appropriate antibiotics and our job now is to see whether he can go on breathing on his own." Maggie looked meaningfully at the girl: Come on, take over, be the doctor for crying out loud! Dorothy handed Marjorie a blood gas syringe, and Marjorie, with that continued air of just-what-I-was-about-to-suggest, went to work feeling for a pulse in the baby's wrists.

To Maggie's surprise, and maybe to her own as well, Marjorie Fallon succeeded on her second attempt at getting a small sample of arterial blood out of the newborn's wrist artery. She was so visibly triumphant at this small victory that Maggie did not have the heart to say to her, Get the air out of the syringe — put pressure on the wrist. Instead, she took the syringe from Marjorie and carefully bubbled the air out of it herself, while Dorothy held pressure on the small blue bruise forming at the site of the blood draw.

The gas was lousy, sure enough. When the little blue slip of paper came back from the lab, Marjorie took it and read the numbers out loud, waiting, Maggie thought wearily, to be told what they meant. "So what do you want to do?" Maggie asked.

Marjorie considered, in that irritating way she had, irritating because it suggested that she was carefully weighing well-understood pieces of information to arrive at an educated decision, and of course she was doing nothing of the kind. "I guess we could intubate him," she said, very hesitantly, and Maggie felt like the proprietor of a carnival game facing a rube who has just managed a lucky toss: Well, give the little lady a prize!

"I think that would be a good idea. Let's just let Dorothy get another line in — meanwhile, you check and see whether you have everything you need."

At that, Dorothy looked up and seemed about to speak: You're going to let this useless intern try to intubate this sick baby? She said nothing, though, so Maggie did not answer, I'm going to let her try once — she got the blood gas, didn't she?

> *Dear Doctor Weintraub, it is my painful duty to inform you that Doctor Maggie Claymore's last two published papers and maybe others beyond are based on data she fabricated and will be unable to justify and since this puts the entire good name of your distinguished program in jeopardy I am writing to suggest that it is very important that you step in now and prevent this from going any further and causing a scandal which will discredit your whole institution which she is also endangering with the substandard medicine she practices and parents have a right to know that their children are not receiving good care. If the hospital authorities cannot put a stop to this unscrupulous doctor then it will be the obligation of those who know what is really going on to inform the public in any way necessary to protect innocent babies and prevent a disaster and we can no longer remain silent.*

The ambulance was jolting along, and the baby was doing well in his little transport unit, and Dorothy was occupied bending over him and checking and rechecking his monitor leads, assessing the pinkness of his skin, fiddling with his two IVs. There wasn't much for Maggie to do, and it was becoming oppressive, her sense that she needed to say something to Marjorie, that she didn't know exactly what to say.

She looked over at the intern, at her brave little smile as she rode along with this baby she had done so little to help. "Marjorie," she said, and Marjorie started, turned toward her, nodded eagerly.

"I'm sorry about that," Marjorie said. "I really do know how to use a laryngoscope, of course, and I just got nervous with so many people watching me — I feel really silly." And she laughed a silly little laugh.

"That's okay," Maggie said, as if she hadn't even been going to mention that, as if it didn't bother her at all that a Blessed Innocence intern, in front of three or four nurses at an outlying hospital, had tried to intubate a baby by putting the laryngoscope in the wrong way, as if she were trying to insert the breathing tube up into the baby's head rather than down into the baby's neck. Good going, Swifty — show us you really don't know which end is up. Which end of the baby, which end of the trachea. Maggie had silently reached out, turned the laryngoscope around in Marjorie's hand, and Marjorie had gone ahead with her two failed intubation attempts; Maggie had then intubated the baby and here they were.

"What I wanted to talk to you about, Marjorie, was when we go to meet with the parents, when you're about to transport the baby out and you go get consent? Now, I know there were a lot of family members there, and it was probably a little confusing, but I think we should go over some of what you need to communicate in that meeting."

"It would probably help a lot if you spoke Spanish," Marjorie said thoughtfully. "I'm going to learn medical Spanish, I think."

"Yes, that's a good idea," Maggie said.

Dorothy looked up from the baby and said quietly, to Maggie and most definitely not to Marjorie, "He's really fighting the tube. I think we need to snow him a little more or he's going to have problems."

Maggie didn't bother asking Marjorie what she wanted to give; she just ordered the appropriate sedation and Dorothy gave it; later on, back in the NICU, the baby safely plugged in, Dorothy would write out orders for all the various medications she had requested and Maggie had authorized, and Marjorie would ritually sign the orders.

"Marjorie, you have to remember that these families are usually not really prepared for this kind of situation — remember at the end when Dorothy brought in the baby, in the incubator, when we had the parents reach in and touch him — that's really important. See, after you tell them the baby's really sick, they don't have any idea what's going to happen next. For all they know, the baby's dead, or about to die. You make sure they touch the baby and say goodbye."

"Sure, that's really great that you do that," Marjorie said.

No, Maggie wanted to answer, what's really great is that I know how to intubate the kid and Dorothy knows how to get the lines in and give the meds, and between us we'll keep the baby alive, and in the meantime maybe you should go count your toes. She thought of the large Colombian family, gathered in the mother's room, waiting for news, the lamentations of the baby's grandmother, awkwardly consoled by another of her children, the brash seventeen-year-old nephew who had interpreted for the parents, the father and mother, both small, dark people in their early twenties, the father standing rigid next to his wife's bed, very close to her but not touching, the other aunts and uncles standing quiet and concerned around the walls. And Marjorie babbling away about whatever happened to come into her mind.

And right now, this month, she, Maggie, could not afford any problems in the NICU. No lapses, no departures from the standard of care. Everyone in the fucking hospital, she felt, was watching her, wondering about her, and any disputes, any even mild disasters, would make people think there was really something wrong, wrong with Maggie. In her mind at night, as she tried to fall asleep, tired and overtired and past tired and out the other side, echoed imaginary conversations, conversations she might have overheard in elevators or echoing up the stairwell. So what's all this fuss about Maggie Claymore — they're saying she's not good clinically? Well, I don't know, but I heard there was some fuss about a baby in the NICU last night — the kid got into trouble and Claymore wasn't even there. Yeah, well. No smoke without fire, I guess.

She had overheard no such conversation, of course. Probably only a few employees at Innocence were even aware of the letters or the posters, and those would by and large be people who knew the scoop, knew who was persecutor and who was persecuted. Wouldn't they? And last thing at night, and again in the jolting ambulance, there rose to Maggie's imagination the image of that poster, of that headline: WARNING TO ALL PARENTS!!!! Maggie leaned forward to look into the incubator and check out the baby's color, and what she was thinking grimly was that it ought to be Marjorie's picture on that goddamn poster.

And that thought annoyed her, made her angry at herself, since obviously it ought not to be anyone's face, and what was happening to her to make her have a thought like that about an intern, five months out of medical school, a child, who was hers to teach and guide and counsel? Surely if Marjorie had made it this far, through the schooling and the tests and the clinical training, surely there must be enough in her head to make her into a passable doctor. No one's face should be on that poster. Marjorie, let's get to work.

The baby looked fine. Not fighting the tube now, well oxygenated, blood pressure holding steady. Maggie snapped her head up, leaned back against the awkward strip of cushioning, and began to fire questions at Marjorie. When we get this baby back to the NICU, what vent settings are you going to start him at? What are your goals for his ventilator management overnight? What are your biggest worries?

. . . My biggest worry is that at some point she will commit another crime either through failing to meet medical standards which is true of almost all of her practice or else a real crime with malice aforethought as she did in the case of little Heather Clark a child whose only crime was to have some disabilities so I beg of you if you do not believe me please do yourself and your hospital the favor of verifying at least some of her so-called credentials so that you will see what a fraud has been working here for years without anyone knowing even if they did wonder why she does not keep to the same standard as the other doctors . . .

Dorothy was suctioning the baby once again. Suctioning can be a matter of life and death in patients on ventilators, patients who depend on open plastic tubes to breathe; in fact, the residents' joke name for the chronic care hospital where sick and lung-damaged babies went after they "graduated" from the NICU was Our Lady of Perpetual Suction, rather than Perpetual Succor. This baby was making lots of thick frothy mucus, and the secretions could plug up the tube, or drip down into his lungs unless they were regularly removed with the flexible plastic suction catheter attached to the portable suction pump.

Maggie let Dorothy deal with the suctioning, a nurse's job done efficiently by a good nurse. Meantime, she concentrated on Marjorie Fallon, on this poor stupid intern who, whether she knew it or not, was even now taking the first uncertain steps on the road that would lead her to at least marginal competence. Okay, Swifty, here is where I take things in hand and you start to shape up. Someday, perhaps, if Marjorie had enough brains to understand what happened in her own life, she would look back to this ambulance ride, or at least to her time in the NICU with Maggie, as the turning point, the key moment, the fork in the road.

"Okay, so let's say the baby starts retaining CO_2 — what are your options?"

"Retaining CO_2 — so he isn't breathing it off —"

"Right, that's what I said. What are your options?"

"We could probably — well, we'd start by dialing up the pressure, increase the PIP."

Maggie let out a loud breath. God give me strength.

"Marjorie, explain to me please, first of all, what the possible variables are when you're adjusting a ventilator? Why don't we just start with that, back at first principles, and then very slowly we can figure out what it is you think you're doing with this baby."

Marjorie blinked at her. Nodded vehemently, as if agreeing with Maggie in a loud and ugly fight, backing Maggie up. "Well," she said, and nodded again. "Well, I think —" Then she shut her mouth, her face working vigorously, her eyes squeezing shut and then flicking open. An elaborate pantomime of someone fighting back tears.

Oh, spare me, Maggie thought. She's already broken down once on this transport. Why doesn't she just say, I'm sorry, I don't know, tell me. I'll tell her. She ought to know, there's no excuse for her not knowing, but, okay, I'll tell her.

"Marjorie —" she said, and her voice was sharper than she'd meant it to be.

But Marjorie's voice was even sharper, and was much, much louder, so loud that the two EMTs up in the front seat of the ambulance heard it and turned their heads.

"Why don't you stop picking on me all the time?" Marjorie yelled. Well, maybe not yelled, but certainly said much too loudly.

"Marjorie —" Now her main goal was to calm Marjorie down; they had a sick baby here, and a nurse and two EMTs listening in, and it was not the moment.

"Picking on me and always asking questions and never supporting me and getting me all embarrassed in front of other people so I can't answer anything at all!"

Dorothy bent over the baby and began to suction again; an additional hiss of noise adding a little more erasure value to the background noise of moving vehicle and outside traffic. In fact, at that moment, the siren, which had been off, came on again; maybe the driver felt the same impulse as Dorothy to create a little more noise and remind people that this was an ambulance, this was life and death. Dorothy suctioned the baby's nose and mouth, around the plastic endotracheal tube, then disconnected the tube from the ventilator to slip her suction catheter into the ET tube itself, a thin flexible clear plastic straw inside the thicker, firmer straw that was keeping the baby alive.

"Okay, Marjorie," Maggie said, gently, reasonably, "I didn't mean —"

"You didn't mean what?" Marjorie was crying now in great, gusting sobs; her face was contorted and there was stuff coming out of her nose, which an efficient nurse would have suctioned immediately. "Maybe you don't ever mean anything, but, you know, there are signs about you in the hospital — that's how much damage you do! Signs hanging up warning parents that you don't care who you hurt!"

She scrabbled in the drawer of the incubator unit, looking for a box of tissues probably but knocking against Dorothy's arm just as she had reconnected the tube to the ventilator and was putting away her suction catheter.

"Careful!" said Dorothy sharply.

Maggie was so angry she could hardly speak. She watched Dorothy, efficient and obviously eager to protect her patient from further attacks, locate a hospital-issue box of tissues in another drawer and hand it to Marjorie, who blew her nose vigorously.

"You," Maggie said in a low and very serious voice, a husky voice of absolute self-assurance, "are the poorest excuse for an intern that I have ever seen in my life. You are a constant danger to your patients, and the only reason you haven't killed them all is that the nurses protect your patients from you, the other interns protect your patients from you, and I protect your patients from you. You know less than any other intern, less than most medical students, you can't do the simplest procedure, and most of all, your instincts are terrible. And when you are asked perfectly reasonable, perfectly simple questions about patient management, questions that any of your fellow interns could answer, questions that relate to your ability to manage this baby in the NICU, you burst into hysterical tears and then attack the person who is trying to teach you." This is out of line, Maggie knows, even as she is saying it. I am angry at her because of what she said about the posters. I should not be saying such things.

"Maggie, could I get you to take a listen to this baby?" said Dorothy.

"Sure." Maggie stuck her stethoscope earpieces in her ears and listened; she could still hear the siren, dimly and far away, could hear the vehicle rumble. She tried to blank those out and listen to the breath sounds, wondering whether Dorothy really thought something was going on or whether she had just wanted to create a diversion.

Maggie straightened up. "He's definitely moving less air."

"I'm afraid the tube's getting plugged. I've been suctioning, but it's getting harder — and I've gotten some big goobers out, but there's a lot of them."

"I should have put in a bigger tube," said Maggie. She had initially planned to use the normal full-term-baby-size tube, but when she had looked down the baby's throat, after Marjorie's unsuccessful attempts to intubate him, the opening had looked small and swollen and she had gone down a size, muttering that there might be some swelling, that there might perhaps have been some trauma — so in a way, it was all Marjorie's fault; she had evidently been rough as well as incompetent. And when Maggie had slid the smaller tube in, it had felt snug to her — but now it was plugging.

"We're home," Dorothy said, in obvious relief, as the ambulance screeched around the tight corner leading to the Blessed Innocence ambulance dock, the one Maggie could see from her office window. Dorothy took her suction catheter and prepared to give the baby one more good vacuuming before the dash to the elevators.

Maggie looked at the intern. Marjorie was still blotting at her face with the wad of tissues, still crumpled and red-eyed, though no longer sobbing. Maggie said to her, "Listen, I'm sorry. I got carried away there. We'll get this baby upstairs, make sure he's okay — then we'll sit down together and have a talk. Okay?"

Marjorie nodded — at least, Maggie thought she nodded, because just at that moment the ambulance came to a jolting halt at the dock, all three women riding in the back lurched a little, and Dorothy, who had been holding the end of the baby's endotracheal tube in her hand, after taking out the suction catheter, pulled on the tube just a little.

"Oh, hell!" Dorothy said, looking down at her patient. "Maggie, I think I may have just extubated him."

The ambulance doors were flung open and cold air rushed in; the EMTs stood there, ready to lift the incubator down, ready for the dash to the NICU. But Marjorie was the only one who looked at them; Maggie and Dorothy were both bent over, listening to the baby's chest. The ventilator continued to pump, but there was no answering mist of breath coming out through the tube. Now with the ambulance stopped, she could hear clearly through her stethoscope: no air was moving in the lungs. The tip of the tiny tube had been jarred a few millimeters, a small jar, the tape hadn't even come loose from the baby's lip, but the tube was no longer in the trachea. And because of the medication, because they had snowed the baby to stop him from fighting the tube, he couldn't breathe at all for himself now, not even the labored largely ineffective respirations that had kept him alive in the nursery. They had suppressed his own respirations because they had promised to do it for him, and do it better.

Dorothy was already pulling off the tape. Maggie slipped the tube out of the baby's mouth, and Dorothy clapped a face mask on, a little bowl of transparent plastic over the nose and mouth. She had the bag ready to hand over, and Maggie took it, holding the mask on with her right hand and squeezing rhythmically with her left. She was in an awkward position, twisting herself around between the baby and the wall of the ambulance.

Maggie was thinking a number of things at this moment, in a kind of mental seven-layer cake. On top, first and foremost, she was thinking about getting oxygen into the baby. Never mind the overtones of broken promises — we said we'd breathe for you and now we're not doing it, or the overtones of blame — and to tell the truth, she was much more inclined to blame Marjorie, who seemed more and more like a jinx, than she was to blame Dorothy, a competent and honorable nurse who had proved her professionalism by noticing the mishap as soon as it happened and announcing it as soon as she'd noticed it. Maggie was aware of all that, but it was down very deep.

Anyway, all this was down very deep. What Maggie was thinking was, Oh shit, we aren't really moving his chest with the bag and mask. Oh shit, he's really hard to bag; his lungs are even stiffer. Am I going to have to crash intubate him here and now? There's no way to get him upstairs without his losing brain cells if we can't bag him. Images moved quickly through her mind: herself, holding the baby, running up the stairs, herself on the Stairmaster at the gym, an ambulance intubation, cramped and poorly lit, Dorothy trying to bag the baby —

Maggie straightened up, looked past Marjorie, who had flattened herself against the wall of the ambulance, to the EMTs.

"Take the incubator out, bring it right inside the hospital doors. Dorothy will be bagging the baby as you go. Marjorie, take the blue duffel and bring it inside. We have to reintubate him because I'm not getting anywhere with the bag and mask. Move quick!"

From the inadvertent extubation of the baby to the moment when Maggie stood over the open incubator in the hospital vestibule, laryngoscope in hand, was perhaps a minute and a half. Dorothy was squeezing the air bag, but the baby's chest was still not moving. She had tucked a rolled blanket under the unresisting neck — how does a NICU nurse whose hands were both occupied with bagging a baby find, roll, and position a blanket? Maggie didn't know, or even think to ask. She had found the proper size endotracheal tube in the duffel even as she had stepped through the automatic doors of the hospital.

"Hold the incubator steady — don't let it roll — lock it if you can," she said to the EMTs. "Okay, Dorothy, suction him, then a couple more breaths, do what you can."

Dorothy's hand squeezed the black rubber bag once, again, and both women watched the indicator on the pressure gauge travel up past thirty, to a higher pressure than anyone would ideally want to use to force air into newborn lungs. Dorothy shook her head. She pulled the mask off the baby's face, and Maggie slipped the metal lever of the laryngoscope into the mouth, bent and looked forward along the curved steel path into the baby's throat. At the end of the path, a light bulb the size of a peppercorn lit the moist pink and red tunnel, shone brightly against the films of mucus and the glistening, salmon-colored curves. Maggie, just at this very moment, was thinking of only one thing, looking for one particular view. She lifted the laryngoscope up a little further, but she was in too far; she was actually looking down into the baby's esophagus. She pulled back: She had already been inside this baby's oropharynx once today, and somehow every baby is a little bit different. The knowledge that she had gotten in once easily enough made her sure she could get in again: I know the trail, I know the landmarks, I know the way.

And there it was, suddenly slipping into view in front of her. The vocal cords, the divided white circle, the two linear structures with the slit in between — the baby wasn't breathing, so they didn't move, but there they were. There was too much bubbly mucus — it was hard to see and hard to keep the laryngoscope steady, but it was clear enough and worth a try. She slid the tube in, immediately obscuring most of the view she did have, keeping her eyes focused on that one target, on that little circle of vision that included the path between the vocal cords. The tube bent around to the bottom, refused to curve up the way she wanted it to. Maggie pulled it back, just a little, tried again, eyes still fixed on the target. It was impossible to see where the tip of the tube was; all she knew was that it wasn't where she wanted it; it was somewhere in the mucus and the bubbles and outside her field of vision. Pulled it back a little once again, angled it against the laryngoscope and tried again. Saw the tip — right at the cords. Paused, steadied her hand, guided the tube a little farther. Tip looked like it was going to bend against the wall of the oropharynx. Twirled the tube slightly, slid it in. Saw the tip travel between the vocal cords, slide in just a little bit more. A tiny bit farther and there. Stopped. Held the tube in place, took the laryngoscope out of the mouth. Dorothy stuck on a hasty piece of tape, hooked the airbag up to the tube, squeezed it once, then again. Maggie listened over the chest.

"Harder," she said.

They both saw the chest move. Maggie heard through her stethoscope the air in the lungs. Oxygen, air, right where it needs to be. Squeaky and stiff in the lungs, obviously severe lung disease, but enough to get us up to the NICU.

"Tape it down while we wait for the elevator to come," she said, smiling. "Don't bother hooking up the vent again — we'll just bag him through the tube till we're upstairs." She straightened up to see that she had a small audience, a couple of residents, a nurse, people who had come to use the back service elevators. To Maggie's surprise, the first thought that came to her, as she met the various gazes directed at her, was Fuck you all, I'm not a side show. You have a lot of nerve watching me.

"We'll need the elevator," she said brusquely.

"You okay?" asked one of the residents hesitantly.

"We are now," Maggie said. She tried to recapture her smile, tried to meet this perfectly nice young fellow halfway: Crash intubations in the vestibule! Maggie Claymore saves the day! But all she could think was, He's probably heard stories about me. He's probably wondering what I'm up to — he's thinking about that sign. Warning! Danger!

"Anything you need?" asked the resident, and she imagined him

190

telling this story all over the hospital — but what story? A story about Maggie saving a baby, or a story about Maggie doing something weird?

"I need you to get out of the way," she said. "I need to get my patient upstairs." And she helped the EMTs push the incubator into the elevator, with Dorothy walking alongside squeezing the bag rhythmically, with Marjorie trailing behind carrying the blue duffel. And she left the others standing there, staring after her.

15

The Infertility Problem

I T WAS FOUR YEARS AGO that Maggie and Dan started trying, as they say. Before that, they had been in the habit of referring to a possible baby occasionally, but usually more in the negative sense than in the positive: Well, we won't be able to take a trip like that after we have a kid, so let's go to Barbados now. But Maggie's fellowship was over, she was settled in a job, she was no longer on call most months of the year, Dan had been at the clinic for a couple of years, and they had bought the house in Jamaica Plain. Things were no longer marginal, life was no longer desperately fatigued, they were no longer living on student incomes, even if they were both paying back enormous loans. And they had gotten the house cheap because of that downstairs apartment that wasn't really a completely separate apartment but would be fine for an au pair.

Mind you, Maggie had qualms about starting a baby. The usual ones, the predictable list. For one thing, she didn't exactly yearn for a child, didn't find herself looking with envy at children in the supermarket or children running around the park. She liked the idea of a complete family, father, mother, baby. She assumed that the baby would bring with it all the necessary attachments and yearnings. Goodness knows, she had seen it often enough in the hospital, that predictable delivery room miracle, the mother reaching out with joy to accept from the pediatrician's arms, from Maggie's arms, this new, blood-smeared center of the universe, had seen the softening eyes, the paternal tears.

The problem was, of course, that Maggie had seen a lot of other things happen in delivery rooms as well. She tried hard not to think of the delivery room only in terms of death and disaster, but she had just spent three years as a neonatology fellow, called to all the worst deliveries, welcoming into the world one serious congenital anomaly after another, greeting the extremely premature, the badly asphyxiated. Normal deliveries, healthy babies, were only a small part of her experience, and there was no question that as she contemplated a hypothetical delivery room with herself at center stage, she worried more than a little about all the things she knew so vividly could go wrong. An occupational hazard, she knew. She told herself most firmly that her fears were merely predictable, ironic, statistically foolish. She knew this and believed this, but still she worried.

She also worried, naturally enough, about what having a baby would mean for her at work, about women she had seen grind to a halt after having babies, worried about constraints on her time and about being distracted in some fundamental way from the work that she loved, that she finally had the chance to do, now that her training was done. But they would get an au pair; the house was big enough. She would demonstrate textbook perfection at work: This is how you take a maternity leave. This is how you come back from it, hit the ground running, never look back.

So they started trying; she put away her diaphragm and felt slightly bothered every time they made love, worrying that she had forgotten something, something important. Every cycle, when she was ovulating, they calculated when a baby conceived that month would finally be born. A May baby, a June baby, a July baby. And then those months of obsessive record keeping and sex on schedule. And then after a year or more, maybe not a baby at all. And their sex life turned to something sad and mandatory and discouraged. And then they stopped — stopped calculating, stopped tracking, stopped trying. If it happens, they said to each other, then it will happen. And it may not happen.

And now, four years. After a year of trying and not getting pregnant, you go to the specialist and start the infertility workup. These are, after all, two doctors here; Dan and Maggie both know a fair amount about infertility workups, but they rarely discuss in any detail the fact that they are not pursuing one themselves. All that has passed between them are some exchanges about how neither one of them is interested in the extremes of modern child-bearing, in vitro fertilization or egg donation — or in artificial insemination or surrogate parenting or even adoption. Both of them have been willing to let nature take its course; she would get pregnant or she wouldn't. And in fact, she didn't. And both of them have apparently accepted this: they are not, after all, going to have a baby.

In accepting this fact, they have rendered themselves medical dinosaurs. All around them their contemporaries are proceeding along through gonadotropin injections to stimulate ovulation, intra-cytoplasmic sperm injection, gamete transfer. Maggie and Dan do read about some of the snazzier developments, the ones that make it into the *New England Journal of Medicine* or the *Boston Globe,* but read about them is all they do.

They're smart enough and well trained enough to understand that age matters, that these years they're letting get away from them can't be recalled, that it will just get harder and harder for her to get pregnant — she will be in her forties soon. The truth is, Maggie is completely terrified of finding herself a patient in the medical system, terrified of beginning a workup of any kind on her own body. She has always been healthy, and in her heart she expects to be always healthy. She doesn't even have a regular internist of her own, just the gynecologist she sees every two years or so for a Pap smear, and with whom she resolutely does not discuss her attempts to conceive. As Maggie, who likes hospital adages and maxims, herself might say, denial is more than a river in Africa.

If something about her body doesn't work properly, well then, perhaps a baby is not meant to be. Or maybe it's Dan's body — he doesn't seem eager to find out either. She cannot contemplate with any degree of calm the idea of the two of them putting themselves, their sexual life, their sexual organs, in the hands of Medicine. Medical instruments, blood tests, sperm samples, hysterosalpingograms — she can think about them objectively, or at least she thinks she can, when they apply to other people. Not for herself, not for Dan. And anyway, she tells herself, she would have been one of those people who go through the whole million-dollar workup and then nothing. Million-dollar miscarriage, if that. Not to mention all the NICU superstitions about the jinx of premium fertility workup babies.

So what they say to each other, Maggie and Dan, every now and then, is "So okay, then, it's just the two of us." Penelope and Sarah live downstairs in that apartment where they would have put an au pair. Maybe Maggie will have other godchildren, maybe she'll be a presence in the lives of her friends' children — and then, of course, she'll be a presence at the beginning of hundreds, thousands, of children's lives. And none of that seems so bad. And no, she has not minded working surrounded by babies; they are her patients, her mission, her problems to solve.

Oh, she has her moments of regret. After all, she sees all her private doubts and her infertility problems all reflected again and again in magazines, TV news, newspaper headlines. At work she listens to Claire anguish over how little she sees her baby, and hears other people complain about how Claire is always leaving early; at home, there is Sarah's life to look at, Penelope to cherish.

People ask, of course, though less and less as time goes on. And at least she had never, thank god, told anyone that they were in fact trying; one of the NICU nurses has been going through the whole infertility song and dance with everyone in on every step of the way. One of the other nurses gives her her injections when she has to work nights, and when she gets to the right point in her cycle, they send her home early with dirty jokes and encouragement. Maggie listens and smiles politely, affects somewhat less knowledge of the medical facts than she really possesses, thus, she hopes, deflecting any suspicions that she might have gone partway down that road herself, even in her imagination.

She is no good with failure. It makes her medically vulnerable; it makes her a sad story. She would rather have people assume it's all about her career, rather have them think that she never wanted children, that she has chosen her life in this respect, as she has in every other that is within her control. She doesn't think so much about all this anymore, certainly not obsessively, certainly not with any suspense in those days right before her period is due, and she certainly no longer feels any strong sense of disappointment when it comes. It's almost reassuring: her body performing as it has before, predictable and functional; it does what it does and it does not do what it does not do.

16

Data

MAGGIE DOES NOT WANT to go to work in the morning; she wakes up already attacked by her first thought at the sound of the alarm clock. It makes her angry with herself, each and every morning: Why am I taking this so seriously? She disciplines herself to think about work — to think about work properly and sensibly, not about the crazy acts of a crazy enemy but about the real and true details of her job, usually so easily all-consuming.

Good news: Little Justin is going to get transferred to a hospital in Vermont. Nearer to home. Little Justin and his whole extended communal family and their *primum non nocere* T-shirts and their crystals and their mantras and their chants. And the special herbal tea, which exploded in the microwave last week; you can still smell the weedy aroma. Better news: We took good care of Little Justin, we helped make him better. Bigtime surgery on a very new baby, and then a careful, slow recovery. Good work in the DR, good work in the OR, good work in the NICU. And now we found a place to send him; Big Justin was so proud of himself yesterday when he announced the transfer. Maggie punched his shoulder and said, Strong work. And commended him as well for the way he had kept things under control medically in the NICU all month, the management decisions he had made. He's a good, smart resident, Justin.

He will be a good doctor. She wanted him to remember her as someone who helped him along that way, someone who encouraged and praised and taught. Bad news: The memory of Marjorie Fallon's voice, *how much damage you do, how much damage you do,* even worse, the memory of her own angry voice, trying to do damage, to take this idiot intern apart.

And here it is again. Why had it all thrown her this badly? Is it possible, Maggie has wondered, that these anonymous letters attacking her competence, her integrity, her intentions, have somehow spoken aloud her most private inner doubts about herself? Is that why she hears these accusations over and over in her mind?

Why is this so bad? She has spent her whole professional life braced for a terrible lawsuit, a medico-legal professional disaster — all doctors do, and rightly so, especially those who deal with the very small and the very sick. Here there is no lawsuit, no evidence of bad medicine, no open accuser to say anything at all — but it is taking over her life. The letters are not even threatening — the detective keeps asking her whether any threats have been made, and Maggie tells her no. No threats against my safety, just a threat against everything I am and everything I do. And worst of all, it is all happening right out here in the open. Maggie is a private person; she does not discuss her inner doubts or her fears or her worries, not even with her friends. She has always dressed and carried herself so as to say, Here I am. I am a doctor. She would have preferred, and this is the simple truth, almost any letter sent directly to her, no matter how obscene, how frightening, how incisively on target, to these letters that tell other people at the hospital bad things about her, that attach interesting rumors like colored plastic clothespins to her clothing.

I need to do my work, Maggie repeats over and over to herself as the day goes by. Let me do my work. She smiles and nods as Justin shows her a chest x-ray on that baby she and Marjorie brought in by ambulance: doing great. Will go home in three days. Pneumonia almost completely gone. And another x-ray — a much, much tinier chest. A new premie with premature lung disease. The babies come and go; they fill her brain, but she is completely attuned to the rhythms of their illnesses. As they get better, they are of less and less interest, or perhaps it would be more to the point to say that they are crowded out of her brain by the newer, sicker babies. She had tried to explain this to Marjorie Fallon: You should always be thinking most about the sickest baby. Well, that is second nature to Maggie herself; it is how her mind structures her world. She is at her happiest, her most completely understood and understanding, at a moment like this, running the list with Justin, a smart doctor who speaks her language. Baby Boy not-those-Kennedys: lung disease continuing to resolve very slowly, baby getting better. And now Justin is asking if she would come to a care conference on Surviving Twin Grassini tomorrow. We really need to plan for long-term care. Maybe, he says, clearly a little hesitant, maybe we should involve the ethics committee?

There's no need, Maggie tells him, the baby's not brain-dead, we aren't using any extraordinary measures to keep her alive, she's just a very low birth-weight newborn with bigtime lung disease and a lot of other problems. But still, Maggie tells herself, be open to it, praise his initiative, encourage and stroke, smile and compliment. Good thought, though, Justin, she tells him. Good idea, setting up that meeting.

The babies came and went. Most of them she knew quite well after a fashion; she listened to their breath sounds and pored over their nursing sheets. She adjusted their ventilators and stared at their x-rays. She nudged the interns, she reined in Justin when he tried to push past what he actually could do. And the babies got better. They got better, came off the vents, gained weight, went home; fell into their filing places in her mind full of newborns, among all the other babies, all the other months. Only a few of them really stuck in her mind, either because they were special problems or because she had spent particularly memorable hours over them. Baby Boy not-those-Kennedys, for example — she still felt proprietary about that scrawny little fighter; he was still on the vent, but only to spare calories that he would otherwise use up making his muscles work to breathe. He needed to hold on to every calorie he could get. But he was a fighter, and he was hanging in there. Surviving Twin Grassini was another matter. Still alive, to everyone's surprise. But no progress, just one damn thing after another. A new infection, this time fungal, a question of her belly getting bloated after a tiny increase in her drop-by-drop feeds. Maggie crossed her fingers; you never know. But in her heart, she was not so sure anymore that she believed Felicia Grassini would make it to each and every one of those milestones Maggie had imagined for her once, after saving her life, the first time around.

Donna Grey, leaving the clinic where Maggie Claymore's husband Dan worked, was eager to get home. It had been an interesting and not unproductive day, but a long one. And she was disconcerted to find herself ending it in this rotten neighborhood, to be walking along this cold and littered street in the darkness. She should have parked in one of the doctors' parking spaces, right up against the clinic, guarded at least by proximity and by whatever authority the squat brick clinic building itself could summon. But Dan had not mentioned the special spaces when he gave her directions to the clinic, and when she had passed an empty street space she had grabbed it with all the alacrity of a Boston driver.

Probably it had been an act of covert hostility, not telling her where to park. He resented her coming to the clinic, and he was trying to make her life difficult. Donna reached her car, noted with relief that it was undamaged, pressed the button on her remote and listened to the car beep in welcome and reassurance: No one has bothered me. She checked her back seat for intruders, got in, locked all the doors with the automatic door lock button, turned on her lights, and pulled out into traffic, glad to leave behind the little knots of men and boys huddled in the cold wind outside the convenience store and the check-cashing place.

Oh, boy, was she eager to get home. Her apartment. She had bought it almost ten years ago, and it had taken her father's entire legacy, money he had probably thought would provide for her forever, send her children to college, if she ever had children. It was in Back Bay, a big airy two-bedroom apartment near Commonwealth Avenue, her refuge and her castle and the only place she ever wanted to live. Let's face it, she wasn't about to marry again, or to have kids. She dated every now and then, but it never led to anything. Which was more or less the story of her life, though four thousand dollars' worth of therapy when she was freaking out about being thirty-five years old and not likely to get married ever again had convinced her that it was in fact her own decisions that kept her out of relationships. Four thousand dollars well spent; Donna went into therapy to solve a problem, solved the problem, and then stopped the therapy. A smart therapist helped her to see that she was attracted only to men who were not interested in getting involved. When she was a kid, she married one, and she got what she deserved, and good riddance. The next step, no doubt for another four grand, was supposed to be to help her reshape her tastes so she could fall for someone who wanted intimacy and involvement and all the rest. She put the money into wall-to-wall carpeting instead.

Snow-white wall-to-wall carpeting. You would not look at Donna's apartment and think of granola and saving the rain forest any more than you would think of them to look at Donna herself. She liked things clear and stripped down, but by that she meant white walls, white carpets. Donna slipped her shoes off in the hallway, lined them up neatly under a small table. The thing she liked best about Maggie Claymore so far was how neat her office was. She knew better than to go judging all the doctors according to those standards — she knew that there were smart, important people who liked to live with mess and clutter — but she didn't truly respect it and she wouldn't have let one of those people into her own home.

She stripped down methodically, putting her clothes away with an almost savage orderliness. She wrapped herself somewhat ritually in a phenomenally expensive cream silk robe, floor-length, heavy silk, the output no doubt of millions and millions of worms. But silkworms are not in danger; they are a domesticated resource. And a completely natural fiber; Donna ordered her underwear from a catalogue that sold cotton raised without pesticides or chemicals. Next to her skin, in secret, she avoided dyes and poisons. The natural cotton underwear was not cheap by any means, which was fine; she loved luxury, loved things that cost money. Maggie Claymore, for all her carefully chosen and appropriately expensive clothes, had never in her life felt the rush of joy that came to Donna as the folds of lush cream silk slid over her body. Maggie did not really understand the women's magazines, but Donna, who didn't read them either, did understand; this is the thrill they promise.

She sat in the one armchair that rose as lonely as an iceberg from the white rug of her living room: one single armchair, covered in pale leather. Heaven knows, cows are not endangered. In a world where so much agricultural land is used to graze cattle rather than raise crops, it's good to make use of those hides. Soft as butter, the salesman had said. What does a person need in a living room, anyway? One armchair, if she lives alone, one television to watch, one thousand-dollar aquarium for color and life. Space is the luxury, white space around the chair, blue watery space inside the tank. Not one of those tanks choked with plants everywhere, not one of those rooms in which you trip over a coffee table as you stumble away from the lamp. She would sit in her armchair and write up her notes, she would watch the news and eat baby carrots with bean dip for dinner, and tomorrow, maybe, she would catch a few of these damn doctors up with the lies they had been telling, either directly or just by I'm-so-busy-saving-lives omission.

Maggie went to the gym — she was faithful — two weekdays and once on the weekend, every week except when she was on service. She sat on an exercise bike and pedaled out her anger. Or at least pedaled. She sat now on the exercise bicycle and churned her legs with grim, bored determination. The health club was oversubscribed, and they had squeezed in yet another few exercise bicycles and Stairmasters; there was another woman riding the bicycle right next to her, and there couldn't have been more than six inches between them. She could hear the other woman's every breath and found herself wondering why anyone would want to exercise in a tight white leotard with a scarlet bikini bathing suit worn over it. And obviously expensive black and green and yellow aerobic shoes, and a matching yellow Walkman. She was a rather heavyset woman, and she huffed and puffed fiercely as she pedaled, her eyes closed, lost in whatever she was listening to. Maggie kept her own eyes fixed on the illuminated grid that told her when she was riding up a simulated hill.

She did not enjoy the bicycling, or the atmosphere of the gym, but she rather liked sweating. As her T-shirt began to stick slightly to her body, pulling gently at her as she leaned forward, she felt her usual pleasure in this evidence of exertion, in this pure and unstoppable body function. And on up the next imaginary hill, a little higher this time.

She was onto the fourth and hardest hill by now, and suddenly the woman next to her broke her rhythm. The lace of her sneaker had gotten caught in the bicycle pedal; another turn or two of the pedal had untied the sneaker and wound the lace around and around the pedal, and now suddenly the bicyclist realized that something was wrong, as her shoe tightened inexorably around her foot. She stared wildly around the room, trying to figure out what was happening, then stopped pedaling, tried to pedal backwards to unwind the lace, and ended by taking her foot out of the shoe and getting off the bicycle, leaving the shoe still fastened to the pedal. She knelt in the constricted space between her own bicycle and Maggie's, trying to get the laces untangled.

He had a perfectly good reason to be in here. His balls itched. He was allergic to this new organic laundry soap that Cindy had started buying; he had told her that at least twice. So why the hell did she continue to use it? Did she think it was some kind of a joke, sending him off to work in clothing that always itched him? Well, he wouldn't scratch himself in public, that was for sure. He just happened to be passing by the NICU, so he took refuge in the tiny senior call room, big enough for a cot, a bedside table with a telephone, and a chair. There was just enough space for a person to stand between the chair and the table. He had spent plenty of nights in this room, and he noted on behalf of tonight's occupant a familiar grievance — housekeeping had not yet come in to make up the bed. The room, windowless and always overheated, smelled to him of dirty sheets. It was always a little close in here, but the disheveled bed, the blanket dragging onto the floor, the wet towel in the sink, all exaggerated his sense of squalor. He put his hand down inside his underpants and scratched luxuriously, but the smell of the room and the sense that he was hiding in order to perform an act that people would find unpleasant to watch brought back a very distinct memory.

He had been a fourth-year medical student, almost fifteen years ago, five hundred or more miles away, another state, another status, doing an optional advanced medical student rotation at the hospital where he hoped to do his internship, working every third night, doing the job of an intern. Busting his ass. He saw it as his make-or-break month; if they liked working with him, thought he did a good job, he would get the residency he wanted, and he devoted himself to making that perfect impression, stayed up all night preparing his presentations, jumped to do scutwork for the interns, to check labs, to run errands, to draw blood. He remembered the call room precisely, even smaller than this one, furnished with bunk beds. And he had gone out of his way to ingratiate himself with the intern who was supervising him, offering her the bottom bunk, getting her clean towels from the laundry cart.

When the supervising senior resident had asked to speak with him, he had honestly expected to be told, We'd like you to come here, we like your style. Instead, the senior resident, Marvin, one of those folksy I'm-okay-you're-okay pediatric types, who wore Birkenstocks and thick socks with his white hospital pants, took him into the conference room and told him, gently, that he seemed to be having a problem with personal hygiene. The intern who shared the call room had complained, and so had the other interns on the team, who had to work with him closely. They wondered, said Marvin, looking intently into Hank's eyes, if maybe the rotation was so stressful that he wasn't having enough time to take care of all his personal needs? Like what? Hank had asked, dry-mouthed. Like your laundry, said Marvin. Like, well, your personal hygiene.

Hank had finished out the month, but he had not even applied to that hospital. They had given him a good, though not wildly enthusiastic, evaluation; he went down south, where he manifestly didn't belong. He also, ever since, never wore any article of clothing twice; it was why he was so angry now with Cindy. She knew that everything he put on came straight out of the laundry; how did she dare soak it all in substances he couldn't tolerate? He used the strongest deodorant on the market, kept one container at home, one in his overnight bag, and another in his desk, reapplied it by noon every day. He showered every morning. He had tried a variety of colognes and aftershaves, but they made him feel silly, and some of them, it seemed to him, affected his sense of balance. It was a recurrent nightmare still in his life: the people he thought respected him were actually talking about him with disgust. His body, his smell, his clothes. If he could have erased himself into an outline, fleshless, without sweat glands or sebaceous glands or any other smelly or oily secretions, he would have done it.

When he had been himself a senior resident, an intern had come along who reminded him strongly of Marvin: same too-long curly brown hair, same sincere manner, same fucking Birkenstocks. The nurses loved him, thought he was sweet as could be. Hank had happened to pick up a phone one night when they were both on call and overheard a phone conversation, this intern calling home for a loving good night. The very same week, the series of letters began, warning that there was no place in this hospital, this city, this state, for a pediatrician who was a faggot and probably a child molester and probably had AIDS. It was a fairly conservative hospital in a southern city known for its Bible-thumping politicians. The intern had gone elsewhere for his next two years of residency, but for the remainder of that first year, Hank had had the satisfaction of watching him, tense and on guard at work, never able to relax and joke again with the nurses, someone who had learned that he was being watched by unfriendly eyes, learned that he did not and would not ever belong.

"What are your greatest strengths?" Dan asks, putting his fingers together, puffing out his cheeks with pompousness.

Theresa giggles, then cracks up.

"Come on," Maggie tells her. "That's a real question."

"Your greatest strengths, young lady?"

"Okay." She is wearing Maggie's gray wool suit, left over from Maggie's own applicant days; it does not quite fit her, but she insists she has the sewing skill to alter it a little. It's clear enough that she thinks it will bring her luck, and she's determined to wear it. "I'm very — I'm honest. At least, I try to be honest, and I think that's very important for a physician —"

Dan makes a loud buzzing noise: mistake, bad answer. "You have to blow your horn more than that. Forget honest — tell them you're incredibly goal-oriented, driven, strongly motivated. Tell them you're persistent."

"No," Maggie interrupts. "Save persistent for your greatest weakness. 'My greatest weakness is that I just can't let things go, I'm so persistent. When I start something I just go at it a hundred and ten percent, and I don't stop till I reach my goal!'"

Theresa is laughing and shaking her head; *I could never say those things.*

"Theresa," Dan says, "repeat after me. 'I would drive a tractor over my grandmother to get into your fucking medical school.'"

"I would drive a tractor over my grandmother to get into your medical school."

"'My only goal in this interview is to suck up to you,'" Dan recites.

Theresa smiles and ducks her head.

They work her through all the questions they can think of: What do you think are the most important trends in health care today, and which medical discoveries of the past five years do you think are most significant? What will it be like for you going back to school after you've been out? And even, over Dan's objections that the question is illegal, How do you plan to combine a medical career with your personal and family life? Theresa goes home with Maggie's suit in a dry cleaner bag over her arm.

"You guys — thanks so much," she starts, as Maggie sees her down the front steps.

"Forget it. Just get out there and tell them how wonderful they are and become a doctor, okay? Dan did it, I did it, you can do it."

Maggie goes back up the stairs, listening for sounds from Penelope and Sarah, but all is quiet.

She takes out a thick folder that has been nagging at her mind all evening. My dossier, as compiled by Donna Grey, Useless Detective. Containing, she assures me, many documents that establish my credentials, prove I attended medical school, passed my courses. Oh, good.

She flips it open: a photocopy of a transcript. But she is reluctant to leaf through these pages of her own recorded achievements. Answers the phone with relief; accepts Sarah's invitation: I'll be right down. And she will find a tactful way to mention that the other day when she got home, the front door was unlocked, Sarah and Penelope having come home and run out to get a container of milk. Leaving a pile of backpack, lunchbox, macaroni and yarn collage, and biology lab reports right inside the unlocked door. We live in the city, Sarah. It isn't safe. Just be glad it wasn't Dan who discovered it.

"Dan," she says, watching him fuss with the newspaper. "Will Theresa get in?"

He looks up at her, as if surprised. "She'll get in somewhere. She has the grades. People who meet her will see she's smart. And by the end of medical school she'll be an arrogant, self-assured asshole, just like you and me."

And he looks back down at his paper. Then up again. "I might go to a swim meet tomorrow night, if that's okay — the *Globe* might cover it. I want to make sure they interview Marco De-Andrade — he needs a college scholarship, and this might help."

Maggie watches him. Is that what I am? Is that what you are?

"Better go for the bigger dome tent — capacity three to four. That will take the two of us and Penelope, no problem." Precisely, Sarah dog-ears the page in the L.L.Bean catalogue. Her whole kitchen table is spread with shining catalogues, comfort and possibility. You can order ten pounds of macadamia nuts dipped in dark chocolate, or a set of a hundred and twenty wooden blocks. Cashmere and jersey and piqué and linen and knife-pleated rayon and sand-washed silk in colors with names like Seahorse and Chervil.

"Look at this chart." Sarah comes to stand beside Maggie, slaps the catalogue down. "I say we go for the zero degrees cold-weather bag — the only question is mummy or rectangular? Mummy is supposed to be warmer."

Maggie studies the picture, imagining herself zipped into the bag, zipped into the tent, safe in the dark with Sarah and Penelope on a mountainside somewhere. Safe on a mountainside — you have got to be kidding. Safe like an avalanche, safe like frostbite, safe like lost forever.

"You can't move your legs around in the mummy bags," Maggie says. "I think it would be claustrophobic." Especially after the avalanche.

They pick out the boots and the thermal underwear and the parkas, the packs and the sock liners, the gloves. Hundreds and hundreds of dollars. Very restful, Maggie thinks, gratefully, as they dwindle into Swiss Army knives and campfire cookware. It takes her all the way back to medical school; even then Sarah's idea of a study break was to spend imaginary money on lives constructed out of consumer possibilities. One night, very late, before their gross anatomy exam, both of them buzzed beyond belief on muscle names and branching blood vessels, Sarah actually did call L. L. Bean and discussed orienteering compasses for a good ten minutes with the operator.

And of course, Sarah is baking for her. Come down and taste my cookies, she said, and Maggie came down in time to kiss Penelope, warm in footed pajamas, on her way to bed. Icebox cookies, rolled and frozen and sliced; they come out little chocolate and vanilla checkerboards. Sarah sweeps the catalogues grandly into a slightly unstable pile, sets out glasses of cold milk, little saucers of hot cookies.

"Why haven't you told me about what's been going on?" Sarah asks, her back to Maggie as she puts the milk back into the refrigerator.

Her mouth is full of cookie; she swallows.

Sarah sits down, faces her, looks at her straight. "I wasn't going to mention it. I wasn't going to tell you if you chose not to tell me. But I can't stand this anymore."

"Did Dan tell you?"

"No, Dan did not tell me!" Now Sarah sounds mad; now Maggie can feel the edge of her anger through the warm sugar smell of the cookies, the slightly metallic vapor of the milk. "If you really want to know, I bumped into Kenny Weiss — remember him? Actually I was in your neck of the woods — I took two of my students over to the Reichmann Children's Cancer Center — they want to volunteer for their community service requirement. Turns out the jerks won't let anyone under sixteen volunteer — the whole trip was a waste of time. But there in the lobby was Kenny, all buttoned into his white coat."

"Sarah," Maggie tries, but she doesn't quite know where to go.

Sarah continues to stare at her. "He told me there's been a detective talking to him, asking about you. Signs hanging up in the hospital? Why didn't you tell me any of this?"

Maggie pushes back her chair, away from milk and cookies, away from comfort.

"Because I wanted there to be one place in my life where no one knew about it, I guess," she says, somewhat lightly, trying for a tone of interested self-examination, *Gee, that must be why.* "I wanted there to be one room —" Her breath catches in a sudden ragged sob, and she looks helplessly around this kitchen, this messy room. Tent, frostbite, avalanche, subzero, insulation, quilted mummy bag. Out on the ledge.

Harvey Weintraub does not sound happy. "This time he says you faked your data for those last two articles."

"Faked my data?" She tries to keep her voice calm, but to her dismay it is hitting her again just as hard as ever, the same disbelief, the same pain, the same desire to hide, to duck, to step outside of herself, of this self who is so much a target. And yet, also a feeling of *Oh right, this again.* It begins to be possible to imagine a life in which she takes these letters for granted, a part of her day. Ho hum, what is it this time? Murdered a child, faked my data? What kind of a life would that be? She is repelled — but even more repelled, more offended by the way that each new accusation provokes this grim-faced concern. Look at Harvey: Okay, we don't think you killed Heather Clark, but tell us, did you fake your data? Harvey, who knows my mind as well as anyone, who shaped my mind, who used to be proud of my mind.

"Yes — it's fairly explicit, says you duped your co-investigators, that most of the experiments were never performed."

Maggie laughs, a false and tremulous sound. "Well, I guess if it's not one thing it's another."

"Maggie, you know I have complete confidence in you and your integrity as a physician, as a researcher." He pauses, clears his throat. "I take it all those experiments were performed exactly as described, by the way?"

"Of course they were." She swallows. She wants to yell at him, How can you even ask? And he knows her well; he knows what she wants to say.

"Do you want to see the notebooks?" Her mouth is dry.

"Maggie, of course not. I just want you to be sure you can lay your hands on them if anyone *does* want to go over them. Consider it a heads up. Better safe than sorry."

He had asked her to come have lunch in the cafeteria, if the NICU wasn't too crazy, of course. And she had gone, assuming this was meant as a public gesture. But then as they sit there, eating lunch, it occurs to her that the really splashy public gesture of confidence would be for him to announce her appointment, her promotion, to that new job. Oh, she wants it so badly. Feels so entitled to it, after what she's been through. After what they've let her go through, the hospital big shots and their pet security firm. Think how her enemy would feel when she was promoted — maybe even wonder whether the anonymous letters and Maggie's bravery under fire had helped!

She straightens her shoulders and smiles at Weintraub. She tells him how grateful she is to him for backing her up when the lawyers and detectives wanted her pulled out of the NICU to cover the hospital's ass. I appreciate it, she tells him. It meant a lot to me. Some people might not have seen how significant this could be in the general perception of my situation.

Maggie takes a deep breath, smiles again, pushes herself on. I've done a good job in the NICU this month, she tells him, a very good job. I had a real problem intern, and I had to play intern myself some of the time to cover her, but those babies got damn good care.

I'm sure they did, Weintraub says. He turns his fork sideways and scrapes up the strawberry syrup film off his cheesecake plate.

I just want you to know, Harvey, that if you have other jobs for me, clinical, teaching, administrative, you don't need to worry about me. The NICU was the perfect place for me to be this month, you know — it distracted me from all this nonsense. I had more important things to think about than who wrote dumb letters about me. Anything you want to load on me, feel free. I'll appreciate the vote of confidence, I'll do a good job, and people will see that you believe in me and that I'm worth believing in.

Weintraub has put his fork down and is watching her closely. She knows he knows what she means. He doesn't look evasive, he doesn't look troubled. He looks interested. Good, good, give me the promotion! Make all the people who've been enjoying feeling sorry for me feel stupid, all the people who've been wondering if I really did do the things those letters say, make them change the way they look at me! She has wanted this before, but not with this grim competitive desperation. If he promotes her, puts her in a more powerful, more visible position, then that will be the definitive final answer to all the letters: Sorry, sucker, but you are wrong. The person in your letters is not who I am. This is who I am. The poison in your letters is not the way my world talks about me.

Maggie goes back up to the NICU not at all displeased with herself. Maybe, maybe not — but maybe. And anyway, she tells herself, after a furtive look at the bulletin board near Dorothy Ramirez's hallway desk, after checking to see there is no notice assailing her, and anyway, I didn't fake my research. I am a compulsive record keeper. I have all the notebooks. Shit, if I were going to fake the experiments, I'd have come up with more remarkable results. But that research was real and those experiments were done. I am not a fake any more than I am a murderer. I have never faked anything.

Oh, she thinks, suddenly, and stops dead, standing silent at the sink outside the NICU door. Oh. Oh, yes I have.

We need to talk about necrotizing enterocolitis. Justin, maybe you would bring everybody up to date on what went on last night with Felicia Grassini, why we started the NEC watch. This will affect all of you when you're on call, so you need to know. Necrotizing enterocolitis, or NEC, is one of the really bad things that can happen to a premature baby — or, much more rarely, to a very severely stressed full-term baby. Now, pretty much everything about this illness is controversial, what causes it, how it happens — etiology, pathogenesis, management. What do we actually know about the pathogenesis? Neil? Exactly. Thank you. Something damages the bowels, probably oxygen deprivation. Then, bacteria, probably introduced in milk or formula, invade that damaged bowel, and you get a hideous internal infection. I mean, hideous. That's the enterocolitis part, the infection of the bowel, the growth and overgrowth of bacteria, producing their poisonous gases, eating away at the loops of the intestine. The necrotizing part is that the bowel tissue can die, rot away inside the abdomen.

A NEC watch is what we call it when we get suspicious. A premature baby's gut stops processing formula through, and most of it stays right there in the stomach. The baby's belly gets distended. There's blood in the stool. And so on. So very late last night, Felicia Grassini's nurse sounded the alarm. The baby had blown up her belly; there was mild abdominal distension. So we stopped the feedings of expressed breast milk, even though we were only giving her a tiny bit, and we sent off blood tests and from here on, everyone hovers close. NEC watch.

The folder is open. But Dan is nowhere to be seen; only the sound of the shower, remote from the third floor, almost a vibration rather than a noise. Bedtime, the day is over. The newspaper is already gone, neatly folded, Maggie knows from experience, neatly placed on the recycling pile. How can he care so much, read it with such absorption, follow the details on the news? How can anyone keep such track of the world? It's all she can do, she sometimes feels, to keep track of her own tiny field. Her own field of tiny beings. And yet there is Dan, cheerfully responsible for every organ system in great big, decrepit adults. A generalist. And so, on to the world. A generalist.

And a creature of routine. So she is surprised when she hears Dan's slippered feet on the stairs, coming down. He should be getting into bed, slippers aligned to be stepped into in the morning, taking up his night table book, his historical novel about the British Navy, setting down his eyeglasses. It's the only time all day he reads without his glasses; she can imagine the oceanic dimness all around him, around his book, before sleep.

But he is coming down the stairs. He is walking into the living room, where she sits unoccupied on their couch. He is wearing his glasses, also, of course, his pajamas and his bathrobe. His mother buys him his bathrobes. This one is thick lush white velour with a blue and gold crest on the front pocket, like something a ridiculously overpriced hotel would hand out in its spa.

Why is he looking at her like that? Why does everyone look at her like this tonight, with anger and reproach, and could it be betrayal?

When necrotizing enterocolitis is severe, overwhelming, fulminant, you move quickly into a life or death situation. What do we see, Iliana? Right, air gets into the bowel wall, *pneumatosis intestinalis,* fatal bubbles visible on x-rays. Bacteria disseminated throughout the body via the bloodstream, throughout the abdominal cavity by perforation of the bowel. There is no treatment except to get the baby to surgery and cut away as much as necessary of the rotted loops of intestine, trying to remove the infection before it kills the patient. Which it often does, anyway. And when it doesn't, you are often left with a baby who does not have enough gastrointestinal tract left to absorb nutrition.

But with Felicia Grassini, we're seeing the other kind of clinical picture, a slow and puzzling is-it-or-isn't-it story of a little abdominal distension, a tiny bump in the white blood cell count. So we watch and wait. Last night we x-rayed her abdomen, started broad-spectrum antibiotic coverage. Yes, that's right, Marjorie, we left a tape measure in place under her so you can pull it round and check her abdominal girth every hour. See if her belly is swelling up. Watch and wait, watch and wait.

In the Donna Grey file, which she did not bother to read. Her medical records from medical school. First Sarah, asking reproachfully, Why didn't you tell me? And now Dan.

"I didn't mean to pry," he says so stiffly, so coldly. "You left it right here on the table, and I thought it might have something in it about their investigation." He hands her the file, open to the medical record, and she sees it just as she realizes what it must be. Clear on the page to Dan, to her, dear god, to anyone at the hospital who looks. And who have they given it to, who has been looking at it with eyes that can read these symbols?

Her medical school physical exam. 24yoG_3TAb$_3$P$_0$. Universal medical notation, the way all medical histories of women begin. Age and reproductive status. Twenty-four years old — her medical school physical. G_3, gravida three, pregnant three times. Para zero, never gave birth. TAb$_3$, three therapeutic abortions. As opposed to SAbs, spontaneous abortions, that is to say, miscarriages.

"Don't you think it's a little strange that this is news to me? When you were trying to get pregnant — when you weren't getting pregnant — did you ever think of mentioning it? Oh, well, I've been pregnant three times, I know I can get pregnant no problem? Or even before that — did it ever seem important enough to mention?"

"Dan, this was in high school. High school." Well, actually, the last one was in college. But long before she even knew Dan, long before she became the conscientious, grown-up, sexually responsible caretaker of her own fertility who cheerfully suggested to Dan that they stop at a drugstore and buy condoms on the way back to his apartment for their very first encounter. A first encounter he might not have been absolutely certain was even about to happen until she suggested the drugstore stop. And suggested it with a good-natured, slightly rueful straightforwardness gleaned from past encounters with slightly goony graduate students and even the occasional professor, none of them the sort to carry supplies in their wallets. Oral contraceptives upset my system, my diaphragm is back at my place, if you don't have any condoms at home, let's stop at that pharmacy. But that was already a decade after the first therapeutic abortion, more than half a decade after the last, okay?

NEC watch. We started her on a NEC watch last night. Cultured blood and urine, stopped feeds, checked a white blood count and diff. Her abdominal girth was up, but now it's stable. Her blood pressure's holding. But I don't know, she sort of smells like NEC.

And you know, this has not been a lucky baby. If anything can go wrong. Baby Girl Murphy's Law. Surviving Twin Grassini.

Mrs. Grassini in the breast-pumping room, as usual, when they get back from x-ray rounds. Someone has to go in and talk to her about this. Maggie wants to add, And Marjorie, whatever you do, don't make her feel it was her breast milk that caused the problem, okay?

As if you could stop parents from feeling it was all their fault. The premature deliveries, the undeveloped lungs, the delivery room deaths. As if you could truly, truly convince them ever that we live in a cruel and random world. Sometimes you act and make decisions, and then you live with the consequences, which are by no means always what you thought they would be. But sometimes consequences overtake you when you meant only well, when you did only everything you could.

"I can't believe you didn't tell me. Especially with what we've gone through."

He stands there in judgment, wrapped in his damn white robe. Hands sunk deep in the pockets, shoulders hunched. More in sorrow than in anger.

"I was embarrassed about it — more than embarrassed. I felt really bad — it made me ashamed. I was fifteen the first time — can you imagine a fifteen-year-old member of my church sneaking into New York City to get — to go to Planned Parenthood?"

"Can you imagine what it feels like for me? Right now?" No, not more in sorrow than in anger; there's plenty of anger there too.

"Dan, if you're thinking this proves that you're the reason I never got pregnant you know you're wrong. This could easily be secondary infertility —"

"Or maybe one of the abortions did some damage. Ever think of that?"

She thinks of it all. *One of the abortions,* she hates the sound, hates what it says (truly) about her youth and confusion. She thinks about how stupid she was, and how glad she is that at least she didn't have to risk her life, because she would have done anything to end those pregnancies, and she thinks about how they may be

215

the only pregnancies she'll ever have, the only times implantation will take place. And yes, she wishes one of those implantations could have been theirs together, hers and Dan's, but what can she do? Wishing won't make it so, telling him wouldn't have made it so.

"I'm sorry." Downstairs, with Sarah, tears came so quickly, so easily, sending her in retreat out of the room; she would not cry in front of Sarah. Now no tears are coming, though they might perhaps soften Dan. "I should have told you."

"But you never would have. If not for this thing, I would never have known." He is paging through her file again, and she imagines the transcripts and certificates passing before his eyes, the many accumulated pieces of achievement and effort. And why on earth had she ever told the doctor at university health about the abortions, anyway?

"Or were you thinking maybe that if we went to see an infertility specialist, that would be an excellent time to mention all your previous pregnancies, all your abortions? Would that have been my little surprise? Or is that why you never wanted to go see a specialist? Tell me your thinking, Maggie. I'm genuinely interested."

"I said I was sorry. But you don't have to keep beating on it. It all happened years and years before we met. It's not like it was your baby I aborted without telling you." It was mine. And mine. And mine.

She gets up to leave the room, to go get ready for bed. Thinking, to be honest, of Harvey and whether she has ever faked anything: Oh, yes, I have. Not letting herself think of Dan. But he grabs her arm as she starts to push past him out of the room, and she stops, standing right there up against him. He shakes his head, and she imagines that his eyes have tears in them, though they probably don't. Maggie puts her arms around him, reaching inside the velour robe to embrace his chest, still very slightly damp.

"I'm sorry," she whispers. "I'm so sorry."

"I'm sorry too," says Dan, hugging her back, apologizing back, just exactly as if this were the end of a bad-tempered fight about nothing, faults on both sides.

17

Bethlehem Pines

MAGGIE AT FIFTEEN, a counselor-in-training. Sent off to camp, in truth, partly because her mother was worried about her. Maggie was a good student, always. She had always been a straight-A honor roll student, and she still was. But her mother was worried that she had started running wild. Maggie didn't say where she was, or she said she was at a girlfriend's house — an approved girlfriend always, from the youth group — and then she wasn't there. Maggie loved her mother and she took the trouble, always, to lie to her: *We went out with a whole group of girls from church and we ended up at Linda's house and I know I should have called but I forgot.* But Maggie came home smelling of the things that fifteen-year-olds imagine that their parents cannot detect, cheap wine and cigarettes and marijuana, and when the phone rang she ran to answer it first, and there was definitely something different about the way she looked. Not just the specific battles fought and won (from Maggie's point of view, not her mother's), for example, to wear blue jeans when she was out with her friends — Maggie's mother could see clearly enough that the other girls wore blue jeans too. But there was something new about the way that Maggie moved, about the way she wore her blue jeans, or even wore her skirts for school, and the something, of course, was sex. And Maggie's mother must have known that, as every mother of every fifteen-year-old girl must know it on some level, but Maggie's mother could not say that to Maggie. Not quite. She could say, running wild. She could say, mixing with people too old for you and not from our church. She could say, Don't make a mistake you will always regret. She could even say, Avoid the occasion of sin. But she could not say, and she did not say, Don't do what I did — don't end up pregnant and forced to get married before you're twenty. And therefore there were certain direct lies that Maggie did not have to tell her.

That first summer, that fifteen-year-old summer at Bethlehem Pines, Maggie was at the same time more pious and more promiscuous than she would ever be again — or, at least, that was how she later formulated it, when she had, in her own mind, grown up. When she had left home and gone off to college and was in the business of mocking her childhood and its strictures, when she sat around with friends and competed to tell stories of parents or high school or small-town stupidity. *So they sent us off to this Bible camp in the Poconos, and guess what, it was all sex, drugs, and rock and roll — well, actually, sex and Boone's Farm apple wine.*

Her freshman year in college, Maggie would take a fairly generic American literature course and read novels by a long string of authors she had not particularly liked in high school, where she had written the requisite A papers on the deep meaning of *The Old Man and the Sea* and "A Rose For Emily." Reading these books in the comparative privacy of her own dormitory room, in the heady air of college intellectual freedom, she suddenly felt that the world had opened before her — not to reveal secret places and exotic lives, but to include the stories and secrets of her own life. Her childhood and her mother and her religion and her dreams and her sins began to seem to her almost deliriously part of American history, American culture, and she found ways to identify powerfully with almost everything she read — with Jay Gatsby, for example, coming from nowhere, from nothing, and making himself up as who he wanted to be. With Hester Prynne, of course — now there was a book she was glad they hadn't ruined for her in high school, as they had for so many of her college classmates; Maggie's high school stuck rigorously to the less controversial *House of the Seven Gables*. In college she found *Elmer Gantry* so fascinating that she actually made her way through *Main Street* and *Babbitt* — not in term time, because she was and always would be a slow and careful and precise reader, but over the following stay-at-college-live-in-a-dorm-and-work-in-a-lab summer, the summer that really once and for all proved to her that home was behind her and she was ready to invent her life.

But there was an especially dramatic moment as she read *The Grapes of Wrath*. It was a book she loved, another one of these books she read with astonished fascination, with this sense that things had been kept from her, that there had been an actual active conspiracy to keep her in ignorance — and of course, in Maggie's case, that was to some extent true. Her church did in fact circulate parental advisories, did in fact recommend keeping almost all adult fiction away from adolescents, with certain exceptions made (James Fenimore Cooper was allowed, but not Willa Cather, say — and *The Scarlet Letter* was explicitly forbidden, as perhaps it is anytime a humorless minister makes up the list). Maggie's mother had indeed sworn allegiance to certain codes of keeping-it-away-from-the-children, but the books that Maggie had been most careful to conceal when she lived at home had been the current best-sellers, the books of information or hot current action, the books that came after her early flirtation with James Bond, the books that had been passed around at school or found in a bedside table while babysitting or read aloud at smoky gatherings in Eleanora Davenport's garage. It would not have occurred to Maggie or any of her friends to sneak around with the classics of American literature — but they would have been at the very least not recommended and in many cases forbidden, so she did have the joy of reading them in college with that extra sense of salt.

And anyway, there she was in the middle of *The Grapes of Wrath*, and there in chapter four was Preacher Casey: "Tell you what — I use ta get the people jumpin' and talkin' in tongues, an' glory-shoutin' till they just fell down an' passed out. An' some I'd baptize to bring 'em to. An' then — you know what I'd do? I'd take one of them girls out in the grass, an' I'd lay with her. Done it ever' time.

Then I'd feel bad, an' I'd pray an' pray, but it didn't do no good. Come the nex' time, them an' me was full of the sperit, I'd do it again."

Maggie read it again, slowly, deliberately, as she read everything. Then read Tom Joad's response: "Joad smiled and his long teeth parted and he licked his lips. 'There ain't nothing like a good hot meetin' for pushin' 'em over,' he said. 'I done that myself.'"

And Maggie sat there, eighteen years old, in the squalid splendor of her college dormitory room — not absolutely private, perhaps, but she and her roommate had two small rooms for two young women, and her roommate spent most of her time at the library, leaving Maggie to enjoy the room, the books, the disorder. She sat there and thought of Bethlehem Pines, and she was thinking, So all of this makes sense. All of this is known and understood and predicted and part of America.

And closed her eyes and remembered hot nights and prayer meetings and shouting out responses, and believing. She remembered believing. She remembered, though already she had so completely stopped believing that she wasn't sure she was quite remembering it right. But she remembered being part of a happiness, part of a certainty, part of a sense that right here, right now, the question had been asked and the answer had been given. She remembered being on her feet, clapping and shouting and singing, and knowing she had given up the bad, the evil, the sinful part of her and that she was loved.

And then of course, she could remember helping to put the little girls to bed in her cabin, and watching their eyes close in their tired, radiant, sweaty faces, and feeling a kind of exalted nostalgia, for her own childhood and innocence, for the time, not so many years ago, when her own evening would have ended this same way. And instead she and the junior counselor and the senior counselor would all three slip away to the bonfire, to the clearing back in the woods where all the other counselors gathered, and where the evening would go on and on into the summer night.

Her very first week of her very first summer at Bethlehem Pines, Maggie scored big. She attracted the attention of the boys' sports director, who also worked as one of the waterfront lifeguards, and of course later she would understand that he noticed her because he was on the prowl, because he was a college student boy with an eye out for the new high school girls, one after another. At the time, he was a prize, pure and simple: older — in *college* — good-looking, and extremely cool.

His name was Leon, which was cool because he was so cool, and because of his position of responsibility he had keys to various camp buildings, which meant that he and Maggie had sex in, among other places, the building where the volleyball equipment was stored, the boys' changing room down by the lakefront, and the rather creepy canoe shed. It was not, of course, Maggie's loss of virginity, that first evening (the first week of camp — Leon worked fast!) on a blanket out in the woods beyond the bonfire. Maggie had managed to lose her virginity several months earlier, with a boy her own age at a high school party. They had neither of them known exactly what they were doing, and they had both been somewhat high, and Maggie, thinking it over later, had decided not to count it; it was neither romantic and exhilarating nor cool and degenerate. She and all her friends were by this point quite expert in what they did or didn't count, and all the mental gymnastics that went along with that; it was the thing she was least able to explain, later on in college, to people who had not grown up as she had grown up. Anyway, she therefore decided to count as her loss of virginity a chilly evening spent in the famous Eleanora Davenport's garage, sharing a sleeping bag with a boy two years older who was at least someone she knew fairly well, someone she had been seeing occasionally in youth group for years but who lived in a comparatively distant town. And who did, more or less, know what he was doing. And there had been a series of encounters, and a pregnancy, and a trip to Planned Parenthood — but that was something she was already expert in not thinking about. In not counting.

Leon, however, was her first great romance. They were, very quickly, an acknowledged couple; she sat encircled by his arm at the campfire, she stopped as she herded her charges past his life-guard chair, admired his bronzing shoulders and arms, and let the little girls see her admiring him. She thought about him, and his shoulders and his arms and his hands, pretty much all day long, and at night she did things with him that she was pretty sure even Eleanora Davenport had never done.

And it all lasted about two weeks of the eight-week summer. Maggie was not the only high school girl to pause admiringly at that particular lifeguard chair, and after two weeks or so, Leon moved on. There was a Bible pageant in the dining hall that Friday night, and Maggie was in charge of the Rebecca-at-the-Well scene; she and the little girls had spent the day making a papier-mâché well, which they carried carefully into the stage area near the juice dispensers. Maggie had draped the chosen Rebecca (long, dark hair, of course) in the most appropriate bedspread she could find, and they had covered a red plastic cleaning bucket with brown paper. Maggie stood at the side of the crowded dining hall, watching Rebecca step uncertainly (her sandals had been borrowed from another girl with somewhat bigger feet) toward the well, paper-covered bucket balanced on her shoulder, when she noticed Leon, across the hall, whispering intently in the ear of one of the prettiest of the counselors-in-training, a girl Maggie had twice in recent days encountered at the foot of Leon's chair on the waterfront. No more evidence was needed — nor ever is. Through tear-filled eyes, Maggie watched Rebecca draw up her bucket and react to the approach of the blanket-draped Hebrew men. Rebecca's sisters and female relatives, wrapped in the less appropriate bedspreads, huddled in the background, whispering to one another. The boys' cabin, in an excess of imagination and competitive spirit, had turned two boys into a camel, and their coordinated stepping was without question the hit of the evening.

An evening that Maggie ended alone at the campfire, drinking way too much Boone's Farm. Leon and his new conquest didn't show up at all — or perhaps the conquest was even then under way. Maggie drank herself sick, which is not that hard to do on the particular substance in question, as she would always point out when she told the story later on, in college, by then a far more sophisticated consumer of tequila sunrises and black Russians. But back by the campfire, she drank apple wine until the summer night sky was spinning over her head, and she might never have made it back to her cabin had she not been helped by the junior nature counselor, a boy named Michael, who, surprise surprise (as Maggie would later put it, telling the story), became her very next Bethlehem Pines boyfriend.

It would be easy, you know — very easy — too easy — to see this as a story about religious hypocrisy and superficial beliefs. Maggie herself did that, at least for a while, telling stories on herself in college. Can you believe it, the name of the lord on our lips all the time and there we were, going at it like rabbits all night! Admit it, you who went to regular, normal summer camps — it wasn't like this! We were off the scale, off the fucking scale, no pun intended. That kind of thing — but, to be fair, that is the way that college students make hay of their childhood and adolescent institutions; it is how they build the necessary structure of superiority and sophistication. And Maggie had the sense and the perspective to recognize that, partly because of *The Grapes of Wrath* and the other books she read. She had the good grace and good fortune to discover that the world was wider and deeper not only than her own experience, but than her too easy recastings of that experience, and she stopped making certain kinds of jokes about her childhood, her church, her mother.

My mother does believe, I did believe, we did believe. It brought us joy. It complicated our lives. It changed the balance. Maggie no longer believed. It had gone from her during her final year of high school, no dramatic realizations, no epiphanies of rationalist thought, just the dawning awareness that she was going through motions, chanting words that had lost their meaning. She was young enough and tough enough and realistic enough to face the world without believing, but even so, she knew it was a loss. Something was gone. How strange to find the words in the books that no one had given her to read, back when she believed. But there they were — and Maggie, who no longer believed, was able to feel a little regret, a little nostalgia, a little gratitude, and to feel it young enough and close enough to the actual experience of growing up that it must be accounted a true, if secular, state of grace.

18

Sharing

MAGGIE: She should never have agreed. Go bother someone else — I'm busy practicing medicine, she should have said.

"Clinical discussions are often disempowering for many doctors and nurses. I'd like to thank Dr. Weintraub for offering me some opportunities to work in real clinical settings to help you see the advantages of building consensus." So speaks Graham Shipley.

A bad idea whose time has come. And boy, has it come. Into her conference room, where she should be in charge. Her boss, Harvey Weintraub, and the hospital change expert himself, Dr. Graham Schmuckley, Mr. Employee Empowerment. And a couple of other neonatologists, Hank Shoemaker and Claire Hodge, lassoed by Harvey to come watch this great innovation in action. Employee Empowerment Through Sharing.

"I think it might facilitate things for you if I started out by reminding you that everyone in this room is united in wanting what is best for the patients in this hospital. We may have different views about what is best, and all those views are equally valid, and that's why we need to bring everyone to the table and make sure that all the voices are heard and that we are all on the same page."

Why doesn't he go away with his mixed metaphors, why is he

wasting her time while Felicia Grassini gets sicker and sicker? What on earth can he think he means, "all those views are equally valid"? Maggie's fingers drum on the conference table.

The world is full of people who look at our patients and say, Too small, give up, let them go. Too sick, stillborn, better off dead. Those people speak out of ignorance, out of their own limitations, out of the human tendency to give up on a hard fight. *My* babies are the ones who don't necessarily look like they have a chance, but turn out to draw on determination and strength and a will to live that would make most fleshy, robust adults look like powder puffs. It has always been and still is a miracle, that in seven hundred or eight hundred grams of human cells, of unfused bones and translucent skin, there is that drive to grow, to heal, to live, to survive. Look at Felicia Grassini, who came out fourteen weeks too early and already infected, who needed a high-frequency oscillator to breathe for her, who went into shock from her infection so that water leaked out of her blood vessels and into her tissues and she blew up like a sick, sad balloon — she fought off that infection, that pneumonia, that septic shock, and her lungs are healing, do you hear? Healing and growing, and if that much power is wrapped up in the unlikely, unpromising package of Felicia, then who would dare stand up and say, She doesn't want to live, doesn't need to live, doesn't deserve to live. Yes, it's one damn thing after another, yes, different systems keep failing, but that's what it is to be born fourteen weeks too soon. This is our job, coping. Get used to it.

Justin tries hard to argue the dopey defeatest point of view: Felicia Grassini is too small and too sick for surgery; now her belly is blowing up and we may be getting into an abdominal emergency, in which case the only way to save her would be to take her to the operating room and take out who knows how much of her gastrointestinal tract, and we're just plain being too aggressive here, medically. We gave this baby a good shot — she's just too small. Everything is against her. It's time to face facts. It's time to present this to the parents: they need to make some very hard decisions. If something else goes wrong —

"As it surely will," Maggie says. "When you say *if*, you really mean *when*. You mean, ask the parents to decide to let the next infection, the next treatable problem, kill the baby. Is that what you mean? Stop giving antibiotics, stop checking vital signs?"

"I think we have to decide how aggressive we want to be," Justin says, not for the first time. "I mean, this is a baby with bigtime head bleeds. The odds are, this is going to be a severely damaged kid — don't you think we're pushing things too far?"

"The outcome for kids with head bleeds is extremely variable, as I think you know."

"How far would you go?" Justin demands. "Major surgery? Organ transplants? Renal dialysis?"

"Mind if I interrupt here?" Mr. Empowerment.

Yes, of course she minds.

"Sometimes it's helpful to remind ourselves that there are certain things we can all agree on. Often, it turns out people aren't as far apart as they think they are. Here we have a group of really caring individuals, highly trained, all committed to working together to benefit this baby."

Oh, for the sweet lord's sweet sake. He wants to go around the fucking table and have all of us say where we're coming from and what we bring to this discussion. Maggie shoots a look at Harvey: Can he really be taken in by this? He looks as pious as can be. Almost desperate, she looks to Hank; surely grumpy old geek-boy Hank isn't interested in this nonsense?

He is filling a mug at the coffee machine, taking the last dregs of coffee, putting the pot back empty, and Jean Dreyfus gets up and pours in more water.

Hank: He'll call the newspapers, that's what he'll do. He'll call the *Globe*, the *Herald*, *USA Today*, call them from a pay phone with a hot tip: a doctor at Blessed Innocence who isn't safe — they've been warned, and they're still letting her take care of babies. People are so concerned about this doctor, there've been signs hung up on bulletin boards all over the hospital — and still the administration protects her.

Headlines: BLESSED INNOCENCE DOC DANGEROUS TO PATIENTS. Maggie Claymore's smug I'm-so-great face looking out at the world. Then let her try and show off, then let her act like the crown princess. Not as smart as you think you are. Not as smart as I am.

He thinks, I will call the newspapers, I will call the TV stations, I will hang you out to burn in the sunshine. He says, Maggie, I worry that this decision is being influenced too much by the mother's pregnancy history. Turns to Weintraub and explains, This woman has been through years of infertility treatments, and I'm concerned that may mean her baby gets inappropriately aggressive interventions. That everyone is unwilling to level with the mother about the baby's real chances.

Maggie: She smiles encouragingly at Jean Dreyfus, the nurse who has been with the baby and the family from the beginning. Who does not want to give up on the baby. Who speaks directly to Maggie, ignoring the go-around-the-table idea. "We're committed here —" she says this hesitantly. "It would be one thing if we had to ask her parents whether to dialyse her. But are we really going to withhold antibiotics?"

"No," Maggie says. "We're not. And dialysis is completely irrelevant. There's nothing wrong with her kidneys. The question is whether she goes to the OR if she needs abdominal surgery, and the answer is yes, she does. That's what her parents want and that's what will happen."

Justin glances over at the representative surgeon; the surgical powers that be, even more impatient with meetings and talking than Maggie, have sent a surgical intern, who is asleep at the table.

"Don't you think," Justin begins, careful, polite, questioning, holding himself back, "that the likely outcome for this baby includes long-term rehab, neurological deficits, now you're adding in short-gut syndrome — it's not benign, it's not painless, the life you're saying she has to live."

"Is that definitely true?" asks the social worker.

Maggie defers to the neurologist, who gives a long and garbled speech. The gist is that the baby has suffered severe head bleeds, and numerous episodes of oxygen deprivation and neurologic damage could be localized to several regions or possibly extended beyond them, or possibly not, and the effects could indeed be global, and several particular functions are of concern, but it's very hard to predict beyond saying that there may be both mental and motor delay. Thank you so much. Very helpful.

"Sounds like this baby won't make it out of the OR," says Hank. "It's an anesthesiology nightmare."

She wants to hit him. She wants to grab his poisonous coffee and throw it in his face. She wants to tell him, right here in front of all these people, that no one asked for his opinion. How dare he speak in such terms about her baby, about the baby she has kept alive? About the baby who has tried and tried to stay alive.

"I think that's an exaggeration," she says calmly. "A good anesthesiologist should be able to handle it; her lung function has been improving steadily."

"Do the parents fully realize she may need surgery?" The social worker, checking in.

"Marjorie?" asks Justin, bringing into the discussion for the first time the person who should have been leading it, the intern who is supposed to be the baby's doctor. Who was here the night the baby came in and should have been the one holding the pieces together all along, following the baby step by step through her hospital story and learning what there was to learn, good outcome or bad outcome. That's what internship is supposed to be — except that's not how it's worked, not this time, not this baby, not this intern.

"I mentioned to her mom yesterday that we were concerned about her abdominal girth," Marjorie says.

"But did you tell her about the prognosis for short-gut syndrome and a lifetime of IV nutrition?" Hank again. What the hell is he doing in this meeting, in this conversation? Is it possible that Weintraub has told her colleagues that he's worried about Maggie and how she is functioning? Are they checking up on her? Has Justin gone to Hank for help and support in murdering Felicia Grassini? Maggie knows that Justin, who made this meeting happen, is not pleased with the way she is behaving. Essentially, she has wrested control away from him, she is presiding in an obvious, maybe even heavy-handed way: *I'm in charge.* Too bad. Justin will grow up to be the kind of doctor who handles power and meetings in a way commonly described among the female doctors as let's-all-just-put-our-dicks-on-the-table-and-see-whose-is-bigger; unfortunately for him, at this meeting, Maggie has the biggest dick.

"Let's everybody take a piece of paper," says Graham Shipley. Speaking of dicks. "Let's try a little exercise. I want everyone to diagram your feelings about this decision. Draw an arrow for each emotion you feel, and position the arrows so we can see whether you feel pulled in different directions, or whether your emotions are really in sync."

Maggie bends over her paper and draws a stick figure caricature: Mr. Empowerment. Draws all the arrows sticking into his torso. Saint Sebastian, martyred for insisting that the Romans should share their feelings.

Hank: He does not like classical music, and he resents the idea that he is supposed to like it. It actually comes up more often than one might expect; lots of doctors, maybe especially in Boston, are classical music enthusiasts. They play in little chamber music groups with friends, they give money to the BSO, they spend ridiculous amounts on new CDs for their already ridiculously expensive CD players. And, it seems to Hank, they go out of their way to name drop: this conductor conducting that piece with that soloist, the best ever, the only performance that counts. Well, yes, the way doctors tend to talk; Hank, as a male doctor, is not familiar with the female summation of let's-all-put-our-dicks-on-the-table, but he certainly knows the style.

Harvey Weintraub, his boss, is so proud of the particular pair of seats that he and his wife now sit in as their symphony subscription that he has been known to draw a seating plan of Symphony Hall on a napkin at lunch to demonstrate to David Susser that his, Harvey's, seats are in the acoustically ideal situation, far better than most more expensive seats. And David Susser, a man who otherwise talks only and endlessly about cloning, would draw sound vectors on the napkin to show that in fact, when there was a piano soloist with the symphony — as there would be at some goddamn concert or other that Harvey was very proud he would be attending — the piano sound would actually pass over the heads of people in Harvey's seats, and the ideal acoustic placement would be somewhere on the right side of the balcony — where David had been sitting for some other goddamn concert.

Hank sits silently when music is discussed. Hank spent two years of his life in a lab where the boss kept the radio permanently tuned to some fruitcake classical station that didn't even run commercials to break up the monotony. When Hank himself listens to the radio, always in the car, he likes news, and especially traffic reports. (In a way, his feelings about music are just one more point on which Hank is more in accord with Maggie than he is with most of his other colleagues. Maggie likes gospel of course, cares about it more than Hank cares about anything musical, but her feelings about classical music, the mixture of profound boredom and skepticism about the motives of enthusiasts, those feelings are actually not so different from Hank's. Of course, Maggie is a much more secure and less crazy person, and it would not occur to her ever that doctors who talk at length about their trips to European music festivals or their new Deutsche Gramophone four-CD sets are actually trying to make her feel inferior. Still, if you were giving an award for Least Likely to Be Found at Symphony Hall in the neonatology department, Maggie and Hank would have to be among the finalists, Hank probably the winner.)

But here he is at Symphony Hall, complete with the chip on his shoulder: Look at me, I'm not dressed up. I will not do you the favor, you stuck-up fuckers, you stuck-up fakers! He pushes his way a little bit too roughly among the crowds of better-dressed people, the occasional fur-coated woman, the business-suited men. He smells a thick and strange perfume as he gives one final shove, enters the doorway, sees a sleek blond head turn to give him a dirty look, a triple string of pearls around her neck. He sticks his tongue out, once, quickly, then leaves her behind to wonder.

His seat is in the middle of a row on the left side toward the back on the main floor. The stage is already busy with musicians, coming and going and plinking on their instruments as he settles in his seat, and the gold rectangle of the hall is unexpectedly familiar to him. He has been here twice before, both times for the same reason, but that does not make it home ground. The last time was more than two years ago; Dudley Chen does not visit Boston all that frequently. And out comes the conductor, and everyone claps.

Then Dudley Chen comes out, crosses to the center, and shakes the conductor's hand, and Hank rises slightly in his seat with recognition. Yes, that's him, I know him! Dudley Chen is easy to pick out of a crowd. Over six feet tall and skeletally thin, he stoops forward slightly from the waist. He has longish limp dark hair falling forward over his high forehead. He wears a tuxedo, and Hank finds himself wondering what it would feel like to stand on that stage, wearing a tuxedo, knowing that every single person in the hall has come wanting to hear you. He will never know that feeling, he supposes, but neither will Weintraub or Susser or Maggie Claymore. The woman sitting next to him, small and shrunken in her green wool outfit, is clapping like a crazy person, almost stomping her feet; you can see her legs twitching. Hank moves his own left foot away from her. He thinks of confiding in her: Dudley Chen is an old — what would he say? Acquaintance? No, in for a penny, in for a pound — an old friend of mine. We went to college together, and I always come to hear him when he does a concert in Boston.

Actually, he feels a certain fondness for this woman; she is just so goddamn ugly — plain, shriveled face, hacked-off dull brown hair, no makeup, no jewelry, just that awful grass green wool thing covering her from neck to feet. He imagines that she is not someone who regularly comes to Symphony Hall, that it was a big deal for her to buy a single ticket and come tonight. She idolizes Dudley Chen, collects all his recordings, yearns for the nights he comes to Boston and she can leave her lonely, strange life of eating takeout food and listening to music and waiting for phone calls that never come, wrap herself in her ugly green outfit, spend a whole week's money on a seat in Symphony Hall. And imagine if she knew that the man sitting quietly beside her was an old friend, an actual acquaintance of that man up on the stage, that man she would always worship, who would never know her name or her face, that tall figure now lifting his violin, not yet ready to put it under his chin, but holding it in both hands, angled across his abdomen.

Maggie: I go into the parents' room and see the Grassinis with Jean and Erika, and I assume they're talking about me. I can't face Mr. Grassini; I have barely exchanged a word with him since I found out he was asking about me, about the posters. I have never in my whole career taken care of a child and been unable to face a parent; I face parents when the babies are brain-damaged, when they're diagnosed with fatal cardiac conditions, when they're dying. And I have to ask myself, am I so set on being aggressive with this baby because I am worried that if she dies, he will complain, he will tell the hospital he never wanted me as her doctor, he saw the signs about me? Maybe sue?

I have to ask myself something else, also. Those letters about me, the accusations about Heather Clark, *Maggie Claymore killed this child because the child wasn't perfect.* And of course I know my reputation is exactly the opposite. I'm supposed to be an extremist, always aggressive, with the most busted babies. And I am; I am the last person on earth to snuff out a child's life because the child is disabled. So I have to ask myself here, am I taking this as my chance to prove that, loud and clear?

No. There is no way this has affected my medical judgment. It has not, it will not. It never will. They can accuse me of murdering every child who dies, and I will still take proper care of the ones who are alive.

I go into the parents' room and see the Grassinis with Jean and Erika. I make myself look at them. At him, at this man whose baby is alive because of me. No, that's wrong, that's off. At this man who has been trying to have a baby now for years. Who lost a baby in the delivery room. Who has to worry now that something weird is going on with the doctor who is entrusted with his one fragile surviving child.

I imagine myself in a delivery room, on the table. The babies I would never let the specialists try to give me. The memories of all the procedures I would not, would never, will not, undergo. The million billion dollar, ninth time around IVF pregnancy. Finally, too early a birth. Contractions, the terrible certainty that it has all gone for nothing, or maybe the wild hope that in spite of the wrong dates and all the other risks, it is finally about to be okay.

The Grassinis turn and look at me, and what do they wonder? Who is this woman whose mess swirls around her like a cloud, swirls around our baby? What, oh what, is happening, who, oh who, can be trusted?

I go into the parents' room, and I look Mr. Grassini in the eye. We are worried about your daughter again — not her lungs this time. Her belly. What we call necrotizing enterocolitis, another diagnosis you had been able to live your life up to now without knowing about. "No one knows what causes this," I tell him. "Probably it's another end result of oxygen deprivation. But if Felicia shows any more evidence of intestinal problems, we're going to have to operate."

I am on the delivery table. My insides are out of control. I am pushing out the babies I would do anything to keep safe inside. My guarded ones, my precious ones, pushing them out into the bright lights of the world. My son is dying, drowning in air. My daughter they are holding, keeping, saving.

Mr. Grassini pounds a fist against the wall. Twice. Two thuds. I wait for him to say, Get us another doctor, this must be your fault. We've heard about you, Dr. Maggie Claymore. But what he says is, "She's already been through so much!"

"I know," I say.

"Surgery! Cutting her open!"

"There isn't really any choice," I say, though I've been at a meeting arguing about choice for the last hour. There isn't any choice, and I told them so at the meeting. "If her intestines start to become necrotic — that's when tissue is deprived of oxygen —"

"Then she could die, right?" Mrs. Grassini, calm and to the point. Thank you.

"Yes," Jean and Erika and I all say together. We've all seen it happen. We've seen babies' bellies turn black. We've seen them die even with surgery.

"There isn't any choice," says Mrs. Grassini. Then calmly reaches for an FAO Schwarz shopping bag, removes a stuffed bear, cotton-candy pink. "I brought this for her," she says. "For luck."

I am on the delivery table. I am screaming. I am beyond control. Everything is beyond control. I am turning inside out. But nothing is being born. I am bringing forth only emptiness, the emptiness inside me, out into the lights of the hospital for all to see.

Hank: He really did go to college with Dudley Chen. Even at the time, it had been kind of a big deal, Dudley Chen choosing not to go to any of the conservatories that would have welcomed him eagerly, going instead to a small liberal arts college. Giving interviews about wanting to be well rounded, guest starring with the student orchestra every now and then with amiable we're-all-in-this-together condescension, then running off to give big-deal concerts and be the teenage violin prodigy. Hank had been aware of his famous classmate, and in fact they had taken at least one class together, a big lecture course on voyages of discovery that had presumably attracted them both by its reputation for easy A's. The professor had made a big fuss one morning, starting the lecture by telling the class that the night before he had had the privilege of hearing one of his own students in concert, that he wanted to tell everyone what a remarkable musician they had in their midst, would Dudley Chen please stand up and take a bow. Dudley had stood up, smiling modestly, and the students, most of them well aware of his celebrity, had applauded.

It had seemed to Hank, for a while after that, that he ran into Dudley Chen everywhere. In the science library, lining up ahead of him for readings on reserve, waiting to get into the dining hall to see *2001: A Space Odyssey,* even at two A.M. one night during exam period in the all-night convenience store near the campus. He remembers quite distinctly that Dudley Chen had begun to nod at him, smile in recognition, and he had anguished for hours, both at the time and since, over his own failure to introduce himself — to stick out his hand and say, Hi, I believe we're both in "Sails and Trails" — make the connection, be noticed, be someone who really did go to college with Dudley Chen.

The interesting thing is this: Hank *knows* that in fact he has never spoken a word to Dudley Chen, that Dudley has never known his name, that any chance to be a friend of this famous person he had tossed away back in college, when of course you did rub shoulders with strangers and classmates who might go on to be famous. He knows that, and yet he also knows something else, some other truth.

There is music playing now; the orchestra, though not yet Dudley. Playing something; who cares what. And now Dudley does lift his violin and does play, and though Hank is not moved by the music, does not exactly enjoy the music, he permits himself a sense of awe at the trick of it. So much sound coming from one little instrument way up at the front of the room, coming through and over all the noise from so many other musicians. Hank knots his hands together in his lap, presses his elbows tightly to his sides, avoiding contact with the people next to him, with the woman in green.

One thing at least you can say for Symphony Hall: By and large, people in the audience keep their fucking mouths shut. You don't have to be on your guard all the time, ready to start a fight with some loudmouthed asshole. Cindy won't go to the movies with him anymore. She says she's scared because someday he'll tell some kid to shut up and the kid will pull a gun. Says he makes her crazy, twisting around in his seat to locate who's talking, says he starts worrying before the movie even begins, scoping out the people around them, deciding who is likely to be noisy.

Well, fuck Cindy. She has gone off and left him, walked out on him yesterday, and look at him, here at Symphony Hall. Cindy is gone and he does not care. He does not fucking care. Look at him, he's doing fine. And between that and the sense of his own connection to the soloist up on the stage, and who knows, maybe even the music, Hank relaxes a little bit, and in this unlikely setting, so calculated to remind him of so many slights and grudges and exclusions, he settles back into his seat, more or less at peace.

Maggie: She knows she should not have lost her temper at Hank. But he had a lot of nerve, coming to that meeting on her patient like that, sticking his nose in where it didn't belong. Daring to ask her, was she sure her medical judgment wasn't being affected by the family's situation. In other words, are you being this aggressive only because this is a well-to-do, desperate-for-a-baby family? Would you push for surgery if this were some fourteen-year-old's unwanted accident?

Yes, she said, firmly, thinking of Baby Boy not-those-Kennedys.

Hank Shoemaker, sitting in judgment on her, on her baby. Showing off for Harvey and Mr. Empowerment, or just getting on her case? What about the neurological damage? What about the fact that this baby will probably not be normal?

I don't see myself as here to take care of just normal kids, she told him. I think I have a mandate to care for children with handicaps, disabilities.

But do you have a mandate to *create* them?

She should not have lost her temper, but she did.

This baby is here. I didn't create her. I didn't even save her in the delivery room. She's *here.* She's been through pain and suffering and she's lived from day to day and she hasn't always had enough oxygen, but she is over there in the NICU with a heart and a brain and kidneys and a liver and with every day she is another day old. Don't you come marching in and tell me to kill her —

Mr. Empowerment interrupted: Let's remember that we all share some very important values.

Maggie cut him off. Let's remember that this is *my* patient. That I have discussed her situation extensively with her parents, and they want us to be as aggressive as possible. And I intend to support that. If she needs surgery she gets surgery. She leaned over and shook the sleeping surgeon's shoulder, a little bit roughly. Go back and tell that to your team, okay? *If she needs surgery, she gets surgery.* Tell them I want her evaluated every couple of hours for the next several days, and if I don't see you guys coming by the NICU, I'm going to file a formal complaint.

He goggled at her sleepily. Where am I? you could see him thinking. Am I operating? No. Good.

Let's start from the place that we're all basically good people, and we all have our emotions, and that's okay. Dr. Shoemaker's feelings are valid because they come out of his experience, and your feelings come out of a different experience.

He has an idea, Mr. Empowerment does. He wants them to try some teamwork exercises. They will pretend that the floor of the conference room is quicksand, and they will work to get their whole team from the door to the table without touching the floor. Maggie notes to her satisfaction that Weintraub looks a little taken aback by this idea.

Wish I could stay and play, she says. Justin, you and I need to get back to our patients. And out they go, leaving the rest of them unwillingly taking off their shoes, building a pontoon bridge of chairs.

Hank: He goes to the mailroom. A big envelope from the *American Journal of Perinatology,* rejecting his article, which had already been rejected at two other journals, and they take their goddamn time about it. This study has now been making the rounds for almost two years, what with having to revise it and reformat it every time it came back. He grabs the rest of his mail, a couple of journals, a lot of circulars, a few lab results, and stomps out of the mailroom; the fat idiot who is supposed to be in charge of the place is sitting in the back doing something weird. Jerking off or whatever — probably ought to be locked up. But hey, Hank tells himself, it could be worse. Just as well to have someone who doesn't know what's going on in the mailroom. Comes in handy every now and then.

Hank's research involves the cultivation of cells from the lungs of premature babies, the stimulation of these cells by the products of the thyroid gland. The biggest thing in neonatology in years had been the discovery that you could give newborns with respiratory distress artificial surfactant, the substance missing in premature lungs, and the babies would do better. Surfactant is what makes the air sacs pliable, and the absence of it is what makes the lungs stiff and unable to expand properly to take in air. Hank had long ago jumped on the thyroid-hormone horse; thyroid hormone would stimulate surfactant, just as it stimulated so many other things. But then along came artificial surfactant, and now no one is very enthusiastic about thyroid hormone as the wave of the future. And now this one particular paper keeps coming back with comments about the shaky experimental methodology and doubts about whether it actually contains anything very new, given similar experiments with animal models by blah blah blah and you know who. And the stupid idiots out there who publish only their friends' work are laughing at him.

His office is a small cubicle just off the lab, only a closet, really, and a total mess, journals haphazard on the shelves, cell biology supply catalogues on the floor. He has shut himself into his office only to fume, only to glare at the comments that had come back from the *American Journal of Perinatology*. And now he finds himself looking with fury at the two new issues of two other journals that had come in the mail, absolutely certain that those journals are full of papers by people he knows. His hand is actually trembling as he grabs up the slick covers, scans first the blue one with the green border, then the white one with the red titles. If there is anything by Maggie Claymore, for example, he will — well, he doesn't know what he will do, but he will do something. Just let him find another of her bogus pieces of so-called research, fancy statistics trying to show that what you don't find is just as important as what you do find. Or even worse, one of those self-aggrandizing little commentaries she likes to write about how important it is to do follow-up studies.

So Hank sits down in his chair, first clearing away a sludgy coffee cup and the minutes of the last hospital staff meeting, and allows himself the luxury of a detailed fantasy: Maggie Claymore unmasked. The entire department of neonatology assembled, Weintraub announcing that with much regret, he has to break the news that one of their colleagues has been found conclusively guilty of scientific misconduct. Apologies and retractions will of course be sent out to all relevant journals, and Dr. Claymore has submitted a formal letter of resignation, which I have accepted.

It works. Hank relaxes, smiles, his lips move slightly with the words. In his fantasy, Maggie is packing up her office, loading journals into cartons. Her eyes are red, her hair greasy and disheveled. Unmasked, found out, disgraced, goodbye.

Does he forget, even for a moment, that there is no reason at all to believe that Maggie actually has ever fabricated a single point of data? That he has made the accusation up out of nothing more than his dislike of her, his resentment of what seems to him regular and splashy publications, though in fact there is nothing particularly remarkable about the couple of times her name has been in print over the last year? Does he believe it, really and truly, that because he made it up, because he might pass on his story to other people, because it would give him pleasure to have it be true, therefore it is true? In that answer, of course, would lie some estimate of how crazy, what kind of crazy. Just paranoid, or downright delusional? Does he recognize the world and, recognizing it, dislike it, or does he not actually know what is real and what is conjured from his own dislike?

Hank is not crazy, and he knows it. Have you not, after all, ever worked with someone you came to hate? Has there never been some voice in your workplace whose very timbre clenched your body up with fury and resentment? Has there never been some one particular person whose achievements rankled, whose defeat and disgrace you craved? Perhaps you faced it openly and indulged yourself in endless fantasies of that defeat and disgrace, or perhaps you tried hard to discipline yourself into collegial feeling, or even justified your visceral responses, proved to yourself conclusively that you disapproved rather than disliked, disapproved of someone who was not a good person, not a good worker, ungenerous, gratuitously unpleasant, lazy, and so on and so forth.

But of course not everyone sends anonymous letters. Hank is rather inclined to look on his own recourse to that technique, and to others still more unusual, as evidence of his own superior intelligence. Others may fume and hate and resent, but he, Hank Shoemaker, is smart enough to do something about it. To hit out at the people who annoy him, disrupt their smug peace of mind, their satisfaction in their looks, their professional success, or their social comfort. He has found a way to do it that leaves him safely hidden with his hatred and yet lets the objects of that hatred know its strength and its fury.

Don't say there isn't any figure who comes dancing into your brain. Don't say you've never been tempted.

Part Three

19

Faking It

MAGGIE LAY AWAKE and worried. And lay awake and worried. This was their weekend off, their time together, their time away, and she had been game and cheerful all day. Game and cheerful driving north out of Boston on a suspiciously gray afternoon that had turned by evening not into white and drifting snow, but into a full-fledged sleet storm. The last half-hour of the drive into New Hampshire, Dan had crouched forward over the steering wheel, driving more and more slowly, both of them flinching whenever a passing truck sprayed their windshield with thick frozen mud. They had arrived late at the hotel, and the dining room was closing, so they had had to sit down immediately, no time to go up to their room and unwind a little, maybe shower, maybe even make love. Come down in different, slightly dressier clothes, their hair damp, exchanging secret couple smiles. Instead they dropped their luggage at the desk, occupied their table in the restaurant, and then took turns in the restaurant bathroom.

Maggie had washed her face, combed her hair, stared at herself in the unfriendly mirror and smiled. This is our time. Everything else is far away, behind a wall of sleet. Don't let Dan get worked up, don't let him bristle at the waiter, don't let him eat slowly on purpose, don't let him start finding that the food is disappointing, the room uncomfortable. If she went out to him and smiled and distracted him, he would relax, he would forgive, it would all be okay. This was her job in the travel dynamic of their marriage. When Dan was not wound up, he would acknowledge it himself: *One thing goes wrong and I start thinking everything is wrong.*

But in fact it worked out fine. When Maggie got back to the table, the waiter was commiserating with Dan about the drive, telling him that considering the weather, he had made excellent time up from Boston. Dan, allied now with the waiter, was ordering a fairly expensive bottle of wine; a very good sign.

The hotel was part of a ski resort in the winter, though the ski season had not yet fully begun. In style, it was an overgrown country inn — eight rooms in the original old house now expanded to thirty rooms by building an ersatz Victorian extension in the back. The restaurant was moderately famous, a place people might drive up to in the summer, a chef whose recipes would appear in Boston food articles, with maybe a sort of patronizing, not-bad-for-New-Hampshire clause. The kind of place Dan would remember and want to go to someday for the weekend.

The dining room was almost empty; over on the other side, one group of four lingered over coffee. There was very little light, only a candle on each occupied table, a short, fat white candle in a little glass lantern, and beyond that only a fire now down to its embers and some ridiculously low, expensively subtle house lighting coming from god knew where. Nothing so obvious as a wall lamp or, heaven forbid, a ceiling fixture. Maggie could see only dim outlines of the other diners: two couples, the men in dark suits, the women both in sweaters that glittered in the candlelight, sequins or sparkles, something that reflected. She caressed the highly polished tabletop, slightly uneven, rough-hewn wood with metal joists on the square corners. Everything in the room was like this, opulently rustic. The fireplace, for example, which she had passed on the way to the bathroom: great odd-shaped granite hunks and then a white marble mantel. The array of weathervanes displayed on the wall, positioned to catch the beams of those mysterious lights along their battered metal edges. The room smelled slightly of woodsmoke. It was warm and quiet and dim, and Maggie could feel her shoulders relaxing after the drive. She opened her menu, looked at it without seeing it, closed it and smiled at her husband. Whatever sounds good to you. He would have a plan, of course, or he would not have ordered the wine.

The waiter materialized again, displayed the label on the wine bottle to Dan, did his routine with the white napkin and the corkscrew. Maggie, watching across the table, felt her eyes suddenly swimming with tears as Dan lifted the wineglass, tasted the wine, full of his silly, endearing expertise. The candlelight caught in her tears, refracted in this extra film of fluid, so that for a moment her eyes seemed to be filled with light. Dan nodded his approval of the wine, opened his menu, and began to order, the waiter bending low to confer with him, and Maggie took the moment to dip her head down, raise her napkin, and apply its starched white corner quickly to each eye. Her vision cleared; the flame was back in its proper place. But the intense sadness was still there, and sharp and unwelcome in her mind was still the thought, *If they find out, I will kill myself.*

And that was the thought she could not drive from her mind in the dark, in the soft, king-size, four-post bed. Dan was asleep; the storm outside had calmed so that there was only an occasional gust of wind loud enough to shake the window panes a little bit or whistle past the corner of the building. Earlier, when they had been making love, the storm had been much more intense, and they had laughed a little at its noises and its violence; no longer vulnerable in their little car on a sleet-covered road, they were safe inside and all the howling and the gusting was merely a suitably passionate backdrop.

For all that, actually, Maggie thought, it had been obligatory ceremonial lovemaking: Here we are in our fancy room, fresh out of the Jacuzzi, stuffed with expensive food, well, there's only one thing to be done about it. And Dan of course with his little surprises, his little jar of almond oil, which she had not really been glad to see just when she was finally all washed and clean and bathed.

Oh, she had done her best, she had been gung-ho and ready for anything and full of her own sound effects, not exactly faked but certainly exaggerated and emphasized. And Dan had also been full of enthusiasm. It had been, Maggie thought, one of those connubial collaborations: Let's not admit that we'd both rather go right to sleep. Or maybe not — what does she really know about him, anyway? Maybe he truly felt all sexy and romantic, maybe it was a real and true sexy and romantic moment, and she was just trapped in her stupid endless circles of tension and anxiety and sorrow. *If they find out, I will kill myself.*

And Dan was asleep now, his breath whistling slightly, the thick comforter tucked tightly round his legs. He would toss it off during the night; he tended to feel warm when he slept, and though he gladly snuggled down at night with blankets, he always ended up sprawled in his cotton pajamas on the mattress, uncovered and unrestrained. Maggie herself rolled her side of the comforter well under her body; she did not tend to feel warm when she slept and had woken up shivering often enough to find that Dan had thrown the blankets overboard. There was in fact a very distinct kind of chilly dream that she had come to know, a dream in which images and pictures were haunted by an anxious sense of something gone, something missing, something cold, and she finally moved toward consciousness as toward the wall of a pool, shimmering at the end of a lane of underwater swimming, finally reached for it, touched it, and hauled herself up and out and into the full awareness of how cold she was.

If they find out, I will have to kill myself. There it was, simple and unadorned and flat and so, so sad. What made her eyes fill with tears, earlier at the dinner table and now again in bed, as she blotted them against her pillow, was a sudden notion of the world after her death, moving on without her. The bleakness, the absolute, convincing, matter-of-fact bleakness of it: They find out, I kill myself. I am dead, and the world goes on.

This was, she knew perfectly well, insane. If she were not so numb and sad, she would be shocked and horrified at herself. She had no patience for melodrama, hated the very idea of suicide. Back during her training, working on the adolescent ward with anorexic girls starving themselves into cardiac arrhythmias, punked-out boys who achieved toxic levels of alcohol, she had taken care of those patients full of her silent fury, balancing their electrolytes and nudging their bodies back toward the vigor they had so deliberately wasted. And in the next room, down the hall, all through the hospital, people who would have given anything for a little bit of the health these idiots threw away. And now look at her: She works only with newborns, with babies who are doing the damn best they can with the little that was given to them. Look at Felicia Grassini, Baby Girl Grassini, Surviving Twin. I bang on the table and tell those fools, Full court press! If this baby needs surgery, then she gets surgery — she goes to the OR just like you go to the OR. Period, end of discussion! And they look at me like I'm a crazy extremist — but Felicia didn't have to go to surgery — no, she didn't — we rested her stomach and the baby started to get better. All by herself. And that means I was right all along, doesn't it? She *wants* to get better. Every gram of her wants to get better and grow up. You don't give up on a baby like that.

If they find out, I will have to kill myself. Maggie tossed restlessly in her blanket cocoon, as if she could rid herself of this stupidity by shaking it off. Of course I won't have to kill myself. Number one, no one will find out. Number two, if they did they wouldn't care. Stop it, stop thinking about it, go to sleep. Think about other things.

And she did think about other things, but then it came back. It had been coming back and coming back for a couple of days now, ever since that first moment in the hallway, ever since she remembered. All along, Maggie has not been afraid. After all, as she keeps telling herself, there are no threats against her in the letters. But now she is afraid. She had been able to do her job, watch over the babies. Ease up the vigilance on Felicia Grassini a little, as she seemed to respond well to the antibiotics. Felicia stabilized, her belly got no worse, then started to get a little better; it might be time to try feeding her again in a couple of days. But when Maggie encountered Felicia's father, when she caught him looking at her with what she thought was suspicion, she would feel that reflexive familiar anxiety. *What if they find out? What if he finds out?* Whenever she wasn't bent over a baby, it seemed to her, the same thoughts intruded, unwelcome and insistent in her head. It was so familiar it was almost ridiculous by now, already, and work was her only good defense, and when she had signed over the service to David Susser for her weekend off, she had felt a certain foreboding, as

247

if she were giving away her only props, leaving herself completely unsupported, undefended, wide open.

In fact, she had already made up her mind that if Felicia Grassini was getting sicker, she would not take the weekend off, tradition or no tradition, hotel reservations or no. She knew Dan would be very upset, that he would be hurt, that he would ask her angrily how it was possible that she was the only doctor in the world who could take care of this patient. Grandiosity, delusion, loss of proportion — she knew how it would look. But she would not go away and leave this child whose father did not trust her; she would prove herself and win his trust and get the baby through. But then the baby got a little better. So she signed over the service and got gamely into the car with Dan, and he headed them north into New Hampshire, where they had a reservation at that overgrown country inn with the celebrated restaurant that Dan had read about and remembered. And so she lay in bed now in a room far away from the familiar traffic noises of her own home, and worried.

If they find out. If they find out. Okay, look. When she was a graduate student, when she decided to apply to medical school, her adviser was not pleased. He was a rather removed man, frequently chagrined at what he considered some small slight or other to his own academic importance, but generally fair to his students as long as they worked their asses off. Maggie had had several tentative conversations with him on the subject of medical school and her own evolving plans, and he had nodded absently. But then, when she actually applied, he took it as one more slap in the face; he essentially stopped speaking to her. He looked right through her, he made nasty references to doctors and their science-blind stupidity, and even to the money Maggie would earn as a suburban dermatologist, all disguised as jokes offered to other underlings in her presence. Maggie became frightened: Without his backing, she would not get into a good medical school. And, if she did not get into a good medical school, maybe did not get into any medical school at all, then what would become of her? Her scientific future was shot to hell, her adviser had turned against her, she would be nothing.

So one night when she had been working late in the lab when no one else was there, she went through the connecting door into his secretary's office, turned on the computer, and found the letter of recommendation he had written for her. She had given him only one envelope so far, one medical school to send it to, but she had another twenty ready at home. It was in fact a crummy letter, luke-warm and grudging. *I am writing to recommend,* not *I am happy to recommend. I support her application,* not *she has my most enthusiastic support. She has my recommendation,* not *my highest recommendation.* All the secret code words for mediocre. You would have read it and felt that Maggie's adviser was trying to say something nice about her, hard though it was, because he hoped against hope that she would get into medical school and get out of his lab.

This was, after all, the beginning of the computer age: Maggie made a few changes. Nothing big, nothing dramatic. *Adequate* to *accomplished, careful* to *competent and conscientious.* Added the *I will be very sorry to lose her but I fully support her decision* sentence that seemed so conspicuous by its absence. The *one of the two or three best students I have ever worked with* sentence. She knew the secretary would proof the letter only for spelling (or perhaps had already proofed it, before sending it out to the first school) and would sign it for her boss, as she signed all his correspondence.

And the secretary did, and the letter went out — or so Maggie assumed. Certainly she never heard anything more about it, and certainly she got into a couple of medical schools. And to be honest, she forgot quite quickly and handily about that little late-night act of word processor vandalism. She had not, after all, faked any credential that she didn't have. And at the time, really, if she had thought about it at all she would probably have seen it as sort of a good joke, a clever way to turn the tables on an adviser who had behaved like a jerk because he had to take it personally that she wanted to do something a little bit different from what he did. Truly, she had not thought of that evening in years, of her solitary tap-tapping in the secretary's office, of her slight nervousness, telling herself that if someone came in, some other student with an experiment to do, she would just say she was typing up an abstract —

but of course, no one came. No one saw her do it, no one noticed it had been done. And she had not thought about it in years, and no one else had ever thought about it, and no one ever would.

Oh, but now they might. Maggie sat upright in the unfamiliar bed. Picture the accusations continuing: *She faked her research, there are lies on her resume.* Eventually, just to satisfy itself that there is no truth to any of this, the hospital investigates. After all, they've already pulled her medical school information, her health services records, her transcript. Maggie winced at the memory of the health services records; she and Dan have not discussed that since he first read her file, but surely they will have to again, someday. But once the powers that be start investigating, who knows what's next. Easy to imagine: They ask to see her research notebooks, all well and good. They go through that accreditation folder more carefully, check her residency years, her medical school transcript — and then, when they check her medical school application, there it is. And of course they will check it; right now in the middle of the night it seemed clear and obvious that they would have to check it. People fake things all the time, research of course, but not just research; they try to go to medical school when they never graduated from college, or they calculate their grade point averages the wrong way to make themselves look like better science students — the hospital would definitely check her out as far back as college. And then they come to her old adviser, a famous scientist whose name might even be familiar, whose academic halo will be reassuring to all, and they ask him, Did you in fact have Maggie Claymore working in your lab? Did you in fact write this letter about her?

She got out of bed, moving quietly. The bed seemed very high off the floor. She would not risk turning on a light, since sometimes Dan slept badly in strange rooms. She took refuge in the bathroom, a showpiece of gray and yellow tile, that deep yellow bathtub. Maggie sat on the edge of the bathtub, which would no doubt figure in Dan's scenario for tomorrow, and instead of thinking even vaguely of sex and wet, tangled bodies, she was thinking of her old adviser's face, of his delight as he looked at the letter plucked from her old file, as he realized that he had her, he had her, he was going to bring her down.

250

She covered her face with her hands, flinching at the chill they transmitted from the tiles where they had been resting. This is ridiculous, this is absurd. Okay, the list of reasons why. The list was as familiar as a prayer; she had been offering it again and again over the last few days, on the ride up to New Hampshire today, across the table in the restaurant, making love to Dan. The list of reasons why. Even if they start verifying things, they'll never go that far back. They might conceivably check formally to see that I really did get my M.D., but that's as far as anyone would go. And even if they did want to verify that I worked in his lab, they'd never bother going to see him, handing him the letter. Just a phone call, probably just to his secretary: Was she there from this date to that? Thanks, just checking. And if they did for some unbelievable reason give him the letter, he wouldn't remember that he didn't write it this way. After all, that's more than fifteen years ago, a lot of graduate students and letters of recommendation under the bridge.

"It was what I deserved," Maggie said softly into her hands. She pushed back her hair, then stood up, looked earnestly into the mirror over the dove gray sink. A triptych mirror with angled sides; three reflections to choose among. Her face looked quite ordinary and familiar to her, marked neither by the tragedy of an entire career going down in flames nor by the off-base look of a crazy woman.

"The thing that bothers me," she whispered to the three mirror faces, "is that once they find one thing that I faked, once it sounds like one of the accusations does have some truth to it, they may start feeling that there's bound to be some truth in all of them. If I faked a credential, then maybe I did fake my research."

Hearing the words, even whispered, gave them a certain frightening reality. They were in the air, they existed. But oddly enough, at the same time, Maggie found that the melodramatic hiss of her own voice also shifted the perspective back: You are an overtired, overfed, overstressed crazy person in a nightgown hissing at yourself in the mirror. It's time to go back to bed and get some sleep.

The next morning it was no longer storming, but a sleety drizzle streaked the windows and dappled the muddy fields outside. There was an enormous "country breakfast," complete with overflowing breadbasket and quantities of pancakes, and then one group of guests headed for a nearby factory outlet shopping mall. They were sociably determined to recruit as many people as possible for this enterprise, but Maggie and Dan went instead to the big living room and sprawled in front of the fireplace, sitting and not reading the local paper while behind them a very bright twelve-year-old boy beat his father three times running at backgammon.

Dan reached over and stroked the back of Maggie's hand, stroked it with his own fingers turned away, so that the nails rubbed against her skin. He smiled at her, and once again she had that sense of marital connivance, of a deception aimed at proving what a wonderful time they were having. She told him softly what a great place this was, how they would have to come back in summer when there were walks to be taken, in foliage season, in winter maybe, to ski cross country, and then was suddenly afraid she had made it sound as if there was no point to their being here right now.

"Let's go back to the room," he said. "It's a good day to be lazy."

"Okay," she answered, smiling at him, nodding, feeling once again that she was acting, that she was covering up, that she was faking it.

Maggie Claymore and her husband were going away for the weekend, and Hank Shoemaker knew it. He had eaten lunch on Friday with her, part of a big group of doctors, Hank keeping quiet, keeping himself to himself, listened to a bunch of idiots commiserate with Maggie: How awful about those posters on the bulletin boards, we hear there were more of them this week, isn't it creepy. And those crazy letters — have there been more letters, Maggie? What's the hospital doing about it, anyway?

Hank cut his soggy tuna melt into even little square pieces, ate them one by one with a knife and fork. Eating with his colleagues, he tended to get paranoid about anything they might see as gross, might laugh about later — food on his clothes, big bites, the smell of tuna on his fingers. Listened with pleasure as Maggie whined on about how clueless the hospital security people were. *Because they're up against a fucking genius avenger, that's why.* And when she said, No new letters recently, he bent his head so no one would note with surprise any hint of a knowing smile on his face. The new letters would be arriving today. And they were, he felt, particularly clever; instead of making it seem like a campaign of random complaints about Maggie, this that and the other thing, everything but the kitchen sink, this new suggestion that she was drunk or drugged out gave the whole thing a pleasant cohesion. She's dangerous, she's out of control — you can't trust her, not her judgment, not her word, not anything. Everyone's always worried about the impaired physician — well, here she is!

Now Maggie was modestly agreeing that it had been a little rough being on service with all this going on, but then she switched over to showing off: Clinical work was so absorbing, so good for distracting her, taking her mind off these crazy letters. Hank smiled to himself: he'd just bet. Well, true or not, welcome back to full-time wondering about it, Dr. Claymore. What a self-dramatizing, grab-the-spotlight bitch she was, anyway, using the letters and the posters to make herself out as a heroine for doing her goddamn job. Wait till people started to wonder what little molecules were pumping through her bloodstream those nights when she was watching over those patients. Wait till people looked at her and thought, Well, where there's smoke . . .

As he ate his last little square of tuna and white bread and melted American cheese, Hank heard something that truly interested him: Maggie Claymore and her husband were going away for the weekend. To some inn up in New Hampshire, where it turned out that two other people had already been, where she said Harvey Weintraub had also been. It was more boasting, showing off: We're just going to drive away and spend the weekend eating and drinking and fucking — I'm so lucky, my husband loves me, he knows all about wine, I'm so brave. And listen to all the others murmuring, Good idea, you really need that, you need to get away.

Hank did look up from his plate now, looked right at Maggie Claymore. Looked at her blankly, telling himself there was after all no way that she could possibly see anything strange in his gaze; he was only looking at her to note what she was wearing, what she was eating. A light blue sweater with the collar of a white blouse sticking up, a necklace made of what looked like a length of gold rope.

He liked knowing that to her he was just one more colleague, sitting at lunch and eating cafeteria food and talking shop, standard stuff. He even liked nodding in unison sympathy with the others at the table: Poor Maggie, hardworking Maggie. He liked knowing that none of them noticed a thing. He was quiet Hank who cut his food up small. And so he looked at Maggie but did not quite meet her eyes, looked instead at the remains of the salad on her plate.

And it was right then that the idea hit him: what he would do while she was away. Do something to her house! He would make her feel she wasn't safe even there. Go to her house, maybe write something on the door, maybe just hang up signs all over it. He would do it late Saturday night. There would be no one there to see him, no one who could recognize him — and then when she and her husband got home, all fat and proud and lovey-dovey on Sunday, they would find proof that there was no safety, no escaping. He was both frightened and thrilled by this idea — so risky! Hank was so careful, so law-abiding — never vandalized anything, never, heaven knows, actually attacked anyone. He had already taken chances that made him anxious and excited — going into Maggie's office, or especially hanging up those posters. But this would be much chancier — after all, he had every reason for being anywhere in the hospital, as long as no one saw him actually hanging a sign. He had no reason for being at her home.

And so he sat there, among his colleagues, and chewed with his mouth closed, and laughed at someone's hospital joke, congenial and unremarkable, and thought about going to visit Maggie Claymore's house while she was out of town. If he went late, after dark, if he knew they were gone until the next day — he was transfixed, delighted, thrilled by the idea of the two of them coming home, walking up to the house, arms around each other, and stopping, seeing signs on the house. DOCTOR MAGGIE CLAYMORE MURDERS CHILDREN. Something like that. Welcome home.

20

Maggie in the Caribbean

ANOTHER BATHROOM: Maggie in the shower in the Caribbean, to be exact, in a small but perfectly nice hotel bathroom in a resort on an island with white beaches and blue water. Getting ready to go out to dinner; no drive, no sleet, no hurry. Reflecting, as she arranges her little bottles along the side of the tub, on the number of products a woman needs to pack, to carry, to use. On the soap and the shampoo and the conditioner and the facial scrub and the shaving lotion and the moisturizer. All this, and I'm not even particularly pretty. And Dan will unwrap the little white cake of hotel soap and not think about it for a single second.

It does definitely make you more conscious of your appearance, a day on the beach watching other people's bodies, women in bikini bottoms cut so high on their thighs and buttocks that you can plainly see they have no pubic hair at all. Long-legged, bare-breasted women, athletic beautiful-bodied ease, Europeans lying out in the sun, coating themselves with coconut oil as if no one ever heard of skin cancer. And, needless to say, smoking, and making it look kind of glamorous, even to a moralistic doctor.

Maggie rubbing conditioner into her hair. They go regularly on vacation, Maggie and Dan. Somewhere warm every winter; Dan chooses. They both like ocean swimming, and Dan has been known to go windsurfing, but most emphatically they do not hang-glide or aquaplane or even water ski. Maggie lies on the beach and reads thrillers. She watches Dan swim. She's willing to do various silly tourist activities as required, wander in the market, watch a dinner show with native dancing, take a short drive in a van to see a historic building. She lets Dan lead her first to the most expensive restaurants, where he is inevitably disappointed, and then to some well-publicized off-the-beaten-track local dive that he can enthuse about when they get back. She doesn't bring home baskets or pottery, and she doesn't remember the facts about the historic buildings. Settled by pirates, or fought a war with Spain or France or England, based on a traditional courtship dance or a harvest celebration, fort built two hundred years ago or four hundred years ago, used as a church or now a local craft cooperative, incorporating African rhythmic elements with Spanish flamenco steps — it has to be said that it's all pretty much the same to Maggie.

Getting out of the shower, wrapping her head in one big white hotel towel, her body in another. Marching out into the cool of the air-conditioned room, looking down at Dan, who is lying across the bed, watching TV. Maggie thinking, Well, Mr. Hotel Soap, Hotel Shampoo, never think twice about it — here I am, scraped and scrubbed and conditioned, and behold me. Not beautiful. His body, already slightly brown, conjuring up the memory of his body in the water. Talk about beautiful. But even this is a sort of automatic and fond familiar moment, a marital recognition of who she is and who he is, which is not without its tiny tinge of smugness. He's mine, I'm his.

These vacations they take — they are easy and pleasant and in their minor variations and their major resort hotel samenesses, they are as relaxing as they are supposed to be. And of course they are also evidence of a certain kind of success, financial, professional. And marital: Look, here we are together, here we go together on vacation, a recommended resort, a nice big bed. But the vacations are also still a reaction against those weird and cut-rate boardwalk boarding house summers when she was little, those fraught and promiscuous weeks at Bethlehem Pines when she was in high school. Here I am now. I am a grownup; I am normal. And maybe also a reaction against her mother and that bed-and-break-fast she runs with her second husband in Arizona, a bed-and-breakfast decked out with Victorian furniture and tasseled pillows, with marble-topped washstands and flowered china pitchers, with Bible mottoes on the walls and devotional books in the bookcases and the night tables, a regimen of informal morning prayer gatherings before the homemade muffins are laid out in the breakfast room. Her mother sends out a newsletter every couple of months to all her regulars, keeping them up to date on renovations and new antique acquisitions, and also on her family life. She sends a copy to Maggie, of course, and Maggie has been more than a little mortified to find her own doings reported: my heroic, baby-saving doctor daughter (oh, and of course she can guess how they feel about abortions, the people on this particular mailing list). Pray for her and for the babies she cares for.

Maggie is grown up enough to tell her mother, Thanks for the kind words, great job on the newsletter. Even, mumbling slightly, Thanks for the prayers. But she will never drag Dan to stay at that bed-and-breakfast, no matter how many invitations. Occasionally she has thought of suggesting to Dan a driving trip in the United States, a trip to Luray Caverns to see if the underground chambers are as she remembers them. But she doesn't mention it; they don't do that kind of vacation trip. No, she will go with Dan on trips that make sense to them both, and he can consult the wine list, or sample the local beer or the rum cocktails, thank you very much. She and Dan will bake in the sun and eye the bodies of sleek strangers, more or less surreptitiously or conspiratorially. They will go together to normal hotels, to anonymous rooms, anonymous showers, anonymous clean white towels.

21

Search Needs

HANK: Saturday night as he was driving there, it occurred to
him that he had never before been curious to look at her
house. He didn't want to know the details of her life, resented those he did have to know. Who cared where she lived, who
cared what she thought, who cared about her stupid trips away
with her stupid wretch of a husband. It was a cold, clear night, and
Hank wore a winter coat and a heavy wool hat; he would pull it
down in front, tuck his chin down into the coat collar, and no one
would ever be able to identify him, even if someone saw him. In his
briefcase beside him on the seat were ten copies of the sign, tape,
thumbtacks. He was wearing wool gloves, and under his gloves
were plastic hospital gloves, surgical gloves. He had worn them
when he was printing out the signs, would wear them when he tore
the tape or pressed the thumbtacks. He was smart, thorough, careful. Like the way he had located her house on a Jamaica Plain street
map, and now parked three blocks away, parked carefully in a legal
spot, his car neatly in line with a row of other cars. Hiked up his
collar, tucked in his chin, pulled down his hat. Put the briefcase under his arm, pressed it close with his elbow, dug his gloved hands
deep into his pockets, and started out. Hope you've had a nice day,
Maggie. Hope you've really enjoyed getting away, and you haven't

been worrying about what might happen at home. Hope you've been feeling safe.

Maggie and Dan: But this time, when they go up to the room and make love, it does work. Sex, right here and now, drowns out the insane chorus in Maggie's brain. Ordinary sex, no new little vibrating toy produced out of Dan's suitcase, no fancy leather straps to take advantage of the antique bedposts. The two of them, full of food and contented from their breakfast, sit together on their big soft bed, staring out the window, past the flowered curtains and the lace undercurtains, out to the silver-gray day. They kiss and kiss, fully clothed, and then slowly slide their hands under each other's clothes. Maggie lets the beginning of her beach movie scroll out in her head, and she's there, she's on the beach, she's dizzy, bemused with arousal, overwhelmingly grateful to be enjoying the moment. Not to be thinking about letters of recommendation and being found out.

Dan is off the bed, kneeling between her legs, tugging her jeans and her underpants down around her ankles. She kicks them off, and her feet, still in their warm blue socks, she laces together over his shoulders, behind his neck. His tongue as he licks his way into her feels thick and just a little warmer than her own body. He likes to do this, loves to do this; when they first started sleeping together, she remembers, she was embarrassed that he would want to do this — to eat her out, he had called it, the first time she had ever heard that expression — and go on doing it, and sometimes even do it instead of intercourse. And he did not necessarily do it so that she would pay him back, he did it because he liked to; he was more aroused afterward than he was to begin with, which made him, according to Sarah, Maggie's roommate way back then and therefore the only person with whom Maggie had discussed this in detail, many women's true dream lover.

Now she lies back on the bed, naked legs, nice warm feet in her woolly socks, looks up at the ceiling, at the aggressively countrified border of stenciled sunflowers marching around the walls. Her hand moves gently in Dan's hair, and she pictures him, all those years ago, when they first met in medical school. And a little alarm in her brain: *Getting too close, think about other things,* but she doesn't think about other things. She thinks about Dan, back then; she can hear his hoarse voice, saying in bed, in his dorm room, back all those years ago, saying, I love to eat you out.

Unfortunately, as soon as Maggie allows herself to think, Oh good, I'm not thinking about that, she is thinking about it again. Not crazily, not even enough to keep her from enjoying herself, but steadily with one small part of her mind.

In books, Maggie has noticed, people stop thinking when they have sex. In trashy novels maybe they disappear into clouds of flowers or great ocean waves or something stupid like that, or they lose all grammar and punctuation. Is it abnormal to think in a straight line right through your own orgasm? The orgasm is real enough, not like that trumped-up stuff she pulled last night, but as her feet twist together more tightly, as her butt clenches and lifts slightly off the bed, pressing her into his face, as she makes her perfectly genuine noises, what she is thinking, clearly and distinctly, is, In the end, after all, if worse comes to worst, if they show him the letter and if he knows it's different from the letter he wrote, even then it would only be his word against mine — and he'll have to explain why he signed the letter in the first place.

Dan lies down beside her, and she traces his slippery lips with her finger, traces her hand down around his neck and begins to unbutton his shirt. Both naked, they wrap themselves in the comforter together, and Dan points to the window, where the sun is coming out. He strokes her hair, and they lie there, bodies pressed skin to skin, full length. He is hard against her belly but content for the moment to hold her and be held.

"I just want to tell you" — his mouth close to her ear — "you've been incredibly tough about this whole thing — about all this crazy stuff going on. I've been really impressed."

"Thank you." Maggie rubbing against him, but feeling . . . no, not entirely pleased. Will it end eventually, this sense of being disgraced, marked, and shamed?

"Do you think maybe we should hire a lawyer?" He is still talking softly into her ear; she can feel his warm breath.

"There's Elaine Oliphant — the hospital lawyer — I told you about her. She's smart." Stop it, leave it behind. Make love to me, for crying out loud.

"She doesn't represent you. She represents them. She's not on your side, Maggie!" For Dan it so quickly becomes us and them. Maggie wants to say, But if she represents the hospital, then she represents me, but she says nothing.

He is slipping inside her now, and in fact her body is still so roused and so attuned to him that in spite of all the nonsense, all the noise in her brain, she is moving against him, moaning, reaching down to grab his ass and pull him against her. They are suddenly sweaty in motion, wrapped in their blanket, then Dan raises himself up on his hands, shaking off the blanket, pulling their upper bodies apart so that only there at the center are they connected. Maggie lets her arms flop back over her head, lifts up her feet and centers them neatly on the round hills of his bottom as he goes into his piston act, his pushups. She closes her eyes and listens to his heavy breathing and his grunting and the slap of his body into hers, and then she lets go of it all, lets go of everything, loses herself in the rhythm, in the run-on sentence, although the beat in her head is the same: This makes it better, makes it better, makes it better, hide the letter, hide the letter, hide the letter.

Still, when they are up and dressed and out together, enjoying the suddenly pleasant day, she feels that certain smug domestic triumph that comes when a weekend away is going well. The room is fine, the food is good, we're getting it on, even the weather is cooperating. The only odd thing is this sense that she is congratulating herself on pulling something off, some silly movie-of-the-week stunt, smiling through the trip to Paris without letting on that she is dying of radiation poisoning. Smiling and playing along and all the time, carrying her terrible secret: *If they find out, I will kill myself.*

Hank: He had not intended to go in. He was imagining only that shock of violation they would feel when they came back and saw their house marked with the posters. He had not even meant to try the front door. It felt risky and daring enough already, this climb

261

onto her porch with his hands in surgical gloves and his pockets full of signs — it was the most dangerous thing he had ever done. In fact, he had never done anything remotely like this before; he meant to hang his signs and hurry back to the car, and he could already imagine the sense of relief as he started the engine and drove away. But the house was dark, through and through, and he stood there on the front porch, keeping carefully to the deep shadows up against the wall. His hands were safely gloved, after all, gloved in surgical gloves and then in ordinary gloves; there was no reason he shouldn't reach inside Maggie Claymore's mailbox — perhaps he would fold up one of the posters, leave it in there. He should have brought a special letter to leave for her right here in her own mailbox. *Dear Doctor Claymore I know who you are and where you live and what you are and I will not rest till you have been exposed and the world knows you for the criminal and the fake that you know you really are.* Hank was particularly proud of that last batch of letters, the ones about the drug abuse. He had been better than clever, look how skillfully he had made himself sound like a nurse. *(If I can collect enough evidence about so-called Doctor Claymore to prove my case then I will present it even if it means my own necessity to retire early but it is hard to make an accusation against a doctor and press the charges . . .)*

So go ahead, check out the nurses; the hospital brass know perfectly well that when a nurse makes an accusation like substance abuse or erratic behavior, takes that heavy, fraught step of calling out a doctor, she usually knows what she is talking about. Oh, they would be worrying and worrying, wondering what to ask Maggie, and even more what to ask *about* Maggie. And maybe she would in fact get all tense and anxious, maybe medicate herself a little bit. That's all it would take, a tranquilizer every now and then, and things could look very bad for her. Let her do it, let her prescribe something for herself, let her steal something out of a med cabinet and let some sharp-eyed nurse notice her: Isn't that the doctor all those letters were about? Well, I saw her doing something very concerning, very inappropriate, so I just felt I needed to let you know right away, Dr. Weintraub.

The fucking front door was open! He had tried the knob, the

262

same way he had slipped his hand into the mailbox; it was intriguing, that was all — intriguing to be here, shadowing her, touching the things she touched every day. But what the hell did it mean that the fucking door was open? Even if they were home, people presumably didn't leave their doors unlocked at night in fucking Jamaica Plain — they must have gone away in some kind of flurry, upset maybe by the latest accusations; they must have forgotten to lock up. And even as these thoughts presented themselves, Hank had opened the door, folded himself silently into the shadows of the dark house, pulled the door silently closed behind him. This was dangerous, he knew, this was far from what he had intended, but then again, what a gift, what a sign from heaven. Her house delivered up to him like this, welcoming him in. He knew they were away — he'd heard her say it yesterday at lunch, they had reservations. And here it was, nine o'clock at night, and the house pitch dark — empty and unlocked and waiting for him. He would stay here and listen for a while, make sure no one was there, and then he would go into her house, go upstairs to her bedroom, say, and leave her some messages. Why, if someone were to ask what he was doing there, he would just say, I'm a colleague of Dr. Claymore's. I was in the neighborhood, thought I'd drop in, then got worried when the door was wide open and the house was dark. I have no idea where she's been all day, or what she's been doing. I hope she's okay. I hope nothing's happened to her.

Maggie and Dan: They drive into the nearest small town and browse dutifully through a string of antique stores. Maggie finds a pitcher that almost exactly matches the one her mother had when she was a child; bulbous, thick, lime green frosted glass with small gilt stars scattered over it. Does that one still hold pride of place in her mother's new home, or could it in fact have found its way here after some wanderings, the same pitcher that presided, frosting over with iced tea in warm weather, over the vinyl National Parks place mats and wood-grained plastic salad bowls of her childhood? She does not point it out to Dan, who is much occupied with a vintage game of Go to the Head of the Class, the same exact edition he played with as a child. Is this what people do in antique stores, match random items up against their own histories, like some great game of bingo?

"Did you win?" Maggie asked, returning the pitcher hurriedly to its shelf, concealing it in fact behind a tall white vase and a crystal decanter.

"I was an ace. I think my parents used to let me."

He closes the game and puts it back on the shelf, and Maggie thinks about her mother's dining room table and sees herself back from college on one of the vacations that she kept as brief as possible. Sitting at the table, so carefully set for two, pitcher in the center. Eating her mother's salad, festive with canned mandarin oranges, and pontificating about genetics and the meaning of life. And her mother smiling and nodding and waiting, perhaps, for Maggie to finish up and get moving so that she could invent her own life — like mother, like daughter. Maybe they were both in a hurry to get on with it, and Annalisa just did a better job of covering up her eagerness.

Maybe she's no more nostalgic for it than I am, Maggie thinks. Maybe that really is her pitcher and she gave it away as soon as she could, gave everything away and started over. And she suppresses a brief urge to go back and find the pitcher, and buy it and take it home.

Instead they stroll on, arm in arm, to a self-proclaimed country store, linger briefly among the novelty potholders and maple sugar candy. Objects decorated with pictures of cows or colored leaves, though the foliage season is recently over. They are not shoppers, not souvenir buyers — they do not like to live with clutter. Maggie buys some leaf-shaped maple candy for Penelope, and Dan chooses a postcard to send his friend who had recommended the hotel, a postcard of the nearby hills taken when the fall foliage was at its height. Now the colors are gone, but we know they were there.

Hank: He waited and he waited. The house was silent. Light came in through a round window just above his eye level and showed him the entrance hall. A large staircase led up to the second floor; oddly, it was fenced off with a child safety gate. He would go upstairs, find her bedroom, yes, make her feel she was not safe or private even there. Maybe leave one of the signs neatly on her pillow? Or even under her pillow? Imagine that: Doctor Maggie gets into bed, not suspecting a thing, then feels a paper crunching under the pillow, reaches under, and there it is, smack between the eyes. *I see everything. I am everywhere.*

It was time to move forward, to do his errand. He unhooked the baby gate. What the hell did she mean having a baby gate? He folded the gate neatly to the side and climbed the stairs as silently as he could, keeping close to the wall, reminding himself firmly that someone just might be up there, someone might be asleep, someone might suddenly appear, switch on the lights, cry out. His hat was pulled down as far as it would go, and he would remember the way out; any noise and he would run. But surely this was meant to be; even the full moon shining through the big windows all through the house was meant to be. No one would interrupt him, no one would ever find him out. He had never done anything like this before; no one who knew him would ever imagine him as he was right now, but that only made him stronger. He had power and righteousness and absolute invulnerability. He felt himself moving with grace, as he never moved in the hospital or in his own home, as if he knew his way.

It was, therefore, mildly disconcerting to climb the stairs and find himself not in her bedroom as he was expecting, but in her living room. In the dim light it seemed surprisingly plain, an anonymous room bordered by smooth-cornered furniture. Anyone's room. Hank thought, with some pride and some disgust, of his own living room, of the colors and complexity his wife had introduced and had now left behind her. He was not taking care of it; it seemed to him now, in fact, that he had resented it for years, resented having to live amid her artifacts, her spindly legged bits of furniture, her standing lamps, her droopy Indian scarves. At home now he was left watching the carefully arranged rooms deteriorate into squalor, as he dumped his dirty clothes on the couch in the evening, undressing in front of the TV, left the newspaper on top of the plastic tubs that had held his microwaved frozen dinner. He still did his laundry, dressed carefully, went out into the world careful and dignified and neat and clean and normal, but at home, he knew, things were slowly crumbling. Still, what did it matter, as long as he looked okay to the rest of the world? The house could damn well go ahead and disintegrate; it served his wife right. Sooner or later, he supposed, he would shift the TV into the bedroom. What would become of the rest of the house, ignored, untouched, and haunted?

And here he was instead in a room that was a temple to someone else's marriage. The light coming in through the window glinted off only a couple of framed pictures, fronted with glass. Most of the walls were bare; the room was empty by his standards, by his wife's standards, not much furniture, walls almost blank.

He passed through a set of open double doors into their dining room. Just one big oval table, six chairs set around it, once again nothing on the walls, nothing in the center of the table. Cindy had gone in for candlesticks and arrangements of flowers and vines, pinecones and dried grasses. Hank had never really liked them, had occasionally even complained that they took up too much space, but he felt now a kind of pride; he was still married to someone who understood how to live more gracefully than these people.

A door opened off the dining room, and he went in and found himself in a small and crowded study. A bookcase higher than his head, a desk loaded with a computer and stacks of paper, the desk a board placed across two filing cabinets, and yet another filing cabinet against the wall, leaning slightly toward him, it seemed to Hank, as if the floor was not quite even. And the whole room was really only the size of a big closet. He was eager to look through the papers, to see what was there — did he dare turn on the light? He tiptoed back through the dining room, into the living room, stood listening to hear if there were any footsteps, any noises, any suggestion of anyone at home. Nothing. Silence. The slight hum of an empty house.

Well, then, he would be brave. His hand was sweaty inside its two gloves, and he set the briefcase down neatly on the couch. Okay, he would allow himself ten minutes in the study, then up to the bedroom and leave the note under her pillow, then get the fuck out of here. His feet were soft on the carpeting as he went back into the study, turned on the architect's lamp over the desk. It was an unexpectedly bright light, illuminating the whole room but casting in particular a glaring bright spot on the desk. He squinted against the brightness, then slipped off his thick wool gloves, flexed his fingers in their pale elastic coating. I am the burglar, I am the spy, I am the Avenger. I do what I want and no one is safe from me.

He could do anything. He could tear the papers into shreds, he could smash the computer screen. But of course he would do no such thing, no vandalism, nothing so crude, nothing so easy. He was, after all, not crazy, not out of control. She was the enemy, and she had left her door unlocked, and because he wasn't crazy, only clever, he would take advantage of that to do something clever and cruel, something that only a true Avenger would think of doing. He just had to think of it, that's all. He wanted her to come home and see what he had done and feel not only fear, not only violation, but also the scary, cold certainty that her enemy was on to her, knew more than she knew, held her in his power.

A pleasing fantasy: What if he altered her computer, changed it so that whenever it was turned on what came immediately to the screen was a long catalogue of everyone who despised Maggie Claymore and why? Or what if, buried deep in one computer file or another, was a paragraph about how she had faked her data, or maybe how she had invented her whole CV — imagine that, a confession — she might not ever see it, might just print it out as part of something, maybe even submit it to a journal. But he had neither the skill to reprogram her computer nor the time to go through the files.

In fact, however, what he found on the desk was an odd mixture of tantalizing and disappointing. It was really sort of a household desk, the stuff was all bills and tax forms and papers about refinancing the mortgage. Everything was sorted neatly, receipts for bills already paid, mortgage papers. Hank looked with some interest at the copies of their income tax returns from last year, Maggie and her husband's. As he had suspected, Maggie's salary was higher than his own. He felt a surge of hot, sick anger. Yes, indeed, together Maggie and her asshole husband made quite a lot of money, what seemed like way too much money for two people. He and Cindy, after all, had managed on less than half of what Maggie and her husband threw away on their lives in this bare and boring place. Though if Cindy thought she was going to get any of his money now, she had some news coming to her. It was one thing to support her while she diddled around and thought about going back to school and getting some bullshit nutrition degree, shopped, and took care of the house. But he was not going to pay her any goddamn alimony. Go ahead, let her practice herbalism and support herself that way.

It pissed him off, though, Maggie Claymore and her dweeb husband with so much money. Ever since Cindy had left, cleared out just as she had been promising to do, he had been even angrier at Maggie. As if it were her fault or something, though once again he knew it was not her fault. Not anyone's fault but Cindy's. But he hated Maggie, and he hated her more now, and that was Cindy's fault too. And you can go straight to hell, Maggie Claymore, wherever you are.

Maggie and Dan: Their second night in the hotel, Saturday night. A long afternoon walk over a nearby hill, slogging over muddy ground under a progressively brighter sky, another big fancy dinner, coffee in front of a blazing fire in the living room. Very nice. Marveling to each other about how tired they felt, all that fresh air. Wink, wink, and up to bed. And yes, Dan had noticed the bedposts and did indeed produce straps, and fine. Maggie likes that kind of thing well enough, and she does, truly, respect the impulse that makes Dan so determined to work on their sex life, to introduce variety and act out fantasies. Has he actually ever had a fantasy about making love to a woman tied to a four-poster bed? Or does it only seem like the kind of fantasy a man might have, should have had, might be expected to have had?

The great thing about being the one who is tied to the bed, of course, is that you are relieved of all responsibility; if you feel particularly energetic, you can writhe against your bonds and moan, but essentially you can assume that you are doing your part by lying there, arms splayed apart, toes pointing. If your foot starts to feel cramped, you can surreptitiously flex it against the leather strap, and this will probably be perceived as just more writhing.

Maggie's own preference would have been for total darkness, since she was after all the one splayed out and exposed, but she was generous enough to be able to imagine that the sight was part of the fantasy, so they left the bathroom light on.

Actually, there have been times when Maggie has found this kind of sex really wildly exciting, unexpectedly, almost embarrassingly exciting. Tonight, this weekend . . . let's face it, she's just kind of preoccupied. And in fact, right in the middle, she gets this sudden and very horrible thought: Imagine if my enemy had a picture of this. And she begins to imagine photos of herself, photos on the hospital bulletin boards, even in the newspapers. Which makes it that much harder to relax. And it seems to take Dan a very long time to come; he's getting older, Maggie thinks, protectively, and three times in twenty-four hours maybe he can't manage so easily anymore. And she thinks deliberately about Dan younger, about Dan when they were in medical school, only to lose that thread of thought and see the newspaper headlines return. KINKY SEX DOC SCANDAL. *This was in private, between consenting adults," protested Dr. Claymore.* It's crazy — she knows it's crazy — but she almost wants to say to Dan, Maybe this is risky. I feel so exposed — maybe we should untie me, turn off the light, maybe we shouldn't take any chances. Think about what's going on, think about my position. My position, indeed! But she says nothing, of course; she stays in her position and waits him out.

Hank: He did not think about Maggie in a sexual way. He thought about her — some days it seemed he thought about her constantly, but it was not sexual. He did not imagine her embraces or even her undressings; it was not that kind of obsession. He hated her, and he desired her humiliation, and he hated her in part, presumably, because she was a woman, felt reproached and mocked by her in part because she was a woman, and therefore one of a long chain of women who had laughed at him or ignored him or thought him insignificant and unappealing or just, perhaps, not really worth noticing. But to be fair, if she had been a man, then she could have joined a similarly long chain of men, grouping together in casual hallway and tennis-court friendships, excluding him, sizing him up and rejecting him or, most often, just not noticing him. Maggie and many of her friends would probably tell you that the medical world is full of male bonding and boys' clubs; Hank, who would never use those terms, could tell you that not all boys are necessarily included. Of course, Maggie would turn right around and say that until you have been female, you don't know what it really means to be excluded, but would that be any comfort at all to someone who has the anatomic credentials and yet feels passed over? He could not, after all, blame this on any group characteristic and therefore was left face to face with personal disqualification, hurt and angry, while Maggie had righteous wrath to sustain her.

He might in some ways seem like an easy villain, that successful-woman-resenting, insecure male who is so ready a bugbear to the professional woman and who does in fact run resentful through corridors everywhere, but he is not actually a rapist manqué. Give him credit for that: He has, in actual fact, paid Maggie the compliment of wanting to see her broken and defeated and humiliated on professional grounds, as a colleague, as a doctor, as a researcher. That these are his fantasies rather than sadomasochistic images of her naked and sexually subjugated body should perhaps win him a few points, even if all accounts are being kept on the negative side of the ledger.

He leafed through the papers on the desk. Could he somehow fuck up the refinancing of the mortgage, could he ruin her credit rating? It didn't seem very satisfying — how would she know that he was behind it? And anyway, too private. It was frustrating to feel so close and yet not be able to see the great gesture.

Hank turned on the computer. The ping as the monitor screen lit up scared him badly. The computer went right into a medical literature index, asked him if he'd like to search. He could run up a big bill, he supposed, tell it to find all articles with the keyword "cell." But it was a puerile idea. He would get out of the medical index and see what else was there, maybe something more personal. But the computer was not like his own, a completely different system, and he was not actually clever about computers. He was a little too old; when he was a science-smart college boy, students had not had their own computers. He had learned how to use the hospital system, of course, but it was the only system he knew. And he was a terrible typist, so word processing irritated him — one mistake after another. It was faster to write things out by hand and give them to the departmental secretary. Now, as he pulled out the desk chair and sat down, facing the monitor, he felt a stiffness in his neck, a tension in his shoulders. The fucking computer would fucking well do as he told it to. He punched the ENTER button with his gloved finger, harder than he needed to. Once again the computer flashed some logos at him and returned him to the beginning of a medical literature search; courteously, it inquired whether he required a full menu of prompts to select his search needs. And he wonders where she is right now, Maggie Claymore, and whether she's thinking about the letters.

Maggie and Dan: Dan unties her, kisses her, and falls asleep immediately — well, three times in twenty-four hours, he's getting older. But Maggie is not tired, and there's no point in lying in bed and agonizing over imaginary headlines, waiting no doubt for other anxieties to take over. In one of the antique stores there had been a shelf of beat-up paperbacks, and for fifty cents she had bought a ratty old copy of *Goldfinger.* She hasn't read any of the James Bond novels since early adolescence, but surely James can get her through a bad hour or two.

She slips out of bed, pulls on her nightgown, and roots around in the little pile of paper bags they brought back from their expedition into town. Maple sugar candy, a tiny, flat packet of postcards. Then the too big, recycled plastic bag from the antique store; she recognizes it with her fingers in the darkness, retreats with it into the bathroom. Quite comforting to be back in this bathroom, to find it waiting here for her, familiar from last night's watch, but also alien, a place she will never see again. She takes her place on the side of the big bathtub, holding her plastic bag. Catches sight of herself in the mirror over the sink, that triple view again.

Suddenly she shivers: Unreasonably enough, after love and food and a day with no hospital reminders of her troubles, she feels cold and frightened and alone. Leans over the deep yellow tub and turns on the hot water faucet, full blast. The water pours down with a comforting noise, drumming hard at first against the tile, then a softer splashing as the tub begins to fill a little. And great clouds of steam billow up at her; the room feels safer, warmer, immediately. She opens the plastic bag and takes out her book and with it a small notebook covered in thick paper printed to look like old and weathered maps. The notebook had been on a rack at the counter of the store, along with a quantity of other little useless stationery things, stickers and fancy memo pads and pencils topped with little plastic animals. Maggie had picked it up and paid for it along with her paperback book, thinking vaguely, Well, if I can't sleep, I'll read or I'll write.

Now she goes quickly and quietly back out into the comparatively clear and cold dark air of the bedroom in order to find a pen on the roll-top desk. Back in the bathroom, she huddles on the corner of the bathtub, now about a quarter full of steaming water.

It is most unlike her, this impulse to write things down. Never kept a diary. Doesn't enjoy writing up projects at work; disciplines herself to march through and do it on schedule, but without pleasure. Never generates a memo unless she has to. And yet when she picked up the notebook today, surely what was in her mind was some idea that she might write down the obsessive worries that were torturing her, that she would write them out of her mind, put them down on paper and laugh at them. In fact, the sentence that she has been imagining writing, has been imagining all evening, she suddenly realizes, is *If they find out, I will kill myself. I will have to kill myself. If they find out.*

But she can't do it. Can't put down anything on paper that might in any way incriminate her. Can't write down anything that would shock Dan if he read it, or that would be of any value whatsoever to an enemy. Just last night she entertained the ridiculous fantasy of breaking into the medical school admissions office, stealing the letter of recommendation out of her file, destroying it — if that paper were gone, she had thought, I would be safe; while that paper exists, I am in danger. Ridiculous, maybe, but how can she now create some other dangerous piece of paper? She holds the notebook open to the first blank page, leaning it against *Goldfinger*, holds the pen in her other hand. She aches, actually aches, to write it down: *If they find out, I will kill myself. I will jump off a building*— no, I will steer *into a one-car accident so no one will ever know for sure* — no, I will *inject myself with potassium chloride* . . . But she doesn't write it, doesn't write anything.

Interestingly, she has started praying again. Every single day, falling easily enough into the ritualized phrases and promises, petitions and rhythms of her childhood. She has not prayed in years. She would have said, shrugging, that she doesn't believe, or doesn't know whether she believes, or in what. Besides science, of course, besides medicine. But now she prays, and not for the sick babies. She prays for herself, for help and strength, so she can help the sick babies and face what she has to face. She prays now, silently, in the bathroom. Looks at the notebook page and thinks of promises and threats. Please don't let them find out. If they find out — but she doesn't write it down.

Turns instead to James Bond, sitting in Miami Airport, reflecting on his trade as a professional killer. What a man. Maggie giggles to herself. "Bond picked up the body and laid it against a wall in deeper shadow. He brushed his hands down his clothes, felt to see if his tie was straight and went on to his hotel." She reads her way through the first four chapters, reading slowly because she always reads slowly, because she is not capable of skipping through a thriller with anything less than the word-by-word attention she brings to scientific articles. And maybe because of that, maybe because this kind of writing can't stand up to that kind of scrutiny, she finds herself losing interest, the book losing its hold on her as she reads. James Bond drank and smoked and savored the good things in life, took his gun out of its hiding place in a hollowed-out book, sneaked into a hotel room and found a beautiful blond woman. "It was at the top of the afternoon heat and she was naked except for a black brassiere and black silk briefs." Yes, well, of course. What else would you expect?

How strongly these books had affected her once, that powerful tickle of sophistication and sexual cruelty — but it's a memory of conviction, not a reawakened thrill. She closes the book and opens the notebook again. An idea for what she might write, what she wants to write; though she exercises a continued anxious censorship, watching carefully for anything that might be dangerous to put on paper, she is writing with unexpected speed and fluency, covering the first few pages in the notebook. The air in the bathroom is wet and heavy now, and she has turned off the running water. This is comfort, this is safety. Maneuvering herself carefully onto the rim of the luxurious yellow bath, leaning her back against the tiled wall and drawing her knees up so that she's balanced on the ledge. On one side the bathtub wall drops straight down to the floor, on the other it slopes more gently, invitingly, down toward the steaming water. Maggie leans her notebook against her knees and writes and writes in the warm, wet air, in the clouded bathroom, with her husband asleep outside.

Penelope: She is awake now, but it's dark. Not all the way dark, but nighttime dark. She doesn't call because if she calls Mama will come but be angry: You are in bed and you have to stay in bed. See how dark it is? It's nighttime. Instead she tries again at the corner of the crib, stands on Bear, squishing Bear with her bare feet. Arms go over the side of the crib, pull hard. Kicks with her feet. She's leaning over the rail now, it hurts a little on her stomach, her feet kicking up off of Bear. Brings one hand up to grip the top of the rail as hard as she can, and wriggles sideways so her head won't go down. Now she's lying along the top of the rail, holding tight. Doesn't want to fall. Slides her legs up and wobbles there, then, quick, one leg down on the outside. Now the rail is pressing on her bottom and her legs are stretched too wide apart, and she lets the other leg down outside too and falls with a bump into the story-reading chair right beside the crib. The bump makes a noise and so does she, more out of surprise than pain, but not a big noise.

Getting down off the story-reading chair is easy; she does it on her stomach. And now she is out the door of her room and out of her room and walking in the dark nighttime. Mama will come and find her and pick her up soon and tell her, See how dark it is? Time for little girls to be in bed. And maybe shake her head and laugh and say, How did you get out! And try to sound angry but laugh some more.

But the hallway is dark and she doesn't hear Mama coming. All she hears are her own feet padding gently on the wood boards, the soft swish of her legs against the paper diaper on her bottom, hanging down, full of pee. Pad-pad-pad, swish-swish. She stops, stands still a second, pees a little more down into the diaper so it feels warmer against her for a second where the pee comes out. Then she is at the bottom of the stairs, and when she sees the gate is open, she is past it and going up before she can even feel surprised. That gate is never open, but now it is open. Up and up and up, holding on carefully to the banister.

At the top of the stairs the floor under her feet changes to rug, soft and just a little bit scratchy, and now her feet make no noise at all. One room she can see into has more light, windows full of big light, so she heads for that one. Soon Mama will come and pick her up and say, Nighttime, dark time, time for little girls to be in bed. She wants Mama to come and hold her up off the floor, but she also wants to go as far as she can and do as much as she can before Mama comes, because Mama will take her back to her crib.

She has been in this room before, sat on that couch, banged her head once on that table because the top is glass like a window, and she went under it and then tried to stand up. Maggie put a washcloth on her head where it hurt. Maybe Maggie will come and pick her up. She puts her hand on the table; the glass feels cold and smooth. Bends over and licks it, and it tastes like ice but warmer. Spits a little spit on it and rubs it in with her hand; it isn't so dark in here, but it isn't light enough to see her spit on the glass.

It is light enough, though, to see that there's something on the couch, something dark on that white couch. She leaves the cold, smooth table and checks: it's a bag like Mama carries. She knows how to open that. Takes out the papers one by one and drops them on the floor next to the couch. Finds a calculator — Mama has one too but she isn't supposed to touch it. She pushes some buttons, but no noise, no lights, no beeps. Drops it on the floor. Reaches her arm way down inside to the bottom so the edge of the bag is pressing up under her arm. Moves her hand around inside the empty bag, taps against the sides. Finds at the bottom a little bottle and pulls it out. Shakes it and it makes a rattle noise, something inside. Tries to get the top off, but it hurts against her fingers, doesn't move. She bites down against the top of the little bottle, likes the taste, the way her teeth can press into it a little bit, not like the glass, which is so hard. Then her bottom teeth slip in under the lid, and it almost goes into her mouth, but she spits it out. Little candies in the jar, she puts some in her mouth. Sweetness moves away along her tongue, and the smooth little balls turn slightly rough and grainy. She scrabbles her fingers in the bottle, takes out some more. Bangs the bottle in triumph against the glass table, and some candies fly out, clatter and ping on the table. She goes chasing them, feeling along the table and putting them in her mouth when she finds them, and suddenly the big light goes on, so she can't see anything at all except the inside of her own eyes for the first second. She hugs the little bottle protectively against herself; Mama will try to take it away. Then the brightness clears out of her eyes and she sees a grownup standing there and looking down at her and it isn't Mama at all, so she starts to cry, so Mama will come and pick her up.

22

Poison Center

TRULY, HANK did not see what the fuck else he could have done. He turns on the light to see what is making the sounds, thinking maybe it's a cat, and he sees a little kid in pajamas printed with cartoon dinosaurs, and first he thinks there's something wrong with her mouth, she's bleeding, then he takes a horrified step closer and the little kid is clutching what he knows with a sinking feeling is the bottle of Sudafed from out of his briefcase, which, he notices, is sitting there empty, all the papers strewn on the floor. And the medicine bottle is open, and the red around her mouth is the coloring off the little pills, and as the kid opens her mouth and starts to howl, he can see a couple of pills sitting on her tongue, in varying shades of pink.

What kid? What fucking kid? Maggie and her husband had no kids. What is the kid doing here? But Hank had certain reflexes bred into him after his share of sessions in the emergency room, years ago, and the first thing he did was grab up the kid and do a finger sweep of her mouth, get out all the pills in there. At least ten of them. And there were more pills, he saw, on the couch, on the carpet, most of them sticky and licked.

And the kid herself, whose age he would have put at maybe two, was remarkably strong, writhing in his grasp, screaming her fucking head off. She kicked him, hard, caught him right in the chest, and he almost dropped her.

Almost, but not quite. Hank is the villain of the piece, Hank is a weirdo and a sicko and a crazy person, all right, but you could say in his defense that he did not consider even for a second the possibility of dropping the child, hurting the child in any way, even of running away and leaving her behind. The very best of Hank, perhaps, is the doctor in him, the pediatrician, and it was the pediatrician in him that took over now. He was looking at the child with horror — who was she, how had this happened, would someone else be coming in after her, would he be discovered? But he was also thinking, ingestion, pseudoephedrine, ipecac, gastric lavage. Call the poison center. He didn't know, of course, any details about this particular drug taken in overdose; he was not an emergency room doctor. He worked with babies who took only the drugs they were given. But he found he still knew by heart the phone number of the poison center. He put the furious, kicking child down on the rug, picked up the cordless phone with its antenna and its built-in answering machine and its ten different kinds of memory and automatic redial. Managed to turn it on, got a dial tone. Punched in the number, got the recording warning him the call would be recorded. Oh, shit. But what else could he do?

"Poison center."

"Hi," Hank said in a falsely high voice, and the child was still crying, loud and clear in the background, and that almost offered a kind of camouflage — though of course it probably increased the danger that someone would come. Why didn't someone come? Who the fuck leaves a little kid alone in an unlocked house at night? "I need to know how dangerous a pseudoephedrine ingestion would be in a two-year-old." Come on, tell me it's nothing. Tell me the kid could take the whole bottle and just get a little hyper for a while. It's an over-the-counter med — how bad can it be? But Hank had his vivid memories; during residency, he had seen a toddler bleed to death into his gut after ingesting his pregnant mother's prenatal vitamins with iron. He had taken care of a suicidal eleven-year-old who had tried to make his parents sorry for taking away his television privileges by swallowing a whole bottle full of Tylenol and had almost needed a liver transplant. *Come on, tell me pseudoephedrine can't do any harm.*

"How much did the child take?" asked the calm woman on the other end of the phone; to her, of course, it was all in a night's work.

"I don't know — she opened a bottle, there were at least ten pills in her mouth, I got those out, but I don't know how many others she might have swallowed."

"Can you take a look at the bottle and tell me how many pills were in it originally, and what the dose was?"

"Hold on a minute," said Hank, and put the phone down. It made peculiar little zapping noises at him, and he hoped it wasn't going to cut him off altogether. The child was still clutching the pill bottle — in fact, she had another pill in her mouth, which he immediately removed. She didn't want to let him have the bottle, screaming "No! No! No!" at him and pulling her hand away, and again he was struck by the sheer strength of her. He had to immobilize her wrist with one hand and pry her fingers off the bottle, one by one, with her yelling and the tears running down her face and snot dripping out of her nose and getting into her mouth. It wasn't easy, but he got the bottle away.

"The bottle had a hundred tablets, thirty milligrams each, in it originally, but it wasn't full," he said. "The problem is, I don't know how empty it was."

"Can you count the pills that are still in it and all the ones you've taken out of the child's mouth, please?"

To do this, he had to pour the pills out on the top of the bookcase, count them back into the bottle. Thirty-six of them, plus another thirteen he had cleaned out of her mouth, plus nine more he found on the floor. Fifty-eight pills accounted for, he reported. And he'd had the bottle for several weeks, and took a pill or two almost every day — he must have taken between twenty and thirty of them, at the very least.

"So that would leave between twelve and twenty-two pills that the child might have ingested?" asked the poison center woman.

"Well, I could perfectly well have taken more pills than that, I just can't be sure — is it a problem?" Why didn't she just give him the information that he needed.

"And the child's weight?"

Well, she seemed to weigh a hundred pounds, all solid, squirming muscle, but in fact it was again a good question to ask a pediatrician. In Hank's training, there had been plenty of times when he had had to guess a weight and calculate emergency drug dosages.

"Call it about fourteen kilos," he said, with confidence. The little fourteen-kilo monster had stopped crying, seemed to have wiped her face more or less clean on the couch, and was staring at him with suspicion and what he took to be malevolence.

"Okay," said the woman at the poison center, and again a burst of faraway static intervened.

"Could you repeat that, please?"

"I said, at that weight, if she ingested even four thirty-milligram tablets of pseudoephedrine, she could be at risk for systemic effects. She needs to have her stomach cleaned out."

Oh, shit, oh, fuck, oh, the hell with everything. "What kinds of systemic effects?"

"There is a risk of cardiac arrhythmias, of respiratory disturbances —"

"A high risk? Are those things common?" But what did it matter whether they were common or rare; he was going to have to take the fucking kid to an emergency room, and how the fuck was he supposed to explain it?

"My card doesn't say how common the effects are." Now she sounded almost prim. "The child is going to need to have her stomach emptied — do you have ipecac?"

"Look, I'm not actually sure she swallowed any pills at all — she seems to have been mostly sucking off the coating —"

"Even four of those tablets could have systemic side effects," repeated the woman, sounding a little impatient, as if she was wondering what was wrong with him. "After she gets the ipecac, they'll be able to see whether there are any pills or pill fragments in the vomitus. What part of the state are you calling from, please?"

Hank hung up. That is, he tried to hang up, but there was no obvious little hang-up button on this fucking futuristic phone. Finally he turned a little switch to "off" and the phone went completely dead, no dial tone, no nothing. Could they trace the call? Was the poison center woman calling the police, even now? Ah, shit, why had he given the weight in kilograms — they would know he was a doctor. Shit!

An unexpected giggle caught his attention, and he looked over at the child, to see that she had removed her pajamas, and was in the act of peeling off her paper diaper, which looked like it had masking tape wound round and round her waist, holding it on. She had nevertheless managed to pull the diaper away from the tape, and was laughing with what Hank considered malicious delight as she stripped the soggy diaper down to her ankles, leaving a belt of masking tape and diaper fragments around her waist. She looked up at him, met his eyes, and smiled at him, and the smile was so pure and ecstatic that he actually smiled back.

All right, ipecac. He couldn't just stand there and wait for the cardiac arrhythmia to hit her. He would give it two minutes, check out the house to see if people who left a child alone at night to wander around the house and poison herself had the consideration to provide themselves with ipecac, and then, if he didn't find it, he would load her into his car and buy some on the way to the emergency room. Okay, decision made. He gathered up all his papers, checked the couch, the floor, stuffed everything into the briefcase. The Sudafed bottle too, the pills. The kid's pajamas. Grabbed the heavy diaper too, just in the interest of leaving no traces in the room. Then dropped it; fuck that. It would be hard enough to carry the kid and the briefcase. But when he reached out his hand, she stood right up and took it, held on to his three middle fingers with a sticky, happy grip, and toddled right along with him out of the living room. As he switched the light off, he felt a certain relief; he had left things undamaged in the study, in the living room only the diaper, and after all, the kid had come in under her own steam, taken off the diaper herself — he had done no damage, left no traces, hung no posters — no one would ever know he had been in the house, if he could just get the kid safe. And if he could get her safe, he would disappear. He would never try anything like this again. *Only don't let the baby seize or choke or die . . . don't let her do anything bad . . . don't let her die on me . . . don't let her heart stop beating . . . please, please, please.*

He looked quickly into the other rooms opening off the central hallway, the kitchen, a coat closet. Then a bathroom — turned on the light, checked out the medicine chest. He was still wearing his surgical gloves, but he did think to wash them off quickly under the tap; by now they must have Sudafed and baby spit and god knew what else on them and might be leaving traces. No fucking ipecac in the medicine chest, of course. Not much of anything, actually, just some Motrin and a few cosmetics. Probably their real, personal bathroom was upstairs with the bedrooms; pity he hadn't thought of checking that out. There might be something useful there, some interesting pharmaceutical secret that could be used to embarrass Maggie.

He was almost shocked by this thought, as though he had forgotten his reason for being in this house, as though he had forgotten his entire campaign, forgotten Maggie Claymore herself. The little girl was pulling him back out of the bathroom and he went along with her. Okay, downstairs and out — but he'd need something to wrap her in, it was cold out and she was naked. She leaned on him a little bit, going down the stairs, pulling down on his hand every time she moved down a step. As they passed through the open baby gate at the bottom of the stairs, it occurred to him to wonder whether maybe she lived down here, maybe her clothes and stuff would all be here. He looked into what seemed in the dimness to be a stupendously messy dining room, crap strewn all over the table and piled in boxes against the wall, then into another bathroom. Bingo: a changing table with diapers and baby clothes stuffed higgledy-piggledy into the shelves; when he pulled out a diaper, a party dress fell out onto the floor. He opened the medicine chest and saw the little brown plastic bottle of ipecac sitting there, waiting for him on the bottom shelf, and felt a physical relief so strong he almost sat down on the floor. It would be okay. He would get the pills back out of her stomach; she wouldn't die. It would be okay. And here were all the other medicines of childhood, liquid Tylenol and cough syrup and vitamin drops, and a plastic spoon

282

for measuring out doses, and an eyedropper, all jumbled together on the shelf with a packet of birth control pills and several partly empty prescription vials, erythromycin, he noticed, and Bactrim.

He diapered her, reasonably efficiently, right over the band of masking tape. She seemed surprised but not outraged to find herself flat on her back on her changing table. Then he pulled a sweatshirt over her head, and she started to scream. It was even louder and more resonant here in this cramped bathroom than it had been upstairs in the living room, but Hank ignored it and crammed her legs into a pair of pink striped stretch pants. She was kicking and fighting, but, after all, he was an adult male and he was stronger. There was a pair of blue sneakers at the bottom of the changing table, with unmatched socks stuffed into them, and he got the socks onto her feet and the sneakers on over them, fastened the Velcro. Shit, now she wasn't just screaming. She was saying, Mama! Mama! Well, he would just give her the ipecac and then they would head for the emergency room, and if Mama were here where she was supposed to be, none of this would have happened.

What followed, Hank's attempt to give ipecac to a strong and angry toddler who did not wish to take it, would have made a reasonably comic piece of slapstick. When he brought the spoonful of ipecac near her mouth, the child stopped screaming and began to spit; he had been holding her hands together over her head, but she wrenched one away from him and gave the spoon a whack. Most of the ipecac went on the floor, some on Hank's coat. So he filled the eyedropper, held her arms down even more firmly. The nurses in the emergency room used to say that if you pinched the child's nostrils, the mouth would open, but how the fuck was a person with only two hands supposed to hold a kid down, pinch the nostrils, and administer the medicine, all at the same time?

The child was spitting steadily now, making loud Bronx cheer noises with her mouth. He got some of her spit on his face. Okay, he would wait till she drew breath, then put the dropper in her mouth and squeeze. Okay. Jesus, she was strong. She did pause for a gasping, sobbing breath, but he somehow didn't quite have the nerve to stick the dropper in. The next breath, however, he was ready; the plastic nozzle went into the back of her mouth, and he

283

squeezed hard on the rubber bulb. Next thing, the air was full of ipecac spray, on his face, in his eyes, everywhere. Had she actually swallowed any at all? Who the fuck could tell? Grimly, he put what was left in the little brown bottle into the eyedropper and squeezed that in too. Out it came. Okay, he had done what he could. Maybe she got some ipecac, maybe enough, maybe too much. He would have twenty to thirty minutes before it took effect, plenty of time to get her to the emergency room at Blessed Innocence, this time of night. And then they would take care of her, his problems would be over. He dropped the ipecac bottle into his pocket, grabbed the child up and slung her over his shoulder, took his briefcase, and he was out of there. He paused going out the front door, but there was no one around, no one coming home, no one looking. He closed the unlocked door behind him and started down the street.

The child had stopped crying; she seemed to like being in motion. She wriggled around in his arm so that she was facing off to the side. It was only when he heard two soft thuds that he realized that she had taken off her shoes and dropped them on the sidewalk; she crowed with pleasure and began trying to take off her sweatshirt.

So he stopped and gathered up the shoes, which meant making her stand in her socks for a minute on the cold sidewalk. He decided to put the shoes back on her, remembering the energetic way she had walked through the house holding onto his hand; it would be a relief not to have to carry her. But when he tried to get the shoes back onto her feet, she fought him and screamed and he realized he couldn't afford to attract attention like this. The hell with it. One shoe in each coat pocket, pick her up again, and hurry.

He was back at his car; with relief, he got the door unlocked, decided to strap her into the back seat. It was extremely awkward leaning around the front seat to strap her in, and he found he seemed to have a cramped muscle in his shoulder, probably from carrying that heavy child. And she didn't want to be strapped in, and she was howling again, but he pinned her with one hand and stretched the belt around her middle. The back seat was cluttered with reprints and journals; it seemed a long time since he had looked back there, but he swept them all to the far side. And at least he could get into the front and slam the door closed and things would be private.

The little girl quieted down when the car started to move. Hank was worrying over what he would do at the emergency room — could he leave her in the waiting room with a note pinned on to her shirt telling what she might have taken? No, too incriminating, a note in his handwriting. Better to leave her in the emergency room, go to a pay phone and call in, disguising his voice. He could even try to sound like a woman. This is crazy — this will never work, he thought, but it was still a weaker thought than the idea of the little girl dying. He had seen small children die; he had to get her somewhere where she wouldn't die. He gripped the wheel so his hands wouldn't shake. He passed a hospital sign and suddenly realized that he was right near a small private Boston hospital; they didn't have a pediatric ward, he didn't think, but they had a twenty-four-hour emergency room and they could surely handle a kid — much safer, a place where no one would recognize him even if they saw him. He made a U-turn and headed into the hospital parking lot, which turned out to involve some complicated driving around the back of a modern building and in between two much older ones. Okay, he would park off to the side, leave the kid in the car, go out and scout the emergency room, then he would drop her and be out of here. Out of here! Drive a mile or two away, make his call.

Unfortunately, when he came back to the car, having chosen a brightly illuminated entrance with sliding glass doors — he would just put her on the rubber mat, the doors would open, and with luck she'd move in toward the light, and once inside surely a nurse or someone would take care of her — unfortunately, he came back to a car full of vomit and a little girl who was energetically producing more. The stink hit him as he opened the door, then he heard her retching. She had puked all over the seat, on his reprints, on her own clothes. He almost heaved himself at the smell and the sound and the sight, but at the same time he pulled out a tissue and wiped off her face; she looked so tortured and so wretched, so stripped of all the spirit that had shone out of her before.

He was a man who frequently, in the line of duty, performed procedures on young babies, who put needles and tubes in through skin that was not anesthetized, who cut when he needed to cut and caused pain in the name of healing. And yet he felt peculiarly guilty for what he had done to this little girl, for her misery, for the pills he had left in her reach and for the emetic he had administered. He also, of course, felt with a kind of bewildered disbelief that the whole evening had spun way far away from his control; the child in his car, the vomit everywhere, the position he would be in if he were discovered.

She stopped vomiting and looked at him with a helpless kind of appeal, which made him wipe her face again. "It's okay, honey," he told her. "Everything's going to be okay. You just had an upset tummy."

Jesus, but it smelled awful. And then, as he looked with a kind of despairing disgust at the ruin of the back seat of his car, it occurred to him that he could do just what the woman from the poison center had said, he could check the emesis, and if there were no pills or pill fragments, he could determine that in fact no pills had made it down into her stomach. And there were no pills, no fragments. The ceiling light was on, and he could see reasonably well. He was yet again grateful for his surgical gloves as he explored the mess on the seat, suppressing his own gag reflex. Explored the mess on her clothes. There was nothing red, nothing pink, nothing hard. Nothing to suggest any pills whatsoever. So it made sense: She had only licked off the coatings. Of course it made sense, babies didn't like to swallow pills. She didn't need to have her stomach lavaged, and she didn't need medical monitoring. Of course not. She needed to go home.

He felt a little uncomfortable with this decision, to tell the truth. He had checked as carefully as he could, but was it possible he might have missed some fragments? Or that a pill or two could have been pretty thoroughly dissolved by now? Well, yes, possible, but unlikely. If she had really taken several pills, he would have found the evidence. Now he would take her home, leave her in her own house — maybe find a crib. Remember to take off the clothes he had put her in; when her mother or whoever got home, they'd just find her naked there with her pajamas next to her — remember to take the pajamas out of the briefcase. And if she'd thrown up some more, that would just cloud the issue further.

Okay. He sat down in the stinking car, rolled his window down all the way, and started to drive. The little girl was retching again in the back seat. "We'll be home soon," he told her. "We'll see Mama." Whomever the hell Mama was, Mama who left her alone in the house at night and didn't even bother to lock the door. Some Mama! Hank allowed himself the luxury of righteous anger as he drove back toward Maggie Claymore's house. Not quite admitting to himself that he could not bear the idea of abandoning the child to wander alone into a strange emergency room, could not send her, miserable and alone, through that sliding door.

But when he had made his way back into the complex streets of Jamaica Plain, almost dizzy from the sour odor, he knew suddenly and certainly what he would find at the house. It loomed in his mind as a house of evil and misfortune, his enemy's shelter, which he had not been able to sabotage, after all. The house that had lured him in and then loosed this cascade of misadventure, that literal cascade of half-digested food, which he would never succeed in cleaning off his back seat. And so when he came driving slowly up the hill, he was not at all surprised, really, to see that all the lights were lit up on the first floor, that someone, obviously, had come home.

Probably it was the child's mother, whoever that was — but suppose it was Maggie instead, after all? He drove on, parked carefully a block away, then took the child out of the car. It was disgusting to lean in close to her, a relief to have her out of the car in the cool air. But what to do? It was time to be clever, he felt, time to defend himself. He retreated into his coat, pulled the collar up around his neck. He stripped the filthy clothes off the little girl, then pulled her pajamas from his briefcase, but she screamed when he tried to put them on her, and he gave up immediately, afraid of the noise. He left her in the diaper only; it was already quite wet, he noticed. He wrapped her up inside his coat, vomit and urine and all, holding her against him, and ran the block to the house. All right, he was there, at the bottom of the steps leading up to that now illuminated front porch.

And the child knew it; she was wriggling in his grasp, eager to climb the stairs. And now he understood what it was she was saying: "Go up!" she cried out. "Go up!"

He set her down and watched her, watched how she made her determined way up the steep wooden stairs. She had opened her mouth to cry but hadn't cried yet. Good. Let her neglectful mother, whomever she might be, think the baby had gone out naked on this cold night. He flung the pajamas up onto the front porch, then withdrew into the shadows near a big tree and watched the little pale figure toiling up to the top of the steps. She was at the door, she had stopped. And he knew what would come next, and he knew it would work, and he was all the way down the hill, waiting at the corner, when she started to scream, and he waited only long enough to see the door open, and he was out of there, moving fast, back to his stinking car.

23

Custody

S O THEY COME BACK Sunday afternoon to the police in their house, to craziness and upset and confusion. Police asking questions, Sarah crying. Maggie comforts her and listens, and slowly works out the sequence of events: Sarah got a call from a student, a fourteen-year-old girl calling to say, *I'm depressed. My parents, they're unbelievable. I'm trapped in a family that doesn't know who I really am. I might as well be dead. I'm only a few blocks from where you live, Ms. Hartz. I remember from when you had us over to see your garden. To identify all the plant strategies for surviving the winter, chart the annuals and perennials, discuss pollination and dispersal. When you served us little crescent-shaped biscuits flavored with cheddar cheese and poppy seeds, and hot cider stirred with cinnamon sticks. I can never speak to my mother again, not after this afternoon. I might kill myself.*

So Sarah goes running to the rescue, leaves Penelope there in her crib, leaves the door unlocked because, and isn't this cute, Sarah's lost her keys again. And Sarah can't find the student at first, because the student has been asked to leave the bar where she used the telephone; they aren't interested in troubled fourteen-year-olds. And then when Sarah finds her, they let a little more time go by in intense arm-around-the-shoulder conversation on a damp, dark street before Sarah draws her back to the house, promising hot co-

coa and perhaps a book of poetry to borrow, and it won't look so bad, you'll see, this is how it is with parents and children sometimes. Maggie can imagine it all so easily: wise Sarah, maternal Sarah, adults-can-be-cool-like-me Sarah!

Except Penelope is missing. Penelope's crib is empty. And maybe Maggie can't really imagine that at all, the panic, the ninth-grader standing, scared, off to the side, faced with real terror and real tragedy, then gratefully sent home with her parents, who arrived only a beat before the police. And soon after the police came, while two officers were still searching the house, while Sarah herself took one more hopeless look at the empty crib, the stepped-on stuffed bear, there was a noise on the porch heard by the policeman who was just starting to go up the staircase, the staircase with the open child gate, which Sarah has already told them and told them she did not open, she never opens. Sarah, too panicked and desperate to conceal anything, had said, Yes, I went out and left her alone. Yes, I left the door open. Anyone could have come in. Someone came in and stole my daughter! And the police kept asking for details about Sarah's boyfriends, about Penelope's father, and when she told them she had no contact with him, they looked even more interested. And then there was the noise on the porch.

And there on the porch, sad and sick-looking and naked in the chilly night, there was Penelope. Sarah came running when the policeman called, and as he was asking her if this was the little girl, Sarah of course had already snatched her up, holding her chilled and smelly little body close and weeping the tears parents weep on such occasions; Sarah had never imagined them, but Maggie could have told her about them. Maggie has actually seen them wept in the hospital, when a child whose death and disappearance was feared, reasonably or unreasonably, is restored safe and unquestionably alive.

But all happy endings are not so simple. The police were suddenly not interested at all in Sarah's certainty that someone had broken into the house and taken Penelope; they did not seem to feel that an opened baby gate and a diapering table that Sarah thought was in slightly different disorder from when she had last seen it were compelling evidence of anything at all. There was no evidence of a break-in, no evidence of theft — they had Sarah, still clutching Penelope, come upstairs with them and verify that the computers and the VCR and the CD player were all undisturbed, that nothing was missing, that nothing had been touched. There was no intruder, there was only an irresponsible, dipshit mother who left a two-year-old alone in the house while she went out for some stupid, selfish reason, maybe mixed up with drugs or drink, who probably left the front door not only unlocked but wide open so the baby went wandering, but who for all anyone knew had just sent the kid outside to play naked in the middle of the night. And then she notices the baby's not in her crib, so she decides the bogeyman's been here and she calls the cops and says there's been a kidnapping. The police had already searched Sarah's apartment, already seen the level of chaos, they had already made up their minds about Sarah. They went home at last, late Saturday night, but only after warning Sarah that they would be back in the morning, and she had better be there. And they had already notified the Department of Social Services. Emergency, emergency, child at risk. The social worker had twenty-four hours to investigate, and she showed up in the early afternoon, maybe five minutes before Maggie and Dan drove up, back from their holiday weekend.

So she comes back to Felicia Grassini, who has not had a good weekend. They started tube feedings again late Saturday, too much too soon by Maggie's standards, and by Sunday the baby had blown up her belly again, and she had some blood in her stool. Maggie stands over the warming table on Monday morning, having taken sign-out from David Susser and thanked him for her weekend off and called him various names inside her head for a lab-oriented, clinically obtuse dweeb, and says to Justin, Call the surgeons. And tell them I want somebody senior over here, not that intern who can't keep his eyes open.

"What is it?" Justin asks. "Her white count isn't up. Her pressure's okay."

"She looks rotten," Maggie says matter-of-factly. This is a matter of fact. "She doesn't look like herself at all. I don't think she can mount a white count. I think she's already septic."

291

Erika Donnelly is pressing a gauze to the baby's tiny heel, bruised like a plum from all the pinpricks, all the blood draws. She looks up, ignores Justin, meets Maggie's gaze. "And look how she's oozing here," she says, her voice worried. "I think she's losing her ability to clot."

And then everything happens fast, because it has to happen fast. Maggie was there at the right minute, she saw it only a little while before surely everyone would have seen it. And Erika, who knows this tiny baby better than anyone else does, sees it too, and the two of them, standing shoulder to shoulder, railroad a somewhat dubious and reluctant surgeon. Felicia Grassini is in the operating room by midday, and she loses most of her loops of intestine. Infected intestine, air in the bowel wall, necrotic bowel. A risky, difficult operation, but not as risky and not as difficult as it would have been a couple of hours later.

The Grassinis wait it out not in the surgical waiting room but in the NICU parents' room, which has come to seem familiar and maybe even a little reassuring: so many pieces of bad news, so many scary moments, and the baby has come through every time. Maggie, busy out in the big room with a new baby with severe pneumonia, sees Karen Kennedy come sashaying along and wants to block her: *Stay out. Someone else's baby may be dying on the operating table. They don't want to see you and think about your comparatively sturdy twenty-four-weeker. Believe me, they don't.* But she says nothing, watches the girl go into the parents' room, a teenage girl dressed all in black, haunting the hospital in her pallid makeup, and Maggie remembers how she looked that morning a month ago in the emergency room, hurt and alone and giving birth, strapped to a stretcher. A screwed-up kid. And she thinks of the student who called Sarah up, so Sarah went running out of the house to meet her, to help her, to save her, and Maggie, who is not, after all, particularly interested in the well-being of adolescents, thinks, Oh, damn all screwed-up kids. And then turns back to the baby with pneumonia.

She goes into the parents' room a little later, having just gotten a call up from the OR — the baby is holding her own, but it's touch and go — basically just a notification that as of now, as of this moment, Felicia is alive. Mrs. Grassini is hooked up to the electric breast pump, which chugs quietly. The milking machine. Breast milk dripping drop by drop into the plastic cylinder she holds up under her elegant black chenille sweater. You can tell she's distraught because the sweater is just hiked up any which way, the breast is almost revealed; normally Mrs. Grassini manages this too, with a certain delicacy, a certain careful gentility. Mr. Grassini is pacing, which is what fathers do. The rhythm of the breast pump repeats itself in his gait, and also in the rocking motion of Karen Kennedy, who is not pumping breast milk but is encamped firmly in the rocking chair.

Maggie delivers her news: Holding her own, touch and go. Mr. Grassini presses her, of course: What does this mean? Are you sure you're telling us everything? Everything? Mrs. Grassini continues to pump, or, rather, the machine continues to pump.

It is Karen Kennedy, her face powdered to a ridiculous pallor over her acne, her bright red mouth inexpertly and unglamorously drawn on, who seizes the moment.

"Can they adopt *my* baby?" she demands, looking straight at Maggie.

It certainly gets everyone's attention. They all turn and look at her. A painted child. A problem child. How can she have a baby in the next room?

"If their baby — if Felicia doesn't make it," Karen says, and now a tear is making its way down through the powder, trailing little pepper specks of mascara. "I'd like them to have my baby. My parents will never be glad about him. They don't want me to bring him home — they say I should put him up for adoption. Really, they probably hope he would just go ahead and die."

"No, they don't, darling," says Mrs. Grassini. "No one would hope a thing like that."

"But they'll never be glad he was born. I'm not even sure I could be glad he was born." The tears wash down her face, but she doesn't sob; she looks straight at Maggie.

Maggie thinks for just a second about all the tears in this room, the ones she's seen and all the others. Tears of anxiety, tears of having just visited a sick baby, tears of reaction to hospital paraphernalia. Tears over every ungained gram of body weight, every set-back. Over the really bad news, the infections and the holes blown in the lung and the head bleeds and the necrotizing enterocolitis. The congenital malformations and the neurological disorders. Your baby will always. Your baby will never. She has broken so many pieces of bad news herself, and it seems briefly strange that all her bad-news sentences must always include that one unquestionably sentimental word, *baby.* You would never use any other word, never say to a parent, Your infant has meningitis. Your neonate has a heart defect. Later Maggie will make herself think of all the good news, all the babies who make it and grow up, but she cannot think of them right now, and as Karen rocks and cries, her powdered, pallid face for an instant looks blurred to Maggie, as if the tears were in her own eyes. She sees instead a mother from years and years ago who sat in that chair while Maggie explained, and drew out on a piece of paper, her baby's inoperable heart defect. A short, stocky black woman, a stranger, as all of them are strangers, all the parents, a stranger who appeared out of the night, following the ambulance that had taken her baby away from the hospital where he was born because even when they put him in 100 percent oxygen, they could not get enough oxygen into his bloodstream. Maggie remembers her own hand drawing out that misconnected heart, and the look of complete disbelief on that mother's face as she cried. *You mean there's nothing you can do? Nothing you can do? Nothing at all?*

"I've thought about this a lot," says Karen. "I want them to have him — especially if their baby dies. They'll take very good care of him — even if he has problems. Even if he's, like — you know — re-tarded."

Mrs. Grassini has turned off her breast pump, carefully discon-nected her precious cylinder of expressed milk, capped it and set it on the table, pulled down her black chenille sweater, and gotten slightly unsteadily to her feet. Karen stands up forcefully, leaving the rocker to rattle back and forth a little wildly, and the older woman hugs her, and they stand there together.

And Maggie doesn't know what to say. And neither, she would

guess from his expression, does Mr. Grassini. It is not their moment. It is, perhaps, not a moment for anyone except mothers.

But Felicia Grassini does make it. Makes it out of the operating room, at least. There's a lot less inside her than there used to be, and she's still on a cocktail of the strongest antibiotics known to man, or at least to surgery, and she's a very, very sick, very, very small baby, but she's alive. She's hanging in there. And Maggie feels fiercely proprietary. The next day, when things are quiet in the NICU, she goes in search of Peter Cannon; this is his kind of story. The way they were all so prepared to let this baby go, to say she wasn't worth the surgery. The way Justin is still hitting her at morning rounds to say, What about the quality of life? What about short-gut syndrome? Okay, this baby will have problems, no matter what. Okay, she may need to be on intravenous nutrition for years. Okay, but this morning Mrs. Grassini has a living daughter, and that daughter has a chance, and what is this whole damn expensive pile of a hospital here for if not for that?

So Maggie says to Peter, "Wanna go sneak a smoke and look for more criminal activity?"

"I've quit," Peter says to her, sadly. "Want to see my nicotine patch?"

They are in the waiting room of his clinic, watching the last few families of the morning pack up and go. A boy with cerebral palsy, zipped into his Red Sox jacket by his mother, his father standing ready with the baseball cap, and then they push the wheelchair off toward the elevator. One of those special wheelchairs with a headpiece to support his arched neck, with plastic leg pieces to strap his contorted legs down. His arms sway out to the side, spastic, flailing, and his father tucks them carefully away from the elevator door. A little girl, some syndrome or other, her face obviously abnormal. Tiny, strangely shaped ears, a disconcerting grin. Peter's people. Short-gut syndrome would be just another problem for just another kid; Felicia Grassini will be one of the lucky ones if she has full use of her arms and legs, if her brain is normal. Which, of course, it may well not be.

"You've really quit?"

"It's too cold to smoke outside. I fear they've done me in with their smoke-free environment. Soon I hope to be as self-righteous as everyone else. A good example to my patients, and a marathon runner. In my spare time."

But he won't look at her. Something is wrong.

Instead of going to the cafeteria to get lunch, they go into Peter's examining room, where he has a special system of ropes and pulleys rigged up to help his patients negotiate the scale, the examining table, even the blood pressure cuff, without too much help. He is restringing a complex arrangement of weights and cords that allows him to test the muscle strength of a child seated on the table. To do this, he kneels on his own examining table, absorbedly passing nylon cord through hooks, rigging the weights.

Something is wrong.

Maggie has a new policy, invented for herself on the drive back from New Hampshire. Out there, open, confrontational, confident. Maybe this is the time to try it.

"Is something wrong?"

"Could you hand me the two-pound bar?"

She hands it to him. "What's wrong, Peter?" And then, because she can't help herself: "Peter, did you get a letter about me? Did you hear something about me? Tell me!"

"Your detective? I mean, the detective who's supposed to be solving this, about the letters? Well, I guess she was investigating people who were your enemies and also — people who were your friends. Anyway, she was investigating me."

And she found out you're gay. Or something like that, something about who you sleep with and what you do. Oh, god, Peter, I know how private you've tried to be, but nobody, truly nobody, is going to care —

He does not look at her. He digs his hand deep into the pocket of his pants and pulls out a chunk of closely folded papers, hands it to her like a tiny weight. She starts to pull the papers open; they're slightly warm from his body. He doesn't look at her. He is kneeling on the table again, tugging gently against the pulleys hanging from the ceiling.

Maggie spreads the creased papers out on her knees. Xeroxed news clippings. Peter's face?

"This was ten years ago," she says, almost accusingly. LOCAL DOCTOR. BRAIN-DAMAGED BABY. PARENTS' CLAIM. She feels a tiny, involuntary frisson of fear, of identification. There but for the grace of god.

"In Wisconsin," Peter says softly. "Before I came here." His voice is muffled, he is facing the wall, looping cords over an ascending series of pegs.

"But what does that have to do with anything — what does that have to do with her investigation?" Maggie, outraged.

"See, I won — I won the case."

"Good," Maggie says, bewildered but on his side: Of course you won the case. You're a good doctor.

"But a lot of people thought I was guilty — I lost patients. I got some phone calls, I got some letters — it was a pretty hard time. Well, you can probably imagine." He shifts clumsily around on the exam table, tearing the paper, moving to sit facing her. "And the really stupid thing I did — I buried it, I didn't mention it. I just wanted to leave it behind me."

"I still don't see what this has to do with the detective." Maggie, still outraged, but also thinking, What kind of idiot lies about something so easy to check?

Peter sits quietly, legs dangling off the examining table. His voice continues, sad and reasonable, and she wonders suddenly about the conversations *he* has with parents — probably here in this very room. It's part of his job too, just like it's part of hers: Your child will always. Your child will never.

"Your detective," Peter says slowly. "Her job, I think, is to find out things. Maybe to find out things about people around you. Someone's lying. Someone's not who they seem to be. So this is something she found out."

She wants to ask about the malpractice case, but doesn't want to ask if he doesn't want to talk about it. She wants to apologize, which is surely ridiculous. Wants to say, But Peter, you're such a good man, such a good person, such a good doctor. And wants to ask, and knows she never will, Is this why you do the work you do,

Peter? Are you making amends for something? Or are you protecting yourself by staying away from the normal children and making your place with the children who are already damaged?

"What I think is," Peter says, staring past her at the eye chart, "when something like this happens, things just get poisoned. The atmosphere. The workplace." And though he does not say it, she knows what he means: the friendship.

Maggie cannot help anyone. She wants to help, to make things right, and she cannot figure out how.

Use me as a reference, she told Sarah, over and over. I'll talk to the Department of Social Services. I'm a doctor, an expert on children. They'll listen to me. And never mind, thought Maggie, that I think you were crazy to go out and leave Penelope sleeping, that I think you were little short of criminally irresponsible, that I can't forgive you for leaving my house unlocked all the time — never mind that. We need to get the social workers to close this case, to get out of your life, Penelope's life, my life. Out of our house. We need this investigation closed, this probationary period over, all doubt resolved. No more unexpected visits at all hours, no more snoops poking into our business. I will tell them what a good and loving mother you are. I will tell them that Penelope needs to stay with you.

But Sarah looked right past her. Sarah maybe even resented this assurance that Maggie was an authority, that she could presume to give approval, that the social workers and investigators would listen to *her*. Sarah was still offended that no one — not the police, not the social workers, not even Maggie, believed her theory about someone coming into the house and taking Penelope, that everyone thought she had just left the door open and Penelope had gone out by herself. Sarah was angry maybe because Maggie had confirmed that nothing was missing, nothing disarranged, just a wet diaper on the floor in her living room and some smears on the coffee table, showing Penelope had explored upstairs when she was alone in the house. No, Sarah was not interested in Maggie's help. Sarah looked right past her to Penelope, playing happily with a snake made of old socks sewn end to end. Penelope coiling the snake around her fat little middle.

So could she help Peter? Could she go to someone about Peter? Demand they call off the detective? Demand that the hospital take no disciplinary action against him since the investigation was really about something else? Should she go out and hire a lawyer of her own, ask the lawyer to make sure that no one was harmed in her name, that this stupid, clumsy detective concentrate on Maggie and Maggie alone? Yes, and draw more attention to Peter's problem, that's what she would do. Maybe there were ten other doctors whose secrets had been uncovered. She had passed Weintraub in the hall and imagined him thinking, G_3TAb_3. For example. Not that that was the same as lying about professional credentials. And, damn, she had to admit, she didn't really approve of what Peter had done. Or what Sarah had done. But she didn't approve of what had been done to them, either.

Donna Grey clutched her black binder, always. Wherever she went, she had it with her. She was back interviewing Hank Shoemaker now for the third time, and she seemed to be peeping at him from behind her great big notebook. She was fussing about dates and times, as she always did. Where he was on Thursday night. What time he left the hospital. Whether he saw anyone else after he left, whether he stopped in at any restaurants or bars, whether he got any phone calls after he was home. Finally he lost his temper with her: Why the hell, he wanted to know, should he be subjected to this kind of thing? Again and again and again? No, he didn't keep track of what time he left, no, he didn't go out drinking after work. So what? He worked until things were done, and then he went home and made himself something to eat, okay?

And the next thing to be done, anyway, was to renew his suggestions about Maggie Claymore's research — they would have to investigate, and when you investigate, who knows what you might find. He had been watching her — it seemed to him that he was running into her all the time lately. She was always dressed up, and she always smiled at him nowadays, but he could tell what it was.

Inside, she was falling to pieces — he knew it. He could recognize the effort because he took such trouble himself, so careful to look professional and act normal and friendly all day long. He knew that Maggie was smiling at him because she wanted everyone to like her, because of this new idea: If people didn't like her, they might begin to wonder whether she had killed Heather Quirk, whether she had faked her research. And all the rest. So all of a sudden she was Miss Friendly.

The only thing was, every now and then these days, Hank found his own thoughts drifting to David Susser. Another splashy publication this month, a paper with five names on it, but Susser's name first. And now David Susser was supposedly having an affair with Marie-Claire Armand, who had come from France to do four or five months work in his lab; she was an intense, bone-thin woman with almost colorless hair and eyelashes, who was always hanging around right outside the ambulance entrance, smoking, but she was unquestionably a visiting young scientist from France, so it was possible that Susser thought very well of himself for that. And most immediately, the secretary over in neonatology had flatly refused to retype a lecture handout for Hank, because, she said, she was working on a long grant application for David and wouldn't be done for days.

It would not take very much to remind him that he was no fucking superman. A few letters — start maybe by telling him that French bitch was stealing stuff, ripping off his cell cultures, planning to smuggle all his secrets home to France. Only screwing him to lull his suspicions. And then go from there into the research — letters to the other four coauthors, warning them that a major scientific scandal was brewing, asking them whether they had really verified each and every data point — and of course, you knew they wouldn't have. They would have obediently signed those requisite letters that had to be submitted with the manuscript: Yes, we all take full responsibility. Yes, we are all the real, true authors, not just people with tenuous connections to the research and claims on the first author. They would shake in their shoes when they got the letter, written with an obvious command of scientific vocabulary;

they would imagine themselves dragged down in a horrifying investigation.

So first Susser stops trusting his girlfriend, then his colleagues stop trusting him, start coming around and asking him questions, bugging him to show them proof that he really did what they've all published a paper saying they did, that he really showed what they've all gone on public record as saying they showed. And then, after that, when he's really started wondering what the hell is going on, maybe risk one, just one little letter with a threat in it. *The next time you go to your special seat at Symphony Hall, watch your back carefully.* Or maybe, *Make sure the burglar alarm is turned on at your house.* Something like that, so he would have to decide between going to the symphony and worrying the whole time that he was being stalked, or staying home to protect his house. Of course, it would be a little dangerous, the police would probably be interested, because it would be sort of a threat — but the beauty part of it was, Hank himself would do nothing further. Wouldn't go near the guy, wouldn't even bother to find out where his house was. Hank was through, once and for all, with going to people's houses.

Interestingly, it never occurred to Hank to bother sending David Susser the messages that he was quite sure had helped unhinge Maggie. Hank would probably not have been able to explain clearly his sense that David Susser would be at most mildly perturbed by letters telling him that everyone hated him and no one trusted him as a doctor. David Susser might be irritated, but on some very profound level, he would not give a real big flying fuck. And surely this has something to do with gender; Maggie's vulnerability, her willingness to entertain the possibility that her colleagues thought badly of her, and her horror at the idea, surely has to do with her being female, with that woman's need to be liked, to be nice, to be approved of. David Susser needed all this much less, and Hank understood that, even though Hank himself was as sensitive to the possibility of being disliked, excluded, disapproved of, as anyone could be — and Hank was male. This world has become so complicated and self-conscious that Hank Shoemaker, a man, a relatively out-of-it weirdo geek, a sexist surely by anyone's definition, and at least a bit of a secret nutcase, was rather pleased by the idea that his next enemy would be another man; it was almost as if he were thinking righteously, Now they can't say I do this because I don't like women! Take that! Yes, in fact, he had turned his nasty fantasies about persecuting David Susser into some kind of self-congratulatory certification of his own free-thinking immunity to prejudice, the way a pediatric intern may report a father for suspected child abuse and feel a thrill of pride because the family is white, and this report surely justifies, excuses, and validates any past reports of black parents, the investigations of their families, the removal of their children into protective custody while the investigations take place. See, I do it to everyone. It isn't what you think.

In three days, Maggie will go off service, her stint in the NICU done. And Felicia Grassini is very much on her mind; she wants to leave a baby girl so clearly declared on the side of life and aggressive intervention, which to Maggie are often one and the same, that no one will ever, ever, ever suggest anything else. Ever.

Felicia Grassini. Many of her colleagues would say that Maggie is being a little crazy here. They know, as Maggie herself knows, what is probably in store for this baby. Yes, she's alive, and yes, she's healing from her surgery, but it isn't clear that she will ever be able to absorb food through her intestines. Which means a life of implanted central intravenous lines and total parenteral nutrition, protein and calories and fats flowing right into her veins. And that is not the way the body is supposed to work; the body was designed to absorb nourishment through the gut, and intravenous nutrition is an inadequate, usually temporary second choice. Felicia's future is surgery and more surgery, bacterial and maybe fungal infections creeping from her skin to her IV line, problems with her liver — if Felicia's brain is normal, what Maggie will have helped create is perhaps a bright, endearing child, adored by her parents and her nurses, who faces constant hospitalizations and medical scares, and eventually, probably, an early death.

Or maybe not. And Maggie knows that too. Bad things happen, but so do good things. What if Felicia "flies," as they say? What if her intestine works better than expected, not worse, what if she has fewer line problems, not more, what if a couple of years from now she's a pretty healthy kid with some hairy medical stuff in her past? Stranger things have happened. Anyway, in Maggie's mind the die was cast at birth; Felicia made it out of the delivery room, so she deserved every chance. And now, as Maggie prepares to sign off the case, she knows that even for her colleagues who might have played it differently, the die is now finally cast: She got sick, her doctors advised surgery, and her parents agreed, and the surgeons fixed her. A definitive vote has been taken. She deserves every chance.

24

Maggie's Notebook

S HE LIVES in a little tourist resort town in New Hampshire near a lake, or maybe mountains, or both. And rents a room, cheap, and works when there is work, which is to say, when the tourists are around, in the summer and then for the foliage, then sometimes in winter, at a not very famous ski resort. She sells postcards and candies and thrillers for the tourists to read and answers questions about the roads and the weather report as if she were a native. In her room are piles of used paperbacks that eat up most of her salary and a green glass pitcher she bought in a junk shop, and also a beautiful, warm quilt. She bought it from the woman who made it, who learned how to quilt from her own mother back before the Second World War. Buying the quilt made her feel like a tourist, since that is what the tourists do, buy quilts and maple syrup and wood carvings and jewelry made to look like leaves. But when the tourists go home, she is still in her rented room, under her quilt. She has sex maybe once every couple of weeks with the married man who owns the souvenir shop, who is very nice. And nobody knows where she comes from and nobody knows who she is.

On Nantucket in the off-season it is certainly cheap to get a room, though she has been warned that she will of course have to move when the summer people come and the rents are quadruple or more. But she doesn't plan to be there then. For the first time in her life she is free of possessions, owns two pairs of cotton sweatpants and four shirts, a flannel nightgown, and nothing else at all, no objects. She waits for the snow and she doesn't do very much, she just idles through the day. She takes long walks on the beach, and the cold wind blows sand into her hair. And she isn't pretty enough or strange enough or anything enough for people to really wonder about her or take the trouble to find out. She knows all kinds of things, she has studied and studied and studied, but you couldn't tell that by the books that she reads. She has memories of a much more complicated life, but for now she doesn't show them or talk about them. Maybe she thinks about them, or about all the things she knows, and maybe she doesn't. She buys boring groceries and eats them alone. No problem leaving when the season starts; she has no wish to run into anyone she knows. Someplace off-season in the summer, she imagines. Maybe someplace in Florida. Beaches and high-rise condominium buildings and alligators. More walking along the beach.

Or one of the mountain states — Cheyenne, Wyoming — or Boise, Idaho, or Boulder, Colorado. And working maybe as a waitress. Somewhere where there are a lot of men and you can take them or leave them. Very strange and foreign for her, but still it's America, with safe water and normal brands in the grocery store and of course everyone speaks English. She sees every single movie that comes to town, except maybe the horror movies, since all her life she has had trouble sleeping at night after scary movies. Childish nighttime terrors. Then maybe one day she goes to see a scary movie, and so she learns that the terrors have left her or, rather, that she has outgrown them. Folks in this place are friendly but they don't really expect you to be complicated. They know she's from the East, came here they suppose because life is better near the mountains and the air is clean. She doesn't recognize herself at all in this clean air. She's lost a lot of weight and she never wears makeup. At night, she likes to read women's magazines. Once when she was at a movie, a little boy choked on a peanut M&M and she

25

Donna Solves It

N o," DONNA GREY said, firmly. "I don't have proof, and
you're not going to get proof unless you're very lucky."
Maggie was not there to hear this; she was explicitly excluded from this meeting as she had been from the several other
update briefings that Donna Grey had conducted. They were for
the head of security and a hospital vice president and someone
from the attorney's office; they were not for Maggie. She was not
supposed to know, not allowed to know, the details of the investigation. It was at these updates that it could be said out loud, Do you
think she's really guilty of any of the things they're saying about
her, do you think there's anything funny about her, do you think
she might be sending these letters to herself? *No smoke without fire,
no smoke without fire.* When Donna had initially raised the question of whether Maggie could be behind the campaign, an obvious
unlikely-but-possible to anyone who had ever investigated poison-
pen letters in a workplace, she found that the head of security and
the hospital vice president, at least, were downright eager to seize
on that particular explanation, and even now, when Donna had essentially ruled out that possibility, they would still ask her in wistful
voices whether she was sure Maggie wasn't making some of this
trouble herself.

The meeting was held, as the other meetings had been, in the office of the hospital vice president, large and neat and blessedly free of the medical journals and reprints that had begun to irritate Donna as she made her way from doctor's office to doctor's office. Why the hell did each doctor need a separate set — why not just one for everyone to use? Save a tree, shoot a doctor. It was a relief to admire an office without journals, in fact by and large without shelves, and also without framed diplomas.

And it was a pleasure to take center stage, here in the middle of the slate blue carpet. The vice president, whose name she could not remember, though she knew she had it in her notebook, had chosen to watch her from behind his vast, polished, pale wood desk, not to come out and join the lawyer, Elaine Oliphant, and the head of security, Sandow, at the more informal grouping of black leather chairs around the chrome and glass table. This put Donna in the middle of the floor between desk and conversation area, turning to one side and then the other as she made her presentation. Center stage.

And they didn't like what she had suggested. The vice president was drumming the fingers of one hand on his desk, chewing thoughtfully on the corner of his mouth, waiting for someone else to talk. Elaine Oliphant was making notes, staring down at her pad, not meeting anyone's eyes. It was left to the head of security to challenge her, as one expert to another, and clearly he didn't like it, either. Finally he came out and said it: "This kind of activity, it's usually a woman. Anonymous letters, all that."

Donna had been expecting this; she felt now, in fact, rather remarkably close to what Maggie would have felt in her place: The bastards — they want it to be anyone except a male doctor! Let it be a crazy secretary, a menopausal nurse, that would make them happy.

"But you have no proof," said the head of security, one more time.

"He's clever," Donna said. "He's a very smart man. I've been through his hospital wastebasket every evening for the past two weeks, I've even gone out to his home and checked out his home garbage. Nothing. But then, there haven't been a lot of new letters over the past couple of weeks. I can certainly keep up the surveillance, but it's my opinion that he takes extraordinary precautions."

"But all of this is without any proof — you're talking like you know he's guilty," said the vice president. "And you're basing the whole thing on a couple of coincidences."

Donna opened out her folded chart again. She was prepared to explain herself as many times as necessary, and she hoped, in her heart, that they would give her permission to forge ahead with the investigation; they should congratulate her and encourage her to go on, to search the wastebaskets again and again and to trail Hank Shoemaker home from work. And eventually, surely, he would slip up and she would catch him.

Had she known it the first time she sat in his grimy office? To be honest, no, not a bit — she had had no more instinct about him than she had had about several other doctors she interviewed; like the others, he seemed uncomfortable in conversation, uneasy talking to her. Were these guys on edge because she was female, because she represented some authority not their own, because they had guilty consciences? No, it was Donna's considered opinion that they were just nervous because she compelled them to talk about something outside of medicine. Hank Shoemaker had seemed twitchy and resentful. She had flagged his name early in her investigation, however, because it had been suggested to her twice, first by Maggie herself on her incredibly reluctant and half-assed list of guesses, and then again by another woman in her division, this battle-ax, Dr. Gravenstein, the one who had told her that Hank was crazy, no question about it, something should be done about doctors like him. Of course, Dr. Gravenstein had then launched into a lengthy dissertation on why, it started to seem to Donna as she listened, every single other goddamn doctor at Blessed Innocence was dangerous, or crazy, or incompetent, or at the very least lazy. So how far was she supposed to trust the word of someone with that kind of megachip on her shoulder? Especially when Elissa Gravenstein's own name had already been mentioned by Maggie as a possible suspect, Maggie saying apologetically that she hated to admit it, but Elissa sometimes seemed to resent other women doctors.

But with Hank's name coming out twice like that, two different people perceiving him as more than a little bit off, Donna had looked at him carefully. Not at his manner and personality, but at his comings and goings, at the times he could justify and the times he could not. And she had found her pattern, nights when things were hung on bulletin boards or leaflets put up in bathrooms, those were without exception nights Hank Shoemaker worked late. There had been not a single such incident during the two trips he had made to medical conferences, though one letter had been delivered by in-hospital mail on the day after he left. All the other names she had pursued, those people mostly had spouses or families at home to verify their hours, those people did not work late, or if they sometimes did, the dates didn't match. Donna was proud of her meticulous charts, which reminded her, actually, of the nursing work she had seen in the NICU. Hundreds of numbers, hundreds of tiny pieces of information, sorted onto the right grid, could tell you anything you needed to know. Her vague sense that nurses were more essential than doctors, more reliable, more knowledge-able, had only been increased by this investigation. Nurses kept better records, knew where they were and what they had been do-ing at any particular time, because they wrote it down, and in read-able handwriting. It had been her greatest fear, to tell the truth, that the person behind the campaign against Maggie would in fact turn out to be a convenient woman-doctor-hating, on-the-rag psycho nurse, the one she knew all these bozos were hoping for.

The others studied the charts, passed them around. The room was full of reluctance. The hospital vice president, the hospital law-yer, the head of security. No one wanted to say, Well, good job. No one wanted to acknowledge what she had shown them, what she had diagrammed for them in red ink to represent the incidents, blue to show Hank Shoemaker's movements, green for corroborat-ing evidence, all against a black timeline.

"It seems to me," said the vice president rather weightily, as if conscious of the obligations of his office, "that the fundamental weakness of your approach is that you've investigated only a small, select group of possible people — the ones who were named to you as having possible grudges against Dr. Claymore. And out of that small, select group, you've picked the person who seems most plausible in terms of times and places. And that's all very well. But if the person doing this is really just not on your list — someone who's kept their feelings well under wraps, someone maybe whom Dr. Claymore doesn't even know — I mean, you could be totally barking up the wrong tree here. All you've done is show which one on this arbitrary list is the best fit."

"This is not an arbitrary list. It is a carefully culled selection of names of those people named by Dr. Claymore and by others as disliking her, combined with names of hospital employees who have been noted for strange or vindictive behavior patterns. That's how you investigate — you generate a list of possible people, you explore out along connecting lines. There's always more people in the world. We aren't in a mystery novel where the only suspects are a small group of people in an isolated country house."

"Yes, I appreciate that," said the vice president, though he obviously didn't. Snippy little bastard. Snippy little mustache. He stroked it tenderly. "So your idea would be to focus in on Dr. Shoemaker now and look for further indications —"

"I don't like it," said Elaine Oliphant. "I don't like sending investigators after one of our own doctors, with no more evidence than this — what if she's wrong? What if he finds out someone's been going through his trash? What if he's not guilty?"

"You think he could bring suit?" asked the vice president.

"Maggie Claymore already came to me — just the other day — about wanting to hire her own attorney," said the hospital attorney. "I talked her out of it. I don't think that would help one bit. Let's try to keep things from becoming adversarial if we possibly can. And similarly, I don't think we have to express our support for one employee by undercutting another."

"I agree," said the hospital vice president. Then turned with elaborate courtesy to his head of security. "What is your evaluation?"

"Well," Sandow said, with professional heaviness. "Well, I do think that Miss Grey is to be commended for the careful detail work she's put in. And I think all of us will without doubt keep her theory in mind if further developments should — well, should so indicate."

It's her last day on service. Tomorrow, goodbye to these babies, these interns, goodbye to this room. Hello to the rest of my life, such as it is. To everything that's been on hold.

Maggie is making out her usual meticulous notes on each and every baby, ready to sign them out to Claire Hodge. It's hard to give them up, as it always is; she's always relieved to feel the hospital wheel turn a notch, happy to slide the weight onto someone else's shoulders — but after a month of involvement so intimate, it's also hard to believe that someone else will care as she has come to care, will take the appropriate amount of trouble. The underlying message in Maggie's carefully enumerated problem lists is just that: Pay attention. These babies are mine and I do not yield them lightly.

So this is what is on her mind as she comes hurrying out of the NICU, clutching her little pile of index cards. She is wearing scrubs; another long night in the hospital, or, rather, a very early morning; she came in at three A.M. to hover over a baby with meningitis, transported in from a hospital in one of the very ritzy suburbs, where he had been hanging out in the well-baby nursery for almost two days since birth, nobody apparently looking at him too closely (as Justin told the story), and looked almost dead at the end of the transport. So they gave him some IV fluid and he started to seize. Even Justin was scared, glad to have Maggie there to help, though she took pains to let him know he had already been doing everything right. He was okay, Justin. Would be okay.

Anyway, she's a little tired, and a little wound up, and very preoccupied with holding all possible information about all possible babies in her head at once when she comes marching out of the NICU and the secretary looks up at her with a worried expression and says, "They just asked me to stat page you to the parents' room."

The parents' room? Stat? She is running through the swinging doors before she has even conjured the horrible possibilities: a breastfeeding mother, a baby suddenly gone limp and blue. Shit. Shit. Not on my last day!

She crashes through the door and into the parents' room, braced for the worst, ready to take command and bark orders, and almost falls into the sheet cake. THANK YOU, DR. CLAYMORE! LOVE, FELICIA ornately scrolled among the sugar roses and forget-me-nots, Mylar balloons from the ceiling, streamers dipping down almost into the faces of the nurses and residents. And everyone is applauding, led by Mr. Grassini, who has jammed his video camera under his arm long enough to bang cupped hands together for a round, fully resonant sound so loud that she thought at first balloons were popping.

Maggie is dizzy and grateful; no disaster, no blue baby, just smiles and friendly noise and also a familiar strangeness: how important she has been in their lives, in all their lives. The recurring miracle of this profession, this job. Felicia, Baby Girl Grassini, Surviving Twin Grassini, will be just a baby among babies in Maggie's memory, not *the* baby of babies. She happened to be born when Maggie was on, so Maggie took care of her. A fact of life, a fact of work.

They are cutting the cake into neat squares, heavy with blue flowers and green leaves, thickly paved with frosting. Mrs. Grassini is handing her an enormous flower arrangement, real flowers, roses and lilies surrounded with a cloud of baby's breath. What an appropriate flower, Maggie wants to say, but she cannot speak.

No, Felicia is not a baby who has marked her particularly. Just a baby, a sick baby. It happened to be Maggie's month, that's all. Except they all mark her, all the babies. And so Felicia is alive, so she goes on to join that invisible army, the babies, the children, now even the teenagers, alive because of Maggie. Not something she can quite think about on a daily basis, but yes, a pillow, a comfort, a shadow thought to hold close through all the dark nights.

Karen Kennedy, now, looking even younger than usual. Less makeup, cheeks a little pink as she stuffs them full of cake. It will never work out, Maggie believes, this new plan of Karen and her baby going home with the Grassinis, a difficult adolescent daughter adopted at the same time as a fragile baby. But look how happy Karen looks, look how she carefully selects the soda without caffeine and pours a cup for Mrs. Grassini, who drinks nothing that might affect the breast milk she so faithfully pumps and stores. Look how Mrs. Grassini accepts the clear plastic cup, holds it steady so it won't slop over, since Karen has filled it too full, bends her head to slurp a little foam off the top. Look, oh, look, at Mrs. Grassini's hand caressing Karen's shoulder briefly, look how they smile at each other. Maggie, who now prays every day, can recognize grace when she sees it.

Maggie's own mouth is full of cake. It is the standard bakery sheet cake of a thousand hospital occasions, but she has never tasted anything so delicious. The sweetness fills her up like love.

the natives, have stopped noticing her when she walks by. They can see that she has washed up here for a while, and that even though she doesn't belong here under this sun and under this sky, it's the place she needs right now, far enough away from wherever she started out. And they probably can't even guess where she started out. And they aren't even interested.

In Seattle where it rains all the time, but she likes it that way. She wears rubber boots and a blue waterproof jacket. She plays on a women's softball team but she doesn't have any real friends. She works in a xerox place, efficient and polite, and copies things for people and collates them. Notices to hang on telephone poles when they're selling their bicycles or renting out rooms in their apartments, CVs on which she notices words misspelled and doesn't say anything. Every now and then a scientific article, and then she smiles to herself. She is one of those people who serves you during the day, like a person in a coffee shop or in a bank, back when people went to banks instead of just to machines. Or a person in a mailroom. She is one of those people you don't really notice except to be glad that she's clearly kind of smart and efficient at her job, but you wouldn't wonder about her and you wouldn't really talk to her. On the way home she stops in a market and buys fresh vegetables; at the boarding house where she lives, she doesn't have kitchen privileges. Just a small room all her own, a window with a view of the mountains when it isn't foggy outside. She pulls her chair up to the window and stares out at the mountains and with her knife cuts strips off the peppers, the celery, the fresh tomatoes. Looking out at the mountains. Maybe she thinks about what it was like, once upon a time, to be visible to everyone, to be hypersupervisible, and very important in what happened to lots of people — but maybe she doesn't think about it at all. Maybe she thinks about things that took a long time to learn — important skills, technical skills, things she practiced and practiced until she was as good as she would ever be, and maybe sometimes she finds her hands going through strange motions. Or maybe she has just let it all go. On the weekend when she doesn't have a softball practice she goes on long walks around the city, getting to know it better than she ever got to know a city where she lived much longer. Walks and walks, getting in better shape than she's ever been, tiring herself out. Oh, and she goes to church.

She is in Mexico, in a town no tourists ever go to because there is nothing there to see. One of the well-to-do families is renting her a room, a corner room in a whitewashed house that is built in a square around a courtyard planted with flowers. Every day she has a Spanish lesson with the daughter of the house, a beautiful laughing young girl, who sometimes tries to find out about her and where she has come from but smiles and accepts it when she does not answer those questions. Once she and the daughter of the house were on the local bus to the market, and she made the girl tell a woman with a baby across the aisle to take her little one to the doctor right away, that the baby had a dangerous infection around his eye. The mother said no, said it was just an insect bite, but finally agreed to go to the clinic, convinced by the intensity and the certainty of this strange English-speaking lady. But then at her next Spanish lesson, she wouldn't answer any questions again.

In her room, she has only a cot and a carved wooden dresser, and there is a painting of the Virgin Mary hanging on the wall. The weather is very hot, even at night, and sometimes she cannot sleep. The family has told her she must not go out walking alone at night; it is not something young women do. Still, the family surely knows that a certain young man, or maybe not quite so young anymore, a smart fellow who went away to the big city to go to the university, then came home to care for his elderly parents, that he sometimes comes on the not too hot nights to be let in through her window, and to keep her company until the very early morning. When they make love, her mind empties, the way it never used to do, in that other life she had elsewhere. Now it's different, now she can feel what she feels without interrupting herself and bothering herself with terrible thoughts. No one knows anything about her here, not the family she rents from, not the daughter, not the young man. Perhaps he thinks he knows about her, but he doesn't. He brings her bunches of heavily scented flowers, so that often in the morning her room is full of their color and their smell.

27

Losing

MAMA IS PUTTING EVERYTHING IN BOXES. The boxes are big enough to climb in, though when her foot breaks the side out of one, Mama yells. "Broken," Penelope offers, her new word, and for good measure she tries, "Uh-oh!" which is Penelope's old word for *broken* and *mess* and all the other bad things that have their own special names now. But Mama is still yelling. Having everything in the big boxes makes a bad feeling anyway, so when Mama won't stop yelling, she grabs on hard around Mama's leg and holds on tight, smelling Mama close. And soon Mama reaches down and touches her hair, then comes down beside her on the floor — where's my Penelope? where's my girl? where's my hug-a-bug? — and then, better. Not all better — the big pots with the handles are still in a box, and her own special cereal bowl with stars on it, and even the yellow blanket — but better when she can smell Mama close.

But something wet on her cheek not from her own eyes: something silly, Mama crying, but without noise. But Mama put the yellow blanket in the box, and Mama took the picture with her hands in red and blue fingerpaint off the refrigerator and put that in a box, and so many books. Mama could take them out, but Penelope can't — Mama would be mad — but now they sit with faces close together and Mama cries. And a kiss on the cheek, rubbing cheeks together, which almost always works with Mama when Mama is sad, does not make her stop.

A Necklace of Needs. That's what you do in Employee Empowerment Through Sharing sessions. You make a Necklace of Needs. Maggie, who was shanghaied into this completely against her better judgment, who is doing it solely because it was a direct request from her boss, sits at a big round table sorting through discs of construction paper. The man sitting next to her, an insectlike fellow she would swear she's never seen before, reaches past her to grab a blue circle labeled SELF-ESTEEM.

"Sorry," he says to Maggie, "did you want that one?"

"No. Is there one that says 'chocolate'?" He laughs appreciatively, but he is already gluing SELF-ESTEEM next to POSITIVE REINFORCEMENT. Maggie senses a theme.

So here she is. With a random selection of hospital employees; she has no idea who most of them are, since badges and titles have been rigorously left at the door and introductions made only by first name. She recognizes one other doctor, an earnest young man from, she thinks, Psychiatry, and a nurse from the renal dialysis unit who once worked in the NICU. But the other people could be custodians or lab techs or Nobel laureates in biochemistry. Maggie likes titles and badges, thank you very much. You can call me Doctor because that's what I am. She looks at her own necklace, completely barren. Be a good sport. You can do it. Reach over there, pick up the orange piece of construction paper. Smile at the woman across the table, ask if you can borrow her glue. There you go. Good girl. ENOUGH TIME glows prominently on Maggie's necklace. Maybe if she took a Magic Marker and made it ENOUGH RESEARCH TIME.

And the great Dr. Schmuckley is in his element. Circling the table, looking over people's shoulders, urging them on. Think it through, tend to all your different needs. What, after all, is EMOTIONAL SUPPORT without A HEALING ATMOSPHERE?

Funny how all words lose their meaning; *healing* is actually a technical term at Blessed Innocence, but its true technical meaning has nothing whatsoever to do with this idiocy. These people aren't thinking of the patients, the ones who are actually sick, when they talk about healing. There is no healing from gibberish and stupidity.

Here is my personal Necklace of Needs: NO CRAZY PERSON WRITING LETTERS TO ME OR ABOUT ME, NO POSTERS HUNG UP WARNING PARENTS THAT I'M DANGEROUS, NO BEDPANS LEFT ON MY DESK, NO DETECTIVES WANDERING AROUND ASKING PEOPLE ABOUT ME. Very negative, my dear Dr. Claymore. Oh well, here's a positive one: I NEED TO BE THE CLINICAL DIRECTOR OF THE NEW EXPANDED NEONATOLOGY PROGRAM. Thank you very much.

And now, of course, they have to talk about their needs. Excuse me, *share*. Pick a need from the necklace and share how it is or isn't met in the workplace.

Well, one thing about medical training: it teaches you to zone out. Once upon a time, Maggie would have said she could just about sleep with her eyes open; a necessary skill for the tired resident, forced to listen to the pontifications of her elders and betters. Now that she herself is an elder and a better, and certainly is better rested, as a general rule, she contents herself with what Dan calls internal psychic exile.

She thinks about Penelope, about holding Penelope on her lap. About that heavy and vigorous body, about Penelope squirming off her lap. Okay, it's time to take some control here, Maggie thinks, remembering all her godmother resolutions, all these years, about being the source of strength and order and discipline in Penelope's life. Yes, Sarah is embarrassed and ashamed, and yes, it's been a hard, hard time, with the police, with the department of social services — but I've been wrong, Maggie thinks. I've been letting Sarah push me back and put me off just because she's embarrassed and ashamed, when the truth is, she needs me and Penelope needs me. I will go home, I will knock on their door, I will tell Sarah to leave all the nonsense behind. I'll take them to the circus, to the Children's Museum, I'll take them out for ice cream, I'll tell Sarah she has to let me help a little more. Ask me to babysit when she needs to go out. Ask me to talk to her social worker. Even make out a schedule, if she needs to, where I watch Penelope a certain number of hours a week. I'll go to court for her — I'll make Sarah let me go to court. And she'll be grateful, she will, in the end. And Penelope will be — Penelope will be fine. Strong and smart and never ever left alone again. Maggie closes her eyes for just one second: Penelope, looking exactly as she now looks, only taller, in a graduation gown, curls flying in all directions.

But then she zones back in. Dr. Schmuckley is telling the guy next to her not to use names, please, and the guy is nodding, but Maggie has already heard the name he used.

"Theresa?" she repeats, too loudly. "Theresa in the hematology lab?" she asks him, and he nods, nervously, before Dr. S can remind them, Once again, no names please.

"So what happened? What were you just saying?"

He looks at her nervously; her tone is not nurturing to his self-esteem.

"People don't realize that being a supervisor is stressful — having to give criticism or terminate a staff member makes you really vulnerable."

"I can identify with that," says a large woman across the table, whose necklace features not one but two circles labeled VALIDA-TION.

"When this — this person — acted disrespectfully to me and refused to obey direct orders from her supervisor, I had no real choice other than to terminate her. I have my job responsibilities, and I take them seriously —"

"What happened?" Maggie's voice is way, way, way too loud.

"Would you like to share a little more?" Dr. S's voice is friendly and gentle.

"As I was telling you, I made a perfectly innocent remark about some of the disturbances we've had in the hospital. About breaches of security. People in this hospital — even doctors — don't realize how important it is in a serology lab to maintain absolutely consistent standards in every way."

"The doctors are the worst," says the large validation woman across the table.

"Absolutely." He nods happily, no doubt validated. Nurtured. "So when you get warnings about a particular doctor — letters and even a flier under the door, you have to keep an eye on things — that's all I'm saying. No smoke without fire. So then this young — person — absolutely goes for me, uses strong language, insults me in front of people I supervise — and she has the nerve to tell me I have to take back what I said."

Heads are shaking all around the table. But at least a few people, the dialysis nurse, the psychiatrist, a couple of others, are shooting looks at Maggie, shifting in their seats, staring down at their Necklaces of Needs.

"And what happened after she said that?" Maggie can barely speak to him.

He arranges himself prissily in his seat. "We had a somewhat prolonged exchange. She used terminology that truly shocked me. Truly. To her supervisor!"

"Obscene?" someone asks, hopefully.

"Verbal abuse?" asks someone else.

"Not precisely obscene, but severely disrespectful of my position and my professional expertise. And then this morning I called her into my office and I told her she was being terminated. Two weeks notice. Note that I didn't do it in front of her coworkers, though I think I would have been perfectly well justified. After all, she called me names in front of those same coworkers."

"I once had a cafeteria worker threaten to sue the hospital," begins the Validation lady, reminiscently, but Maggie cuts her off.

"You will rehire her this afternoon, with a full apology!" Maggie gets to her feet. "I said, you will rehire Theresa this afternoon, and apologize to her!"

Dr. S is making gestures at her. "We have to be very careful not to let anything said in this room, in this forum, turn into something it wasn't meant to be, Dr. Claymore —"

In his agitation, he has used her title — and her last name. And her name is all it takes. The guy is staring at her, plainly stunned. She looks down at him, trying to look down on him with all the contempt and animosity and power she can manage. *I am losing everyone, and everyone in my life is losing; I will not lose this. You are a bug and I could squash you.*

She puts out her right hand, and he stares at it, then extends his own forelimb and shakes it, clumsily, from his sitting position.

"I am Dr. Maggie Claymore. I believe I was the subject of those letters and that flier. And anything you care to say about me, you may say right now so the whole table can hear. Though I warn you, I intend to go immediately to the head of my department, and the hospital attorney, and the senior vice president, and repeat it verbatim, and explain that you fired a young woman for taking exception to your slanders." And who knows, I just might get a lawyer of my own, even though they don't want me to, and if I get a lawyer, your goose is cooked. We'll sue your ass off.

"Dr. Claymore!" Well, well, well. Dr. Schmuckley can raise his voice, can he? "I have to absolutely insist that whatever anyone shares in our workshops remains absolutely confidential. This is an oasis in the workplace, a stress-free setting in which honesty is rewarded and people can share what is in their hearts."

"Really!" agrees the Validation lady across the table.

"I would never have brought this up —" begins the man, the bug, Theresa's boss.

"But you did," Maggie says. "You brought it up. And when Theresa and I bring the lawsuit, we will make sure that every single person at this table is subpoenaed as a witness. And every person in your lab who heard you slander me. And I promise you, I absolutely promise you, that you are not valuable enough to this hospital to keep your job once I start raising hell over this. I have the personal assurances of the executive vice president and the chairman of the hospital board that if anyone is identified as spreading these slanders about me, the hospital will take swift action."

"I didn't write the letters! I had nothing to do with any of this!"

Of course he didn't write the letters. She knows that. Really, she does. But she almost feels like she is finally face to face with the person who did.

"You repeated slanders about me and fired an employee who objected. In front of witnesses."

She looks down at him; he looks up at her. Then he shrugs.

"Let's not fight about this, Doctor. I'm sure you've been through a hard time." You can almost hear the little gears clicking in his brain.

"You'll rehire her?"

"I will. I will do that. She's always been an excellent employee —"

"You'll go right now and rehire her?"

"Right now?"

"Perhaps if we move on to the next stage of our empowerment exercise . . ." Dr. S suggests, not quite smoothly. Passing out more cutouts, big construction paper socks.

"Right now," Maggie says. "Right now. I'll walk you over to the lab."

The lab director pushes back his chair, squeaking it across the floor, and gets to his feet, keeping his eyes fixed on Maggie's. As they move together to the door, Maggie hears Dr. S, a little squeakier himself than he was a while ago.

"So now that we've identified some of our needs in the workplace, we need to look to the strengths we bring to help us there. What we're going to do is look at these stickers and assemble a Stocking of Strengths —"

"Like support hose?" asks a woman at the table, and that is the last thing Maggie hears before she is out of there.

Mama Mama Mama. Mama! No, she does not want to be in her crib, not night-night time. Not in her PJs. No story, no song, no kiss, no nightlight! Mama! Mama Mama, up up up now! She holds the rail and pulls her head as high as she can, and she sees the place in the hall in front of the door, and Mama is going out again with a big box. Again. Mama! Holding the box like she is going to sit right down, sit down on the floor. She leans against the door, pushing it more open, then she goes out down the steps. Penelope calls after her, calls, Mama! and calls, No! but she doesn't keep crying, not again this time, because Mama keeps coming right back, like a game of hiding and coming out, except that Mama doesn't smile at her, Mama doesn't start laughing, or tickling, Mama doesn't look at her at all. Mama goes to get another big box. All gone, the big box is all gone. Mama took it away.

*   *   *

Maggie had already, that same week, been through the miserably awkward experience of meeting with the Clark family's lawyers, because the Blessed Innocence lawyers had finally decided that the accusations about Maggie and the death of Heather Clark were so widely disseminated that the hospital had to inform the Clarks' lawyers. Elaine Oliphant had emphasized, over and over, that Maggie had no connection to the Clark case, no knowledge of the family, no contact with the patient. As if, Maggie had thought, it would have been perfectly legitimate to argue that some doctor who *did* know Heather might well have murdered her.

The victory seems to be, according to Elaine Oliphant, that the Clarks' lawyers decided not to "depose" Maggie for now; they aren't going to interrogate her formally, on the record, though when Maggie heard the expression *depose you,* she registered more *knock you off your perch, take away your power.* But one way or another, they aren't going to do it now, though of course they reserve the right to do it later on.

And this is all explained at great length first by Elaine Oliphant, and then by the head of the legal department, and then once again by Harvey, and it is all being done for the benefit of the vice president, this debonair old guy with the biggest office of all. The vice president sits behind his gleaming desk, hands laced neatly on the polished wood in front of him. A full head of smooth, silver hair, a well-groomed mustache, a vigorous, intelligent face that belongs in a Yankee family portrait, and a single small facial tic — he chews the left side of his mouth while he listens, pulling the lip further and further in between his teeth so that every so often you catch a funny glimpse of him in which his face looks like it's starting to disappear into itself.

Maggie understands that here is power, here is the Hospital with a capital H. But the hospital so removed from its function that it has become an institution, any institution. You can look at Harvey Weintraub and see some relation to medicine, some former self that moved among the babies, stethoscope at the ready. You look at the vice president, and you could be talking bank, you could be talking brokerage firm, you could be talking foundation. Institutions live and die a life quite apart from their function; they struggle and compete and flourish and fail against a backdrop of boards of directors and bottom lines. Well, Maggie thinks, why not? Professional function is a luxury of good institutional health, just as people live and die quite apart from what they do in their jobs; all the things that are most meaningful in one's life become quite by the way when one is reduced to a sick and failing body.

The vice president speaks, low and cordial and definitive. "Excellent. So that's taken care of. And the detective's investigation is concluded as well."

"It is? What did she find?" Maggie looks around at them all. This is only her damn life they're talking about. "Well? Did she find anything?"

Elaine Oliphant and Harvey Weintraub exchange what looks almost like a furtive glance, but the vice president looks straight at Maggie. "She found a variety of tantalizing leads, but no definitive evidence pointing to any one person. Needless to say, if the activity escalates again, we can pursue this further, but I hope that won't be necessary."

"Now that you're off service, Maggie, it's clearly dying down," Harvey puts in.

"These things have a life of their own — I mean, they tend to run their course and then stop." The head of the legal department, as if he knows what he's talking about.

Elaine picks it up again. "But Maggie, now that you're no longer working in the NICU, we want to warn you to stay completely away from there."

"What?"

"There have been a great many rumors floating around, a lot of accusations, a lot of anxiety. We feel it's particularly important, over the next few months, for you to avoid any ambiguous situations."

"The appearance of evil," intones the vice president, and shoots her a not particularly warm little smile.

"The last thing you need right now, Maggie, is to be seen hanging around some patient care location where you don't absolutely need to be, and then something goes wrong with a patient," Elaine continues.

326

Harvey Weintraub leans forward and puts it straight, doctor to doctor. "Stay out of the NICU. We all need to put this behind us and get back to work. And we all know you're a superb clinician, Maggie. Just give everyone some time to put this whole thing to rest. Take some time to catch up on your research. Don't kibitz with your old patients. Stay off the wards. Don't work late, don't be seen here at odd hours. Whatever you do, don't go into a room alone with a patient."

She sat at her desk, forcing herself to work on these damn protocols. The project was overdue; she had set her own deadline on this one, and it had slipped by almost a month ago. The odd thing was, the writing went much more easily than usual; the screen seemed to fill up remarkably quickly, the sentences came one after the other. Of course, she wasn't writing up data, didn't need to stop to consider each and every sentence and check it back against her numbers. But still, usually she found writing that was not straight data exposition hardest of all. She had a peculiar feeling that she was talking directly into the computer, that she was explaining herself through her fingers. She was writing with a kind of urgency, the way she liked to lecture, to explain things to students out loud. But she didn't usually write that way, and now she wondered, briefly, Could it have anything to do with that notebook, with the longer and longer stories she had found herself writing at night? It was such an unfamiliar thing for her to find herself doing, sitting at her desk last thing before going up to bed, scribbling pell-mell without stopping to consider. Hiding the notebook at the back of a desk drawer, and good night. She had never kept a diary, never written poems, practically never in her life written anything that was not due in somewhere — college paper, grant application, journal article, or occasional letter to her mother. They did not add up to very much, even taken all together, but those meandering lines of semireadable handwriting on those blank, lineless pages were something altogether new in her life. How strange, and here she was tapping away at the computer, line after line after line, the cursor moving forward and forward, with few hesitations, none for long.

And then a phone call: Harvey Weintraub was wondering if

you could stop by. She tried hard to be annoyed, tried hard to click her tongue in irritation as she saved the computer screen, stood up, checked out her clothes. But of course she was scared, and also a little bit excited; maybe yet another meeting about her troubles, about yet another letter, another poster, another accusation — maybe something new and bad. But maybe something else: Rumor had it that the merger with St. Catherine's was now finally out of the woods; the Boston diocese had found some double-talking administrative loophole that allowed everyone to ignore the birth control pills and condoms given out to teenagers, whether they wanted them or not, in the Blessed Innocence adolescent clinics.

So if the merger was going to happen, it was just possible that Harvey was in fact about to promote her, that he was finally ready to restructure the division. And if he promoted her, if he promoted her! Silly to look at it as if it would save her life, but that's what it would do, it would save her life. She had been campaigning, and he knew it, and she had sat there like a good girl and she hadn't hired her own lawyer because they clearly didn't want her to, and she had let him tell her to stay away from the patients until things died down — but there it was, he had said, right in front of the hospital vice president, We all know you're a superb doctor. And I am, Maggie thought, and added reflexively in her mind, *and the bastards need to promote a woman.* She had been bombarding Weintraub with evidence of her research activity, her administrative skills. Flow diagrams of the followup clinic she supervised and a proposal for an expanded neonatology curriculum for the residents. She had been making her ambition plain enough, putting it directly in the pipeline to Harvey. *They need to promote a woman. I am a woman and I need to be promoted. I need the hospital, the whole hospital world, to see what they think of me. I need my enemy to see that I am still winning, that I am marching forward and forward and that none of this has held me back. I need to win.*

She left the computer humming on the orderly desk, locked her office door behind her, and went off again to show a brave face and act the part of what she was, a busy person with a new article cooking on her computer screen and a head full of useful knowledge.

*   *   *

And now finally up and up and up, and the coat of course — Penelope doesn't cry about the coat and Mama says good girl when it's all zipped, but Penelope doesn't like the coat tight on her belly, but Penelope is glad to be going outside. She says bye-bye as they go out the door, but Mama does not laugh and say bye-bye in a Penelope voice. Mama just squeezes her too tight and carries her down the stairs.

Car seat. These days she likes the car seat, and she climbs in herself, and Mama starts to say, Good girl, then sees the shoe is off, and Mama pushes her all the way into the seat, pulls down the belt hard, and goes to get the shoe; Mama's face is mad again. Penelope sees one of the big boxes resting on the seat and puts out her hand to pat it, then bang it. Mama back in the car, puts the shoe on too hard and ties it too tight. But she likes the car seat, and she has a special game she can play because now she can reach the back of Mama's seat, and she is peeling off the fuzzy stuff, a little at a time because it's very sticky. A big piece is already off but she doesn't do it till Mama gets in and the car starts. She likes the little bumps and the cough noise when the car starts.

Say bye-bye, Mama says but she doesn't turn around. Penelope said bye-bye on the porch but she says bye-bye again and waves to the house. She slides her hand into the top of the big box and she can feel something soft, and rubs it with her hand, then slides the edge up between her fingers the way she does at night so it fills up that space because she knows, she knows, she knows, it is the yellow blanket, right there, coming in the car, and that makes Penelope happy as they drive away.

This was the worst homecoming ever, the worst drive home from work.

She was driving like a crazy person, though of course everyone in Boston drives that way. She was perfectly well aware that she was driving recklessly, and even muttered under her breath, "Death wish!" as she cut off the black BMW that had been moving up fast in the left lane of the curving Jamaicaway. Let him jam on his brakes and honk his stupid horn. Fuck you. Fuck you all.

She had come home often enough with bad news. And worse

329

news, you might think, than this; okay, so she wasn't getting the promotion, okay, so she had been passed over. Dan would ask, Didn't you sort of suspect that was coming? He had offered once or twice a don't-get-your-hopes-up warning, Everything is political, you can't ever count on these things, but not ever exactly saying, And maybe the target of an anonymous-letter campaign might perfectly reasonably not be a new expanding program's choice for its shiny new figurehead. Which she had known too, of course. She had been braced, or so she had thought.

She took the left-hand turn off the Jamaicaway at high speed and with an audible screech of tires that gave her a certain satisfaction; there was oncoming traffic in the other lane, and the sensible thing to do would obviously have been to slow down and stop and wait at the light — maybe wait right through the green and the next red for that little moment's grace when her side would turn green before the other. But she was damned if she was slowing down, if she was waiting for them, if she was sitting this one out. She didn't want to get home, particularly, but she wanted to win every possible small contest on the way. Don't make me wait, don't get in my way, don't fuck with my brain. Not today.

So I'm coming home to say, Guess what, that bastard Harvey Weintraub has made David Susser clinical head of the new program. Someone who only cares about research and now he's the clinical boss. And then he calls us all into his office, that bastard Harvey Weintraub, and makes this announcement like he expects us to cheer. It should have been me, and I'm not the only one who knows that. I would do this better than David, though almost anyone would do this better than David. David is a sweet little lab nerd who's gotten lucky. So now he gets a big office and a secretary and some power, and soon he'll be a great big lab nerd asshole who jerks other people around.

For a moment she truly hated David Susser. Then she switched her angry energy back over to Harvey. Fucking men. Fucking Harvey Weintraub, pretending to be her protector, telling her over and over, That was an interesting proposal, an interesting memo, *I can see you've been giving our teaching curriculum some very serious thought.* And she couldn't believe she had ever thought there was any chance they would promote her. Sure, they needed to promote a woman — but they needed to because they hadn't done it, because the women don't get promoted — and that was because they were bastards, every last fucking one of them. Of course they had seized on any excuse to freeze her out.

Fucking men. Fucking men. She rapped vindictively at her horn, then pushed her way into a knot of traffic that had stalled behind a green line trolley. Fucking men, get out of my way.

She does not cry easily. This whole thing through, she has barely cried. She has probably been close to it on a variety of occasions, but she does not cry easily.

Maggie is crying in her own backyard. There is no one home, the house is empty, and the cold, gray afternoon is turning into colder, darker night. And there is no one home. She knew as soon as she walked in, as she veered off course to look for Penelope and snatch her up. To tell herself, Here is someone who will never know or care or think twice about who has what stupid job in the stupid medical hierarchy, here is someone who recognizes me and knows me. To tell the story over to Sarah, of course, and to find outrage and comfort and above all find her own way out and back. But she knew right then and there that they were gone.

There is so much of Sarah's junk left behind that you might think the apartment still inhabited, but Maggie can recognize the empty spaces. The beaded wall-hangings taken down off the wall, the books gone and also the brick and board bookshelves, the baskets and the pots and pans. What's left is trivial and easily replaced or else too big to carry, like the kitchen table.

And the note was in the middle of the kitchen table, a folded sheet of paper torn off a yellow pad, Maggie's name printed squarely in the middle, Maggie's name with a period after it. End of sentence.

So here she is out in this pathetic little garden that she knows will never bloom again. Not without Sarah. Not without Penelope.

My dear good friend, I'm so sorry for the mess. You know how I am, but still. If I can, I will have the furniture shipped eventually, but it may be a while, and feel free to get rid of it if it's taking up space you need. And, if you could, would you rake leaves over the beds to mulch them for the winter; I worry that everything will freeze if January is as cold as it was last year. I don't have time. And I don't have time to plant the bulbs, which ironically just arrived today; they are in a box in the hall right next to the bathroom door. I did put some stakes in key places when I was planning next year's garden, and if you could, just dig holes and plop them in, that's all it takes. And you'll be surprised how beautiful it looks when the time comes; I planned great things. So thanks for planting the bulbs, and keep your fingers crossed. And then pray for spring, for all of us. Your own Sarah, forevermore.

And then, so like Sarah, the P.S.: *P.S. The department of social services has substantiated the allegations, that is, found me guilty as charged, and the school has found out and, no surprise, I have been most abruptly canned as a danger to youth. I don't think I'm supposed to leave the state, since they are planning various kinds of rehabilitation and interference and monitoring, so maybe you should shred this letter and any other evidence. I hope your own mess straightens out.*

Weeping in the backyard. What does it mean, rake leaves over the beds? Which are the beds? What if the rake catches in something and pulls it up? There are already dirty dead leaves scattered everywhere; Maggie kneels, in her good dark green tweed skirt, feeling the dampness soaking through skirt and stockings and into her kneecaps. She gathers the leaves by hand off the flagstones that make up the short path through the tiny yard, moves the leaves by the handful off the path and onto what she thinks of as the plants. The box of bulbs sits beside her; yes, she can see the stakes. But she is on her knees and crying, and it is all she can do to move the wet and crumbling leaves, a few at a time, patting them down. Everything is being taken away from me.

28

Behind Glass

SHE DRIVES BACK to the hospital, driving much faster than she had driven home, but without the battles, without the honking, without the cursing. Late at night and the roads are empty, no competition. And yes, she's driving dangerously, but who's she going to hurt, after all — only herself. And the speed feels so good; the swaying curves on the Jamaicaway send her adrenaline surging. But then she checks her speedometer and slows herself down, responsible Maggie.

Oh, she has made this trip so many, many times in her life. Home to hospital, hospital to home. Wakened by the beeper, dashing in to help the intern, responsive and responsible, driving fast because the baby's sick, turned sour, crumping on us, crashing. Maggie to the rescue, Maggie on the spot. Or driving home because things are under control, time to let the residents feel in charge. Beep me if you're worried about anything. *Anything.* And driving home to Dan, listening for the next beep. This is her late-night road; she knows what waits at both ends — that's what makes a commute, a journey from known to known.

Her speed is creeping up again, and she panics slightly as she takes a curve too fast, and then panics worse at a flash of a frightening thought: At least if I smash up and die, all this will be over. They'll all be sorry! And at that she lets up on the accelerator and takes the next curve at a more reasonable, if still not legal, speed. And even at a more reasonable speed, it's a short, sweet drive at this time of night.

She has left Dan sleeping in their bed. She has not told him yet about Sarah and Penelope moving out. She has not yet told him about the promotion. They talked about the swimming team, they talked about a possible January trip to Mexico, he asked her if she was glad to be off-service and she said she was, he asked if anything new had happened at work — meaning anything bad, any new attacks from her enemy — and she said no. She didn't want his sympathy, not yet. Or worse, what if he seemed relieved, the complications of Sarah and her messy life all resolved? Or even if he said, Look on the bright side, the promotion would mean even more work, even more hours, and maybe you'd be even more of a target. He wouldn't have said these things, Maggie believes. Would he? Would he have thought them to himself?

You may perhaps think that it is cowardly to make such an accusation and then not sign the letter but Doctor Claymore is powerful and only someone such as yourself can take the step of exposing her and righting this wrong and this danger.

Maggie couldn't sleep. She wanted to be here, to be in the hospital. She pulls into the parking lot, locks her car, hurries to the main entrance, the only entrance open at this hour. The automatic doors slide cleanly open in front of her, and she is in the lofty lobby, with its bright children-of-the-world mural and its soothing peach and aqua color scheme. And she takes a deep breath, feeling a sense of sanctuary, of a haven reached in a world of dangers. Maybe what parents feel, bringing in their sick children.

At the center of the lobby sits the famous security guard. Blond and baby-faced and studying hard, no doubt to get himself a better job. He looks up from his book as Maggie comes in, and, to her shock, he actually does accost her as she heads across the lobby.

"You visiting a patient?"

"No," Maggie says proudly. "I work here. I'm a doctor." And she digs in her pocket for her wallet, surprised and delighted to see that there is actually some security in place — though somehow also a little bit annoyed to be challenged.

But the security guard has already gone back to his book. "That's okay," he says, not looking up, not actually checking the ID she has produced.

Well, thinks Maggie, waiting for the elevator, so much for the myth of hospital security. Forces on alert, indeed, Martin Sandow. You incompetent, self-important, body-building horse's ass.

Waiting for the elevator. She isn't exactly sure where she's going or why she's here, so this gives her a minute to decide — and she can also see her own reflection in the mosaic-bordered mirror positioned between the two banks of elevators. A mirror with a little brass plaque at the bottom: *Donated in loving memory of Katherine Amy Newman, 1986–1987.* Not necessarily the cheeriest thing for parents to see as they go upstairs, you would think. Sorry, Katherine Amy, whoever you were. Wish we could have saved you. We save as many as we can. And it's a nice mirror that her parents gave in her memory, edged with mosaic fish, blue and green and gold.

But Maggie is a little shocked by her own reflection. Her hair is neatly combed, but pulled back into a ponytail. Her face is completely without makeup. She is wearing black leggings and Dan's long loose medical school sweatshirt, and she looks, she thinks, about seventeen years old. She looks almost young enough to be a patient on the adolescent ward, and while she certainly doesn't look like a doctor, she looks peculiarly appealing, smaller than she usually imagines herself, open and undefended to the world.

Who do you think you are???

The elevator door rolls open and she gets in. She hears Harvey Weintraub's voice, warning her, commanding her, setting limits on her life: Stay out of the NICU. Well, the hell with you, Harvey, she thinks, and she giggles, and presses the button. What are you going to do, smack me on the wrist?

Outside the NICU, at the fishbowl, she pauses. It looks quiet in there; an intern she doesn't even know, someone new this month, is hunched over a counter on the far side of the room, writing notes, with a teetering pile of five or six charts beside him, waiting to be attended to. The nurses are busy about their jobs, tending IVs and checking diapers, adjusting ventilators and drawing blood and administering medications and taking vital signs, but they have a calm, unhurried look that tells you nothing bad is happening. Quiet night.

Maggie watches them, standing over on the side, where the curtains are bunched up at the edge of the long window. She feels a tremendous sense of pride, a welling-up of love for all these people, these nurses right here where they are supposed to be, doing their very hard and very careful jobs the whole night through. Whatever happens with the babies, whatever goes right or wrong, the nurses will stay there and stick it out and see it through. Maggie presses her cheek against the glass and finds herself wondering, Why am I here? What am I feeling? What has become of me? They are unfamiliar questions, and she tries to shrug them off, but there's something else, some other calculation or some other insight nagging at her — but she can't quite figure out what. She shrugs it off, or tries to.

Will Maggie be from this time on a more understanding person, aware of her own vulnerability, of the quirks and turns of fate? More understanding, perhaps, of the ways in which disaster is always the potential underside of calm, everyday existence — but surely she knew that already. She did not need anonymous letters and a secret enemy to teach her that particular truth. No, anyone who has been to as many problematic deliveries as Maggie has is well aware of the thinness of the membrane between what doctors call a good outcome and a no-holds-barred tragedy. Thin as the skin, or as she would say, the integument, on a very premature baby; until about twenty-four weeks' gestation, the skin of the fetus is gelatinous, an insufficient barrier between the body and the outside world. Thin as that premature skin, which bruises with every touch, that's how thin. That's all the protection we have.

Inside the NICU, something happens. The intern, a husky young man with a brown beard and mustache, looks around, jumps up off the stool. Maggie watches as he crosses the room. Watches the nurse who called him over, watches the two of them stoop nervously over a warming table. Maggie can't see what's going on, and she can guess from the position of the table that it's some brand-new baby, some baby she doesn't know, though of course she knows the possibilities: Baby pulled the tube out. Baby's blood pressure bottomed out. Baby dropped his oxygen saturation. Baby lost his line.

She could rush in, of course — she lets herself imagine a terrified intern, an anxious nurse, a heroic moment for herself: Maggie Claymore saves the day! They clutch her and cling to her and thank her again and again.

Wouldn't happen. If the tube's out, they'll ventilate the baby, bag and mask, figure out who should put it back in. They know their jobs, these people. In fact, look: The nurse, Maggie would guess, has just successfully suctioned out a big mucous plug and everyone is calming down. Emergency over. And the night goes on. Oh, thinks Maggie, these are my people! This is my place!

And she thinks of Felicia Grassini: This is my baby! Felicia Grassini is still alive — not all her parts are working, but she's got enough, she's got a chance, and she's only the latest one in a long series. The Grassinis have a daughter, not a memory, and no one is ever going to convince Maggie, not now, not five years from now, not fifty years from now, that it would be better to lower her guard, lower her standards, and let a baby slip by. So maybe in many ways the truth is that she is still the same old sure-of-herself Maggie. Just Maggie with an enemy, she thinks, a little sadly. Maggie who didn't get the promotion. Maggie who isn't supposed to be wandering around in her very own hospital — stay out of the NICU, stay off the wards, don't work late — how dare they!

. . . *the dangers posed by an unscrupulous and unqualified doctor who is well known to everyone who has worked closely with her as dangerous to her patients by virtue of her bad judgment and lack of knowledge . . .*

And she takes off suddenly, running. Sometimes, not usually, people run through hospital halls. And into the stairwell, and charging up the stairs. And she bursts through the door onto the ward of all wards where she doesn't belong, West Seven, where little Heather Clark died in the night a year ago, and she marches down the hall. Nods and smiles, says hello to the ward clerk, to two nurses who are making notes on patient clipboards. They look up and nod, don't seem to recognize her, don't seem particularly interested. Maggie strides past proudly, head up high: I belong here.

Maggie can hear a distant electronic beep: someone's IV pump signaling, I'm jammed, come and fix me. All these rooms of sleeping sick children, so carefully monitored, so tagged and plugged into electronic promises, to call for help if help is needed. But Heather Clark died up here, and her machines were silent. Were silenced. Heather Clark when she died would have been only a little bigger than Penelope is now. Maggie, though she doesn't want to, pictures Penelope and Sarah amid their boxes, jammed into Sarah's car on the way to somewhere. On the way out of Maggie's house and Maggie's life. And that feeling begins to come back, that feeling that everything is being taken away from her.

In one of the rooms she is passing, a child begins to wail — loud, heartbroken, frightened crying. Maggie imagines it — waking at night in a strange place, nobody there, waking maybe to fever or pain. But of course, she cannot go into the room — she has no business in the room, she tells herself firmly, and no, it has nothing to do with what Harvey Weintraub said. In all her years at Blessed Innocence, when has she ever gone into a patient room on the ward to comfort a crying child?

"I'm so sorry," Maggie whispers, and she keeps on walking. And finds herself starting to imagine that behind her a nurse comes to attend to the child, that the nurse sees Maggie walking away — and it all comes rushing back, all of it, all the bad stuff.

Maggie gets to the end of the long ward hallway — she cannot see the nursing station when she turns, but she can imagine it: the nurses whispering in alarm, the ward clerk dialing security — and now her imagination is racing, now suddenly it is all out of control, at least in her mind, as she pictures herself dragged, resisting, off the ward and out through the front hospital entrance — she sees all her hospital colleagues standing and staring at her, Weintraub shaking his head and, Oh god, what is he saying? Weintraub making a rueful comment to Hank Shoemaker about how they've just discovered that Maggie faked a letter of recommendation for herself, Hank Shoemaker shaking his head. Everyone watching. *Everyone hates you and is always sorry to work with you.* Erika and Dorothy, Marjorie. Peter. All of them standing there, watching her, thinking things about her, saying things about her. It comes rushing back upon her, all of it, all the worst of it, the sight of her own picture on a poster, the fear of each new trip to the mailbox.

Maggie Claymore is standing in a hospital hall and trembling. Wrapping her arms around herself, feeling cold. There's another stairwell up ahead, of course — in a hospital, you're never too far from an exit — and she makes herself walk toward it slowly, carefully, step by step. Grabs the doorknob gratefully, and into the stairwell she slips, gripping the banister this time, taking the stairs slowly and carefully. Okay, bad idea to walk the wards. Bad idea. I do not need to be the gray ghost doctor who haunts the hospital at strange hours. I do not need to become the person they are all worried I might be. I will beat this whole thing, I will. I will stay myself. Step by step by step.

Step by step by step, it is a long, long way down to the lobby. Maggie comes out to see that same useless guard still sitting and reading. Must be up to lesson two by now, she thinks, how to chew gum and walk at the same time. The elevator doors slide open and an Indian couple is standing there, the woman in a navy blue sari with an incongruous bright red down parka over it, the man in a dark suit. The man is sobbing, visibly, and the woman stands quietly beside him, staring at him, saying nothing.

Maggie steps into the elevator beside them. "Can I help?" she asks, and her own voice sounds unfamiliar, softer and more timid. But damn it, she thinks, in confusion and in anger, I cannot always be walking away when someone is crying.

The man does not answer. The woman says, in accented, musical English, "I think that it will be all right." Before they can exit, the elevator doors slide shut behind Maggie and she feels the lift of moving upward. She has hijacked this sad couple, who were surely on their way home, so late at night.

"Which floor is your baby on?" Maggie asks, absolutely sure that she will hear, In the NICU. These will be the parents of that new baby who was worrying the intern when she looked in earlier, so she will take them to the NICU and reassure them and help them believe that their child can be saved.

"Oh," says the woman, "he is not at all a baby. He is thirteen years old."

The father has taken out a large and very white handkerchief and is blotting his eyes and his nose.

"He has been in hospital so many, many times," the woman says. "Perhaps twenty times, and always it has been all right."

Maggie wants to ask. She has the professional vocabulary to understand the answer, of course, and she wants to ask. But she doesn't. The elevator doors open — they are up at the very top of the hospital.

"I'm sorry," Maggie says. "You were on your way out, I know."

The mother reaches past her and presses the lobby button. "It is all right," she says. "It is kind of you to help us. To which floor are you going now?"

"Five," Maggie says. "The NICU."

"Ah, yes," says the man, speaking for the first time, apparently recovered and completely unembarrassed. "Our son started out in the NICU, thirteen years ago now. It was there that they saved his life for the very first time."

"Here?" Maggie asks. "Here at Blessed Innocence?"

"Yes, indeed," says the father. "He always only comes here. It is the best place, I think."

The elevator stops on five and Maggie steps forward out the door. She turns to look at the couple, standing there side by side. "I'll pray for you — I'll pray for your son," she tells them, and she hears them, in unison, saying thank you as the elevator doors slide closed.

Slowly, Maggie walks back to the NICU. She lets her hand trail along the corridor wall, as if feeling her way. But she knows the way. She thinks about the couple going back down in the elevator, finding their car. She cannot resist making up stories for their son: He had hydrocephalus as a baby and now he has a ventriculoperitoneal shunt draining the fluid from his brain down to his abdomen, and it's always malfunctioning or getting infected. He has terrible, uncorrectable congenital heart disease and he comes in with cardiac failure whenever he catches cold. He has some awful inborn error of metabolism and his body chemistry gets out of whack. Or maybe, she thinks, he's like Felicia Grassini — maybe we took out too much of his gut when he was a baby. Maybe we did something, back that first time when we saved his life. But we saved his life, didn't we? You do have a son, don't you? I will pray for him, like I will pray for Felicia, like I will pray for them all, every day of my life. Every day of my life.

And here she is, at the NICU, looking in the window. But this time she is going in. Nobody can tell me not to. Nobody can take anything else away from me. I belong here. This is where I say my prayers. I am not the villain, and I go where I please. She pushes the door open.

Just beyond the door, two nurses stand talking. Maggie knows them, of course, but it seems to her that they look at her with doubt on their faces, as if they don't quite recognize her.

"Jennifer, Chris," she says, pleasantly. "How's the night going?"

"Can I help you?" asks Jennifer, a small, sturdy woman with an abundant head of dark curly hair.

"I'm just checking in." Yes, that's the tone, pleasant, authoritative. This is what she needs. I need to be here, just don't ask me why. I don't have time to stop and figure it out. And there's something else I need to figure out too, but I'm not sure exactly what it is. Never mind right now, all that can wait. This is where I need to be. I belong here.

But she doesn't, exactly, of course. Not right here, not right now. Still, she steps past the two nurses with confidence, like a doctor stepping past nurses. She walks among the warming tables and isolettes and cribs, and she can feel the nurses at the different bedspaces turning to look at her as she passes, heading for Felicia Grassini's incubator. It's a quiet night in the NICU, the nighttime, turned-down volume of a place that never really rests.

Two people are blocking her way, and she stops: Jennifer, the curly-haired nurse, and this new NICU intern, the man Maggie doesn't know. The intern looks nervous, the nurse looks determined. And every nurse in the place is watching. And she can hear whispers, someone asking what's going on, someone answering, even softer, but Maggie hears her name. And here it is, clear and plain now, everyone staring at her openly the way they've looked at her covertly for months now, all of them, everyone.

The substandard medicine she practices.

341

The danger that this so-called doctor may pose to patients who come to this hospital expecting in good faith to receive only the best of care.

She must not be allowed to endanger innocent children.

Her willingness to sacrifice the lives of children or even we could say kill them neglect them murder them.

"Can I help you?" Jennifer asks again. "You aren't covering tonight, are you?"

"Dr. Claymore?" The intern sounds embarrassed.

Look how they are looking at her, all of them, all of them. Everything has been taken away from me. My nurses, my place, my patients. Looking at me as if I have no business here, as if there's something wrong.

And someone has in fact called security, someone must have called, because here comes security. But it isn't scary the way it was when she imagined it, back upstairs on Seven — there's just nothing scary about hospital security. That doofus with his book from the lobby — here he is, along with a partner, and it almost makes Maggie want to laugh; Hey, you, big guy, down there fighting crime, come up to the NICU, we need you. That baby-faced blond guard and another, tall and very thin and very black, are crossing the room toward Maggie. One of the nurses must have called security to protect the patients from her.

"What the fuck are you guys doing here?" It is Erika, stepping in out of the parents' room, placing herself in the security guards' path. She looks over at Maggie, and Maggie waits for Erika to recognize the situation, to say, Aha, it's crazy, dangerous Dr. Claymore.

"Maggie, you don't look too good," says Erika, who is an excellent nurse.

"I think I need to sit down," Maggie says, swaying. Jennifer recognizes true physical instability and immediately pulls over a chair and helps Maggie into it with strength and skill. One of the rocking chairs parents use at the bedside; like the mirror downstairs, it has a little plaque on it, on the headrest. *In memory.* Maggie doesn't read it; she leans her head against it. She can see Felicia's monitors, can register, from where she sits, that the baby is well oxygenated, that her heart rate is strong and regular. You and me, Felicia, they've taken things away from us. Do we have what it takes? Is our skin thick enough? Do we have the guts? Maggie snorts with laughter, closes her eyes, thinking, Poor little baby, they've taken out almost all of yours. Shakes her head; stupid jokes in the middle of the night.

Erika's voice is most expertly pitched; not loud enough to disturb the babies, who need low lights, a quiet environment, but penetrating enough to reach the security guards, the other nurses, Maggie herself.

"If some particularly clueless individual happened to mistakenly call security, I think we can safely say they aren't needed," Erika pronounces. "This is one of our doctors here, and if she doesn't happen to be feeling well, we can take care of her perfectly well, thank you very much."

The security guards hesitate. Erika widens her eyes. "Out. Home. Leave. Am-scray! This is one of our doctors! We will take care of her! Get lost!"

And off they go. Maggie closes her eyes, because the room keeps moving. She is peripherally aware of Jennifer conferring with Erika. She feels someone's hand brush her forehead, feeling for a temperature. They are taking care of her. And she will be saved.

Whose parents gave this rocking chair? What baby did we fail to save? Felicia is saved, at least for now; if she opens her eyes and leans forward, Maggie can see into the incubator, see inside the thick plastic box to where a tiny pink body lies breathing by machine, warm and safe, though very much in danger. But her lungs are healing and her heart is strong, and the will to grow is powerful. I believe, I believe, I believe. And Maggie trembles, and sinks back in the rocking chair. *Oh, Lord. You who let some people invent their lives. You who let me find this good work to do. Don't let them take it away from me. Don't let me lose it.* She shakes her head: wrong prayer. *Let Felicia live and grow. And those people in the elevator — their son —*

"You've been under a lot of stress, Dr. Claymore," the intern says. Poor confused guy, valiantly working on his people skills.

"Yes." Maggie nods. "A lot of stress. But you know what we say, what doesn't kill you makes you strong." That's Maggie, fond of hospital aphorisms. When all you have is a hammer, everything looks like a nail. If it isn't broke, don't fix it. What doesn't kill you makes you strong. That's Maggie, in spite of everything, a true believer.

Erika brings over a paper cup. Reaches for Maggie's hand and checks her pulse against a big digital watch with luminous numbers. Looks at the intern. "Why don't you go write your charts?" And off he goes — at least he moves a few steps away, where he stands uncertainly at a counter, a chart open in front of him, but looking back at Maggie.

Erika puts the paper cup into her hand, and she sips: flat ginger ale.

"I haven't slept," she says. Then adds, almost to herself, "It's almost morning, and toward morning, I start feeling sick."

"Morning sickness?" asks Erika, half joking.

"Yes." Maggie nods. "Yes."

"Are you really —" The intern is embarrassed, less sure of his ground.

"You're pregnant?" Erika seems unembarrassed and genuinely interested. Jennifer is hovering just beyond.

"I think so," Maggie says. "I think so. I've been figuring it out, just, you know, calculating, and I think I must be." And for a minute she thinks she is beginning to cry, but it turns out to be laughter instead. Not loud, crazy laughter, either, just laughter, rueful and light and bemused. The laughter of someone who has no idea what will happen next, who has lost her bearings. Who has not, perhaps, quite lost control, but who guesses how fragile her control will prove to be. How elusive, how vulnerable, how useless.

"Everything is very surprising," Maggie says quietly. Everything changes, everything is unknown. "Everything is very surprising," she says again, and is not at all surprised to see the others nod. She leans back in the memorial rocking chair. Security has been sent away. Security is gone, she thinks, and smiles to herself. Everything is very surprising.